Sign up for our newsletter to hear about new and upcoming releases.

www.ylva-publishing.com

Other Books by Jae

Happily Ever After 1&2

Standalone Romances:

Bachelorette Number Twelve
Just a Touch Away
The Roommate Arrangement
Paper Love
Just for Show
Falling Hard
Heart Trouble
Something in the Wine
Shaken to the Core

The Hollywood Series:

Departure from the Script
Damage Control
Just Physical
The Hollywood Collection (box set)

The Oregon Series:

Backwards to Oregon
Beyond the Trail
Hidden Truths
The Complete Oregon series (box set)

Fair Oaks Series:

Perfect Rhythm
Not the Marrying Kind

Portland Police Bureau Series:

Conflict of Interest
Next of Kin

The Shape-Shifter Series:

Second Nature
Natural Family Disasters
Manhattan Moon
True Nature
Enemies by Nature
Shifting Nature

The Vampire Diet Series:

Good Enough to Eat

Unexpected Love Series:

Under a Falling Star
Wrong Number, Right Woman
Chemistry Lessons

Sparks

Jae

Acknowledgments

My gratitude goes to my loyal beta readers—Melanie, Trish, Chris Zett, and Anne-France, who have worked with me on so many books over the years. I can't thank you enough for all the time you invest in my books!

I'd also like to thank the volunteers from my Facebook reader group—Bobbi, Jiske, and Mariya, who read the manuscript to make sure Scottie comes across as the competent IT pro that she is. Special thanks to Nance Sparks for going above and beyond by reading it *twice*!

A big thank-you goes to my editor, Michelle, and the entire Ylva Publishing team for their support in bringing this book to life.

And, as always, I'm grateful to every reader who bought this book, left a review or rating, or recommended it to someone else.

Chapter 1

Willow released her stranglehold on the strap of her overstuffed purse, planted both hands on her hips, and rolled her shoulders back.

Several pedestrians slipped past and eyed her as if she were on drugs.

What? Had they never heard of the Wonder Woman pose? It was supposed to boost confidence—or so her sister said. But as Willow stared up at the sleek glass-and-steel high-rise building that housed Kudos Entertainment Inc., she had to admit it wasn't working.

Come on! New city, new job, new me. It'll be great! This was her chance to finally outrun the reputation she'd earned back home, and she was determined not to mess it up.

Right on cue, the infamous Portland drizzle started as she crossed the street.

She smoothed her pencil skirt, adjusted her blazer, and pulled open the glass doors at Kudos's main entrance.

The echo of her sensible flats on the polished travertine floor sounded way too loud as she crossed the lobby.

A crimson couch stretched along one white marble wall, flanked by ferns in large stone troughs. Somewhere in the background, a gurgling fountain drowned out the sound of the rain on the high glass roof.

A young woman with neatly pinned-up, auburn hair looked up from behind the reception desk.

Willow forced a friendly smile. "Good morning. I'm Willow Greene, the new operations coordinator."

"Good morning and welcome to Kudos." The receptionist tapped a few keys, then opened a drawer and pulled out an ID badge on a red-and-blue lanyard. "Here's your temporary badge. HR will take your photo and set you up with a permanent one later today."

She held it out to Willow, who took it, careful not to let their fingers brush. "Thank you."

"Your desk is on the—"

Approaching footsteps cut her off. A woman in her sixties walked toward them from the bank of elevators, her orthopedic shoes squeaking on the floor. "Ah, perfect timing. You must be my replacement. I'm Barbara Peisner, but please call me Barb." Her silver bob swayed as she came to a stop in front of Willow and held out her hand with a warm smile.

Willow discreetly brushed her fingers over a metal brochure stand holding glossy pamphlets that showed off the company's latest toy products. It was an ingrained habit by now—one that she hoped no one would notice. She shook Barb's hand and returned her smile. "Nice to meet you. Thanks so much for coming down to get me."

Barb chuckled. "Now that they've finally hired my replacement, I didn't want to risk losing you in the maze of offices. My husband already booked us a cruise for January, and it's nonrefundable."

"Please tell him he has nothing to worry about. The trip is safe. I look forward to working here." Willow nodded at the receptionist before following her new colleague to the elevator.

Barb gestured for Willow to enter first, then pushed the button for the thirteenth floor.

Thirteen. Good thing Willow wasn't superstitious. At least not much. She resisted the urge to bob up and down on the balls of her feet as the elevator began to climb.

"I hope you had a hearty breakfast. You're going to need it," Barb said with an apologetic smile. "We usually put new hires through a longer orientation, but the months before Christmas are our busiest season, and I'll retire at the end of November, so we'll have to throw you into the deep end."

Willow struggled not to gulp audibly. It wasn't the workload that scared her, though.

Her frown must have slipped through her professional poker face because Barb patted her arm. "Don't worry. I'll be around for the next two months to show you the ropes."

That was exactly what had Willow so worried. Barb would keep a close eye on her. If Willow's string of tech disasters started again, Barb would notice.

"Don't let Celeste, our operations manager, intimidate you," Barb continued. "She's intense, but not unreasonable. She just values efficiency. If you work hard, you'll be fine."

"No problem." Willow's work ethic wasn't what had gotten her fired from her last job. "I'm a quick study and pretty good at adapting. Just point me where you need me, and I'll do my best."

The elevator dinged, and the doors swished open on the thirteenth floor.

Willow touched the cool metal as she followed her out.

"This is us—the operations department." Barb swept her hand toward a frosted glass door with a card reader and stepped aside. "Go ahead and use your badge."

Willow tightened her grip on the ID card and tapped it against the door's sensor. *Please work, please work, please work.*

The piece of technology chose to establish the kind of relationship they would have by flashing a mocking red light.

Not now. She tried again.

Nothing. The door refused to open.

The lines on Barb's forehead deepened. "They gave you one of those temporary badges, right? Maybe it hasn't been activated in the system yet. May I?"

Willow handed over her badge and took a discreet step back.

Barb tapped it firmly against the reader.

The light flashed green, and the door unlocked with a soft beep.

"There we go," Barb said with a satisfied nod. "It's activated after all."

Willow inched forward again. "Sorry. Looks like my hands aren't as steady as I thought. I probably didn't tap it right." She gave Barb a tremulous smile.

Barb laughed. "Don't worry. First-day jitters get the best of all of us. I accidentally locked myself in the supply closet my first week here. Thought I'd have to live off printer paper and mints until someone rescued me." She handed the badge back and swept her arm in invitation. "Come on in."

As she followed Barb in, Willow shot the card reader a quick glare before putting on her game face.

The operations department seemed to take up most of the thirteenth floor.

Even this early in the morning, the spacious open-plan area was already buzzing with activity. The sounds of low voices, the clacking of keyboards, and the soft creak of a desk chair drifted over from a cluster of cubicles.

Floor-to-ceiling windows lined the outer wall, giving Willow a glimpse of a tree-lined street, the MAX tracks curving past lower office buildings, and the blurred green of a small park through the rain-streaked glass. Another wall held a row of whiteboards displaying shipment timelines and inventory graphs. Someone had taped a pink sticky note next to the word *back order* and scribbled *Waiting for a miracle* on it.

The office smelled faintly of dry-erase markers and freshly brewed coffee.

Several employees peeked over their low cubicle dividers to catch a glimpse of the newbie and offer her friendly smiles.

Barb introduced them, and Willow tried her best to keep up with all the new names and faces.

Just when Willow thought she had finally met everyone, a woman in her mid-forties emerged from a larger cubicle in the center of the room, with a frosted glass panel instead of a gray divider. The chatter in the office seemed to dim as she headed directly for Willow.

She carried herself with calm authority, her posture ramrod straight. Her dark hair was swept into an immaculate low bun, not a strand out of place. No wrinkle dared to form on her crisp white blouse or her tailored navy-blue slacks. A faint line was edged between her elegant brows, as if her mind was always in motion, assessing and optimizing everything. "You must be Willow. Celeste Covey—operations manager. Welcome to Kudos Entertainment." Her voice was clipped but not cold.

Willow would have guessed the woman to be her direct supervisor, even before she had introduced herself. She had expected to meet her during her job interview, but Celeste had been tied up in meetings that day. "Thank you. I'm looking forward to being part of the team." She quickly brushed her fingers against the metal handle of a filing cabinet before shaking Celeste's hand.

"Excellent." Celeste gave a curt nod in Barb's direction. "Barbara will show you the ropes. I know you two will have a lot of ground to cover, but I believe you'll find our systems straightforward and our team highly capable. If anything comes up or if you have questions Barbara can't answer, my door is always open. Metaphorically speaking, of course." A corner of her mouth lifted almost imperceptibly as she gestured at her doorless cubicle.

The unexpected hint of humor eased Willow's tension. "I'll knock if I need anything. Thank you."

"Good." With that, Celeste returned to her sleek, clutter-free desk.

Barb didn't give her the time to watch Celeste leave. She lightly gripped Willow's elbow and showed her where to find the essentials: the copier, the supply closet, and, most importantly, the coffee. Finally, Barb ended the tour at her own desk, near the back of the bullpen.

Unlike Celeste's neat setup, Barb's workstation was full of personality. It held family photos, a huge mug with the words *Best Operations Coordinator Ever* on it, one of Kudos's small robot toys, and a rotating calendar that still read *September* even though it was the first of October.

"Your desk is right here." Barb pointed at the workspace next to her own, separated only by a low partition.

The bare desk held not one but two monitors. Willow wasn't yet sure if the extra device was a good or a bad thing. The computer tower sat on the floor, which she knew was a big no-no since it made the machine more vulnerable to accidental kicks, spills, dust, and static electricity from the carpet. But she bit her lip and didn't say anything. If the system malfunctioned, at least they might blame the tower's placement, not her.

Barb pulled out the desk chair for her. "Let's get you logged in. I'll walk you through SAP, Teams, Asana, and all the other fun tools. Just tell me whenever your head feels like it's going to explode and you need a break."

Willow nodded. She already knew her biggest challenge wouldn't be mastering the software. It would be making it through the day without sparks, smoke, or flashing error messages.

Willow glanced at the big clock above the filing cabinet. *Yes!* Just five more minutes and she would have made it through her first day at Kudos without the slightest hitch.

Barb had left half an hour ago for a doctor's appointment, leaving Willow to play around in the Sandbox, Kudos's test environment that was supposed to familiarize newbies with their demand-planning software.

It was kind of fun to enter fictional demand spikes for the new Sparkle Pups line just to see how the system would reallocate inventory. She typed *2,500 units* into the input field and prayed she wasn't accidentally rerouting an actual shipment to Siberia or something. To be on the safe side, she typed in: *Test scenario only—please ignore!*

The keyboard made clicking sounds, but the letters took forever to show up on the screen. Then they stopped appearing altogether.

"Oh, come on. Don't do this to me," Willow muttered, gently shaking the keyboard. "Just a few more minutes."

She typed a row of x's, tapping lightly, then harder.

Nothing.

She pressed backspace.

Still no response from the stubborn piece of equipment.

Willow switched the dongle of her wireless keyboard to a different USB port and held her breath as she typed a few letters.

The keystrokes didn't register.

Not about to give up, Willow slid open the drawer next to her. As soon as Barb had left, she had filled it with an assortment of spare batteries she had carried in her purse.

But replacing the batteries didn't help either.

Maybe she could log out of the Sandbox, restart her computer, and solve the problem without anyone noticing. She didn't want to ask for help and risk getting the same kind of reputation she'd had at her old company.

"Problem?" a clipped voice asked before Willow could even touch the mouse.

Willow jumped and swiveled her head around.

Celeste Covey stood next to her desk, holding a folder. She ran a sharp, assessing look over Willow.

For a moment, Willow considered pretending all was fine, but her new boss didn't seem to miss much. If she caught Willow in a lie on her first day, their working relationship wouldn't be off to a good start.

"Just my keyboard." Willow tried to keep her voice light. "Apparently, it couldn't handle all the excitement and stopped working."

"Submit a ticket to IT," Celeste replied. "They usually send someone up right away."

"That's not necessary," Willow said quickly. "I'm pretty good at fixing—"

Celeste lifted her folder, cutting her off. "Nonsense. Trying to fix a technical problem yourself when we have a perfectly capable IT department is an inefficient use of resources."

Barb had warned her that their manager hated inefficiency, so Willow had to try a different tactic. "I'd love to submit a ticket, but...well...no keyboard." She waved her hand at the useless device.

"The on-screen keyboard should still work," Celeste replied without missing a beat. "Use that to fill out the help desk form."

Damn. Her old boss had been clueless when it came to technology, but she wouldn't be able to fool this one. Willow nodded and forced a small smile. "Good idea. I'll do that."

Celeste tucked the folder under her arm and headed back to her desk, but Willow had a feeling she'd keep an eye on her.

Now she had no other choice. She had to do the one thing that she'd hoped to avoid as long as possible: make the acquaintance of Kudos's IT support.

Chapter 2

Scottie added a quick note to the ticket she'd just resolved, documenting the steps she'd taken, then leaned back and stretched with a groan.

The help desk had finally quieted down. The steady stream of incoming tickets had trailed off, the phone had stopped ringing, and people no longer dropped by for a "quick question" that was never actually quick.

Maybe they could get out of here on time for a change. She glanced left and right to see if her colleagues needed help wrapping up their own work.

To her left, Gordon was speaking softly into his headset, walking someone through what sounded like a password reset. He hated leaving his desk and interacting with people face-to-face, but he had the patience of a saint when handling problems remotely.

His desk was as neat as always, not a cord out of place, and his leather briefcase sat packed up next to him. He looked like a banker ready to head home rather than an IT support specialist.

To her right, Mateo made entries in his daily log, his desk a study in contrast. A chaotic array of sticky notes was taped along both of his monitors, and several empty coffee cups vied for space with a Bluetooth adapter still in its package, a stack of service ticket printouts, and a clipboard buried beneath it all.

Scottie's own desk, sandwiched between theirs, was a cheerful compromise. Her Captain Janeway and Seven of Nine rubber ducks flanked a bottle of screen cleaner, and her rainbow-backlit keyboard added a splash of color to the otherwise black equipment.

The soft ping of a new ticket notification interrupted their momentary peace.

Mateo groaned. "Five minutes to five. We'll never get out of here on time."

Gordon wrapped up his call, hung his headset on its stand, and ran a hand through his neatly parted graying hair. "Let me guess... Someone opened a phishing email despite our training last month?"

"My money is on Mr. Sorensen having accidentally deleted all his desktop shortcuts...again." Mateo fished a wrinkled ten-dollar bill from his back pocket and slapped it on Scottie's desk. "Scottie?"

"Someone can't access the shared drive." Scottie slid ten bucks on top of Mateo's bill.

Wordlessly, Gordon followed suit.

Scottie leaned forward and glanced at one of her monitors, which always showed the queue of open tickets.

Only one remained.

"Keyboard issues," Scottie announced.

They each withdrew their money from the pile and pocketed it.

Mateo laughed. "Maybe they can't find the *any* key."

They all chuckled. It wouldn't be the first time someone took the message *Press any key to continue* literally and searched their keyboard for a key labeled *any*.

Scottie took a closer look at the ticket to see who had submitted it. "Willow Greene, Operations."

"Is she new?" Mateo asked.

"Yeah," Scottie said. "Must be the new operations coordinator."

"They hired someone new?" Gordon asked. "What happened to Barb?"

"She's retiring. You'd know that if you left your desk every now and then—or read the employee newsletter." Scottie nudged him with her elbow.

"At least it's not Mr. Sorensen," Mateo said.

It was an open secret that the company's COO had only gotten the job because he was engaged to their CEO's daughter. He treated every minor computer issue like a full-scale crisis that might plunge the company into ruin. Naturally, he expected IT to drop everything else the moment his name appeared in their ticket queue.

"Thank God," Mateo added. "So, who's going?"

He and Gordon looked at each other. Both were happily married men with families waiting, defying the stereotype of the single IT nerd. Scottie was the only one who'd be going home to an empty apartment. Even after six months of being single, it still felt too quiet.

"I'll take it." Scottie didn't mind staying longer, and she liked interacting with people all over the company.

Mateo playfully clutched his heart. "Our hero." Then he sobered. "You sure?"

"Yeah. Probably a typical newbie problem. Should be a quick fix." Scottie waved toward the door. "You two go home to your wives."

"You need one of those, *mi amiga*."

"Maybe she should start with a girlfriend," Gordon threw in.

Scottie crossed her arms over her chest and gave them a look somewhere between amused and annoyed. "Are you two done discussing my love life?"

"Or lack thereof," Gordon muttered.

"Well, who knows? Maybe our new operations coordinator is cute, single, and just waiting for an IT goddess to reboot her heart." Mateo fluttered his lashes at Scottie.

She threw her Death Star stress ball at him. "No, thanks. I'm still rebooting my own after my big system crash. I'll be in safe mode for a while." She powered down her computer, got up, and grabbed her tool kit and a spare keyboard, just in case. With a cheerful wave, she headed out and called back over her shoulder: "Don't wait up for me, kids!"

When Scottie pulled open the frosted glass door and entered the Operations bullpen, she thought she was prepared for anything: crumbs stuck beneath the keys, a newbie who didn't know a wireless keyboard needed batteries, or someone accidentally hitting caps lock. But she hadn't expected to find the desk next to Barb's workspace empty.

Wasn't this where they had put the new operations coordinator? According to the employee newsletter, Barb would be showing her replacement the ropes, so it seemed like the logical choice.

She looked around.

Half the Operations staff had either already left or was packing up. Of course, Celeste Covey was still working away at her desk, sticking her head out of her cubicle just long enough to steer Scottie in the right direction—toward the empty workspace next to Barb's.

Scottie paused mid-step.

The desk wasn't actually empty.

A pair of long, slender, pantyhose-clad legs and a shapely behind in a pencil skirt were sticking out from under it. Operation's newest employee was on her hands and knees, probably checking the connections.

That was unexpected. Most users just sat there, twiddling their thumbs, while they waited for the cavalry to arrive. This one seemed to be proactive. *Nice.* And so were the lean muscles in her calves.

Jesus, Scottie! Work call, remember? She had no business noticing the woman's calves or any other body part!

Scottie coughed to announce her presence.

A thump and a muffled squeak came from under the desk, then a head of dark-brown, shoulder-length hair appeared. Gracefully, the woman crawled out of the confined space and stood. She unfolded her slim frame to a full five foot nine, the same height as Scottie, which didn't happen very often.

But compared to Scottie, the woman appeared almost delicate, with long limbs and narrow wrists. She looked a few years younger than Scottie, probably in her early thirties. Her cheeks were pink, either from the effort of crawling beneath the desk or the embarrassment of having been caught there. She swept her hair behind both ears, which gave her a studious look, then made sure her pastel-lavender blouse was still tucked in at the waist. A black blazer hung from the back of her chair.

Her outfit wasn't unusual at all. It made her blend right in with the other admin staff, almost like office camouflage. She wasn't wearing jewelry, not even a wristwatch.

And yet something about her made Scottie's gaze want to linger on the new hire. Not because Willow was trying to stand out, but because she clearly wasn't.

She realized she was staring and quickly covered it up by tucking the spare keyboard beneath her left arm and sticking out her hand. "Hi, I'm Scottie from IT."

The woman paused. "Scottie?"

Scottie grinned and shrugged, long since used to that kind of reaction. "What can I say? I'm a Trekkie, and I've always liked fixing things, even as a kid. Plus my last name is Prescott, so the nickname stuck."

"Ah. Willow Greene. No nickname." Her smile was professional and guarded, but her long lashes lent an unexpected softness to the sharp intelligence in her hazel eyes, which peered out from behind glasses with black, rectangular frames. As Willow reached forward with her right hand, she brushed the metal handle of her desk drawer with her left. It looked like a casual, coincidental touch, but that didn't fit the way she moved—elegant yet precise and contained, as if she was always overly aware of whatever she touched. Her slim fingers wrapped around Scottie's with an unexpected strength and gave a quick shake.

"So..." Scottie cleared her throat. "You're having keyboard issues? What exactly is the problem?"

"My keyboard keeps freezing. At first, it was just lagging, but then it stopped responding entirely. I've tried restarting, checking the cables, plugging it into a different USB port, and even putting in new batteries, but it's still not working." Willow gestured at her desk drawer, which was sitting a few inches ajar—just enough for Scottie to glimpse an impressive assortment of batteries: AA, AAA, C, D, and even different button cell batteries.

Oh wow. Scottie had seen hardware stores that weren't as well-stocked! She let out a low whistle. "Impressive collection!"

Willow nudged the drawer closed as if she hadn't meant for Scottie to see its contents.

"Hey, that's a good thing," Scottie said quickly. She offered a smile, hoping to put her at ease. "I like a woman who's prepared for anything."

Willow's cheeks flushed a deeper pink, but she didn't respond.

Scottie took the hint. Time to be a professional. "So, the keyboard problem... Does it happen in all applications or just in one?"

"I was running some simulations in the Sandbox when it first happened," Willow replied. "But as far as I can tell, it happens everywhere."

"Okay, then let's take a look." Scottie set her tool kit and the spare keyboard down. She rubbed her hands together as if to warm them and gestured at Willow's office chair. "May I?"

"Of course." Willow backed out of the way so Scottie could take a seat.

As Scottie settled in, her gaze flicked down to the computer tower. It rested directly on the carpet, not on an antistatic mat or on a rack beneath the desk, as she had first thought. "Um, your computer sitting on the floor isn't ideal," she said as patiently as possible. "The carpet attracts dust and creates static, especially if the cleaning crew vacuums too close to the computer."

Willow ducked her head. "Sorry. The person who had my job before me must have put it there. Maybe they wanted more desk space."

"Hey, no need to apologize. If anything, it's us who dropped the ball. We should've checked your workstation before you started, but we're one tech short right now, and it's been one of those weeks."

Willow waved a hand. "No worries. We've all had those weeks."

"If you need the space, I can set up a rack beneath the desk for you," Scottie said.

"No, thank you," Willow replied. "That's not necessary. We can just put it on the desk."

"All right. I'll do that in a minute. But let's see if I can find out what's wrong with your keyboard first." Scottie glanced around Willow's workspace, checking for physical damage, spills, or debris that might block the keys. But the desk was clean and nearly empty. The only things that stood out were a paper planner and an old-fashioned Rolodex.

It had been ages since Scottie had seen one of those. Everyone in her orbit relied on digital calendars and contacts synced to the cloud. Was Willow one of those tech-averse people who eyed all electronic devices with suspicion and hardly knew how to send an email?

Maybe the keyboard issues were just plain old user error.

Scottie opened the Notepad app and typed a few lines, then tried the same in the Sandbox and a few other applications.

The letters appeared on-screen without even a hint of lag.

"Hmm, it seems to be behaving for me right now," Scottie said.

"I swear it was completely frozen a minute ago." A hint of defensiveness crept into Willow's tone.

Scottie lifted her hands off the keyboard in a placating gesture. "I believe you. We call it the IT effect—the problem vanishes the moment someone from tech support arrives. Let me check all the usual suspects anyway, just to make sure the issue doesn't reoccur as soon as I leave."

She pulled out her small flashlight to peer under the desk and confirm the Bluetooth dongle was firmly placed in the USB port. Usually, she would have popped open the battery cover to make sure they were inserted correctly, but the keyboard was working, plus she didn't want to make Willow even more defensive by implying she couldn't even put in the batteries the right way.

With practiced ease, she checked the accessibility settings and the keyboard properties. The repeat rate was turned up to maximum, and Sticky Keys and Filter Keys were turned off. *Hm. Not that either.*

Willow stayed back and watched quietly from several steps away, but Scottie was very aware of the woman's gaze following her every movement.

She opened the task manager and looked for any runaway processes that might have consumed excessive resources and bogged down the system. A few CPU spikes and slightly elevated RAM, but nothing unusual given the Sandbox simulations Willow had been running.

Willow shifted her weight behind her.

Scottie glanced over her shoulder.

Willow was watching her with an expression she couldn't quite read, maybe a mix of patience and resigned dread.

Didn't she believe Scottie could fix her problem? As the only woman in the IT department, Scottie had encountered that lack of trust in her abilities a few times, especially in the beginning, but something told her that wasn't the case now.

Willow was just as mysterious and hard to grasp as the source of the keyboard issues.

"So," Scottie said while she checked for Windows updates, making sure it wasn't outdated software causing problems, "how long have you worked at Kudos? You're a new hire, right?"

"Yes," Willow replied. "Just started today."

Scottie wagged her finger at the keyboard. "And this is the kind of welcome you're giving Willow? Shame on you!"

Over her shoulder, she caught a hint of a smile on Willow's face, but it was gone as quickly as it had appeared.

Scottie opened the device manager and updated the driver manually, not trusting the automatic Windows process to find the newest version for the wireless keyboard. While she shut down the computer, she turned around in the office chair to face Willow. "I couldn't find any obvious cause. Everything seems to be working normally right now, but I went ahead and updated the driver just in case. I'm going to move the tower onto the desk now, then restart it. Sometimes, a fresh start is all it takes to smooth out the glitches."

Something shifted in Willow's expression, but, again, her face was as unreadable as the two monitors, which now went black as the computer powered down.

Scottie got up, crouched, and unplugged the power cord, followed by the other cables. "Did you move here for the job, or are you from around here?" She always chatted with people while she worked. Usually, it put them at ease.

But Willow looked like a prisoner being interrogated. "I moved here a couple of weeks ago." Her voice wasn't unfriendly, just professional, drawing a clear line.

"Oh, cool. How do you find Portland so far?"

"Rainy," Willow replied with the tiniest hint of a grin.

Scottie laughed. "No one has ever moved here for the weather; that's for sure. But I promise Portland has its perks." Carefully, she slid the computer out from under the desk, lifted it up, and placed it next to the monitors, at a safe distance from the edge. "If you ever need a local tour guide to show you the best food carts, the weirdest festivals, and all the other insider spots, let me know."

"Thanks. That's very generous of you," Willow said, but Scottie had a feeling she wouldn't take her up on the offer.

One by one, she reconnected the cables, then pressed the power button. When the login screen came up, she gestured toward the desk chair. "Let's see if it'll behave for you now. Go ahead and try to log in."

Gingerly, Willow took a seat and typed in her password.

Each key responded without the slightest lag.

Scottie grinned. "Looks like you're all set. But keep an eye on it, and if it starts going rogue again, file a ticket, and I'll hurry to the rescue."

Willow nodded. "Thank you. And I'm really sorry for keeping you so long. It's probably past your quitting time."

Scottie waved her off. "No worries. After hours, when it's quieter, is often the best time to fix stuff. Have a great rest of the day."

"You too."

Scottie took her tool kit and the spare keyboard and walked to the door. After a few steps, she turned back around.

Willow had taken her hands off the keyboard and was watching her leave.

"Welcome to Kudos, by the way," Scottie called back to her.

"Thank you," Willow replied softly.

With a nod, Scottie backed through the glass door, turned, and walked to the elevator.

The keyboard was working. Case closed. Normally, she wouldn't keep thinking about such a routine problem once she walked away. But somehow, she had a feeling she hadn't seen the last of Willow Greene.

Chapter 3

The rumble of the MAX train had long since faded behind Willow by the time she turned onto her sister's street.

Well, it was her street now too, but she hadn't quite gotten used to thinking of it as home yet. The sight of the house still made her chuckle.

Fiona's quirky English cottage looked like something from a fairy tale. Its bold shade of purple made it stand out between the ordinary homes as much as Fiona did among her neighbors. Twin dormer windows with a white trim peeked out from a sharply pitched roof like two raised eyebrows.

The weathered wooden fence that separated the yard from the sidewalk was painted a faded burgundy red. A climbing rose vine spilled through the slats and over the top, with a few stubborn late blooms still clinging on.

Willow tucked her chin into the collar of her jacket against the drizzle as she climbed the few steps to the arched entryway and the white front door beyond. She dug her keys out of her purse and let herself in.

The scents of linseed oil from Fiona's oil paints, melted cheese, and dried lavender greeted her, but the house was unusually quiet.

"Fiona?" she called. "You home?"

"In here!" Fiona replied from the living room.

Willow took off her jacket and shoes by the door. Not that Fiona required it. Her sister had never mentioned a single house rule, other than: "Make yourself at home."

In her pantyhose-clad feet, Willow padded through the narrow hallway and past two well-loved armchairs in the living room.

Fiona was sprawled on the large couch, a chipped mug in one hand and a paperback balanced on her belly. She had her feet up on the coffee table, stretching them toward the electric fireplace, so her mismatched socks were on full display. "Hey, you're back! How was it?" She marked her page by folding down a corner—which made Willow wince—flung the book aside, and jumped up.

Sugar, one of the cats, lifted her head and blinked sleepily, while Spice—who'd been curled up on Fiona's other side—let out an annoyed hiss at the interruption.

"Did you survive day one in the corporate jungle?" Fiona asked.

Willow sighed and dropped her purse next to the couch. "Barely."

"Come on. Sit and tell me everything!" Fiona grabbed her arm and dragged her around the coffee table.

Willow sank onto the sofa next to her. "It wasn't bad. Everyone seemed nice, especially Barb. She'll be there for the next two months to show me the ropes. The work itself seems really interesting."

"Ooh, you mean there are"—Fiona lowered her voice as if whispering dirty little secrets—"color-coded spreadsheets, geeky checklists, and inventory forms?"

Willow chuckled. "Of course there are. But mostly, it involves juggling a lot of moving parts and putting them all together to keep everything running like a well-oiled machine. It's a challenge, but I think I'll enjoy it."

Fiona studied her. "But?"

Her sister knew her too well. Willow hesitated, not sure she wanted to talk about it.

"There is a but, isn't there? Is your boss an ass?"

"No, she's all right, I think," Willow replied. "Well, the jury's still out on my boss's boss, our COO. I haven't met him yet, but our manager seems okay. Barb says she just values efficiency."

"If it's not your bosses, what is it, then?"

Willow grabbed the half-eaten slice of pizza from Fiona's plate on the coffee table and opened her mouth to take a bite.

Fiona snatched it away and pushed the plate out of reach. "There's more in the oven for you, but you're not getting it until you spill. What happened?"

Willow sighed. "The usual."

"Oh no! Tech glitch?"

Willow's lips compressed into a thin line. She nodded. "It all went well until it was almost time to go home. The evil devices lulled me into a false sense of security, and just when I thought I had made it through the day without an incident...bam, my keyboard stopped working and I had to submit a ticket to IT."

"That sucks." Fiona wrapped one arm around her and gently pulled Willow's head onto her soft yet solid shoulder.

Willow tensed for a second, bracing for the familiar zap, but it never came. *Phew.* Maybe she was starting to feel at home in her sister's house after all. The more relaxed she felt, the less often the static shocks happened. Plus it helped that Fiona's house—unlike the Operations bullpen—didn't have carpet. She exhaled and sank against Fiona.

"Could the IT guy fix it for you?" her sister asked.

"It wasn't a guy. It was a woman."

Fiona let go of Willow to clap her hands together. "Ooh, a woman with a tool belt! Isn't that like lesbian catnip?"

Willow shrugged. "I guess."

"So she wasn't attractive?"

How had this gone from being about her sucky day and her traitorous keyboard to being about Scottie's attractiveness? Willow dug her elbow into her sister's side. "She didn't even have a tool belt, just a tool kit."

"I notice you didn't say she wasn't attractive." Fiona flashed her a sly grin.

Okay, Willow had to admit Scottie hadn't been unattractive. She had that capable soft butch thing going, with blonde hair that fell across her broad, open face. It wasn't exactly shaggy, but it curled around her strong jaw with a slight wave as if overdue for a trim. Some people, Willow possibly included, might say it gave her an effortless charm. Her brown eyes had been kind, not judging Willow for even a second, and they had crinkled at the corners whenever she'd smiled—which had been a lot. And, yes, Willow had noticed how well her black chinos fit when Scottie had bent to check out the cables beneath her desk, emphasizing strong thighs and wide hips that tapered into a narrow waist.

"I wouldn't know," Willow said, trying for her most convincing poker face. "I was too focused on my keyboard issues to notice."

"Right," Fiona drawled.

"No, really. My boss's cubicle is in the same bullpen, and I was too busy trying to appear normal. Not that I succeeded." Willow rubbed her face with both hands. "Scottie probably thought I was weird. I'm pretty sure she caught me touching the desk drawer before I shook her hand so I wouldn't zap her."

"Scottie?" Fiona cocked her head. "Is that your boss?"

"No, the woman from IT."

Fiona shoved the rest of the pizza into her mouth and chewed slowly. "So if she saw that," she said once she'd swallowed, "why didn't you tell her the truth?"

Willow groaned. "How many times do we have to have this conversation?"

"I just don't get why you think you've got to keep this a secret at all costs. I know it's what Mom and Dad drilled into you, but you're an adult now. You get to make your own decisions."

Willow pinched the bridge of her nose. "I did make my own decision—the decision to keep it quiet, not tell everyone and their dog."

"I'm not saying rent out a billboard, but why not reveal what's really going on with you to a few select people?" Fiona asked. "Wouldn't it make your life easier if you didn't constantly have to hide or make up excuses? If you told this Scottie person, maybe she could have helped you."

Willow grabbed one of the fuchsia throw pillows and kneaded it roughly. "What exactly should I have told her, Fi?" There was no scientific explanation she could offer for batteries draining and electronics malfunctioning around her, sometimes without her even touching them—at least nothing that sounded halfway reasonable. "I know you mean well, but telling her wouldn't help. People never believe me. They just think I'm weird."

"Maybe it would be different here. Our slogan is 'Keep Portland weird' after all."

Willow shook her head. "This would be too weird, even for Portland."

"How do you know if you don't give it a chance? You said you want this"—Fiona waved her arm in a gesture that indicated the entire city—"to be a new start, so why not try to make new friends?"

Willow dug her fingers into the pillow until they started to hurt. "And then what? Watch another group of people get fed up and stop inviting me to movie night and any other activities involving tech?"

Been there, done that. She had no desire to repeat that experience. It was easier to keep people at arm's length.

"Please!" Fiona huffed. "Those weren't real friends. They were assholes."

"All of them? Including Mia? I thought you liked her." Willow froze. She hadn't meant to ask that. She had spat out Mia's name in frustration.

Fiona went uncharacteristically still. "Yeah, I did like her. But she was more than a friend to you, wasn't she?" she asked quietly.

Willow's head snapped around. "You knew?"

"Of course I knew! It was painfully obvious that you had the biggest crush on her when you were fifteen."

Heat surged up Willow's neck. "Ugh. Was it really? How humiliating!"

"No, it was cute." Fiona studied her with a soft smile. "I never understood why you two stopped hanging out. I just didn't want to ask and dig into something painful. Did you confess your feelings, and she couldn't deal with them?"

Willow picked imaginary lint off the pillow. "No, that wasn't it." Back then, she had been pretty shy. She never would have dared to tell Mia, who was everything she wasn't: cool, confident, popular, and extremely successful at whatever she tried her hand at. "Remember that DSLR camera she took everywhere?"

Fiona nodded.

"It used to be her dad's before he died. One day, she talked me into cutting school and sitting up on the rooftop, talking and taking goofy snapshots of each other for hours. I thought it was the best day of my life...until I tried to take another picture of her and the camera wasn't working. It just turned off and never turned back on, no matter what we tried."

"Shit," Fiona muttered.

"Yeah. Mia got so upset. She tried to get it repaired, but they couldn't fix it. I promised to take a summer job and buy her a new camera, but she said it wouldn't be the same. I tried to explain...told her everything..." The disbelieving expression on Mia's tear-stained face was burned into her memory forever. "She didn't believe me. She accused me of making it all up because I was too much of a chicken to admit that I'd dropped the camera when she wasn't looking. Then she told all our friends that I'd broken her dad's camera and that I'd tried to cover it up by making up some wild story about a tech curse."

That was when Willow had stopped trying to explain the way she affected technology.

In the sudden silence, the hum of the oven from the kitchen sounded overly loud.

"I'm so sorry." Fiona turned on the sofa and pulled Willow into a hug.

Willow sank into her big sister's embrace, not caring one bit that there might be some not-yet-dry paint splattered over Fiona's turquoise overalls. Even the smell of turpentine that clung to Fiona was strangely comforting.

"Why didn't you ever tell me what really happened?" Fiona asked.

Willow shrugged without freeing herself of the embrace. "We weren't exactly close back then. You already resented me enough without me running to you with a sob story about destroying yet another device."

Fiona clutched her fiercely. "Yeah, okay., we weren't as close as we're now. I guess we were too different. But I never resented you."

"Please! *Fiona Aveline Greene! Don't upset your sister; we just replaced the dishwasher!*" Willow imitated her mother's voice. "Don't tell me you didn't resent that!"

Fiona chuckled. "All right. I admit I didn't love that. They tried to lock you away in an ivory tower, and I—"

"Wanted to set out to slay dragons," Willow finished. Even as a child, her sister had always been outgoing and bold and hated any attempt to contain her.

"Maybe not slay dragons, but I wanted to go to summer camp and invite my friends over to play video games, and I hated not being able to do some of that. Always having to be careful. That's just not me."

"I know," Willow said quietly. "I'm sorry."

Fiona nudged her. "Don't apologize for something that isn't your fault. If anyone has to apologize, it's me. For ever making you feel like I resented you. I was only fed up with all the restrictions, never with you."

A lump formed in Willow's throat. She swallowed it down and pulled back a little to grin at Fiona. "Not even when I gave your favorite Barbie a buzz cut?"

Fiona laughed. "Okay, maybe then. I didn't share your fondness for butch Barbies." She pulled Willow back against her. "Thank you for telling me what really happened with Mia."

"You're welcome," Willow murmured against Fiona's shoulder.

They sat in silence for a while, and Willow felt the tension recede from her body. Only then did she realize how anxious she'd been all day. No wonder her keyboard had been acting up! Her effect on electronics always got worse when she was stressed, upset, or experienced any other strong negative emotion.

"By the way, I take it back," Fiona said close to her ear.

"Take what back? Your suggestion for me to make friends and tell people the truth?"

Fiona pulled back but kept her hands on Willow's shoulders. "No. I take back what I said about Mia not being an asshole."

"She's not!" The wave of defensiveness, even after all those years, surprised her. "She was just hurt and didn't understand. It's not her fault."

"I know." Fiona gave a soft squeeze. "But it's not yours either, and I hate seeing you live your life like you're cursed."

The word made Willow flinch. That was exactly how she felt sometimes. But she refused to let it control her life and her emotions any more than it already did. That was why she hadn't walked away from her admin job years ago, even though it required constant interaction with computers, printers, and software. "I'm not. I just need to make it through the first week and establish a new routine at work. Once things settle down and I'm less stressed, my devices will stop glitching all the time."

"Right." A grin returned to Fiona's face. "And until then, you can always call your superheroine with the tool kit to come to your rescue."

Willow smacked her with the pillow. "Shut up and go get my pizza."

"Me? Do I look like a waitress?"

"You look like a woman who wouldn't want her oven to spontaneously combust when I open it."

Fiona gave her a playful glare but got up and padded over to the kitchen, both cats in tow.

Willow watched her with a smile. If she was technologically hexed, she might as well use it to her advantage every now and then.

Chapter 4

A new ticket popped into the queue with a chime.

"Oh, look who it is!" Mateo peered at the notification over the rim of his *IT Ninja* mug. "The new girl strikes again!"

Scottie paused, fingers hovering over her keyboard. Willow had submitted another ticket, just two days after the first one?

"What is it this time?" Gordon asked without looking up from his own work.

"Keyboard issues—again," Mateo replied. "And now her mouse is acting up too."

Gordon let out a low whistle. "What is she doing up there? Declaring war on her peripherals?"

Mateo nodded. "I bet it's user error."

To be fair, everything pointed in that direction. Willow's keyboard issues had vanished the moment Scottie had taken a seat at her desk. She'd been able to type without the tiniest hint of a lag, even before she had updated the driver.

It wouldn't have been the first time a new employee was fumbling with an unfamiliar setup or a technophobe didn't want to admit that it was them, not the machine, causing the problem.

But Willow hadn't struck her as clueless. She had tried to fix the problem herself and had taken all the right steps. Even the way she had filled out the help desk form was thorough, well-organized, and intelligent.

Something wasn't adding up.

"I'll take this one," Scottie said before either of her colleagues could suggest a round of rock, paper, scissors to see who had to go.

"Wow." Mateo reached over and lightly slapped her shoulder. "I didn't know you were into masochism."

Scottie flashed him a grin. "What, your mom didn't tell you?"

Mateo nearly choked on a sip of coffee.

Gordon doubled over laughing. "She didn't just burn you; she roasted you with a flamethrower!"

"Yeah, yeah." Glaring, Mateo mopped up the coffee stain on his shirt, then balled up the soaked tissue and threw it at Scottie. "My mother would totally top you."

Grinning, Scottie batted the damp missile away. "I met her. No doubt she would." She grabbed her tool kit, slid one of the loaner laptops into her bag, and shouldered it like a medic on a mission.

Of course, her volunteering to take this ticket had nothing to do with being a masochist. She was just curious and wanted to figure out what was really going on…with Willow's devices, obviously.

This time, the Operations floor was still buzzing with activity when Scottie got out of the elevator and entered the bullpen.

Two employees were moving around color-coded magnets on a whiteboard, discussing a project timeline, and Celeste Covey sat at her desk, phone pressed to her ear. "Frankly, I don't care about that, Marcus," Celeste said, her tone even but stern. "We've got ten pallets of Sparkle Pups sitting in Newark when they should have been on a truck to Louisville three hours ago!"

Scottie didn't linger to hear more of the tense conversation. Best to get Willow's peripherals issues sorted out fast before she ended up in her manager's line of fire during her first week at Kudos. Scottie's steps were quiet on the carpet as she crossed toward her, so Willow hadn't noticed her yet.

This time, she was at her desk, not beneath it. She clutched her mouse and gave it a little shake. Her gaze was locked on the screen as if she was trying to will her devices into obedience.

"Good morning," Scottie said as she reached her. She waved at Barb, who peeked over her divider, before returning her attention to Willow. "You look like you're about three seconds away from hurling your mouse out the window."

Willow looked up. She released the mouse and let her shoulders drop. "No—but only because the windows up here don't open."

Scottie chuckled. "Don't worry. I'm here to help, and I think my methods are more productive than chucking your devices out the window."

"I'm really sorry to have to bother you again." Willow had averted her gaze.

"Hey, it's all good. This is what I get paid the not-so-big-bucks for." Scottie slid her laptop bag off her shoulder and set it down next to Willow's desk. "So what exactly is the problem? The mouse has joined the keyboard in its rebellion?"

Willow nodded. "The keyboard is up to its old tricks, either lagging or not working at all, and the cursor jumps across the screen, even when I barely move the mouse. It's impossible to click on anything."

"Okay. Let me take a look at your haunted mouse."

Willow winced noticeably.

Scottie paused and studied her. "Did I say something wrong?"

"No, no. It's nothing." Willow got up from her office chair so Scottie could take her place.

Scottie didn't believe her, but she decided not to push it. She took a seat, reached for the mouse, and moved it to the left.

The cursor lurched across the screen like a drunk frog.

She tried to steer it toward a folder, but it overshot its mark and zipped past it.

Definitely not user error.

Scottie glanced over her shoulder at Willow, who seemed almost relieved that Scottie could reproduce the problem this time. "You weren't kidding."

"I tried switching it to one of the USB ports on the back, but it didn't help," Willow said.

Scottie gave her an appreciative nod. "Good thinking." That would have been her next step. "Let's see if it'll behave on the laptop I brought." She connected Willow's mouse and keyboard to the laptop.

Everything worked flawlessly—no hint of a lag, no erratic behavior.

So the peripherals themselves weren't the issue. That meant they were looking at a possible problem with the hardware.

She plugged the keyboard and mouse back in, restarted the computer, and entered the BIOS to see if the peripherals would misbehave even there.

Once the blue-and-gray interface came up, Scottie pressed the down arrow key.

The cursor hesitated for a full second, then jumped down three lines.

Ugh. She shut the computer down and turned the office chair to face Willow, who hovered nearby like a concerned parent waiting for a doctor to diagnose her child. "Well, the good news is your keyboard and mouse are not possessed. The bad news is your computer's got hardware issues."

"Figures," Willow muttered so quietly Scottie almost didn't catch it. "Do you think it could be the motherboard?"

Scottie had gone through her mental checklist of the most likely culprits and had arrived at a similar conclusion, but she hadn't expected it from someone in admin. "I'm impressed. You're thinking along the right lines. My money's on the USB controller. That's the part of the motherboard that handles the communication with your USB devices."

Willow nodded as if she understood every word of the computer lingo.

Scottie's admiration grew. "If you get tired of working in Operations, we could use you in IT."

Willow burst out laughing. It wasn't a polite chuckle or a reserved little smile; it was a loud, unfiltered belly laugh that made Barb peek over the low cubicle divider to see what was so amusing about a computer issue.

Even the two employees next to the whiteboard glanced over.

Scottie scrambled not to stare too, but it was a losing battle.

Quickly, Willow reined herself in, yet her hazel eyes still twinkled as if Scottie had told the best joke ever. "God, no," she gasped out, breathless with laughter.

"Hey, maybe try not to sound so horrified at the prospect of working with me." Scottie aimed for an indignant tone, but she couldn't help grinning reflexively.

A strand of hair had escaped as Willow had thrown her head back in laughter, and now she tucked it back behind her ear. "It's not that. But trust me; you don't want me in IT."

Scottie wasn't so sure. She wouldn't mind getting to hear that carefree laugh more often. The sight of Willow so relaxed, so different from her usual guarded self, still stunned her. She had looked so warm, alive…and beautiful.

Focus. She was here to fix the computer, not to be captivated by its user.

"I'll open up the case and see if I find anything obvious. Sometimes you get lucky and find a loose cable or something else that is a quick fix," Scottie said. "But before I do…have you backed up all your files?"

"Yes, of course." Willow looked at her with an expression as if Scottie had asked whether she had put on underwear. "All my files sync automatically to the cloud, and I run hourly backups to two external drives. Plus I do a manual backup twice a day to a USB drive that I keep disconnected in case of a power surge."

Scottie pressed a hand to her chest and swayed back and forth. Multiple backups were the sexiest thing ever! "You really know how to make an IT professional swoon!"

Willow didn't flirt back or react at all. Her expression, which had lit up with warmth when she had laughed earlier, had become shuttered again—polite and unreadable.

Clearly, Willow wanted to keep things professional. Most likely, she was straight. Which was for the best anyway. It wasn't as if Scottie was looking for another woman to break her heart.

"Let's take a peek under the hood." Scottie pushed the chair back, crouched down, and unplugged the power strip. She held the power button down for twenty seconds to let any residual charge dissipate, grounded herself with a quick touch to the metal case, and turned the tower onto its side.

Willow handed over Scottie's tool kit without having to be asked.

"Thanks," Scottie said with a grin. "Are you sure you don't want a job in IT?" Maybe she said it just to see if it would elicit the same laugh again.

It didn't, but Willow's lips curled up into a mysterious smile. "Very sure."

Scottie took out one of her small screwdrivers and opened up the case. The side panel came off easily, revealing a network of wires, circuit boards, and cooling fans.

Before reaching inside, Scottie touched the metal leg of the desk to ground herself again. No way would she damage one of the sensitive components with static electricity, especially not while Willow was watching.

Then she paused. *Wait a minute!* Was that what Willow had been doing when she had touched the desk drawer before shaking Scottie's hand the first time they had met? But why would she do that? It wasn't as if she'd been about to touch a delicate microchip.

This was getting more curious by the minute. Scottie had to admit she was intrigued.

But for now, she had to solve the mystery of the malfunctioning computer, not the mystery of Willow Greene.

She forced her attention away from Willow and peered inside the open case. With calm, practiced movements, she traced the various cables and connections to a large circuit board. When she lightly pressed against the

USB connectors, they didn't budge. She had done this dozens of times, but Willow's observant gaze made her oddly aware of every motion.

"Hm," she said after a while. "No obvious smoking gun."

Literally. There were no burn marks. No frayed or loose cables. No bulging capacitors. The power supply to the motherboard looked fine too.

"I still think it's either the USB controller going flaky or a deeper board issue," Scottie said. "The computer sitting on the carpet for so long might have something to do with it. Maybe dust got in and clogged the fans, or the extra static stressed some of the sensitive components."

Barb's head popped up over the divider. "I thought static can't harm computer parts as long as they're inside the case?"

"It won't instantly fry your computer; that's true. But in the long run, a lot of small discharges add up. Combine that with reduced airflow from the dust and the motherboard running hotter than it should, and voilà…" Scottie waved at the exposed guts of the computer. "Here's what you end up with."

Barb murmured something about computers being sensitive divas and ducked back behind the divider.

A long sigh came from Willow. "So, what happens now? Do we have to call Dell and wait for them to send someone?"

Scottie grinned. "No. You're in luck. I got my Dell hardware certification a couple of years ago, so I can resolve most issues myself. I'll take your machine back to the IT dungeon to run a few more tests." With a click, Scottie slid the side panel back into place and fastened the screws before dusting her hands on her chinos.

They stood facing each other for a few seconds, neither saying anything.

Finally, Willow shifted her weight. "When do you think I'll get it back?"

"If I have to swap out the motherboard and we don't have a new one in stock, it could take a few days. But I'll leave you the laptop so you can keep working. It has all the software you need." Scottie plugged in the mouse and keyboard dongles and connected the laptop to Willow's dual monitors so she wouldn't have to squint at the thirteen-inch screen. Then she set the laptop to back up to the cloud automatically. "There. You're good to go."

"Thank you, Scottie."

A grateful Kudos employee saying her name was a totally ordinary thing. Just a polite exchange that happened every day. She shouldn't even have noticed—and it definitely shouldn't have sent a wave of warmth through her chest.

Willow was only one ticket in a queue of tasks that awaited her attention. A fascinating, smart ticket with a laugh that stopped the world around her, but still just a ticket, nothing more.

Determined, Scottie shouldered her laptop bag, picked up the tower, and tucked it against her side. "I'll keep you posted."

"Thanks," Willow said—without using Scottie's name again.

There was nothing else to say, so Scottie gave her one last nod, called out a quick "Bye, Barb," and crossed the bullpen. She didn't look back, but she could feel Willow's gaze follow her through the glass door and all the way to the elevator.

Chapter 5

On Monday morning, the scent of roasted coffee beans and the hiss of an espresso machine greeted Willow as she entered the coffee shop closest to Kudos Entertainment.

Oh wow. Apparently, every person working in the Lloyd District had the same idea. The line stretched from the two open registers almost to the door.

Willow thought about turning around and leaving, but the door opened again and someone walked in behind her, blocking her path.

"Excuse me, are you waiting in line or reconsidering whether you really need your caffeine fix before work?"

Willow knew that friendly, resonant voice, didn't she? She turned around and came face-to-face with Scottie.

She was wearing a faded denim jacket over the black polo shirt and chinos that seemed to be her work uniform. Her hair was adorably ruffled as if she'd rolled out of bed just ten minutes ago. It fell into her eyes when she looked up, and she brushed it back with a swipe of her hand.

For a second, Willow considered whirling around and pretending to be engrossed in the menu board above the register, but Scottie had already spotted her.

"Oh, hi, Willow!" Scottie's smile broadened, and she instantly pulled out her earbuds and stuffed them into her pocket. "Sorry, I didn't recognize you from behind."

"You mean without me lingering next to a malfunctioning device." The quip was out before she could stop it. She hadn't meant to say that since she was usually careful not to draw attention to her tech curse.

But Scottie just laughed. "Something like that. Hey, speaking of malfunctioning devices, turns out you were right. It *was* the motherboard. I submitted a request for a new one. The ones we had in stock were either for a totally different CPU socket, or they supported DDR5 RAM, and yours is DDR4, so I would have had to replace half your components, and my boss frowns on that." She gave her an apologetic half smile. "Really sorry about the wait."

"It's okay," Willow said, not wanting her to feel bad. "I'm managing just fine with the laptop."

"Good. I should have your computer back to you on Wednesday."

The line moved slowly, and they inched forward as they talked.

"How was your first week at Kudos?" Scottie asked.

"Fine, thanks," Willow said.

Scottie kept looking at her, not pressuring her, just waiting with an attentive expression.

"Busy," Willow added. "Lots of onboarding meetings, learning new software, filling out paperwork for HR, and familiarizing myself with production schedules, supply chains, and inventory systems. To be honest, I'm still finding my footing, and if it weren't for Barb, I'd be—"

She caught herself, realizing she had once again said more than she'd intended. That was so unlike her! She wasn't one to open up easily, especially not at work. But there was something about Scottie and her easygoing personality that made it hard to hold back.

"Scared of letting something fall through the cracks?" Scottie supplied. Her voice was gentle, and her brown eyes full of compassion.

Willow sighed. "Yeah."

"It's not you. I spent enough time in Ops to know that. Just watching Barb for a while made my brain feel as if it had too many tabs open."

Scottie's use of a computer metaphor made her smile. "That's why I'm braving the long line this morning. I need a caffeine fix before work."

"No judgment from me," Scottie said. "Have they shown you where they keep the good coffee yet? That's always my first priority."

"They did. But I'm actually more of a tea drinker." Again, Willow surprised herself by revealing that little personal tidbit. But it was harmless, right? Revealing her beverage preference hardly counted as oversharing.

"Don't like the taste of coffee?"

"No, that's not it." *Damn.* She should have just nodded. She couldn't very well tell Scottie that she preferred tea over coffee because an electric kettle was much easier and less expensive to replace than a fancy coffee machine. "I drink it every now and then. I'm just not..."

"A card-carrying member of the club?" Scottie finished for her.

"Club?"

Scottie tapped the beat-up canvas messenger bag slung across her chest. It was dotted with several colorful pins. One of them read *Everything is under Ctrl,* another *Be nice to me. You may need tech support someday.*

What caught Willow's attention was the third pin, though.

It was a cute enamel chameleon perched on a branch, its body striped in the colors of the progressive Pride flag.

Willow's pulse quickened. So Scottie was queer. To be honest, the thought had crossed her mind, but she had told herself it didn't matter. But now that Scottie had pointed it out, Willow couldn't help wondering... When Scottie had remarked that she liked a woman who was prepared for anything or told Willow she knew how to make an IT professional swoon, had she been flirting? Or was she joking around like that with everyone?

Scottie tilted her head and tapped the canvas directly above the pins, clearly waiting for a reply.

Oh. Willow stared at the rainbow-striped chameleon. Was Scottie asking whether she was gay too? Heat shot up Willow's chest. She clutched the strap of her purse as if it were a lifeline. "Uh, I...um...yes." To her annoyance, her voice went up an octave.

"Yes?"

"Yes, I'm part of the club."

There. It was out. *She* was out. Outing herself to one of the company's IT techs hadn't been on her to-do list, yet still it had happened. How on earth had they gone from discussing beverage preferences to talking about her sexual orientation?

Scottie still looked at her with that questioning expression, as if she didn't quite understand. "But didn't you just say...?"

"I'm gay," Willow added, forcing herself not to lower her voice to a whisper. If Scottie wasn't afraid to display her rainbow chameleon, neither was she. "A lesbian."

Scottie stared at her.

Was that really such a surprise? Willow knew she could easily pass for straight, but Scottie's baffled expression seemed way over the top, as if Willow couldn't possibly be a member of the LGBTQ+ community. A flicker of irritation flared in her chest. She didn't have to cut her hair short and wear flannel, Doc Martens, or a rainbow bracelet to be queer enough, thank you very much!

Then she was annoyed at her own annoyance. Why would she care about what Scottie thought of her?

Scottie blinked once more, then burst out laughing. "No, no, no!" she got out between amused snorts.

"Yes!" Willow shot back, heat in her face.

"No, I meant..." Scottie finally reined in her laughter, but a broad grin still stretched across her face. "That wasn't what I was asking, but it's delightful to know anyway." Eyes twinkling, she tapped her messenger bag again. "I meant the club of not-so-anonymous coffee addicts."

Willow realized Scottie hadn't pointed at the queer chameleon; she had pointed at another pin, one that depicted a battery icon and a coffee mug next to the words *Coffee-powered*.

Oh my God. Willow wanted to crawl behind the counter and never come out again—pun intended. For once, she prayed for a tech glitch, for every system in the coffee shop to fail...anything to get Scottie's attention away from her and her probably bright-red face.

"No," she finally choked out without looking at Scottie, "I'm not a member of that club."

Scottie reached over, wrapped her fingers lightly around Willow's wrist, and gave a gentle squeeze. "That's all right. We need more tea drinkers in the club—the other club—anyway. To balance out all the espresso-fueled chaos. I'm a proud member of both clubs, by the way. A lesbian with a latte addiction. Just in case you were wondering."

Willow didn't know what to say. She stared at the strong fingers still curled around her arm, then at Scottie's smile that radiated acceptance. At least she hadn't zapped her through the layers of her sweater and coat.

"Next!" the barista snapped.

Thank you, thank you, thank you! Willow had never been so glad in her life to be interrupted by a grumpy barista. She'd been so focused on their conversation and her own mortification that she hadn't noticed the person in front of her finishing their order. Quickly, she stepped up to the counter and tried to act as if she accidentally outed herself in coffee shops every day. "Hi! Could I get a medium chai latte to go, please?"

"Would you like whole milk, two percent, soy, almond, or oat?"

"Whole milk is perfect, thanks."

"Great." The barista typed in her order. "That'll be $6.25."

Willow took her wallet from her purse and pulled out a ten-dollar bill.

The barista shook her head and pointed at a sign on the counter that said, *No cash. Card only.*

Groaning inwardly, Willow pulled out her credit card and tapped it against the POS terminal, careful not to touch it directly.

The screen flickered, then showed an error message: *Transaction failed.*

The barista pressed her lips together. "Try again, please."

Willow did.

The screen went black, and the entire system froze.

"Great," the barista mumbled. She leaned over the register, gave the terminal a hearty tap, and pressed a button.

Nothing.

"Sorry," the barista said. "Give me a sec. I need to restart it."

A collective groan rose from the line behind Willow.

Figures. The day had barely started, and it was already going downhill. Normally, she brought tea from home for exactly this reason. She didn't even want to imagine what Scottie must be thinking.

But Scottie just looked over from where she was paying at the second register to her right with a sympathetic smile. "You've really had a run of bad luck with tech lately, huh?"

Willow forced a laugh, trying to pretend this was something out of the ordinary and not an everyday occurrence for her. "You can say that again."

"Don't worry about it. I've got you." Scottie indicated to the barista at her register to add Willow's chai latte to her order.

When Willow wanted to hand her the ten-dollar bill, Scottie waved her off. "My treat."

Willow frowned. "You don't have to—"

"You can get me next time."

Next time? Who had said there would be a next time? Willow didn't go to coffee with colleagues—especially not queer colleagues she'd just accidentally come out to and who might misinterpret it as a date.

She hesitated, but she was out of options since the coffee shop didn't take cash. Sighing, she slid her wallet back into her purse. "Thank you."

"My pleasure," Scottie said.

Side by side, they waited for their beverages.

Scottie leaned against the pickup counter, hands in her pockets, completely at ease.

Willow couldn't help envying her. She couldn't remember when she had last been so relaxed and comfortable in her own skin. She stood in silence and tried to avoid glancing at Scottie or her chameleon pin.

Luckily, it didn't take long before the barista slid over their beverages.

Paper cups in hand, they headed out.

The drizzle had stopped, and the cool air felt refreshing on Willow's overheated cheeks.

They easily fell into step as they strolled toward Kudos's office building.

"So," Scottie said.

Willow tensed, sure she would ask about her club membership, her constant tech glitches, or some other too-personal topic.

"You're a chai latte person," Scottie said with a soft, knowing smile.

Willow took a quick sip—more to hide her relief than because she was thirsty—and nodded. "That or an Earl Grey. Like Captain Picard."

Scottie's smile grew. "Oh, you're a fellow Trekkie?"

"I wouldn't say that, but I've watched a few episodes."

"Favorite character?" Scottie asked, now all serious, as if she were conducting a job interview and Willow's answer would decide whether she got hired.

Tasha Yar, Willow wanted to say. But then Scottie might think she was into strong blondes with slightly shaggy hair. B'Elanna Torres, the Voyager's chief engineer, was out too because Willow didn't want Scottie to assume she had a thing for women who could fix stuff. And she definitely couldn't name Scotty, the engineer of the original series. "Spot, the cat," she finally said.

Scottie laughed. "Best answer ever. Why do I get the feeling you watched way more than just a few episodes?"

Willow bit back the playful banter at the tip of her tongue. Why was it so easy to slip into this effortless rhythm with Scottie—as if they were old friends…or on their third date? "Who's your favorite?"

"Easy," Scottie replied without missing a beat. "Kira Nerys. She's tough, fiery, and has her walls up at first, but as time goes on, we get to see her vulnerable side. Plus those nose wrinkles are just too damn cute." She scrunched up her own nose in a way that was much too cute as well.

To Willow's surprise, she was almost disappointed when they reached Kudos's main entrance.

Scottie lengthened her step to reach the glass door first, but instead of entering, she held it open for Willow.

The gesture warmed Willow all over, and she quickly ducked past Scottie so she wouldn't see her blush. "Thank you," she murmured.

Willow's low heels clickety-clacked on the travertine as they crossed the lobby. Scottie's steps were silent next to her.

Again, Scottie let her enter the elevator first, then pressed the button for both their floors—thirteen for Willow, ten for herself.

Willow kept her gaze fixed on the floor numbers while the elevator carried them upstairs. Her brain fluctuated back and forth between *Say something* and *Don't you dare*. She had revealed enough about herself for one day.

Finally, the elevator stopped on the tenth floor.

"This is me," Scottie said as the doors slid open. "See you later."

"Hopefully not," Willow responded. "Uh, I mean..."

Scottie laughed, warm and genuine. "I know what you mean. Let's hope you won't need my services again anytime soon."

God, she really was a maddeningly nice person.

"Have a good one!" Scottie lifted her paper cup in a silent salute, then stepped off the elevator.

The doors closed behind her before Willow could decide on how to reply.

Scottie's laughter still seemed to echo in the elevator.

Willow's head hadn't stopped spinning. She stared at her reflection in the mirrored back wall of the elevator. What on earth had just happened?

She had accidentally outed herself to one of Kudos's IT support specialists, not to mention half of Lloyd District's caffeine addicts...and now she owed Scottie a coffee.

Chapter 6

Scottie sat at her desk and scrolled through the patch deployment and vulnerability scan report, looking for any laptops or computers that hadn't updated overnight. Her gaze tracked the column of green check marks, but her mind wandered back to her coffee shop encounter with Willow earlier that day.

She had long since finished her latte, yet snippets of their conversation still played on a loop in Scottie's head. *I'm part of the club… I'm gay. A lesbian.*

Then she cringed as she remembered her own reply: *That wasn't what I was asking, but it's delightful to know anyway.* Delightful! Really? Why the hell had she said that?

A ticket notification popped up on her left screen, pulling Scottie from her thoughts.

This time, she welcomed the distraction and clicked over to the ticket queue immediately.

Windows acting weird, the subject line said. It was from someone in Operations.

Her gaze darted to the name of the employee requesting help: *Willow Greene.*

Willow! Scottie sat up straighter. What was going on? She clicked into the ticket and scanned the details.

Apparently, the computer's windows were minimizing or snapping to the side without Willow clicking anything.

Huh. That was weird. The loaner laptop had worked perfectly on Friday, and so had the external mouse and keyboard.

Mateo glanced over. "What's with the frown? Please don't tell me we've got another firmware rollback."

"No, nothing like that," Scottie said, her gaze still fixed on the screen. "Just a new ticket."

"What's so puzzling about that?" Mateo looked at the dashboard on his own monitor.

Gordon was faster. "Willow Greene again? That's the third ticket she's submitted in less than a week!"

"Yeah, but the other two were because of the defective motherboard. It's not Willow's fault the problem didn't become clear until my second visit." Scottie snapped her mouth shut, surprised at how quick she'd been to defend Willow.

"Still, two completely different issues back-to-back?" Gordon shook his head. "And now it's a loaner that was working just fine before you handed it over. What are the chances of that happening to someone as tech-savvy as you say she is?"

Scottie opened her mouth, about to defend Willow again, but before she could, Mateo lifted his index finger in an "aha" gesture.

"Or," he said, dragging out the word dramatically, "maybe there is another explanation."

Scottie's gaze zeroed in on him. "Go on, Sherlock."

"Maybe she's breaking stuff on purpose," Mateo said.

Scottie clutched her armrests with both hands. It wouldn't have been the first time an employee had sabotaged their computer, but she didn't want to believe that was what was going on here. "Bullshit. Why would she do that?"

Mateo grinned. "So you have a reason to come fix it."

"What?" Scottie and Gordon asked at the same time.

"Think about it," Mateo said. "If she's as clever as you seem to think she is, maybe she has figured out that this is the best way to guarantee a little one-on-one attention from her favorite IT support person. Maybe she's working up the courage to ask you out or something."

Just last week, Scottie would have dismissed it and told him Willow was most likely straight and not interested in her at all. But now she knew that wasn't true—at least about Willow being straight. Of course, that didn't mean Willow wanted to ask her out. She didn't even seem comfortable having to call Scottie for IT help.

Even if she were interested, it wouldn't matter. Scottie had experienced firsthand how quickly a decade-long relationship could dissolve without warning, and she wasn't up for a repeat, especially not with someone as closed-off as Willow. She was clearly emotionally unavailable.

"That's as ridiculous as the socks you're wearing." She pointed at his ankles, where little T-Rexes swinging golf clubs were peeking out. "I can guarantee you that's not it. Something else is going on."

"Like what?" Mateo asked.

Scottie had no answer. She just knew Willow was neither the incompetent technophobe nor the smitten schemer her colleagues were making her out to be. "No idea. But she's definitely not submitting tickets just to see me."

"Then maybe I should go," Mateo offered.

"No, I'll do it," Scottie said quickly, then added, "I'm familiar with her current setup, so it will be faster if I go."

"Her *setup*." Smirking, Mateo painted quotation marks in the air. "Right."

"Yeah, setup. If you don't know what that means, maybe it's a good thing I'm the one going." Scottie grabbed her tool kit and bag and strode to the door without waiting for a comeback.

"This is the weirdest thing I've ever seen." Barb craned her neck to stare across the low divider between their desks and studied Willow's screens as if a time portal had opened there. "I've been working in offices since before computers were even a thing. In all that time, I've never seen anything like this."

The Excel file on Willow's left monitor resized itself and snapped to the top, while several other open apps on her right screen dropped to the task bar, minimizing themselves without Willow doing anything.

Willow forced a smile onto her face, despite her rising panic. She was attracting too much attention. One of their supply chain analysts was glancing over, and she if she wasn't careful, Celeste would notice that she had another tech problem. Last time, she'd gotten lucky: Scottie had chalked it up to the computer sitting on the carpet, even though Willow knew her tech-killing aura was to blame. But she wouldn't get that lucky twice.

Quickly, she dragged the Excel file away from the top until it filled the entire screen again and restored Outlook and the other minimized apps.

"Maybe they gave me the glitchy equipment. Like an initiation prank for the new admin or something like that."

"Maybe they did," Barb replied. "I don't know how else to explain having to summon IT three times in less than a week!"

It was a lot, even for Willow. She usually had a couple of glitches every month, but this was excessive.

Everything had been fine this morning. Her alarm had gone off on time, without her phone battery dying overnight. The microwave had worked without a single passive-aggressive beep. Even her tablet, which often needed several attempts to recognize her fingerprint, had unlocked instantly.

But then she had run into Scottie in that damn coffee shop, misunderstood what Scottie was asking, and blurted out that she was a lesbian. God, she had completely embarrassed herself.

No wonder the avalanche of her emotions had sent her computer into a tailspin.

Calm down! If she didn't, she would risk making another nearby device glitch while Scottie—or one of her colleagues—was there. She closed her eyes, inhaled through her nose to the count of five, then slowly released her breath through her mouth. When she opened her eyes again, her Excel file had snapped back to the top of the screen, but at least the other apps were still where she'd left them.

Okay, that was better. She could work with that. Just as she reached for the mouse, a soft knock sounded on her cubicle wall.

Willow jumped and looked up.

Scottie stood on the other side of the divider, her toolbox in one hand, the fingers of the other casually hooked behind the strap of her laptop bag. She smiled as if she had just walked into a party instead of being called to fix yet another one of Willow's computer problems. "We really have to stop meeting like this."

Her tone was gentle and teasing, but Willow couldn't help feeling guilty. She also couldn't shake her embarrassment over the coffee shop incident or the feeling that she had revealed too much. "I'm so sorry for taking up so much of your time. I know you probably have a million more important things to do."

Scottie walked around the partition. "Other things? Yeah. More important? Nope. I mean, you people from Operations keep telling me your department is what keeps the company running, so if the operations coordinator can't use her computer, that ticket should get top priority, right?"

"Right," Barb said from her side of the divider.

"Hey, Barb," Scottie called. "How are things?"

"Can't complain," Barb answered. "Everything on my end is still working, which feels like a win after witnessing Willow's bad luck."

Scottie set down her bag and toolbox. "So, what's the problem this time? The ticket said your windows are misbehaving?"

Willow nodded. "They keep minimizing or snapping to the sides or the top without me clicking anything. I'll be working on my spreadsheet or sending an email, and suddenly, the windows move when I'm not even touching the mouse."

"I see." Scottie scribbled something down on a clipboard. "How long has it been happening?"

"On and off all morning."

A wrinkle formed between Scottie's sandy-brown brows. She lowered the clipboard and looked at Willow with gentle rebuke. "Why didn't you call me sooner?"

Willow glanced down at her desk. "I didn't want to bother you again."

Scottie took another step toward her. "It's no bother. Really." Her voice was sincere, all teasing gone.

Willow's throat constricted. God, she wanted to believe her. It would be so nice to not be a bother for a change. But that kind of hope was dangerous. Sooner or later, her not-so-little quirk became a burden to everyone.

The clacking of Barb's keyboard stopped. Her head popped up over the divider like a groundhog sticking its head out of its burrow. She studied them with a curious expression before disappearing from sight.

"All right." Scottie cleared her throat. "Let's take a look at what's happening. Mind if I drive?" She pointed at Willow's workstation.

Willow pushed her chair back and stood. "Be my guest."

Scottie sat down at the desk, opened and closed a few apps, moved them around, dragging them to the top, the bottom, left, and right.

The windows behaved like obedient little soldiers, staying exactly where they were supposed to. Not a single one resized or changed its position without a prompt.

Willow wasn't surprised. This was exactly what usually happened, at least when the glitch first started. As soon as she stepped away from the desk and someone else took over, the problem disappeared. "I swear the windows have been glitching all morning."

"Guess I intimidated them into behaving," Scottie said with a lopsided grin.

A snort came from Barb's side of the cubicle wall. "You're about as intimidating as a preschooler."

"Have you ever seen what preschoolers can do to a new sofa?" Scottie asked, her tone full of mock horror. She opened the settings, then checked the multitasking options. "Hmm. I thought it might be Snap Assist being overactive, but it's toggled off. That should have prevented any automatic snapping."

Willow said nothing but kept watching over Scottie's shoulder.

Scottie moved with smooth precision, her fingers gliding over the keyboard without her having to glance down even once. Her expression was calm and focused, her hands steady as she checked for loose or stuck keys, then flipped the mouse over to inspect the sensor.

Somehow, watching her made Willow even more flustered.

Scottie ran a few diagnostics. "Hmm," she said again—not a sound Willow liked hearing from IT support. "I can't find anything wrong. Are you sure you didn't accidentally trigger a shortcut? Sometimes, that can happen when you're using a new keyboard and the layout is slightly different from—"

"I'm sure." Willow dug her fingernails into her palms. She really should be used to that kind of question. Whenever she experienced a tech problem no one else could reproduce, people eventually concluded that she was the one causing the problem.

Well, she was—just not the way they thought. They believed she was incompetent when it was actually her strange, disruptive energy or maybe her mere presence that made devices misbehave.

She couldn't blame Scottie for assuming the same, yet it still stung.

Scottie seemed to notice because she held up both hands. "Hey, I'm not saying you did anything wrong. I'm just trying to consider all possibilities. But if you're sure you didn't hit the Windows key or something, I believe you."

The tightness in Willow's belly eased the tiniest fraction. She uncurled her fists and rubbed the little crescent-shaped indents her nails had left on her palms. While she didn't know Scottie well enough to be sure, the look in her eyes seemed genuine. Maybe Scottie did believe her—at least for now.

Scottie tried a few more things, then shook her head and sat back. "It could be the keyboard or the mouse causing phantom input, but since the windows are behaving now, it's hard to pin down. I could replace them, just to rule them out as the source of the problem."

"No," Willow said quickly. She would bring her own mouse and keyboard if she had to. If Scottie replaced them with new ones and they failed too, IT would become suspicious for sure. "That's not necessary," she added more calmly.

Barb peered around the cubicle wall, eyebrows raised, but didn't say anything.

"All right. Then let's just keep an eye on it." Scottie got up. "Why don't you give it a try? Just to make sure it's working for you now."

Willow took her place, opened a few windows, and moved them around. Everything responded the way it was supposed to.

Scottie's gaze rested on her hands, following her every move, and Willow couldn't shake the feeling that she was focusing on her, not on the way the windows reacted. The subtle scrutiny rankled her, even though she had to admit it was a reasonable strategy. If she were in IT, she probably would have tried to rule out user error too.

"Looks good," Scottie finally said. "But if the windows start to rebel again, call me immediately."

"Will do." Willow stood and backed away from her computer so it wouldn't start to glitch again while Scottie was watching.

But she had misjudged how close Scottie still was—and bumped into her.

Both grabbed onto the nearest object to keep their balance. Their hands collided on the back of the desk chair.

A jolt shot through Willow's fingers. The air seemed to crackle, and a visible spark jumped between them.

Scottie flinched back with a sharp "Whoa!"

Ouch. Willow rubbed her fingers. She was as used to those little zaps as she was to people not believing her. Her entire life, she had always built up more static electricity than anyone else she knew. It was probably part of why she killed so many electronic devices.

She had hoped it wouldn't be as bad in Portland with its wet air, but apparently, that didn't make a difference.

Quite the opposite. The jolt had been stronger than usual.

"You okay?" Scottie asked.

"Yeah, I'm fine. Must be the carpet."

"Right." Scottie lingered for a moment longer, then slung her bag across her shoulders and picked up her toolbox. "Well, then. I guess I'll see you around." She gave her a nod and crossed the room toward the glass door.

As soon as she was gone, Barb's head popped up over the partition, a big grin stretching across her face. "Did I just see sparks flying between you and Scottie?"

Willow's spine stiffened. "It was just static."

Barb leaned farther over the divider. "Hey, I'm not homophobic, if that's what you're worried about."

"Good to know." And it was. At her former job, that hadn't been a given. Not that most of her former colleagues had known she was gay...or anything else about her. For someone who thought TikTok was a breath mint, Barb had amazingly accurate gaydar. "But it was still just static, not Cupid's arrow or something."

"Of course." Barb nodded, but her grin remained. "Just the carpet."

"Exactly." Willow plopped onto her office chair, hoping Barb would get the hint and go back to work. Her hand still tingled faintly—from the static electricity, not from her skin touching Scottie's, of course. She ignored the sensation as she reached for the mouse. Hopefully, it wouldn't start any trouble because under no circumstances would she be contacting Scottie again today.

Chapter 7

Willow pretended to check the time on the wall clock across the office, but she was actually sneaking glances through the glass door toward the elevator.

Scottie hadn't given a specific time, just mentioned that she'd have her computer back to her on Wednesday. Since it was nearly lunchtime, Willow expected Scottie to emerge with the cart any minute.

"You okay?" Barb walked over from the break room and paused behind her, cradling a mug of steaming coffee. "Is the laptop still giving you grief?"

"Oh, no, no. Everything's running smoothly." That wasn't entirely true. The windows were still snapping to the edges of her screen every now and then. But after she had, for the most part, gotten over her accidental coming out in the coffee shop, the laptop had calmed down too. Plus she figured she would return it soon anyway, so the occasional glitch wasn't worth reporting. "I'm just waiting for my computer to come back from IT. I'm supposed to get it back today."

"Ah. So you're waiting for Scottie." Barb gave her a knowing grin before continuing on to her own desk.

"I'm waiting for *my computer*. I don't care who delivers it."

"Right," Barb said.

Willow ignored her and went back to updating the company's vendor list, making sure all contact information was current.

The elevator dinged, then the frosted glass door opened with a beep and the rattle of a rolling cart drifted toward her.

Willow kept her gaze on the vendor list so Barb wouldn't think she was eager to see Scottie. Which, of course, she wasn't. She had never in her life looked forward to interacting with someone from IT.

The sound of squeaky wheels on the carpeted floor grew louder as the cart made its way down the aisle toward her. Finally, it stopped next to her cubicle.

"Hi," came a friendly voice—a male one.

Willow looked up.

The person pushing the cart wasn't Scottie. The man standing there was stocky and about Scottie's height, and a rebellious swoop of hair fell onto his forehead. But that was where the similarities ended. His hair was black and curly, and he looked several years younger than Scottie, with smooth, warm brown skin that was free of the freckles that dotted Scottie's fairer face.

"I'm Mateo Alvarez from IT. You must be Willow. I come bearing gifts." He waved his arm at the cart as if she had won the main prize in a raffle. "I've got your computer here."

Willow stared at him for a moment, then quickly said, "Hi. Thanks for bringing it over."

"Sorry it took a while, but now it's got a brand-new motherboard. Scottie also cleaned the fans and reapplied thermal paste to make sure you won't have any problems with overheating."

So Scottie had worked on the computer. Why wasn't she the one delivering it, then? Willow clenched her jaw to keep from asking.

Mateo unloaded the computer from the cart. "Scottie said to make sure to keep it on the desk," he said with a grin but didn't offer any information about why Scottie hadn't shown up this time.

"I won't move it an inch." Willow backed up the file she'd been working on to the cloud and logged out. Then she got up to give him space so he could disconnect the monitors and peripherals from the laptop and switch them over to the computer.

He handed her the USB drive she'd forgotten to take from the laptop.

Their fingers brushed, but thankfully, she didn't zap him, because she had touched the metal desk leg as she'd gotten up.

"Thanks."

Once all the cables were in place, Mateo pressed the power button. Within seconds, the screens came to life, displaying the login page with Kudos's by-now familiar default background. "Should be ready to go. Give it a try."

Willow took a seat, logged in, opened a couple of apps, and typed a few words.

Everything was working without a glitch, and all her files were there.

"Looks perfect. Thanks so much," she said.

"Great." Mateo gathered the loaner laptop. "If anything else comes up, let us know."

"Will do. Thank you."

A quick wave, then he wheeled the cart back down the aisle.

Willow didn't watch him go. She opened the vendor list to make sure it had synced correctly.

"No sparks with this one," Barb commented from the other side of the divider.

Willow gritted her teeth. "I'm wearing different shoes today."

"Now it's the shoes? I thought the carpet was to blame?" Amusement colored Barb's tone.

"It was, but maybe it likes these shoes better," Willow replied. "Now get back to work and let me focus on the vendor list, or my on-the-job trainer will have my head."

Barb chuckled. "Right. Wouldn't want the mean old biddy to add your head to her trophy collection."

"Exactly." Willow forced her attention back to the list and updated one of the addresses.

No missed keystrokes, no zigzagging cursor, no misbehaving windows. For once, everything was working perfectly.

Then why did it feel as if something vital to the system was starting to go off-track anyway?

"Oh, come on. You've got to come with me. It's Wednesday, which means it's taco bar day in the cafeteria!" Barb did a little dance, looking more like an excited five-year-old than a woman about to retire.

"Tacos on a Wednesday?" Willow raised her brows. "Isn't it supposed to be Taco Tuesday?"

Barb waved her hand. "Kudos does things their own way. Besides, once you taste the tacos, you won't care what day it is. The slow-cooked pork in their carnitas just melts in your mouth, and their guacamole is so good, I might sneak in here every Wednesday once I retire. So, are you coming or what?"

Willow pointed at the reusable container she'd just pulled from the office fridge. "Sounds delicious, but I brought lunch."

"You can have that for dinner." Barb tugged on her sleeve. "I want to introduce you to my friends down in Marketing. I always have lunch with them. Sally is a sweetheart, and Jack does this hilarious impression of Mr. Sorensen that has us all in stitches."

For a moment, Willow imagined how nice it would be to stroll into the cafeteria, chat with colleagues while waiting in line, and bond over company gossip.

She pushed the thought away. She'd never made friends at work in any of her previous jobs. Why would she start now? It was better to keep her distance and avoid the cafeteria. After everything that had happened in the coffee shop, she didn't want to risk another POS system crashing when she tapped her ID badge to it, especially not when someone from IT—or, worse, one of her bosses—might be around to witness it.

"I'm sure they're great, Barb, but I need a little fresh air. Maybe another time." She grabbed her jacket and lunch and slipped out before Barb could try to change her mind.

Quickly, she made her way down to the lobby and crossed the street to a park she had discovered on her first day at Kudos.

It was small, just a strip of green between the glass-and-steel towers and the mid-rise office buildings of the Lloyd District, but it had become her oasis during lunchtime.

Today, it was especially beautiful since it wasn't raining for once. The early-October sun had finally made a rare appearance, and patches of blue sky peeked out from behind the gray clouds. The leaves were turning gold and crimson.

She found an empty bench next to a large maple tree and took a seat. Carefully, she opened the container, balanced it on her knees, and dug in.

Yum. The quinoa bowl tasted as great as it had the night before. The roasted veggies and sweet potatoes offset the tang of the lemon dressing perfectly.

A fountain to her left gurgled softly while she ate, and a fryer at a nearby food cart hissed and popped. The aroma of spicy fried chicken mingled with the scent of damp earth and fallen leaves.

Footsteps crunched across the path, heading toward her.

Willow expected a fellow office worker looking for a lunch spot in the sun or an unhoused person in need of spare change.

"Hi."

Willow nearly choked on a piece of broccoli. She hadn't expected to hear that voice here. Her head jerked up.

Scottie was standing in front of her, both hands in her pockets and her typical easy smile on her face. Instead of the company-issued polo shirt, she was wearing a soft-looking gray sweater, which made her appear even more approachable. Her blonde hair shimmered in the sun as she pulled one hand from her pocket and ran her fingers through the wavy strands. "I spotted you when I parked across the street and thought I'd say hi."

Willow peered up at her, blinking against the sun that formed a halo around Scottie's head, and didn't know what to say other than: "Hi."

Scottie didn't seem to share her self-consciousness. She sat down on the other end of the bench without waiting for an invitation, as if it had never occurred to her that Willow wouldn't want company during her lunch break.

Willow nearly rolled her eyes. *Extroverts.*

Scottie gestured at Willow's lunch. "You don't like tacos?"

"I do, but..." Willow hesitated. She couldn't tell Scottie why she was really avoiding the cafeteria, so she opted for telling her about the second reason. "Bringing my own lunch saves a few bucks." The admission made heat rise to her cheeks.

"I get it." The look in Scottie's eyes was understanding. "Living in Portland is expensive."

Willow nodded. And so was having to replace her phone and laptop every year.

"Did you get your computer back?" Scottie asked as if she could sense Willow had been thinking about her devices.

"Yes, I did. Mateo brought it over earlier. It's working perfectly. Thanks again."

"You're very welcome. Sorry I couldn't deliver it myself. Mr. Haggerty, our CEO, is working from his cabin at the Sandy River today and couldn't connect to Kudos's VPN. He urgently needed access to the toy design files on the company server, so I had to drive out and set it up."

Ah, that explained it. Willow shrugged, aiming for casual. "No worries at all. What matters is that I got my computer back. I don't care who delivered it. Mateo did a great job setting it up." She needed to make it clear that she didn't have a favorite IT support person. It was bad enough that Barb thought she did; she couldn't let Scottie think so too. That could lead to all kinds of complications.

Scottie's smile faltered. A shadow flickered across her face.

Guilt twisted in Willow's stomach, but she knew she couldn't take it back. It was better to draw a clear line. She stabbed at a piece of sweet potato with her fork and dragged it through the quinoa without lifting it to her mouth.

The expression on Scottie's face lasted only for a moment, then her friendly smile was back. "Anyway, glad to hear Mateo got you back up and running while I was off playing tech support in the woods."

Willow wasn't sure whether she should feel relieved or dismayed that Scottie was letting her off the hook so easily and just moved on as if nothing had happened. Probably the latter. She wanted boundaries, right?

And yet she found herself continuing the conversation too. "Sandy River… That's what, about an hour's drive one way?"

"Yeah." Scottie shrugged. "But I didn't mind."

Scottie never seemed to mind anything. Was she really always so kind and easygoing?

"It's a nice drive," Scottie added. "Gorgeous scenery, especially this time of year. Have you ever been out that way?"

Willow shook her head. "I haven't had much of a chance to explore the area yet."

"But you've seen a bit of the city, right?" Scottie asked.

"Oh yeah. My sister dragged me to Powell's, the vacuum cleaner museum, a kombucha tasting, and to get some pear-and-blue-cheese ice cream at Salt and Straw."

Scottie nodded approvingly. "Good choices. All sufficiently weird, which will help you earn your Portlander badge."

Willow bit her lip. With the effect she had on electronics, she was sufficiently weird already, thank you very much. "If you think that's weird…my sister also made me try goat yoga."

Laughter burst from Scottie's chest. She slapped her thighs with both hands, apparently not minding at all that people looked over from nearby benches. "Goat yoga? You're making that up!"

Her laugh was so unfiltered and genuine that Willow's lips curved into a smile. "No, I swear!"

Still chuckling, Scottie eyed her skeptically. "You want me to believe the goats are doing yoga?"

"No, people are," Willow replied. "You're supposed to attempt a yoga pose while a goat claims your mat and another is climbing on top of you."

Scottie's unrestrained laughter rang out across the little park again. "Yeah, okay, that does it—Portlander badge earned."

Willow pierced a slice of carrot. "Well, I admit that I didn't do much yoga, but it was a lot of fun anyway. The goats are really cuddly, and their antics made us laugh."

"Just wait until next year. If your sister is a connoisseur of weird things, I'm sure she'll drag you to the Naked Bike Ride and the Beard and Mustache Competition."

Willow had heard of the Naked Bike Ride, but a beard competition? "No, thanks. I'm not into facial hair." Once again, the words had come out without her permission. That seemed to happen a lot around Scottie. She rubbed her overheated cheek with the back of her hand.

Scottie laughed again. "Yeah, me neither. The Mermaid Parade is more my speed. Sparkly costumes, fishnet stockings, seashell bras, and colorful body paint—it's basically Pride with tail fins!"

The mental image made Willow chuckle along with her. "That sounds interesting."

Scottie nodded and opened her mouth to reply.

Oh shit. Was Scottie about to invite her to the event? Expressing interest in the Mermaid Parade might have been a huge mistake.

The buzzing of Scottie's phone interrupted before she could say anything. "Sorry, hang on. That might be one of my colleagues. They're probably wondering what's taking me so long." She dragged her gaze away from Willow, pulled the phone from her pocket, and tapped open the message.

Willow exhaled. She stared into her bowl, pretending to be occupied by her lunch, while Scottie read the text.

Scottie slid the phone back into her pocket. "Mateo wants me to pick up some donuts on the way back. That man has a secret addiction to pumpkin spice donuts. Want me to pick you up one too? They make a great dessert. I could drop it off at your desk if you want."

Willow fished a piece of sweet potato from her bowl and stuffed it into her mouth to buy herself some time.

Scottie tilted her head like a golden retriever waiting for her to throw a tennis ball.

"No, thanks." It felt like kicking a puppy, so Willow patted her stomach to soften the rejection. "I'm full."

Scottie straightened. "All right. I should probably say no more often too, but life's too short to turn down yummy treats." She flashed her a grin and got up. "See you around."

Willow gave a small, tight smile. "See you."

As Scottie walked away, Willow's gaze followed her, watching her cross the street and weave through the company parking lot until she lost sight of her in the jumble of cars.

"What was that?" she muttered to herself.

Once again, she had opened up and told Scottie more about herself than she had wanted to. She hadn't meant to bring up her sister or their weekend activities or to remind Scottie of her sexual orientation again.

Why was Scottie so easy to talk to? Something about her presence seemed to ease the constant knot of tension in Willow's belly, caused by the knowledge that technological doom was always just around the corner.

But if she wasn't careful, she was risking something even worse. As an IT person, Scottie could easily figure out Willow's secret. She couldn't afford to get too comfortable around her, no matter how nice Scottie was.

Sighing, Willow put the lid back on her container. She'd lost her appetite.

Chapter 8

Willow clicked *print* on the office supply order. It felt good to finally be able to take little tasks off Barb's plate rather than add to her workload. She stood and weaved around her colleagues' desks to collect the document from the printer.

The large gray machine next to the support pillar whirred to life.

Just as Willow reached it, the printer let out an alarming *beep*. An error message popped up on the control display. *Paper jam. Remove paper.*

"Come on." She needed to print one measly page. That wasn't too much to ask, was it?

Quickly, trying not to attract anyone's attention, she pulled out the tray.

The paper was neatly stacked. No ripped pages, folded corners, or sheets crumpled into an accordion.

She opened the top panel, then the one on the side.

Neither showed a shred of paper, yet the printer insisted there was a paper jam.

"Liar," she muttered.

As a last Hail Mary attempt, she switched the machine off and back on, but it continued to flash the same error message.

"Please, no," Willow whispered. "No, no, no, no, no. Don't do this to me."

But maybe it wasn't the printer. Maybe it was her causing the issue—again. Why, oh why had she taken an office job? She should have applied for a job in which she didn't need to work with any electronic devices.

The question wasn't new, of course. Every time she left one job, she managed to convince herself it would be different somewhere else, if only she just gave it one more try and managed to settle in and calm down her emotions.

Besides, were there any jobs left nowadays that didn't involve computers or some other tech? None came to mind, other than yoga instructor, which made her think of goat yoga and her conversation with Scottie in the park last week.

Scottie... Willow had managed to avoid her for the past five days, but now she would probably have to submit a ticket to IT.

Maybe, if she was lucky, they would send Mateo again.

But that thought didn't make her happy either.

"Trouble with the printer?"

The calm voice from behind made Willow jump. As she whirled around, she bumped her elbow on the printer.

Celeste stood in front of her, posture straight and her white blouse crisp. Willow always wondered whether she'd been in the military. The operations manager didn't frown, but she didn't smile either. She just looked at Willow with that probing, analytical gaze that always made her feel as if she was being assessed and found lacking.

Even after two weeks of working at Kudos, Willow didn't quite know what to make of her. Did Celeste like her, merely tolerate her, or hope to get rid of her as soon as possible?

"Um, yes," Willow answered belatedly. "It insists there's a paper jam, but I checked. There's nothing in there."

Celeste stepped closer, her heels making precise, muffled taps on the carpet. "Have you tried turning it off and back on?"

Willow started to sweat. She resisted the urge to wipe her hands on her slacks. "Yes. Didn't help."

Celeste eyed her as if she'd taken a hammer to the printer. "I've noticed you've run into several technological issues in the two weeks you've been working here. Is there a problem I need to be aware of?"

Willow struggled not to gulp. "No, no, of course not. There's no problem. I just... I think they were probably older models, due for a refresh."

As soon as the words left her mouth, she knew it had been the wrong thing to say. Her boss clearly prided herself on running a tight, efficient department, not one that wrestled with outdated systems.

Celeste folded her arms across her pristine blouse.

"Or, you know, just Mercury in retrograde or something," Willow added quickly, trying to recover. She offered a weak smile.

Celeste didn't return it. "There's no scientifically proven effect of planetary movements on technology."

"Right. Of course. I mean, of course not." Celeste was definitely the type who would never believe her, even if Willow told her the truth. She'd dismiss it as a woo-woo excuse.

Celeste studied her for a few more seconds, with the same expression she'd used on the inventory report last week, right before declaring that someone had double-counted four pallets of talking plush giraffes. "Call IT and get this"—she waved a hand at the trouble-making printer—"figured out."

"Of course," Willow said. "I'll take care of it right away."

Celeste gave a curt nod, then strode back toward her desk, her steps fluid and efficient.

Willow sank against the printer. *Crap.* Now she had to summon IT again, and her boss would probably keep an even closer eye on her going forward. Whatever Celeste said, it felt as if the planets *were* out to get her.

"It's your girlfriend again," Mateo announced when a new support ticket popped up on his screen.

"Willow?" Scottie opened the ticket on her own screen, even as she protested: "She's not my girlfriend."

"Yet," Gordon added.

Scottie glared at her older colleague. "You too, Brutus?"

Gordon shrugged. "She's certainly our most loyal customer right now, and I don't think it's because she hopes to finally make my acquaintance."

For a second, she wondered whether Gordon and Mateo were right. Could Willow really be submitting tickets because she would then have a reason to see Scottie?

She dismissed the thought once more. If Willow were interested in her, she would have taken her up on the offer to bring her a donut last week.

"What's the problem this time?" Gordon asked.

"Printer jam, but there's no stuck paper anywhere," Mateo said. "I won't even try to take this one."

"Maybe I should," Gordon said.

That was a first. Scottie gave him a doubtful look. "You want to leave your desk without the building being on fire?"

"I haven't met the infamous Willow yet, and Mateo said she's cute." Gordon slid his wire-frame glasses higher up on his nose and smoothed a palm over his perfectly groomed graying hair as if preparing for the meeting.

"May I remind you that you're a happily married man?" Scottie tried to keep her voice light and playful, but she could hear a bit of an edge sneaking in.

Gordon lifted his hands in a defensive gesture. "What? I said I want to meet her, not go out with her. I'd only be checking her out for you—to make sure she's not an asshole who's going to break your heart." At nearly fifty, he was fifteen years older than Scottie and often acted like a concerned big brother.

It was kind of touching. She knew they both meant well, but she didn't want them to mess with Willow. "Thanks, but I'm a big girl. And like I told you about a million times before, I'm not looking for a girlfriend. No one's checking out anyone, okay?"

"Well, then I'm not going," Gordon said.

Mateo huffed. "We both knew from the start who'd take this ticket."

They looked at her.

Maybe she could solve this issue remotely, just to prove that she wasn't eager to hurry upstairs and see Willow. Which she absolutely wasn't. Sure, she enjoyed chatting with her, but she did that with every employee who needed her help, simply because it calmed them down.

Scottie pulled up the printer's web console and checked the print queue. As expected, it showed a stuck job from Willow. She restarted the print spooler on the server.

The queue emptied, and the stuck job vanished.

Unfortunately, the printer status still showed the same error.

She put on her headset and called Willow's extension.

The call was answered on the second ring. "This is Willow Greene." She sounded a little breathless, as if she had hurried across the office to her desk.

The breathy tone sent a shiver through Scottie. "Hey, Willow, it's Scottie. I got your ticket and cleared the print queue on my end, but the error's still showing. Can you turn off the printer for me? Wait about thirty seconds, then turn it back on."

"I already did that," Willow replied. "Didn't help."

Not for the first time, Scottie told herself not to underestimate Willow. She never waited around for IT to solve the problem for her; she always tried a few things herself and only contacted them when she ran out of options. "Sorry, I should have known you tried that already."

Only silence answered, as if Willow was surprised Scottie thought so highly of her problem-solving skills.

"All right," Scottie said when Willow didn't answer. "I'll come up and check it out in person. Do me a favor and unplug the printer so it's cooled down by the time I get there."

"Will do," Willow said.

"Great. I'm heading upstairs now."

"Thanks, Scottie."

The way Willow said her name sent another ripple of goose bumps down Scottie's arms. She brushed her hands over them, trying to rub away the sensation. *Work,* she firmly told herself. This was work—nothing else.

She took off her headset, grabbed her tool kit, and headed to the door.

"Try fixing the machine this time, not just staring at the woman," Mateo called after her.

"For that remark, I won't stop by the cafeteria on my way back. No chocolate chip cookie for you." Scottie left the office she shared with her two colleagues and made her way toward the elevator.

She hadn't even taken three steps when her boss emerged from his office.

"Ah, Scottie. I was just on my way to see you," Miles Donnelly said. "Do you have a minute?"

Scottie hesitated. She didn't want to make Willow wait too long. "Yeah, sure, if it can't wait. I was on my way upstairs. Operations is having trouble with their printer."

"That's what I wanted to talk to you about," Miles said.

Scottie's chest tightened. That didn't sound good. Was Willow in trouble? Or was *she*?

Miles and their CIO wanted to see single-visit tickets, not multiple visits to resolve the same issue. But they had talked about Willow's motherboard and what could have been done to prevent that problem in the last team meeting, so that couldn't be it…could it?

Her supervisor nudged his office door open. "Come on in and take a seat."

Scottie followed him into the small office, its wall painted the same pale gray as the rest of the IT department. This room was missing the quirky touches of Scottie's office, like the cartoon taped above Mateo's desk, showing an IT person looking at a burning computer, saying *Have you tried turning it off and on again?*

But it did have a bigger window, which gave her a glimpse of the gray Portland sky and the glass facade of a building across the street.

She sank into the visitor's chair and waited with her heart beating slightly too fast.

Miles took a seat behind his desk. He clicked his pen on and off. "I just reviewed the tickets from the first half of October, and I've noticed *four* tickets from Willow Greene in the past two weeks." He paused as if letting the number sink in.

"Four really isn't that many," Scottie said before she could even think about it. Mr. Sorensen had filed more than that in a single day. But self-preservation kicked in, so she didn't add that.

Miles gave her a look. "It is when you zoom out and think about it company-wide. If each of our employees filed as many tickets, we'd need to triple our IT staff to keep response times reasonable."

"Right," Scottie said.

"So the question isn't whether four tickets is excessive or not." Miles clicked his pen again. "It's why those tickets exist. You've been dealing with Ms. Greene most of the time. You must have some idea of what's going on."

"I…" Scottie licked her dry lips. "I'm not sure yet."

Miles rubbed his reddish beard. "Do you think she's just a fumbling new hire who takes a little longer to get the hang of things? Do we need to provide additional training?"

"No, that's not it. She actually seems pretty knowledgeable when it comes to computers."

"Hmm." Miles scribbled something on his notepad. "Then why is she racking up tickets? We're not dealing with another Felicity situation, are we?"

"What? No!"

No one in Kudos's IT department would ever forget the employee who had been caught destroying her computer's graphics card with a pair of pliers, hoping to get a new, better machine. Willow wasn't like that. She might be reserved, always holding back, but she wasn't a liar or someone who damaged expensive devices on purpose.

When Miles raised his brows, Scottie realized how loudly she had defended Willow.

"No," she repeated more quietly. "I'm certain it's nothing like that. She's not sabotaging her devices. I ran every diagnostic known to mankind on her loaner laptop when I got it back, and it's running without any issues. It was a random one-off glitch. I really think she's just having a bit of bad luck with her tech."

Okay, *a lot* of bad luck.

"All right. If you're convinced that's all this is, we'll leave it at that—for now. But please keep a close eye on it. If there's a problem, I want to catch it early, before it affects the company's bottom line."

"Of course. I'll keep you posted." Scottie rose, gave him a nod, and headed to the door. Once she made it to the hallway, she exhaled.

It had been a normal check-in, nothing that should have made her tense up. *Just a bit of bad luck,* she mentally repeated what she had told Miles.

But if that was really all it was, why did she have the weird feeling that she'd lied to her boss?

Chapter 9

Willow felt as if everyone in the open-plan office was watching her as Scottie walked toward her with an easy stride, toolbox in hand. Barb definitely was. Her smirk was visible from several cubicles away.

"Morning, Willow." Scottie's smile seemed genuine. She didn't look annoyed at having to fix a printer problem on a Monday morning. "So, just for a nice change of pace, it's the printer giving you trouble today?"

Willow sighed. "Looks like it."

Scottie set down her toolbox. "All right. Let's see what's going on." She pulled the paper trays all the way out and set them aside, then peered into the now-empty cavity.

Nothing. Not that Willow had expected otherwise.

Scottie opened the top panel, then the one on the side of the printer.

"I already did that," Willow said. "There's no paper anywhere."

"I'm not doubting you, just double-checking," Scottie replied. "Sometimes, the tiniest shred of paper can cause a jam." The muscles in her forearms flexed as she pushed the printer away from the support pillar so she could get to the rear panel.

Willow leaned around the printer so she could see—the interior, not Scottie, of course.

"Nothing here either," Scottie said from behind the machine. "I think it's a false sensor reading. Dust or tiny bits of paper on one of the sensor lenses can block the infrared light beam, and that sends a paper jam signal to the main board."

Willow tried to focus on Scottie's explanation, but her brain was still busy trying to process the way the short sleeves of Scottie's company-issued polo shirt had tightened around her arms.

A sound that was half cough, half laugh drifted over from the direction of Barb's desk.

Willow quickly tore her gaze away and retreated to the other side of the printer. The last thing she needed was to add to the office gossip. She was already in enough trouble because she was pretty sure it wasn't just dust blocking the sensors. It was her weird aura or whatever made devices malfunction around her.

Scottie climbed out from behind the printer and crouched down in front of the gray beast. Her chinos stretched taut over her strong thighs.

Barb coughed again.

What? She wasn't ogling Scottie; she was merely watching their IT person repair the printer so she could learn how to do it herself next time.

Scottie's broad hands were steady and incredibly nimble as she reached into the paper tray bay and gently rotated the paper pickup rollers. Almost without having to look, she located a small flashlight and a can of compressed air in her tool kit. She shone the beam into the narrow cavity, angled the can, and gave a few sharp bursts of air. Then she repeated the process with the second tray.

Next, she opened the front panel, pulled out the heavy toner cartridge, and set it on a sheet of paper, which gave her access to the rollers deeper along the paper path.

She carefully rotated them too, then guided the flashlight's beam over the interior in search of the sensors.

As she leaned down and ducked her head to peer inside the printer, her lanyard with the company ID badge dangled into the cavity, blocking her view. Scottie indicated the flashlight and the can of compressed air she was holding. "Um, my hands are full, and I've got toner all over my fingers. I'd rather not get it on my shirt. Could you…?" She nodded down at the badge.

"Oh. Yeah, sure." Willow's mouth went dry as she stepped closer. *Christ, calm down. She asked you to get the badge out of the way, not to undress her!*

But her body didn't listen. Heat emanated from Scottie, making Willow's own temperature skyrocket in response. The smell of toner and the invigorating scent of Scottie's cedar shampoo filled her nose. She willed her fingers not to tremble as she reached into the printer, careful not to touch Scottie's hand or any part of the machine so she wouldn't zap either.

Her fingers closed around the ID badge's thin plastic. It was warm from where it had rested against Scottie's chest. *Don't you dare think about her chest!*

Finally, she managed to fish the badge out of the printer's interior. Then she froze, not sure what to do with it since the lanyard still rested around Scottie's neck. "Should I slip it around to your back?"

"Not a good idea. Mateo did that once and nearly strangled himself when the lanyard caught on something." Scottie's voice sounded lower, huskier, but that was probably because she was half-buried inside the printer. "It's safer to just stick it under my shirt, where it can't get in the way."

Safer? Willow mentally repeated. Reaching beneath Scottie's shirt felt anything but. Slowly, she lifted the badge.

The top two buttons on the polo shirt were undone, leaving enough space to guide the ID inside.

Her fingers brushed the soft cotton of Scottie's collar as she slipped the badge past a triangular patch of creamy skin into the shirt's opening. She tucked it beneath the warm fabric and lingered for a moment—only to make sure the plastic card wouldn't slip back out, of course.

Scottie held very still, her chest not even rising and falling against Willow's fingers.

Quickly, Willow withdrew and stepped back.

Scottie cleared her throat. "Thanks." She aimed the can into the guts of the machine and sent a few puffs of air toward the sensor.

Maybe Scottie should direct the can's nozzle at her instead. Willow could have used a blast of air to cool down.

"Could you hand me the microfiber cloth and one of the alcohol wipes from my tool kit?" Scottie's voice ripped her from her thoughts.

Willow gave herself a mental kick and went in search of the items, glad to have a reason to turn away from Scottie for a moment. When she handed them over, she was careful not to let their fingers brush.

"Thanks." Scottie used the wipe to scrub the toner residue from her fingers, then reached deeper into the machine with the microfiber cloth, probably cleaning the sensor lens.

Then she moved to the smaller panel that handled the double-sided printing and repeated the process, followed by the sensors in the rear.

Once she was done, she clicked the toner cartridge back into place, closed all panels, and reseated the paper trays. Finally, she plugged the printer back in and turned it on.

Both craned their necks as they watched it power up.

Willow peeked at the control display.

The infuriating error message was gone. *Ready to print,* it said instead.

She pumped her fist. "We did it! Uh, I mean you!"

Scottie grinned at her. Her cheeks were flushed, probably from the exertion of pushing the heavy machine back into its place against the support pillar. "Not so fast. Now comes the real moment of truth. Let's try printing."

Willow rushed to her desk to resend the print job. She was about to join Scottie at the printer again but then stopped herself. It was better to stay back, in case it had been her weird aura, not the dust, that had interfered with the sensors. She leaned against a filing cabinet, trying to inconspicuously keep her distance.

Scottie pulled a sheet of paper from the printer, then carried it toward Willow.

"Did it print correctly?" Willow asked.

"Sure did. Check it out." Scottie handed her the document.

This time, Willow was too slow to pull back a little or to ground herself on a metal object. When their fingers brushed, a jolt of energy shot through her hand. Tiny shock waves rippled along her skin, all the way up to her chest. The sheet of paper slid from her grasp and floated to the floor.

Scottie stared at her fingers, then at Willow. "That was intense."

"It's the carpet," Willow blurted.

"And her shoes," Barb added from her desk, the biggest smirk on her face.

"Yes." Willow nodded several times.

Scottie rubbed her fingers, bent, and picked up the document.

This time, they were both careful not to touch when she handed it over.

"Remind me to bring an antistatic spray for the carpet next time I'm up here," Scottie said.

It sounded as if she already took it for granted that Willow would have to call her for help again.

Unsettlingly, she was probably right.

Even more unsettling, though: Willow realized a part of her didn't mind at all. She was looking forward to seeing Scottie again. *Shit.*

Scottie's fingers still tingled as she hit the button for the first floor to pick up some cookies from the cafeteria. Gordon and Mateo needed the sugar rush, and she needed some time away from it all to get herself together.

As soon as the metal doors closed behind her, she sank against the elevator's mirrored wall. She savored the coolness seeping into her overheated skin for a few moments before she turned and stared at her reflection.

"What was that?" she asked the person in the mirror.

Of course, she didn't get a reply.

The jolt that had shot through her at the brush of their fingers wasn't the only thing that unsettled her. Even before that, the air between them had felt charged with more than just static electricity. If she was honest with herself, she knew what it had been: sizzling attraction. She could diagnose it as easily as she could pinpoint a disconnected Ethernet cable or a failing hard drive.

The moment in front of the printer was seared into her mind, with Willow so close that she could catch the faint scent of her body lotion and feel the heat radiating off her body.

What on earth had possessed her to tell Willow to stick the badge under her shirt? Why hadn't she set down the flashlight or the can of compressed air for a moment to get the ID out of the way herself? Or told Willow to take off the badge altogether? Either option would have been much faster—and less torturous.

Willow's fingers had grazed her collar. She hadn't even touched her skin, and yet the phantom sensation still lingered. The images that had flashed through Scottie's mind in that moment were definitely not safe for work. She had pictured that slim hand sliding more deeply beneath her shirt, trailing down with aching slowness to cup her breast.

Scottie let out a soft groan and forced her thoughts in a different direction—to that zap of energy when their fingers had brushed.

That should have been a wake-up call. *Warning: System error. Do not proceed.*

She wasn't ready to jump into something else; her head knew that, even if her body had apparently forgotten. The self-help article she'd read a while ago had said the same. It advised staying single for one month for each year of a relationship that had short-circuited, and those ten months of singledom weren't up yet. Her heart wasn't done rebooting, so she couldn't trust it yet. Until she could, it was safer to keep her interactions with Willow strictly professional.

When the metal doors slid open on the first floor, she pushed away from the wall and got out of the elevator.

Still, the tingling in her fingers and the phantom touch on her chest followed her all the way to the cafeteria and then back to her office.

Willow dropped onto her chair. She gripped her mouse more tightly than necessary, but it did nothing to chase away the lingering tingle in her fingers.

"Sparks again?" Barb commented with a smirk the size of Kudos's parking lot.

"You need a hobby," Willow grumbled.

Barb chuckled. "I've got one."

"Spying on your co-workers?"

"That and drawing annoyingly accurate conclusions from what I'm observing. I'll really miss it once I retire." Barb's sigh was probably meant to be humorously dramatic but came across as genuine.

"The colleagues you're spying on will really miss you too," Willow said quietly. And she would. Even though she had settled in well and had learned a lot in the past two weeks, she didn't even want to think about handling all of the complex processes by herself yet. Plus she had to admit she liked Barb.

In previous jobs, she had always been careful to keep her distance from her co-workers, worried they would notice how often she got in trouble with tech if she let anyone get close. But since Barb was training her, that wasn't an option. And maybe she didn't want it to be. It felt unexpectedly nice to have a friendly connection with a colleague instead of keeping things strictly business.

"Come over here." Barb waved as if wanting to shoo away both of their sad thoughts. "I'm going to show you how to double-check a supplier's invoice against our purchasing order so we're not paying for more resin than we actually received."

Willow scrambled up from her desk so quickly that she almost sent her chair spinning into the wall. She rushed over to Barb's cubicle, glad for the distraction.

Work she could handle. At least invoices and purchase orders wouldn't make her heart race the way it had back at the printer.

Chapter 10

On Thursday, Scottie walked into the Operations bullpen. She was there to hang a flyer, not to see Willow, but her gaze immediately went to Willow's desk anyway.

It was empty.

Oh. The hollow feeling in her belly was ridiculous.

"Are you looking for Willow?" Barb called across several desks.

Scottie walked over. "Hey, Barb. No, just swinging by to put up a flyer for trivia night." She held up the flyer like a piece of evidence proving her nonromantic intentions.

"So if you're not here to see Willow, that can of antistatic carpet spray is for me?" Barb asked, eyes twinkling.

"Oh, that." Scottie set it down on Willow's desk. "I meant to drop it off all week but kept forgetting." That wasn't quite the truth. She had tried to bribe Mateo to deliver it so she could stay away for a while, but, for once, even the promise of donuts hadn't been able to sway him. "Actually, I did bring something for you too."

Brow furrowed, Barb stared at the small bag of cough candy Scottie handed her.

"You had a really bad cough when I was up here on Monday, fixing the printer," Scottie said. "I thought these might help."

A sputtering cough burst from Barb's chest, sounding suspiciously like suppressed laughter. "Thanks," she finally wheezed out. "You're a sweetheart."

Scottie gave her a nod. "I'll go hang this up. See you later." She walked over to the department's break room, which looked more or less like IT's break room—just minus the empty energy drink cans and the *No trespassing—this means you, Mateo* note taped to the fridge.

A long counter with a microwave, a coffee machine, and a small fridge took up the length of one wall. Two square tables were pushed together in the center, surrounded by a bench and several chairs. A scarred corkboard on the opposite wall was cluttered with takeout menus from nearby restaurants, internal job postings, and an invitation for Barb's retirement party. The faint smell of someone's lunch hung in the air.

The room wasn't empty. Willow stood by the counter, making herself a cup of tea.

Scottie paused in the doorway. Even though she had promised herself to keep her distance, Willow radiated a quiet energy and reserved grace that drew her gaze.

Her gray cardigan fell softly over a plain white blouse, and her black slacks emphasized her long legs. Somehow, even the simple act of looping the tea bag's tag around the mug's handle looked elegant when she did it.

Finally, Scottie tore her gaze away and entered the break room. "Hi."

Willow glanced up from her tea. "Scottie? What are you doing here? I didn't submit a ticket."

She looked so adorably confused that Scottie couldn't help laughing. "Believe it or not, I had work up in Operations before you were hired. Mind you, it wasn't nearly as interesting." She snapped her mouth shut. *Ugh.* That had sounded way too flirty. "Actually, I'm here to put this up." She held up the flyer.

"Trivia night?" Willow read out loud.

Scottie nodded. "Kudos rents out the taproom of a local brewery once a quarter, and the departments take turns hosting. This time, it's IT's turn."

Willow tucked a strand of hair behind her ear. "Oh, that's cool."

"Yeah, it's fun. Plus we get to eat and drink on the company's dime." Scottie hesitated. She was resolved to stay away from Willow romantically. But this wasn't a date; it was practically a work event, right? It wasn't as if she was asking her out. She was just being a good colleague who hated seeing Willow spend her breaks by herself, not socializing with anyone. Maybe Willow was lonely in a new city and too reserved to make friends easily. "You should come," she blurted out before she could change her mind.

Willow set down her mug as if afraid it would slip from her grasp. Her gaze darted from a droplet of water on the counter to the microwave, then to the doorway—anywhere but to Scottie's face. "Uh... Thanks, but...no."

"No problem," Scottie said, aiming for a casual tone. She tried to act as if it were no big deal, even as a surprising wave of disappointment washed over her. "Just thought I'd mention it, in case you were interested."

But Willow clearly wasn't—not in trivia night and not in Scottie either. It was the second time she'd told her no, leaving no room for misinterpretation.

The rejection landed harder than expected, maybe because Willow hadn't even added an explanation or an excuse to soften the blow. No *Sorry, I've got plans that evening.* No *Trivia really isn't my thing.*

Obviously, it wasn't about the date or the activity. She simply didn't want to hang out with Scottie. Like Tanya, Willow didn't think that Scottie was enough for her either—not as someone to date and not even as someone to spend time with.

The thought twisted her gut. Which was ridiculous, of course, because she and Tanya had been together for ten years, while she barely knew Willow at all.

And now that would never change.

She tacked the flyer to the corkboard, ramming the pin in with more force than necessary.

When she turned back around, Willow was watching her with wide eyes, her long lashes fluttering and her rose-colored lips opening as if she wanted to say something—maybe that she would come to trivia after all. But then she pressed them together and silently reached for her mug.

Scottie pointed her thumb toward the door. "I'd better get back to work."

"Right." Willow nodded. "Computers to fix, damsels to rescue and all."

"Exactly."

Neither said anything else, so Scottie lifted her hand in a silent goodbye, whirled around, and fled back to the elevator. This must be why self-help experts recommended staying single for a while.

Chapter 11

Willow's mind was buzzing with delivery deadlines, production schedules, and last-minute logistic issues as she stepped into the elevator on Friday evening and pressed the button for the lobby. She and Barb had worked overtime every day this week as the company tried to hit the retailer cutoff dates in the final sprint toward the holiday season.

It was a lot, but she enjoyed it. She liked the team in Operations and following a clear structure yet also adapting on the fly to any problems that came up. Luckily, her devices had been cooperating for the most part the last few days.

But now she also looked forward to the weekend. She was ready to unplug and leave all tech devices and the constant threat of impending malfunctions behind for at least forty-eight hours.

The only other person in the elevator—a red-haired guy in a suit—got off on the tenth floor and stepped past her with a polite nod.

Willow exhaled as the steel doors started to slide shut.

But before they could fully close, a hand darted through the narrowing gap. It wasn't just any hand. Willow knew those strong fingers and that broad palm. Her heart immediately beat faster.

Scottie! Jesus, how much time had she spent watching her hands to recognize her by a glimpse of them? She wasn't sure she wanted to know the answer to that question.

The doors slid open.

Scottie stood in front of her, blonde hair disheveled after a long workday, her messenger bag slung across a black hoodie that said *Tech Wizard,* with a robed cartoon figure waving a magic wand.

When their gazes met, Scottie paused. "Oh. Hey." She crossed the threshold into the elevator more slowly than usual.

"Hi." Willow moved toward the mirrored back wall to make space for Scottie. Her entire body prickled with awareness, even though Scottie followed elevator etiquette and kept a polite distance.

As the car started to descend, an awkward silence spread between them.

Willow opened her mouth to fill the quiet with small talk, then shut it again. If she asked what Scottie was doing tonight and this turned out to be the day of the company trivia event, that would make everything worse.

Maybe Scottie would even suggest again that she join them, and this time, Willow might not be able to resist the urge to find out what Scottie was like after hours.

But then again, Scottie probably wouldn't ask a second time. Willow's "no" still seemed to hang between them like a wall. Usually, Willow didn't mind walls. They kept her secret safe. Yet with Scottie, she kept poking holes into the concrete, curious to catch a glimpse behind it—or longing to let Scottie see pieces of her.

No. Don't. You know it won't end well.

They both kept their gazes straight ahead, watching the floor numbers above the door.

Seven, six—

The elevator jolted to an abrupt stop.

The lights went out, leaving them in total darkness.

Willow stumbled, thrown off-balance, and instinctively reached for the nearest support to stay upright. Her fingers closed around something warm and solid. That was definitely not the handrail.

Had Scottie moved closer—maybe stumbled too?

The dimmer emergency lights flickered on.

She was clutching Scottie's forearm, holding on for dear life. At least she hadn't zapped her this time, maybe because the long sleeves of Scottie's hoodie had acted as an insulating layer. "Sorry." Willow yanked her hand back.

She waited for the doors to ping open or the elevator to start moving again, but neither happened.

"Shit," Scottie murmured. Even with all the computer issues she'd been summoned to fix, it was the first time Willow had heard her curse. "I think we're stuck."

"Yeah, I think so too." Willow stared at the closed doors. Was this her fault? She had never before caused an entire elevator to get stuck, but maybe the stress this week, paired with all the conflicting feelings when she'd seen Scottie again had short-circuited something.

Scottie jabbed her finger at the *open door* button.

Nothing.

She pressed the button for the lobby.

The elevator didn't move.

"Come on! Seriously?" Scottie frantically pressed the button for every single floor, but nothing happened. "Great. Why didn't I take the stairs?"

"Because you work on the tenth floor," Willow replied.

"There's that." Scottie banged on the door. Her breath came in quick bursts. "Hello? Can anyone hear us?"

Except for the sharp thumps of her fists, everything stayed silent.

"Most folks probably went home," Willow said. "It's way past quitting time."

Scottie stopped her frantic pounding. She slid her fingertips to the crease between the doors and tried to pry them apart with her bare hands.

The metal didn't give an inch.

What was going on with Scottie? She always seemed so unflappable at work, as if nothing could faze her. But now she was the one panicking.

Willow quickly crossed toward her and gripped her sleeve. "Stop. You'll only end up hurting yourself. Modern elevator doors can only be opened from the outside, so unless you've been hiding a Supergirl outfit beneath your work shirt, you won't be able to open them."

Scottie stilled, then turned. A weak smile curved up one corner of her mouth. "You know what's beneath my work shirt."

"What?" Willow stared at her in the soft glow of the emergency lights. "Why would I—?"

"You slid my ID badge beneath my shirt. You'd have seen it if I wore a Supergirl outfit."

Willow's cheeks heated. Was Scottie flirting? But it had been an absent-minded remark. She was probably just trying to distract herself from their predicament. "Just for the record, I didn't peek." Okay, not much. She had noticed the bit of smooth skin the undone buttons had revealed. But this wasn't the time or place to think about it.

Scottie gave up her attempts to open the doors and instead pulled out her phone. "Damn. No service. You?"

Willow fished her phone from her purse and pressed the power button. The screen remained black. It happened so often that it no longer surprised her. "The battery is dead." She dug deeper in her bag and pulled out her backup phone.

Scottie eyed the device as if Willow had just retrieved a stone tablet and a chisel. "Is that an old Nokia?"

"I'll have you know it's a classic."

"Classic, right! That thing has physical buttons!" Scottie let out a chuckle, sounding less nervous now. "I had no idea they still exist outside of museums that display prehistoric artifacts."

"Haha. You'll stop making fun of my phone once I use it to call someone who can get us out of here." But truth be told, Willow didn't mind the teasing. At least the phone had distracted Scottie from her growing panic. She glanced at the small LCD display. "Crap. No signal either. What now?"

Scottie turned on the flashlight app on her phone and directed the beam toward the ceiling. "Look, there's an emergency hatch. I could boost you up. Maybe you can reach the hatch and climb out."

The thoughts of Scottie's hands on her body, her strong fingers gripping her hips, made the temperature in the elevator seem to rise. Willow shook her head to clear it. "Not a good idea. That's how people end up falling to their death in elevator shafts. Besides, I think it's locked and can't be opened from the inside anyway for exactly that reason. The safest place for us to be is inside the elevator. It only becomes dangerous if people try to get out by themselves."

Scottie slumped against the wall. "Damn."

"You okay?" Willow moved a little closer to see her face in the dim light. "You're not claustrophobic, are you?"

"Not exactly. But I'm not too fond of small, confined spaces."

"Really?" Willow wouldn't have guessed that, and she marveled at the ease with which Scottie had confessed a weakness. She definitely didn't have the kind of walls that Willow had erected all her life. "You're in IT. Shouldn't you be used to crawling into tight spaces?"

"I am. But climbing beneath a desk to fix a computer is not the same as being trapped in a steel box, dangling from a single cable five floors above the ground."

"True," Willow said. "But it's actually more than a single cable. Elevators usually have at least four cables, often even eight. Each one could support the full weight by itself. There are lots of safety features, so don't worry, okay?"

Scottie studied her. "Why are you so calm? And how come you know so much about elevators?"

Willow shrugged, trying to play it off. For her, this wasn't new. While she'd never been trapped in an elevator before, she was always expecting things to go wrong. She no longer panicked when technology glitched. "I read a lot."

"Like what? Elevator manuals?" Scottie asked with a faint grin.

Actually, yes. But she couldn't tell Scottie that she'd read up on elevators because she'd wanted to be prepared, just in case. "Thrillers, romances, that kind of thing."

"So in those books, how do the main characters usually get out of the stuck elevator?"

Willow could only remember two novels with a trapped-in-an-elevator scene. Both had been sapphic romances. In those books, the characters hadn't put much effort into getting out. They had been too busy having hot sex with each other. But, of course, there was no way she would tell Scottie that. "They press the emergency button and wait for maintenance to rescue them. It still works, even if the power's out." She turned toward the control panel, glad to have a reason to turn her back before Scottie saw her blushing and started asking questions about the fictional elevator scenarios.

It took a few seconds for her to find the emergency button at the bottom of the panel.

For a moment, she hesitated. Should she get Scottie to press it?

But even if she retreated into the far corner and didn't touch a thing, she would still be close enough to affect the circuitry. Plus how would she explain to Scottie why she couldn't be the one to do something so simple?

Finally, she brushed her fingers along the metal handrail before pressing the emergency button.

A crackle of static burst from the speakers. "T&K Elevators," a tinny voice came through the intercom.

Oh, thank God! Despite her earlier calm, now Willow couldn't help being relieved at this connection to the world outside. "Hi!" She raised her voice so he would be able to hear her without her having to step too close to the speaker. "We're stuck in an elevator in the Kudos Entertainment building, I think somewhere between the fifth and sixth floor. The power went out."

"Yeah, we're aware," the man from the maintenance company answered. "Your whole city block has lost power."

Willow secretly blew out a breath. That meant she wasn't to blame for the elevator getting stuck. Her powers, if you could call them that, had a very limited radius. Usually, she only affected devices in her immediate vicinity.

"How many people are in the elevator with you?" the guy asked.

"There's two of us," Willow replied. As bad as she felt for Scottie, she had to admit that she was glad not to be trapped alone.

"Do either of you have any medical issues like diabetes or a heart condition? Or is anyone pregnant?"

Willow looked at Scottie, who shook her head and mumbled: "Not unless immaculate conception works for lesbians."

"No medical issues," Willow said into the speaker while trying to muffle her laughter, "no immaculate conception."

A snort of laughter came from Scottie.

"Uh, what?" the maintenance guy asked.

"I said no pregnancies!" Willow covered her overheated face with her hand, even though the man couldn't see her. "Sorry, the connection isn't the best."

There was a short pause. "Right. Listen, we're sending someone to get you out as soon as possible, but there are several people stuck in elevators right now. Our maintenance technicians are working as fast as they can, but it might take them a while to get to you."

Scottie moved closer to the speaker. Her shoulder pressed into Willow's. "Define 'a while,' please."

"At least an hour," the man said. "Probably closer to two."

Scottie groaned. "Two hours?"

"Sorry. As I said, we're working as fast as we can," the guy replied. "Sit tight, okay?"

"Not like we have a choice," Scottie muttered.

Then he was gone.

Willow and Scottie turned to face each other. They traded a long look.

"We're not really going to just sit around and wait for an hour or two, are we?" Scottie finally asked. "There's got to be something we can do."

Clearly, she was a woman of action, used to being the one to fix things.

Willow gave her a helpless smile. "Well, there's one thing we can do. It's the first rule of survival for people stranded in an elevator."

"Which is?" Scottie hung on her every word.

"Designate a pee corner."

For a moment, Scottie stared at her, then she burst out laughing.

When Scottie's laughter ebbed away, she straightened. The tension in her shoulders had loosened, and her stomach had stopped churning.

How on earth had Willow managed to make her laugh and forget they were stuck between floors, with nowhere to go? Willow was always so professional and reserved, but every now and then, her dry sense of humor slipped out, almost as if against her will.

Scottie had a feeling there were entire parts of herself Willow kept hidden—parts Scottie would probably like if Willow ever let her see them.

She certainly liked the calming effect Willow had on her, even though their role reversal would take some getting used to. Normally, she was the capable one who knew how to fix stuff and calmed down nervous users. But now she'd fiddled with elevator buttons and frantically tried to get out, while Willow had kept a cool head.

Her composure surprised and intrigued Scottie, and her quiet trust in the safety of the elevator was oddly contagious. Scottie's palms were still a bit clammy, but her pulse had gone from frantic to just slightly too fast.

She would be fine if she continued to focus on Willow instead of imagining scenarios of them plummeting to their deaths in this steel trap.

Yeah, get yourself together. While Willow had already decided Scottie wasn't a person she wanted to socialize with, Scottie's pride still kicked in.

She didn't want Willow to see her panicked and useless. Maybe fate had stuck them in this elevator together to give her a chance to prove that she was a good person to be around after all, even in an emergency.

"I veto the pee corner idea," Scottie finally said. "At least for now. But we could establish a seating area and make ourselves more comfortable." She lowered herself to the floor, drew her knees up, and leaned her forearms across them. "It's not the Ritz, but better than pacing back and forth."

Willow hesitated for a moment, then eased herself down too. "Glad I'm wearing slacks today."

Scottie shifted to the right to give her more space. "Yeah. Skirts and elevator floors don't mix well. Not that anything mixes well with elevator floors."

They sat side by side in silence for a while.

Finally, it was Willow who cleared her throat. "Is someone going to be wondering where you are if you don't get home on time?"

"No. I live alone, and my friends know I work longer hours from October to December, so they probably won't miss me tonight. Well, Miss Figgy might."

Willow tilted her head. "Miss Piggy? You've got a pet pig?"

Scottie chuckled. "I don't think my landlord would be too enthusiastic about that idea. No. Miss Figgy is a miniature fig tree. What about you?"

"I don't have any fig trees or pet pigs, I'm afraid," Willow answered.

"No, I meant, is there someone waiting for you at home?"

"Yes."

Oh. Scottie had sworn off relationships for the time being, but knowing Willow was already in one made the elevator feel more claustrophobic. For some reason, it hadn't occurred to her that she might have a partner. Which was silly because Willow was beautiful, smart, and thoughtful. Scottie had assumed that she was the reason Willow hadn't wanted to meet up—that Willow had formed an opinion of her as not good enough. But maybe it wasn't about her at all. God, Tanya had really done a number on her.

"I live with my sister and two feline roommates for now," Willow added.

Relief shot through Scottie, which was even more ridiculous than assuming Willow was single. *Stop it. Just because she's not living with a partner doesn't necessarily mean she's single.*

Her stomach chose that moment to let out a loud growl, thankfully distracting Scottie from thoughts about Willow's relationship status. "Sorry. Gordon was out sick today, and the COO accidentally deleted his desktop shortcuts and had no clue how to bring them back, so I skipped lunch."

Willow gave her a sympathetic look. Without a word, she reached into her oversized purse and pulled out several items.

Scottie's eyes had adjusted to the dim emergency lights by now, so she could make out a package of Oreos, two granola bars, and a bag of trail mix.

But Willow wasn't done yet. She unfolded several tissues, creating an improvised picnic blanket on the elevator floor, and set the goodies on top, then added a small bottle of water from the depths of her purse.

Scottie stared at the feast. "Wow, you came prepared! That's a portable pantry, not a purse!"

A reddish tint rose to Willow's cheeks. "I tend to get hangry," she said, her tone a little defensive.

"Hey, no judgment from me. If there's ever a zombie apocalypse, I want to be on your team. I have a feeling the only survivors will be cockroaches, your ancient Nokia, and the members of your team." Scottie had never met a person who seemed so well-prepared for any eventuality.

The tense set of Willow's shoulders relaxed, and she smiled. "I'll consider your application, depending on your zombie-killing skills."

Scottie playfully puffed out her chest. "I watched all eleven seasons of *The Walking Dead*, and I can wield a screwdriver like a lethal weapon."

"Well, then, application accepted. Dig in." Willow tore open a granola bar, broke it in half, and held out the bigger piece to Scottie.

Eagerly, Scottie reached for it.

The moment their fingers brushed, a jolt shot up Scottie's hand. In the dim light, a visible spark arced between them. "Ouch." She nearly dropped her half of the granola bar but caught it before it could hit the floor.

"Not again," Willow muttered and rubbed her fingers. "Sorry that keeps happening. Apparently, it's not just the carpet in Operations; my shoes and the elevator floor aren't friends either."

Scottie abstained from jokes about the sparks between them, not wanting to make her uncomfortable. "That's okay. Small price to pay for getting half of the granola bar. The ones with chunks of dark chocolate are my favorite."

"Mine too," Willow said, sounding less guilty or embarrassed now.

They both dug in as if they hadn't eaten all day, which was true in Scottie's case.

When the last crumb of the granola bar was gone, Willow opened the Oreos. But instead of handing Scottie one, she set the pack on their impromptu picnic blanket. "Help yourself."

Scottie didn't have to be told twice. She immediately reached for a cookie.

Willow followed suit and lifted an Oreo to her lips, about to take a bite.

"Whoa, wait!" Scottie lifted a hand to stop her.

Willow froze, the treat half an inch from her mouth. "What is it? Something wrong with the cookie?"

"No, just with your way of eating it."

Frowning, Willow lowered the Oreo. "Uh...open mouth, insert cookie, chew, swallow, repeat?"

"That's what the uninitiated think. But there's only one right way to eat an Oreo—a technique perfected to maximize enjoyment, and handed down through generations." Scottie put on her most dignified expression.

"Everyone knows the superior way to eat Oreos is dunking them in milk," Willow said.

Scottie eyed Willow's now considerably less bulging purse. "Don't tell me you packed some."

"What?" Willow huffed. "No, I'm not walking around with a pint of milk in my bag!"

"Shame," Scottie said. "But even if we had milk, my method would still elevate the Oreo to its full potential."

Willow waved her hand with the cookie. "Please enlighten me, oh Yoda of Oreo Wisdom."

"First, you split it in halves. But you don't pull. The trick is to twist them apart. Like this." As if unveiling the steps of a sacred ritual, Scottie separated the sandwich cookie into two perfect halves, one plain, one with a smooth layer of cream. "Then you eat the plain side." She popped it into her mouth and chewed happily.

"I've seen people do that," Willow said. "And then you eat the other side, right?"

"Not yet. Patience. What's so special about this Oreo-eating technique is that you get to enjoy the cream by itself." Scottie scraped it off with her teeth, letting the sweet vanilla aroma spread over her tongue before eating the other half of the cookie. "See? Try it."

Willow gripped the two halves of her cookie and twisted them apart, her fingers nimble and her expression as focused as it had been when they had worked on the printer. When she scraped the cream off with her teeth, a tiny bit clung to her top lip, and she licked it off.

Scottie averted her gaze. "So, what's the verdict?"

"Not bad," Willow said. "But I think I need a second cookie to confirm the superiority of your method."

Scottie took a second one for herself too. "Can't argue with a scientific approach."

They made their way through most of the package that way, their movements mirroring each other. Around the third cookie, Scottie realized her heart had settled into a steady beat. She was leaning back against the elevator wall, legs stretched out in front of her, crossed at the ankles, as if they were having a picnic on a sunny meadow.

"Something wrong?" Willow asked. "You have a weird look on your face."

"No, everything's fine. That's what put that look on my face. I feel fine. The walls of the elevator have stopped closing in, and I haven't even glanced at my watch or felt the urge to check in with the maintenance team in at least ten minutes."

"That's great. I concede to the superiority of your sacred Oreo-eating technique. It worked like a charm."

Scottie nodded and smiled, but she knew the cookies were only a small part of what had gotten her to relax.

Chapter 12

A few minutes later, Willow had also nearly forgotten that they were trapped in an elevator. The stale air and the faint hum of the emergency lights had faded into the background, replaced by their laughter and the crinkle of wrappers.

They sat side by side, backs against the metal wall, and shared the second granola bar.

This impromptu picnic was surreal yet also one of the nicest things she'd experienced in a while.

Wow. That definitely didn't speak well for her social life. Maybe Fiona was right. Perhaps she should get out more often.

"So," Scottie said once the mango-ginger granola bar and most of the cookies were gone, "what do we do now? You don't happen to have a crossword puzzle or something else to help pass the time in that bottomless purse of yours, do you?"

Willow shook her head. She was well-prepared for tech glitches such as her car not starting and being stranded on the roadside for a while, but snacks were a priority over entertainment. "No crossword puzzles."

"How about we play a game to distract ourselves?" Scottie suggested.

"Sorry, I left my Monopoly in my other purse," Willow said with a smile.

Scottie returned the grin. "There are other games, you know? Games you don't need a board, dice, or cards for."

Willow eyed her skeptically. "You're not thinking of Truth or Dare, are you?"

"Nah," Scottie said. "There aren't a lot of dares we could do in here."

Actually, Willow could think of a few. A scene from a sapphic romance novel came to mind, in which one of the main characters did sexy things to the cream filling of a Twinkie. For a second, the image of Scottie doing something similar to one of the Oreos left in the pack rose to the forefront of her mind's eye. Heat prickled up the back of her neck.

"But we could play a truth-only version—Truth or Drink," Scottie added. "We take turns asking a question, and if we want to pass and not answer, we have to take a shot."

"Won't work." Willow pointed at her purse. "I don't have any alcohol in here."

"We would take a swig of water, then."

"Water? That's not much of a punishment."

Scottie flashed a grin. "You say that now. But if you pass at too many questions, that pee corner will start to look like a great idea in an hour." She tilted her head, again reminding Willow of an eager golden retriever. "So? Are we playing?"

Willow hesitated. She didn't like revealing too much about herself. But they had time to kill, and keeping Scottie distracted seemed like a good idea. If she was honest with herself, she had to admit she was also curious to find out more about her. "All right," she said, hoping she wouldn't end up regretting it. "We're playing. But go easy on me, okay?"

"I promise." Scottie's voice was gentle. "You start."

While Willow thought of a harmless, not too personal first question, she opened the bag of trail mix. "What's the most useless piece of knowledge rattling around in your head?"

A low chuckle echoed through the elevator. "Tough choice. I could write the *Dictionary of Useless Knowledge.*" Scottie rubbed her chin. "Let's go with this one: Turtles can breathe through their butts."

Willow paused in the middle of fishing a peanut from the bag. "You're making that up!"

"No, it's true! It's called cloacal respiration."

"Cloacal—?" Willow nearly choked on the peanut she'd just popped into her mouth. "Maybe you should write that dictionary. If that's the kind of stuff you know, it could be really entertaining."

"Yeah, I'm sure it would be a bestseller. My turn." Scottie took a small handful of trail mix. "What would you be doing right now if you'd left work on time and weren't trapped in this elevator?"

Willow never wore a wristwatch—they always started to lose time, then died within a week—but over the years, she had developed a good sense of time, so she knew it was about seven thirty. "I'd probably be on the couch with my sister, reading, with Sugar, one of the cats, on my lap while Spice swats at the book every time I turn a page." She gave her a wry smile. "Exciting, I know."

"Excitement is overrated," Scottie replied. "Sounds like a perfect evening after a long workweek to me. So...Sugar and Spice? Let me guess: Sugar's the friendly angel, while Spice is the one with an attitude?"

"Pretty much. Sugar is super affectionate and loves everyone, while Spice is the moody one who'll hiss at you for breathing wrong."

"Are they yours or your sister's?"

Willow shrugged. "Depends on who you ask. Technically, they're Fiona's, while I'm just the cool aunt, but if one of them is misbehaving, my sister insists they're mine. And, of course, if cats could talk, they would say that we belong to them. I mean, I haven't lived there long, but Sugar and Spice quickly got used to having two servants instead of just one."

"Naturally," Scottie said with a grin. "As your feline overlords who allow you to exist in their kingdom, they deserve to be spoiled."

Willow returned her grin. "Ah, I see you understand the balance of power."

Scottie nodded. "I grew up with cats."

This wasn't so bad, Willow decided. Scottie had a way of making her comfortable, watching her with an attentive gaze as she spoke, no matter how mundane her answer appeared to Willow. No hint of boredom or judgment showed on Scottie's face, only genuine interest and acceptance.

Willow sorted a handful of trail mix into two mini piles of nuts and dried fruit on her palm while she took her time thinking of the next question to ask Scottie. "What's the last movie that made you cry?"

"Movie? I honestly can't remember."

"Been too long?" Willow asked.

Scottie shook her head. "Been too many. Don't laugh, but I'm the type who cries at commercials or Insta reels. If it involves people being happy, I'm a goner. Marriage proposals, surprise reunions, pets being adopted, babies taking their first steps... I'm done for."

"I would never laugh at that." Willow actually found it very sweet, and she marveled at how easily Scottie let her guard down. Clearly, she wasn't afraid to reveal her soft marshmallow center, and Willow almost envied her.

"My turn," Scottie said. "Why do you carry a second phone, especially such an old-school one?"

Willow couldn't help tensing a little. She didn't want to lie, but neither could she tell the full truth. "Oh, you know..." She fluttered her hand in a vague gesture, scattering peanut crumbs over their tissue picnic blanket. "I don't have the best of luck with battery-operated devices." Then she realized how that sounded and blushed. *Dammit.* She seemed to do that a lot whenever she talked to Scottie.

"Oh, really?" Scottie drawled with a grin.

Ignoring the comment and the warmth in her cheeks, Willow added, "What I meant is that the Nokia is my backup, in case my phone runs out of battery. It holds a charge forever." At least it did for other people. For her, it was just enough to get through the day, but she had to plug it in every night.

A curious expression darted across Scottie's face, and Willow thought for sure she'd ask why she didn't simply carry a power bank instead of a second phone, but Scottie just nodded. "Fair enough. Plus not being constantly online is probably a good thing."

That approval from an IT person surprised Willow. She tucked a stray strand of hair behind her ear and thought of the next question. "What would you do for a living if you weren't a tech wizard?" She pointed at Scottie's hoodie. "By the way, shouldn't it be tech sorceress?"

"Hm, I don't know. Doesn't have the same punch."

"Okay, tech witch, then."

"Ooh, I like that!" Scottie tossed a raisin in the air and snatched it up with her mouth. "Probably a job where I'd be working with my hands and could see the result of my labor at the end of the day. Like a gardener or a landscaper. Something tangible, not just staring at a screen all day, you know?"

Again, the answer surprised Willow. She hadn't expected that from Scottie. "Yeah, I get that. Sometimes, I think the same. Not that I don't love my job."

"Oh yeah. I love mine too," Scottie said. "I just love doing other, more hands-on stuff too. Things that let me create something real."

"Like raising miniature fig trees," Willow said.

"Exactly." Scottie pulled one knee up and leaned her chin on top to gaze at Willow. "Your turn to answer a question. How did you end up here?"

Willow gestured at the metal walls surrounding them. "In the elevator?"

"Working at Kudos."

That was more of a minefield than Scottie probably realized. Willow eyed the bottle of water. Should she take a swig? But she didn't want to answer Scottie's openness with such a cop-out. Besides, if she took a drink, it would only let Scottie know her question wasn't as harmless to Willow as she had assumed. She lowered her gaze and brushed a few crumbs off her lap. "I got fired from my last job."

Scottie reached over and gave Willow's leg a quick, compassionate squeeze. "I'm sorry. Layoffs?"

Willow put her hand on the spot Scottie had just touched. Her leg was tingling, even though this time she hadn't been zapped since she was leaning against the metal wall. "No." She pressed her lips together and hesitated. What if Scottie told one of her colleagues, and before you knew it, the entire company was gossiping about her? But while she hadn't known Scottie for long, she already sensed she wasn't a person who would betray a confidence. She could trust her—at least with part of it. "They said it was because of bad performance. That I wasn't meeting their expectations." That was true, even though Willow suspected it wasn't the real reason. She had simply been too expensive as an employee, needing a new device more often than any of her colleagues.

"Bullshit." Scottie hurled the word through the elevator like a rotten piece of fruit into the trash bin. "That was probably just an excuse."

While Scottie couldn't know anything about her job performance, her trust in Willow's skills felt like a soothing balm on an open wound. "Thanks for not assuming I must be shit at my job, especially after having to come to my rescue so often this month," she said quietly.

Scottie looked away, then back into her eyes. "You're clearly smart and hardworking, considering we seem to be the last ones in the building. I can't imagine you being bad at your job. If your old employer couldn't see that, it's on them, not on you."

Willow's throat tightened. Her mouth felt as dry as a bucket of chalk. She swallowed hard, reached for the water bottle, and took a big gulp.

Scottie smiled softly. "Does that mean you want to pass on the next question?"

"No. I'm just thirsty. Besides, it's your turn to answer a question. Or do you want to stop playing?"

"Nope. I'd love to keep going." Scottie studied her. "Unless you want to stop."

Did she?

"No," Willow answered, surprised at how quickly the answer came to her. Initially, she had agreed to the game mostly to provide a distraction for Scottie. But now she found herself captivated too. Something about the game—about Scottie—was too intriguing to stop. She wanted to find out more about her.

What stunned her even more was realizing she'd been okay revealing little bits about herself in return. She had assumed being asked questions would feel like a near stranger prying open doors she had kept locked forever.

But it hadn't been like that at all, nor did Scottie still feel like a stranger.

That thought sent a ripple of alarm through her. Quickly, she pushed it back and squared her shoulders. "Let's keep going."

Chapter 13

Half an hour later, they were still playing. The trail mix was long gone, and only one cookie remained. Empty wrappers littered the floor between them.

Not that there was that much space separating them anymore. At some point, one or both of them must have moved closer. Now they were sitting so close that Willow could feel the heat radiating off Scottie's body.

Or maybe it wasn't coming from Scottie. Maybe it was her own body producing all that heat. Her skin felt very sensitive, attuned to every subtle movement, every brush of Scottie's knee against her own. Her closeness was like the low, constant hum of the emergency lights.

Scottie caught her staring and lifted her eyebrows. "What?"

"Nothing," Willow said quickly. "Just thinking of a really good question."

"Ooh. Let's hear it!" Scottie waved both hands in a come-at-me gesture.

Willow asked the first thing that came to mind. "What's your biggest guilty pleasure?"

"I don't believe in guilty pleasures. As long as it's not hurting anyone, why would I feel guilty about anything that gives me pleasure?" Scottie met her gaze, calm and unwavering.

The way she said *pleasure,* with her voice dipping low, sent a shiver down Willow's body. The answer also once again surprised her. She'd expected Scottie to name a favorite junk food or a bad TV show she secretly loved to watch. But then again, this answer seemed to fit Scottie. Willow really admired the way Scottie knew exactly who she was and what she wanted and didn't feel the need to apologize for it. "I like that answer."

"Yeah?"

Willow nodded. "And since we've decided there's no such thing as a guilty pleasure, I won't feel guilty for doing this." She swiped the last Oreo just as Scottie started to reach for it and took a big bite without even bothering with Scottie's special technique.

Scottie laughed. "Ruthless. I said *as long as it's not hurting anyone.* That was just cruel." She pouted playfully.

Willow grinned around her mouthful of cookie but then relented, broke what remained in half, and handed one piece over.

"Ooh. Thank you." Scottie studied her portion and seemed to decide it was too small to twist it apart, so she just popped it into her mouth. "My turn again. What's the worst first date you've ever been on?"

The grin faded from Willow's lips. "Does it count if it's more like the worst first date I've *never* been on?"

Scottie raised both brows. "Sounds intriguing. Go on."

Willow swept cookie crumbs off her lap and took her time answering, not eager to recount that particular story. It had been years ago, but she still remembered the painful details. "She worked at the grocery store where I used to shop. We made small talk for months before I finally worked up the courage to ask her out, and she said yes."

"Doesn't sound bad so far," Scottie said.

"It wasn't—until I stood her up because my car wouldn't start. My phone was dead, so I couldn't call her either. By the time I finally made it to the restaurant, she was gone."

"And there never was a second date?" Scottie asked.

A sigh escaped Willow. "No. I tried to explain, but she thought I had blown her off and was just making excuses. She never gave me another chance." She tried to keep her voice light, as if it were no big deal, but being dismissed so easily still stung. What hurt the most was that it hadn't happened only this once. Willow had been accused of ghosting people several times when her dating app had glitched or her battery had died at the worst possible moment. Eventually, she had all but given up on dating.

Scottie watched her for a moment as if she was trying to read between the lines, but she didn't push for more details. "Her loss," she finally said.

Willow wasn't so sure about that. Still, she appreciated the sentiment.

The silence stretched for a moment, then Scottie shifted and leaned one shoulder against the metal wall. "Your turn to ask a question. Make it a good one."

There was something Willow had been wondering for a while, but she hadn't wanted to ask so she wouldn't invite personal questions in return. Now might be her only chance to find out. "What's your real first name?"

Scottie flashed a grin. "Want to take a guess?"

"Mildred?"

A low laugh escaped Scottie. "No."

"Ethel?"

Scottie shuddered. "Okay, okay, I'll tell you. It's Sarah."

"Oh, that's not so bad. I thought it must be something horrible or old-fashioned and that's why you're not using it."

"No, it's all right, I guess. It just never felt like mine. Plus there were three other Sarahs in my class, so my nickname stuck. Other than my great-aunt, no one has called me Sarah since I was seven."

Willow let her gaze trail over Scottie's stocky build; her broad, open face; and the blonde hair that fell in soft layers to just above her jawline. No, she didn't look like a Sarah—at least not any of the Sarahs Willow had ever met. "I think Scottie fits you really well."

"Thanks." Scottie trailed a hand through her hair, pushing back a wavy strand that had fallen onto her face.

They looked into each other's eyes, then glanced away.

"Next question," Willow said to cover for the sudden silence.

Scottie found one last raisin in the otherwise empty bag and popped it into her mouth. "What's something you've never told anyone at work?"

Another minefield question. But then again, maybe it wasn't. She hadn't socialized with anyone at Kudos except for Barb. Her colleagues didn't know anything about her, apart from her name and that she'd moved to Portland from Santa Cruz. So she pretty much had her choice of harmless facts about herself.

"Wait, let me adjust my question since you're new at Kudos," Scottie said as if reading her thoughts. "Tell me something you've never told any of your friends."

Friends? What friends? Willow wanted to say, but, of course, she would never admit that. She didn't want Scottie to think she was even weirder than she probably already assumed. That left something she'd never told Fiona, who was her sister by blood and her best friend by choice.

She twirled one of the empty granola bar wrappers between her fingers. The rustle of plastic sounded overly loud in the echo chamber of the elevator. "I don't think I've ever told anyone that I'm terrified of butterflies."

"Butterflies?" Scottie repeated.

Willow hunched her shoulders and kept her gaze on the granola bar wrapper, not wanting to see the incredulous expression she imagined on Scottie's face. "Mm-hmm. Well, maybe not terrified. I'm fine if I see one from a distance. I think they're beautiful. But as soon as they fly too close, I get really uncomfortable. I know it's silly, but—"

Scottie pulled the wrapper from Willow's fingers, careful not to touch her in the process. "It's not silly. Maybe it's their unpredictable, erratic flight pattern. You never know where they'll land."

At the gentle tone of her voice, Willow peeked up.

Scottie looked back at her without even a hint of mockery. She didn't seem tempted to laugh at Willow's strange fear at all.

This woman was too good to be true. Did she really not have one judgmental bone in her body? "Yeah, maybe. What about you? Do you have any fears that you've never admitted, even to your friends?"

Scottie wiped her crumb-dusted fingers on her pants. "I've actually got something similar, just with dogs. I'm even a little afraid of the small ones—that's the part I've never admitted to anyone." She gave a rueful smile. "I got bitten by a German shepherd when I was five. Still have the scar."

Willow sucked in a sharp breath. Her gaze once again roved over Scottie's body, this time looking for the scar.

Scottie bent down, reached up, and pushed the hair at the back of her head aside. "Right there."

In the low light, Willow couldn't see the scar, but her imagination showed her flashes of a huge dog, sharp canines, and a bleeding little girl. Only when her fingertips brushed soft hair did she become aware that she had lifted her hand, either to touch the scar or to offer comfort. She quickly yanked it back. "That's horrible. I'm so sorry."

"It's okay," Scottie said. "I don't remember much about it. I even like dogs, but if I see a strange dog coming toward me, my body tenses up."

"I can imagine. I bet your body remembers, even if you don't." Willow reached for the water bottle and clutched it with both hands, just so she wouldn't try to touch Scottie again.

What a strange day this was turning out to be. She couldn't believe all the things she had revealed to Scottie.

It had to be the effect of being trapped in this metal box. The stuffy air and the heat in the elevator were getting to her. It seemed to be getting hotter by the second, especially with Scottie sitting so close.

With abrupt motions, Willow stripped off her blazer and popped open the top button on her blouse.

Scottie had never had a thing for collarbones, but as Willow undid a button on her blouse, her gaze flicked to the graceful arc and trailed over the patch of fair skin that peeked out from beneath the open collar.

She quickly looked away. "Uh, what are you doing? We agreed to play the truth-only version, not Truth or Dare, right?"

"I'm not stripping because of a dare. It's just getting a little warm in here. Didn't you notice?" Willow opened another button.

Scottie resisted the urge to fan herself. Oh yeah, it was definitely starting to heat up. "I noticed," she croaked. She peeled off her hoodie and tossed it to the side. The air against her shoulders made her glad she'd worn a tank top.

Out of the corner of her eye, she thought she'd caught Willow's gaze lingering for a moment, but that was probably just wishful thinking. Willow was too busy making herself more comfortable. She rolled up the sleeves of her blouse, revealing more smooth skin, slim forearms, and elegant wrists.

The temperature seemed to climb another few degrees.

To distract herself, Scottie picked a new question to ask. "What's something you used to enjoy but have stopped doing?"

Willow smoothed her fingers over the fabric at her elbow while she seemed to think about it. Her gaze drifted past Scottie as if seeing something in her past rather than the metal walls. "I used to play bass in a band as a teenager, but I haven't played in ages."

Scottie couldn't help staring. The thought of Willow playing the bass, such a visceral instrument that made you feel those deep, low vibrations in your entire body… "Wow. You're full of surprises."

Willow laughed, sounding almost embarrassed. "You seem shocked. Guess I don't look like your typical rock star."

"It's not about looks." Scottie could easily imagine Willow's nimble fingers sliding over the strings. What she had a harder time picturing was reserved Willow losing herself in the rhythm, giving herself over to the music, hair falling wildly into her face as she played. The thought of Willow coming alive like that made her breath catch. "I just didn't take you for a person who'd play in a band. I'd pay money to see that."

Willow gave her head a decisive shake. "No, you wouldn't. We weren't very good. Honestly, we were probably awful. But it was fun."

"That's what counts, right?"

"I guess so." Willow shifted her gaze from the metal wall to Scottie's face. "Your turn. Same question. Something you used to enjoy but no longer do."

Scottie thought about it for a full minute, but nothing came to mind. No hobbies she'd given up, no activities she hadn't done in a while. Well, except for... She bit her lip. "Dating."

"You don't"—Willow nibbled her own lip as if mirroring Scottie—"date?"

"I used to date a lot in my early twenties." Scottie caught the slight lift of Willow's brows. She laughed and added, "That doesn't mean I slept with every woman I went out with. I just enjoyed meeting people. Even if there wasn't any chemistry romantically, it was fun."

Willow turned so she was no longer leaning against the wall, her full attention on Scottie. "And now?"

"Not so much anymore," Scottie said quietly. "I still like meeting people, but I'm taking a break from dating."

Willow studied her with an expression that made it clear she could sense there was more behind it.

"Why did you stop?" Scottie asked before Willow could say anything else.

"Playing bass?"

Scottie nodded.

Willow shrugged. "Life, I guess. After high school, I got too busy to play."

Now Scottie was the one who sensed there was more. "That's not the whole story, though, is it?"

"No." Willow hugged her knees to her chest. "I had a falling out with my high school friends. Some of them were in the band too. After that, I never tried to find another band to play in." She peered over her knees at Scottie. "I'm not great with people."

"I disagree," Scottie said without having to think about it. "You did a great job calming me down, and I think you get along well with Barb too."

Willow tilted her head in a hesitant nod. "Then maybe I'm just not great at letting people get close." She rolled her sleeves back down, either because she needed something to do with her hands or because she felt exposed.

Yeah, that felt closer to the mark. Scottie wanted to say that Willow wasn't bad at that either. After all, she was opening up to her right now in a way that left Scottie stunned and deeply honored, as if she'd been handed an unexpected award. But Willow's openness felt fragile, and Scottie was afraid she would stop talking and retreat if she called any attention to it.

Before she could decide what to answer, Willow buttoned her sleeves and said: "My turn. Why don't you date anymore?"

For the first time since the game had begun, Scottie considered taking a big gulp of water. Was she ready to touch that raw nerve and talk about the one topic she usually avoided?

The dim emergency lights cast shadows over Scottie's face as she sat there without saying anything for a full minute.

"You know," Willow said quietly, not wanting to see her struggle, "you can always drink if you aren't comfortable answering the question."

Or maybe they should end the game here. Willow had already said more than she'd meant to tonight.

But at the same time, she didn't want to stop. She wanted to know what had put that pain in Scottie's usually twinkling eyes—if Scottie was okay sharing it with her.

Slowly, Scottie shook her head. "I don't mind telling you. I mean, it's tough to talk about it. But I want to tell you." A bewildered look settled on her face, as if she was as surprised as Willow at that revelation.

Other than Fiona, people didn't usually choose her to confide in, probably because she kept everyone at arm's length and never let anyone get past polite small talk. Scottie trusting her enough to share something raw felt special. Warmth filled Willow's chest as she waited for Scottie to find the right words.

"I was always a big believer in love and happily ever afters," Scottie finally said. "I saw it between my parents growing up. And I still see it today. Last time I went home for the holidays, they were wearing matching pajamas on Christmas morning."

They both chuckled.

Then Scottie sobered. "I thought I had that kind of forever relationship too. My girlfriend, Tanya, and I had been together for ten years."

"Ten years?" The words came out in a gasp. Willow had never managed to come even close to that.

Scottie nodded, her lips compressed into a thin line. "I thought we were happy. I mean, it wasn't perfect, but what is, right?"

Willow braced herself for whatever came next.

"One day this spring, totally out of the blue, Tanya sat me down and told me it was over. That I was great but not what she needed anymore. Ten years and she was just...done. It was like a kick to the gut." Scottie rubbed her belly as if she could still feel it.

Willow's own stomach churned too. Why would anyone do that? Walk away from someone as kind as Scottie? "Was there someone else?" she asked softly.

Scottie shook her head. "No cheating, no big fight. She just fell out of love and didn't want to share her life with me anymore. In a way, that was worse than cheating. If she'd cheated, it would have been about this other person. About Tanya doing something to hurt me. But this way, it was about me. There was no one else to blame. Just me not being enough."

Her voice was so quiet that Willow had to lean closer to hear her. She wished she could reach over and take Scottie's hand or do something... anything to comfort her and assure her that she was enough. But all she could do was sit there and listen.

"I wanted to fight for us, go to couples therapy, change and become whatever she needed, but Tanya told me it wasn't something I could fix." There was a pain in Scottie's tone that hadn't been there even when she'd talked about being bitten by a dog. Her lips twitched into a semblance of a wry smile. "Me, Scottie, fixer of things, not able to fix something. I didn't know how to deal with that. Still don't." She let her head sink back against the metal wall. "If she could give up on us so easily after ten years, what does that say about forever? About me?"

"Nothing." Willow blurted it out without thinking.

Scottie lifted her head off the wall. "What?"

"Maybe it says nothing about you. Maybe there is nothing to fix. We don't really know each other well, but I can tell you're an amazing person. I bet you gave so much of yourself to Tanya in those ten years. That's not gone just because she stopped doing the same. That person is still in there." Willow reached out and let her hand linger inches from Scottie's chest but didn't touch her. "You just need to find her again. You don't need to change or 'fix' yourself to deserve love." She dropped her hand into her lap and snapped her mouth shut.

What on earth? Why was she of all people speaking up for love and happy endings when she'd never put faith in either? Didn't that make her a fraud or a hypocrite? But she really believed what she had said—not for herself, but for Scottie.

Scottie took a shaky breath and looked at her. Her gaze was intense, searching, as if trying to find the truth in Willow's eyes.

It was almost too much to hold, but Willow forced herself not to look away.

"Thank you," Scottie said, her voice thick with emotion. "I think I needed to hear that." In the dim light, her eyes seemed to gleam with unshed tears.

Willow's heart clutched at the sight. "I meant it. It's her loss."

A smile tugged up Scottie's lips, starting slow, then spreading over her face until it reached her eyes. It softened the pain Willow could still see there. "Thanks." She held Willow's gaze for another moment, then reached for the water bottle and took a long drink, as if to wash a bitter taste from her mouth.

When she capped the bottle and looked back up, the shimmer of tears was gone. "How about you? Are you dating?"

"Are we still playing?" Willow asked. Somehow, this didn't feel like a game anymore.

But Scottie nodded. "Of course. Sorry it got intense there for a second."

"Don't apologize. I was the one who asked you that question."

"So do I get to ask you the same in return?"

The question hung in the cramped space between them as Willow hesitated.

"There's always the option to drink if you aren't comfortable answering," Scottie repeated what Willow had offered before.

But Scottie had laid herself bare, and it didn't seem fair to offer only silence in return for that kind of honesty. Even though Willow couldn't give her the whole truth, she could at least give her something. "No, I'm not dating."

"Not currently or not at all?" Scottie asked.

"Not at all." Willow kept her gaze on the seam where the doors met so she wouldn't have to see Scottie's reaction. "I guess I'm the opposite of you when it comes to relationships. I never believed that they would last forever. That makes it less painful when they don't."

"Who says they won't?" Scottie asked.

"Experience," Willow replied. Her relationships had rarely lasted longer than her electronic devices. Most of them had fizzled out after a short time like a draining battery, while a few had exploded spectacularly, like a power bank overheating and bursting into flames.

Unlike Scottie, who thought she hadn't been enough, Willow had always been too much—too weird, too much of a hassle.

"Did...did someone break your heart too?" Scottie's voice was soft, hesitant, as if she thought Willow might crack under that question.

Willow waved it off with a swipe of her hand. "No. Not someone. Half a dozen someones. But they never broke my heart," she quickly added. "I never fully invested it. I didn't see the point when I knew it would end the same way all over again."

Scottie was quiet for a moment. "That sounds—"

"Cynical?" Willow shook her head. "No, just realistic."

"I meant to say it sounds lonely."

Usually, defensiveness crept up whenever Fiona said something similar, but now a twinge of something else stirred in Willow. She pushed it down and forced a teasing smile. "Says the woman who's given up on dating too."

"I haven't given up on it. I'm just taking a break."

Willow sighed. Taking a break might heal Scottie's broken heart, but it wouldn't change her own situation.

"Let's make a deal," Scottie said.

Willow turned her head and eyed her warily. "What deal?"

That steady, optimistic look was back in Scottie's eyes. "When we make it out of here"—she gestured at the stuck elevator—"I'll go out on a date. No pressure. It doesn't have to result in anything. Just to meet someone and open myself up to the possibility again."

Willow's stomach tightened at the thought of Scottie facing some woman across a restaurant table, laughing at something her date said.

But Scottie deserved a happy ending. She was too great to stay single forever. If anyone could make it work, it was her. Willow gave her an encouraging nod, accepting that part of the deal.

Scottie nodded back. "And you..."

Willow tensed. She knew what Scottie was about to suggest—for Willow to go out with someone new too. In an instant, all of her shields went up.

"You'll start playing the bass again," Scottie finished her sentence.

The tension in Willow's shoulders eased a fraction. She suspected that Scottie had meant to say something else but had changed course when she'd sensed that Willow wouldn't agree to that kind of deal.

Could she agree to the adjusted suggestion?

What she hadn't told Scottie earlier was that the falling out with her friends hadn't been the only reason she no longer played. After Mia—her former best friend and the band's singer—had stopped talking to her, she had tried to continue playing in the band.

But seeing Mia at practice had upset her so much that her weird effect on electronics had flared. The amp and the speaker had kept cutting out. She'd been terrified of accidentally destroying the band's expensive devices, the way she had Mia's camera, so she'd quit.

She didn't think it was a good idea to join another band. At least not right now while she was not yet settled in this new city or her new job.

However, Scottie hadn't said "play in a band again," just "play the bass."

That was something she could do without setting herself up for another disappointment. She could dig out the dusty hardshell case from wherever she and Fiona had stowed it and play her acoustic bass without bothering the neighbors or making any tech implode.

Willow took a steadying breath. "Okay. I can do that."

Scottie's mouth curved up into a warm smile.

For a few seconds, they just sat there, smiling at each other.

"Last round of questions," Scottie finally said. "What's the most impulsive, spontaneous thing you've ever done?"

It was her turn to ask a question, not Scottie's, but Willow didn't point it out. It didn't matter because, for once, the question was an easy one to answer. "This," she replied without hesitation.

Scottie tilted her head. "Getting stuck in an elevator?"

"Talking to you like this." Willow gestured back and forth between them. "Opening up. I don't normally do that."

"Thank you for doing it now," Scottie said, her voice sincere and a little husky. "For trusting me."

Willow had been staring down at her own hands during her quiet confession, but now she lifted her gaze.

Scottie was studying her with that calm, soft look. The warm brown of her eyes seemed to draw Willow in. What she saw in them was a deep understanding, as if Scottie knew exactly how uncharacteristic and how hard this had been for her. Being seen like that felt comforting and unsettling at the same time.

Willow didn't know what to say. A tightness in her throat made it hard to speak. Finally, she got out: "How about you?" She didn't look away from Scottie's eyes. "What's the most impulsive thing you've ever done?"

"This," Scottie rasped. Very slowly, she leaned forward on her knees. Her gaze dipped to Willow's mouth.

Oh God. Willow's pulse sped up. She was very aware of how close they were sitting, no longer shoulder to shoulder but facing each other. Scottie's knee almost brushed hers, and she could feel the heat emanating from it—and from Scottie's lips, which were moving closer and closer.

With only inches between them, Scottie paused. "Willow," she whispered. Her breath teased Willow's mouth, sending shivers down her body. "Tell me if you don't—"

But Willow didn't want to say anything. She didn't want to think or to keep her usual distance. She wanted to feel more of Scottie's heat, more of that connection that had formed between them. Not allowing herself time to reconsider, she leaned forward and closed the remaining space between them.

Their lips brushed in a gentle, tentative kiss.

Before one of them could press closer—or withdraw, a sharp jolt zinged through Willow's lips like a tiny lightning strike.

Both jerked back with a gasp and stared at each other.

Willow pressed her hand to her mouth. She couldn't tell if her lips were tingling from the painful zap or from that tender kiss. She couldn't tell anything anymore. Her head spun as she tried to process what had just happened—what she had done. She had kissed Scottie!

Scottie looked as shocked as Willow felt, not only at being zapped but also about the fact that they had kissed. She reached up and traced her own bottom lip with her fingertips.

The much-too-sensual movement did nothing to calm Willow's raw nerves.

"That was—"

"I—"

They spoke at the same time.

But before either could finish her sentence, the intercom crackled. "Hello in there," the same male voice from before said. "Our maintenance team is there now. They're going to manually lower the elevator car to the nearest floor and get you out."

"Thank God," Willow whispered. Suddenly, she couldn't wait to escape.

Maybe Scottie felt the same because she scrambled to her feet too.

Willow's legs had gone stiff after sitting on the floor for so long. How long had they been in here?

"It'll be a little bumpy, and there'll be some clanks, but that's normal. You're perfectly safe," the maintenance employee continued. "Hang tight and stay away from the doors until our guys tell you otherwise."

Willow busied herself picking up the empty wrappers and stuffing them into her purse, along with their impromptu picnic blanket.

Neither looked at the other.

Within seconds, creaking, grinding noises drifted through the metal walls, interrupted by occasional clanks. The elevator vibrated and shook as it was slowly lowered.

Willow grabbed hold of the railing. She remembered the way she had accidentally clutched Scottie's arm when the elevator had jerked to a stop. That seemed to have happened days, not just a couple of hours, ago.

Finally, the downward movement stopped with a soft thud.

For a moment, nothing happened.

Scottie shifted. She was gripping the railing with both hands.

Was she afraid that they were stuck again?

But before Willow could say anything to calm her, a sliver of light fell through the tiny gap between the doors. A jingle sounded, then a scraping noise came from the other side.

They were opening the doors!

Willow held her breath until the doors scraped open.

Cool air rushed in.

A technician in a blue jumpsuit stood in front of them.

The light from his headlamp made Willow squint against the sudden brightness. The section of hallway behind him was dimly lit by an emergency light. Apparently, the power was still out.

He offered a hand to help her out.

On wobbly legs, Willow stepped into the hallway.

Scottie followed close behind. "Thank you," she said to the maintenance worker.

"You're welcome. You two all right?"

They glanced at each other, then away.

Willow nodded, even though she wasn't sure that was the truth.

Chapter 14

As the maintenance technician led them toward a glowing red *EXIT* sign, Scottie peered back toward the elevator. The doors remained open, so she caught a glimpse of its interior.

It was just an empty metal box now, sterile and impersonal. The wrappers on the floor and any signs of their mini picnic were gone. Already, everything that had happened in there was starting to feel surreal, as if part of a dream.

Dazed, Scottie followed Willow through the staircase and down to the lobby, while the elevator technician wished them a good night and headed back.

Neither of them spoke as they pushed through the glass doors and stepped out onto the slick brick-paved plaza in front of the building.

The power still seemed to be out on the entire block, and the MAX stop across the street was nearly deserted, so the plaza lay in silence. A light drizzle fell, but Scottie didn't mind. It felt refreshing after being stuck in the stuffy elevator for so long. The scent of wet leaves hung in the air.

The streetlights were off, and no glow came from the office windows above them, but otherwise, everything looked the way it always did when Scottie left work late.

How weird that the world outside was nearly unchanged when Scottie didn't feel the same at all.

They both paused and turned toward each other.

An hour or two ago, Scottie had been frantic to get out of the elevator and go home, but now she found herself strangely reluctant to leave.

Would the connection that she'd felt with Willow in the elevator still be there when they went their separate ways?

They stood facing each other in the near dark.

Willow shifted from foot to foot, both hands wrapped around the strap of her purse. After revealing so much about herself in the elevator, she didn't seem to know what to say to Scottie anymore. "My sister is probably worried sick about me. I'd better get home."

Seriously? Willow wanted to rush off without even addressing the kiss? No way! "Wait! Shouldn't we talk about—"

"Can we talk another time?" Willow asked. "I really need a shower, some real food, and a bathroom that isn't a pee corner before I can process any of this." She flashed a wry grin.

But after nearly two hours of being trapped together in a confined space, Scottie knew the way a real smile lit up Willow's eyes. This one didn't.

"All right," Scottie said—because what else was she supposed to do? She couldn't force her to talk if she wasn't ready.

Willow gave her another smile that didn't reach her eyes. "See you on Monday."

Then she was gone, rushing across the dimly lit parking lot toward a boxy little hatchback. The creak of the car door sounded unbearably loud in the stillness of the night. A few seconds later, the engine coughed to life, and the headlights came on.

Scottie stood in the rain, rooted to the spot, and watched the taillights disappear down the street.

It was after nine by the time Willow unlocked the front door and drudged to the living room.

Fiona was curled up on the couch with both cats and a huge bowl of what smelled like popcorn, but as soon as Willow entered, her head snapped up, and she hit *pause* on the remote. "Willow! Finally! I was about to call your boss and tell her to stop working you to death!"

Willow dropped her purse on an armchair and plopped down at the other end of the sofa. "You don't even have Celeste's number, and I wasn't working that late. I left work at seven."

"Seven?" Fiona frowned. "It's a quarter past nine! Did your car break down? Why didn't you call me? Wait, don't tell me... Both of your phones died?"

"No. The elevator did. I was stuck between floors for nearly two hours."

Fiona's blanket slipped to the floor as she sat bolt upright.

Spice hissed, jumped off the couch, and stalked out of the room.

"What?" Fiona stared at her. "Oh my God! You were stuck in an elevator for two hours? No wonder you look so dazed!"

Dazed was right, but it wasn't because of the elevator ordeal. Being trapped in that steel box hadn't rattled her nearly as much as Scottie's lips on her own. Willow still couldn't believe she had kissed Scottie! Why the hell had she done that? She really should have known better.

She managed a shrug. "It wasn't as bad as you might think, even though it took maintenance quite some time to get to us."

"Us?" Fiona asked. "Who's us?"

"Scottie and I. She was working late too and got trapped in there with me." Willow aimed for a casual tone, but she couldn't even say her name without blushing. Thankfully, the only light came from the TV and a lamp in the corner, so Fiona probably didn't notice.

"Ooh, your sexy IT lady?" Fiona put the popcorn bowl on the coffee table and slid closer. "Did she manage to get you out?"

The heat in Willow's cheeks intensified. "No. She's an IT support person, not an elevator mechanic. We had to wait for maintenance to come rescue us."

"Well, could have been worse, right? You could have been stuck with your boss or with some sweaty guy who kept hitting on you. Right?"

"Right," Willow murmured. Spending two hours in a confined space with anyone else would have been a nightmare, while Scottie had made it more than bearable. But then again, with anyone else, it wouldn't have ended in a way that made her heart race.

Fiona slid even closer and nudged her with an elbow. "So? How was it? What did you do for two hours?"

"We had a little picnic, sharing the snacks from my purse." Willow tried not to think of the other things they had done.

"A picnic in an elevator?" Fiona let out a disbelieving laugh. "Sounds cozy! Weren't you freaking out?"

"Scottie was panicking a little at first, but I managed to distract her with a game."

"I Spy?" Fiona asked. "That must have been a very short game. Not much to see in an elevator."

Willow took a handful of popcorn, just to have a reason to look away. "No, not I Spy. We played Truth or Drink with a bottle of water."

"Let me guess. You ended up emptying the bottle because you didn't want to tell her anything?"

Under normal circumstances, that would have been exactly how it went. "I..." Willow rolled an unpopped kernel of corn between her fingers. "I didn't drink even once."

Fiona let out a whistle. "You actually told her stuff about yourself? You never do that!"

"I know. It was the weirdest experience I ever had in my life, Fi." Willow didn't look up from the kernel.

"Weirder than your effect on tech?"

"Okay, maybe the second-weirdest." Willow threw the kernel back into the bowl and crunched on a piece of popcorn instead, giving herself some time to think about how to explain it. "When the maintenance guy said we might have to wait for two hours, it sounded like a lifetime. But then the time just seemed to fly by...or maybe it actually expanded. Like we were in outer space, the only two people in an escape capsule or something. I can't describe it. It was intense. Like getting to know someone at warp speed." The *Star Trek* reference made her think of Scottie again. "After a while, she didn't feel like a stranger anymore, and the elevator felt less like a trap and more like a safe bubble where we could let our guard down and share personal stuff without fear of being judged. I told her things that I'd never told anyone before."

Fiona went uncharacteristically quiet.

Willow peered over.

Her sister was gaping at her. "That really wasn't what I expected when you didn't make it home on time. I thought you were working late, not revealing all your secrets in an elevator."

"Trust me, it wasn't how I expected the day to end either," Willow murmured.

Fiona kept studying her. "So is that why you look so shell-shocked?"

"More or less."

"There's more?" Fiona wrapped her fingers around Willow's arm. Her brow furrowed. "Are you worried that you said too much? Like she'll go and tell your colleagues?"

"No!" The answer shot out of Willow. She didn't want Fiona to think Scottie wasn't trustworthy for even one second. "She'd never do that."

"Okay. Good. But there is something else, isn't there?" Fiona asked. "Did you tell her why you keep having to submit tickets, and she didn't believe you?"

"No, I didn't tell her that." That was the one thing she would never reveal, even to Scottie. *Especially* to Scottie. The thought of Scottie laughing or, worse, looking at her as if she was broken made Willow's stomach twist.

"Then what is it?"

Willow licked a bit of melted butter off her fingers and hesitated. Part of her wanted to keep it to herself and forget it ever happened. But a bigger part felt as if she'd explode if she didn't tell anyone. "She kissed me," she finally blurted out. "Or I kissed her. I don't even know who started it. I think she did, and then I..." She pressed her fingers to her lips, where she could still feel Scottie's warm mouth.

Fiona let out a loud screech that made the second cat jump off the couch too. "What? You kissed her? You actually *kissed her*?"

Willow pressed her lips together, as if that would stop her from reliving it, and nodded.

"And? How was it?" Fiona waved her hands. "Come on, give me all the details!"

How could she sum up that kiss in a few words? Gentle? Full of warmth? Not long enough? It never should have happened? Finally, she said, "Electrifying."

"Don't tell me you zapped her?"

"Hm? Oh. Yeah. That too." It had been electrifying in every sense, even though it had lasted for only the length of a heartbeat.

Fiona half groaned, half laughed. "Oh shit. Poor Scottie. She probably didn't know what hit her—literally! But still, you kissed her! Woo-hoo!" She hopped up and down on the couch, grabbed Willow's hand, and raised it in the air as if she were declaring her the winner of a boxing match.

Willow pulled her hand away. She didn't feel like a winner at all. "Shh! Please don't make a big deal out of it."

"Excuse you! You kiss a near stranger in an elevator and expect me to pretend it's business as usual?" Fiona shook her head, making her dark-brown-and-purple hair fly. "This is totally out of character for you!"

Willow covered her overheated face with her hands. "I know, I know. I don't even recognize myself." None of this was her. She never revealed this much about herself, and she certainly didn't go around kissing women she barely knew, minutes after declaring that she didn't date. Talk about sending mixed signals!

"Maybe that's a good thing," Fiona said softly. "Maybe you needed this space pod experience to stop keeping everyone at arm's length."

She made it sound as if the kiss had been a good thing, but Willow didn't believe that. All she'd done was create a big mess. She didn't even want to imagine what Scottie must think of her now.

"So...what now?" Fiona asked when Willow didn't say anything. "Will you ask her out?"

"Absolutely not! I don't date; you know that. Nothing's changed."

"Really? You shared your soul and an—and I quote—electrifying kiss with a woman in an elevator. Sounds like a pretty big change to me."

"It was an unusual situation that made me act out of character. But as soon as we got out of the elevator, reality snapped back into place." Willow had to think about what she'd told Scottie: *The safest place for us to be is inside the elevator. It only becomes dangerous if people try to get out by themselves.* For an hour and a half, in the contained space of the elevator, things had felt safe. But now that they were back outside, they could be heading into dangerous territory if she wasn't careful. "I'm still me."

"That doesn't mean—"

Willow held up both hands. "It won't work. It never does."

"How can you know that if you don't give it a chance?" Fiona shot back. "Just because it hasn't worked out so far doesn't mean it won't with Scottie. Maybe you got stuck in that elevator together for a reason. Clearly, the universe ships you two!"

"The universe?" Willow barely abstained from rolling her eyes. "Please!"

"What? Getting stuck in an elevator... That's rom-com material, Sis, and you know there's always a happy ending in a rom-com."

Willow regarded her with a shake of her head. "Unbelievable. After everything you went through, you honestly still buy into all of that?"

Fiona's boldness wavered for an instant. "Maybe that makes me even more of a fool after what I went through with Kris, but, yeah, I'd like to believe that love might still be out there for me." Her voice was uncharacteristically quiet.

God, she was really making a big, fat mess of things today, first with Scottie, now with Fiona. Willow brushed her fingers against the metal popcorn bowl, just in case, then gripped Fiona's hands. "I'm sorry. I didn't mean to be an ass. Of course love is out there for you. You're too awesome to not get snatched up by someone much more deserving than Kris. But it's different for me."

When Fiona opened her mouth, probably about to protest, Willow stopped her by squeezing her hands. "I don't have the energy for this discussion tonight. I just want to eat, pee, take a shower, and then fall into bed—not necessarily in that order."

Fiona sighed. "All right. I'll let this go—for tonight. And while I can't help you with the peeing or the rest of your list, there's leftover lasagna in the kitchen."

"Ooh. I knew you were my favorite sister for a reason."

"I'd consider that a compliment if I weren't your only sister."

"Details, details." She gave Fiona's hands one last squeeze, then got up and headed for the kitchen. In the arched doorway, she paused and turned. "Oh, by the way, do you remember where we put my bass when I moved in?"

"I think it's in the garage. Why?"

Willow continued her beeline for the fridge. "No particular reason. Just wondered."

Scottie hurried across the courtyard separating her apartment building from her friend Kassidy's, her pace quickening with every step until she was nearly jogging along the raised beds of the community garden.

Usually, the smell of damp soil, thyme, and rosemary grounded her, but now it barely registered. Her head hadn't stopped spinning ever since that kiss in the elevator.

She needed someone who could help her cut through all the tangled thoughts and emotions—someone who would tell her, without any nonsense, if she was setting herself up to get her heart broken again. If there was one person who could do that, it was Kassidy. Sugarcoating just wasn't in her DNA.

Someone left the building just as Scottie reached it, and she slipped inside and took the stairs to the second floor. After the elevator fiasco, even her exhaustion wouldn't get her to set foot inside of another steel trap tonight.

Softly, she knocked on Kassidy's door.

It took a minute for the lock to click and the door to swing open.

Her friend's bulky form filled the doorway, dressed in a pair of black cargo pants—she never wore another color. But today, her T-shirt wasn't the usual solid black. In big, white letters, it read: *It's too peopley outside.*

Kassidy regarded her with a scowl. "You know I don't like surprise visits."

Scottie put on her most charming smile. "Sorry. When I got home, my phone was dead, so I couldn't call or text. But something happened, and I can't stop thinking about it. I really need to talk." She held out two bottles of ginger beer—Kassidy's favorite beverage—like a peace offering. "I come bearing gifts."

"Bribery is acceptable." Kassidy didn't smile back, but she took the bottles, stepped aside, and opened the door wider. "Come on in."

Scottie followed her in.

Kassidy's studio apartment was the same as always: minimalistic, uncluttered, and all white—the walls, the furniture, and the shelves. She had added even more plants since the last time Scottie had visited, and they kept the space from appearing cold and impersonal. A Heartleaf Philodendron and a String of Pearls spilled down from the exposed silver pipe running across the ceiling, softening the industrial look. On the middle shelf of the bookcase, a regiment of cacti stood in neat formation, each in a white pot. The refreshing scent of peppermint drifted over from the kitchenette.

Kassidy twisted off the caps and set the bottles on the white counter.

Scottie perched on one of the barstools next to her and reached for the closest bottle, not because she was thirsty but because it would give her a moment to think about how to start.

Before she could take a sip, Kassidy gave her an expectant look. "You said you needed to talk, so…talk."

Scottie laughed. Six years ago, when they had first met in the community garden their apartment buildings shared, Kassidy's bluntness had nearly sent her running. But she had seen something in the gentle, patient way Kassidy handled the tomato seedlings, coaxing their thin stems onto the twine without breaking them. So she had decided on the spot that they—two women with *Star Trek*-inspired names and a passion for gardening—were destined to be friends.

Kassidy had insisted hers didn't count since the *Star Trek* character was spelled with one S, while her name had two.

Scottie had replied that her name wasn't an exact match for the *Enterprise*'s engineer either, so she'd adopted Kassidy into her circle anyway—and she was glad she had. Kassidy had proven to be a loyal friend who'd always been there for her when it mattered. After the breakup, she had even offered Scottie her couch for as long as she needed if she couldn't bear to stay in the apartment she'd shared with Tanya.

Her bluntness was just her natural way of communicating, not a sign that she didn't care or wasn't interested in what Scottie had to say.

"Straight to the point, as always," Scottie said with a smile.

Kassidy shrugged. "Small talk is overrated. Let's skip to the interesting part."

"All right. There was a power outage at work today. The entire block went dark, and I ended up being trapped in an elevator with Willow for almost two hours."

Kassidy's eyebrows twitched. "Willow? The Willow of the many IT tickets? The one your work buddies insist must be interested in you?"

Scottie nodded. "The one and only."

"So?" Kassidy asked. "Is she?"

"Is she what?"

"Interested in you."

Scottie took a long drag of her ginger beer. The spicy-and-sweet fizz burned in the back of her throat. "That's what I'm here to figure out. So far, I didn't think she was, despite what Mateo and Gordon keep saying. But then the power outage happened. We played Truth or…well, Truth while we waited for maintenance to get us out. Just as a way to kill some time. But it quickly became so much more than a game."

"How so?"

"It changed things between us in a way that's hard to describe." Scottie played with the ginger beer cap, making it rotate across the counter. "At first, I assumed she'd be reluctant to answer the more personal questions. I thought we would stick to fun, superficial things. Stuff like favorite ice cream flavor. But it quickly drifted into deeply personal territory. I even told her about Tanya, and she—" Scottie captured the cap in her hand. No, she wouldn't violate the trust Willow had put in her by revealing what she'd told her.

"She what?" Kassidy prompted.

"She seemed genuinely interested in finding out more about me, and she opened up to me too. It was incredible, Kass. *She* was incredible. She really let me see her, and I have a feeling that's rare for her. At least from what I've seen, she doesn't even go to the cafeteria for lunch; she always eats alone and doesn't seem eager to make friends at Kudos."

Kassidy gave her a look as if to say, *Why would she?*

Scottie chuckled and flicked the cap in her direction. "Anyway. I finally asked her about the most impulsive thing she'd ever done, and when she asked me the same thing in return, I said 'This,' leaned in, and—"

"Kissed her?" Kassidy asked, eyes wide. "I admit I didn't see that coming. You haven't even flirted with anyone since Tanya kicked you to the curb!"

"No. I mean, yes, we kissed, but she was the one who closed the last few inches between us and kissed me first." Scottie's lips prickled, and she didn't think it had anything to do with her gingery drink.

Kassidy regarded her with a steady, unflinching gaze. "So why the confusion? You leaned in, she kissed you—mutual interest established, right?"

It sounded so clear and easy, but it was anything but. "I'm not sure. She ran off before we could talk about it. Now I don't know what to think…or do. Was it just a heat-of-the-moment thing that can't go anywhere, or do we really have a connection?"

"Hmm." Kassidy rubbed her hand over her buzzed hair. "Are you sure she isn't straight?"

"Oh yeah. Very sure."

"I'm not asking how convincingly she kissed."

Scottie flicked the second bottle cap at her too. "That's not why I'm so sure. She told me she's a lesbian."

"Then why the hot-and-cold treatment?"

"I have no idea. But something tells me there's more behind it than just her not being interested." Willow had told her she didn't date and didn't believe relationships would last. But then she had also talked so passionately about Scottie not having to change to deserve love, and she had encouraged her to date. Something didn't add up.

Kassidy took a slow drink of her ginger beer. "So what's the real question here? You want me to tell you to go for it—or did you come to me instead of Violet or Anisha so I could tell you that it's too soon and she'll stomp all over your heart?"

Scottie paused with the bottle halfway to her mouth. She lowered it and swirled around the tiny ginger pieces at the bottom. Was that why she had paid Kassidy a despised surprise visit instead of talking to one of her other, more optimistic friends? Because deep down, she had wanted Kassidy to warn her to stay away? "Is it?" she asked. "Too soon, I mean. It's only been six months since Tanya and I split up. Not a good time to start something new. I should give it more time…right?"

But instead of nodding, Kassidy waved dismissively. "Forget Tanya. I never liked her anyway."

"You don't like anyone." Scottie pointed at Kassidy's *It's too peopley outside* T-shirt.

Kassidy shrugged. "I don't mind you."

A chuckle escaped Scottie. "Thanks. But even if Tanya hadn't made me seriously doubt myself and my taste in women, I have no idea how to go forward...or even if I should. Willow is a colleague—and given how often she runs into problems with her devices, we'll have to work together on a regular basis. I don't want to make things awkward."

Kassidy huffed against the rim of her bottle, producing a low whistling sound. "A little late for that consideration, don't you think? Since you already kissed her. That's probably not in the *best practices for collaboration* section of the Kudos Entertainment employee handbook."

Argh. She was right, of course. Scottie had no idea how to act if she saw Willow at work on Monday. "So do I just go back to treating her like any other colleague? Pretend it never happened?"

"Can you?" Kassidy asked.

Scottie rubbed her palm, cool from gripping the bottle, over the back of her neck. "I don't know. Something between us changed in that elevator. But is it worth risking my heart all over again? What if she ends up kicking me to the curb too?"

"Well, then you come over with something harder than ginger beer," Kassidy said dryly.

Laughter burst from Scottie's chest. "How do you always make it sound so simple?"

"Maybe because it is," Kassidy replied. "Just talk to her. You want to know if that elevator kiss meant something to her? Ask her. Much better than second-guessing yourself for the rest of the century. If she's worth your time, she'll tell you where you stand."

Scottie regarded her with a shake of her head. "For someone who claims to hate people, you're amazingly good at this."

"I'm not just ten years older and thirty pounds heavier than you; I'm also fifty times wiser."

Scottie snorted. "You mean fifty times grumpier. But, seriously, you are good at this."

"Don't let it get around."

"Don't worry; I won't. Thanks, Kass."

Kassidy tilted her head in acknowledgment. "You're welcome. Now drink your ginger beer before it gets flat and tell me how your kale is doing. Is it still hanging on despite all the rain we've been getting?"

Chapter 15

Maybe this hadn't been her brightest idea. By the fifth floor, Willow's thighs started to burn, and she was gasping for air.

God, she was out of shape! She definitely needed to take up running again.

Thirteen floors was a long way up. What had made her think she could do this without arriving at her desk looking like an extra in a disaster movie?

But, of course, she knew exactly why she had skipped the elevator. After Friday night, she couldn't set foot in one without reliving every minute she'd spent in there with Scottie.

On the next landing, she paused to catch her breath.

Footsteps echoed somewhere below her, slowly coming closer. Apparently, someone else had the same ridiculous idea.

Willow glanced over her shoulder, expecting to see a Kudos employee in a suit, trying to get their ten thousand steps in.

Instead, the person rounding the turn of the stairwell was Scottie. Her face was flushed, and a strand of hair clung to her damp forehead.

Willow's pulse, which had settled down a bit, picked up again.

As if sensing her presence, Scottie looked up from where her gaze had been fixed on the stairs before her. She froze, one foot hovering in midair.

For a few seconds, they just stared at each other.

Then both started laughing. The sound bounced off the concrete walls and echoed through the staircase.

The tension that had knotted Willow's muscles all weekend loosened a little. "You too?" she gasped out breathlessly and gestured at the stairs.

Scottie nodded. "Yeah. For some reason, I wasn't in the mood for elevators." She sent her a lopsided grin that didn't help settle Willow's pulse at all.

"Same here." Well, maybe not exactly the same. The fear of getting stuck again wasn't what had made Willow decide to take the stairs. But she knew she couldn't step into an elevator without remembering the feel of Scottie's lips on her own.

They stared for a moment longer and then, as if by an unspoken agreement, glanced away and started climbing side by side.

Willow was very aware of Scottie's elevated breathing and of her own hammering heartbeat.

They made it two floors higher before they stopped to catch their breath.

"Just two more floors," Scottie rasped out.

It could have been a simple encouragement, but to Willow, it was also an ultimatum. Just two more floors until they reached IT. Two more floors until Scottie pushed through the metal door and was gone, along with Willow's chance to talk to her.

And she owed her that.

Willow had played this conversation through at least two dozen times all weekend, but now the words refused to come. She clutched the railing more tightly. "I think—"

"Listen," Scottie said at the same time.

They both paused.

Scottie made a *go ahead* gesture. Her gaze clung to Willow's mouth the way it had Friday night in the elevator, right before they had kissed.

Not helping. Scottie wasn't thinking about kissing her again; she was probably just waiting, spellbound, for what she had to say.

Willow swallowed. It sounded much too loud in the narrow staircase. "I owe you an apology," she finally said. "For bolting the way I did. And for…for kissing you. I shouldn't have done that."

"Why not?" Scottie finally asked, her voice soft. "Why shouldn't you kiss me, if that's what we both wanted?" She searched Willow's eyes. "You did want it too, didn't you?"

The question made Willow squirm. So far, she hadn't let herself say it out loud—or even just in her own head. Wanting Scottie and knowing she wanted her in return felt like standing on the edge of a cliff. And now Scottie was asking her to take a step forward.

But as much as she wanted to, she couldn't lie. She took a breath. "Yeah. I did. In that moment, I wanted it."

Scottie tilted her head and gave her a quizzical look. "Then why are you apologizing?"

"Because I wasn't thinking. We were in a safe bubble, separate from the rest of my life. But outside of that bubble, this"—she waved back and forth between them—"wouldn't work."

"Why not?" Scottie asked again.

Willow gestured helplessly. For a second, as she looked at Scottie, no good reason came to mind. But Scottie deserved an answer. Willow could see the vulnerability in her eyes. Her running away on Friday had probably brought back that feeling of not being good enough for Scottie. She couldn't allow that. "It's not you," Willow blurted out. "It's me."

Scottie scrunched up her nose. "Right." She set off again, climbing the stairs.

Willow rushed after her. "No, really. I know it's a cliché, but in this case, it happens to be true. Like I told you in the elevator, I don't date. That hasn't changed. Kissing you sent the wrong message."

They climbed an entire floor in silence, then rounded the bend to the tenth floor.

"So," Scottie said, "what you're saying is: What happened in the elevator will stay in the elevator?"

Something flickered across her face, just a subtle shift of her expression, but it was enough to make Willow's stomach churn. Was it disappointment? Hurt? It definitely wasn't just the effort of climbing ten flights of stairs.

"I think it should," Willow answered quietly. *It has to.* This was the real world, not the safe space of the elevator. Out here, a relationship between them would never work. "I don't believe in forever, and you do. Or at least you will again, once you had a chance to heal from your breakup. It wouldn't be fair."

For a second, Scottie looked as if she was about to protest. Then she directed her gaze straight ahead and marched up the last few steps in silence.

Willow followed, her footfalls heavy.

When they reached the tenth-floor landing, they paused in front of the metal door that led to the IT department and turned to face each other.

Willow's heartbeat thudded louder than the echo of their footsteps had as she waited for Scottie to say something.

"All right," Scottie finally said. She rested one hand on the door's push bar as if she couldn't wait to get away from Willow. But she didn't. Instead, she brushed a damp strand of hair off her face and looked at her. "So...friends?"

Willow froze. Friends? With Scottie? Not a good idea either.

Her rational brain shouted at her to say no. She had avoided close friendships for years, and she'd definitely never considered being friends with someone from IT—someone who could easily figure out she wasn't just having bad luck with tech.

She should stay away to protect herself.

But after their time trapped together in the elevator, she felt as if she needed to protect Scottie too.

The look in Scottie's eyes when she'd told her it had been a mistake to kiss her had been bad enough once. She couldn't bear to see it a second time.

After all, what reason would she give for not wanting to be friends? That "it's not you; it's me" explanation wouldn't fly. Scottie would take it as a confirmation that she wasn't enough—not even for a friendship. She couldn't do that to her.

And, truth be told, maybe she couldn't do it to herself either. The thought of saying "no" made her chest ache with something she couldn't name.

"Yes," she said slowly. "Friends."

It would be just a work friendship. They would chat about the rainy weather or the Thorns' latest game or whatever people in Portland talked about with their colleagues. Nothing too deep. Nothing that would endanger her secret...or her heart.

At her answer, a small but genuine smile lifted the corners of Scottie's lips. "Okay." She nodded. "Friends." She held out her hand.

Willow's brain needed a moment to grasp that Scottie wanted to shake on their friendship agreement. She reached out—at the last second remembering to clutch the railing and ground herself with her left—and placed her right hand in Scottie's.

Scottie's palm was warm, her grip strong. She clasped Willow's fingers firmly but carefully.

They shook once…twice, then lingered for a moment before letting go.

Scottie cleared her throat. "All right…friend. I'd better get my ass to work before Gordon and Mateo eat all of the cinnamon rolls our boss brings in on Mondays." After a quick nod, she turned and pushed the bar.

The door swung open, and she stepped into the IT department hallway.

The loud thud as it closed echoed through the stairwell.

Willow leaned against the railing and stared at the gray metal for quite some time. The staircase felt colder somehow now that she was alone, but it was probably just her sweat-dampened body starting to cool down.

With a sigh, she pushed off the railing and started to climb the last few flights to her floor.

Work friends, she repeated with every step. Just work friends. No reason to panic, right?

Chapter 16

Scottie sat at her desk, fingers poised over her keyboard, gaze on her screen, but her mind was elsewhere. Three floors up, to be exact. Her thoughts kept drifting to Willow and their staircase encounter.

A week had passed since then. A week without any tech problems from Willow. Or maybe she had them and was trying to handle them herself so she wouldn't have to see Scottie. Did she feel just as awkward and vulnerable as Scottie did after their conversation?

The previous Monday, she had headed to work, determined to seek Willow out during lunch. But before she could, they had run into each other in the staircase. To her pleasant surprise, Willow hadn't bolted this time, even though Scottie had a feeling she had wanted to.

What she'd said had been less pleasant, though. That "it's not you; it's me" line still made Scottie flinch every time she thought about it. It was basically what Tanya had told her when she had ended their ten-year relationship, and Scottie wasn't sure she could believe it from either woman.

But maybe lumping Willow in with Tanya wasn't fair.

If she's worth your time, she'll tell you where you stand, her friend Kassidy had said. And Willow had told her in very clear words. Scottie had to respect that.

Maybe she should even be grateful Willow had made the decision for both of them. Being friends was great, right? Safe and manageable, not something that would break her heart and throw her into a six-month crisis where she doubted her own worth. Willow was right; friendship was definitely the better option.

If only her damn heart would get the memo. It started to beat faster the second a ticket from Operations popped up on her screen.

Willow! Quickly, she reached for her mouse to click on the ticket, eager to find out what tech emergency Willow was struggling with this time.

But then she paused with the mouse arrow hovering over the ticket. *Slow down.* Was she really ready to face Willow? To embrace a friendship with her without thinking about any what-ifs?

Plus if she appeared too eager, Gordon and Mateo would start teasing her about her "girlfriend in Operations" again. Maybe she should talk one of them into handling the ticket.

Yet when she opened it, the person requesting IT help wasn't Willow. It was Celeste Covey, Willow's boss. *Smart board frozen,* the description field said. *Screen completely unresponsive.*

Okay, she could handle that. And if she got to see Willow while she was up there, she could handle that too. After all, they were just two co-workers who'd agreed to be friends.

All she had to do was to forget those moments of closeness in the elevator and that misguided kiss. Easy, right?

The thirteenth floor was quieter than Scottie had expected for a Monday morning. The usually bustling bullpen was empty.

Her gaze was drawn to Willow's desk. A closed notebook and Willow's Rolodex were neatly arranged in one corner, but otherwise, it was empty too.

The faint murmur of voices drifted over from down the hall, and she followed it to the conference room.

The glass door stood ajar. Scottie peered inside.

A dozen Operations employees were gathered around the long table. Some stared at the digital whiteboard at the front of the room. Others secretly scrolled through their emails on their phones. The energy in the room sagged like a pierced balloon losing air.

Scottie immediately detected the source of everyone's frustration.

The huge smart board was completely frozen. A half-finished chart of some toy production process was displayed on its screen, static and useless.

Celeste tapped at it with a stylus, her jaw tight and her lips compressed into a thin line.

Willow was sitting to her boss's left, across the table from Barb. As she shifted on her chair, her dark-brown hair fell forward. It caught the morning light that streamed in through the window, gleaming like the rich soil Scottie turned in her hands in spring. Absentmindedly, Willow brushed the strands back behind her ear.

Scottie tightened her grip on her toolbox and knocked on the open glass door with her free hand.

Everyone looked up, but Scottie zeroed in on only one of them. Her gaze met Willow's.

"Good morning," Scottie said.

A chorus of answers echoed through the room.

"Morning," Willow answered softly. After a moment, she broke eye contact and returned her attention to her boss.

"Ah, Scottie. Finally!" Celeste waved her in.

Scottie slipped into the room. "What seems to be the problem?"

"It's been a week," Celeste muttered, a growl in her voice. "Just one week and this expensive piece of garbage Joseph insisted we get has already frozen on us. We're losing time—time we don't have. This is our busiest season."

"Let me take a look." Scottie walked around the table and set down her toolbox a few feet from where Willow was sitting. The unobtrusive apricot scent of Willow's shampoo drifted over. After breathing it in for two hours in the elevator, Scottie would have recognized it anywhere.

Focus. She was here for the smart board, not to breathe in Willow's shampoo. Very aware of all the gazes on her, she went to work. She tapped the touchscreen to see if it would register anything at all.

It didn't.

She checked the cables, then tried to access the digital whiteboard's settings, but it was completely unresponsive. Next, she attempted a soft restart, holding down the power button for several seconds.

That didn't get her a response either.

"Hmm." She unplugged the power cord, waited thirty seconds, then plugged it back in.

Still frozen.

This was not something she could fix in the middle of a meeting. She turned back around.

Every single team member was looking at her expectantly.

"So?" Celeste asked.

"Sorry," Scottie said. "This isn't going to be a quick fix. I'll come back after you've wrapped up and take a closer look. In the meantime, I'll get the vendor's tech team on the line to make sure we're not accidentally doing something that'll void the warranty."

Celeste gave a tight nod. "Fine. Everyone, take ten. We'll reschedule this meeting for—"

"Wait!"

Scottie had already turned to leave. Now she snapped back around, along with everyone else.

Willow slowly rose from her seat. Under all the attention, she shifted her weight from one foot to the other. "Why don't we continue old-school so we don't lose momentum? It's the ideas that matter, not the fancy tech that displays them."

"She's right," Celeste said before anyone else could speak. "Let's do this, people."

Willow rushed from the room. What seemed like only seconds later, she returned with an armful of stuff. She spread two taped-together whiteboard sheets over the long conference table and dropped a stack of differently colored sticky notes on top. "Pink for manufacturing, blue for shipping, yellow for marketing." She grabbed a marker, scribbled a few words onto a pink note, and stuck it on the paper, starting to recreate the chart from the frozen smart board.

Celeste took a marker too and added blue notes.

Soon, the conference room was buzzing with activity. People were moving around the table, reaching past each other to place their notes. Even the employees who had glanced at their phones earlier were no longer passive.

Toolbox in hand, Scottie stood in the doorway and watched in awe. Her gaze followed Willow as she gracefully moved around the table, slipping past her colleagues to place sticky notes, each movement precise and fluid. Every now and then, she paused and studied the paper sheets, looking like a general surveying the strategic map before a battle.

Her resourcefulness and quick thinking were amazing! Like in the elevator, she had seemed prepared for any eventuality, even a brand-new device failing. She had stepped in with a creative work-around as if she had seen it coming.

Willow looked up from the table. Their gazes met across the bent heads of her colleagues.

Scottie playfully saluted her and mouthed, "Nice save."

A flush rose up Willow's neck, but she also couldn't hide the pleased smile that curved up her lips.

"You can go," Celeste told Scottie without glancing up from the paper chart. "Looks like we're managing just fine without that thing."

Scottie tore her gaze away from Willow. After one last nod, she turned and walked out.

An hour later, the members of the Operations team filed out of the conference room, chatting and laughing.

Barb snapped a few pictures of the paper chart on the table, then returned to her desk too.

Willow stayed back and gathered the leftover sticky notes into a neat stack, glad to have a moment to herself. Her gaze strayed to the smart board that sat abandoned at the front of the room.

Only when it had malfunctioned had she realized how close to the device she'd been sitting all morning. Was that what had caused it to freeze? A twinge of guilt shot through her, even though she couldn't be sure. Just in case, she would make sure to sit at the other end of the table from now on.

At least Celeste had submitted the ticket to IT this time, so Scottie and her colleagues wouldn't connect the glitch to Willow.

Admittedly, it had been nice to see Scottie again, especially since they had been in the middle of a team meeting, surrounded by other people, so they hadn't been able to talk. Willow still wasn't sure what to say to her.

A shadow fell across the table, wrenching her from her thoughts.

Her pulse picked up. Scottie? Had she returned, as promised, to examine the unresponsive smart board more closely?

But when Willow looked up, it wasn't Scottie who stood before her.

It was Celeste. Her boss's heels clicked on the gleaming floor as she took another step toward Willow. Despite a very frustrating morning, her hair was neatly pinned back, her blouse crisp, and her posture perfect. Now that the meeting had wrapped up without any more waste of time and resources, she looked less grim. She swept her arm toward the paper chart. "That was very resourceful, and I liked the initiative." Her voice was matter-of-fact but genuine.

Willow blinked, then stood a little taller. It was the first real praise she had received from their intense boss. "Thank you. I figured going back to sticky notes was better than letting a tech glitch derail our progress."

"Agreed." Celeste studied her with a gaze that was sharp but not unkind. "I think you're ready to shoulder more responsibility. From now on, I want you to take on Barb's work, while she will shadow you, giving advice and correcting missteps, if needed."

Willow swallowed hard. On the one hand, she felt ready to do more and was thrilled that Celeste trusted her enough to take over Barb's job. On the other hand, she was terrified. More responsibility meant more things could go wrong. As she had settled in at Kudos, the tech glitches had started to ease up a little. The added stress might cause them to flare up again.

Celeste sent her an expectant look, clearly waiting for a reply.

"Of course," Willow said, trying to keep a wobble out of her voice. "Barb...uh, Barbara has taught me a lot, and I'm ready to put it into action."

"Good. I'll let Barbara know." Celeste gave her a curt nod. Then she was gone, the click of her heels fading down the hallway.

Willow leaned on the conference table with both hands, head hanging down between her arms, and sucked in a deep breath.

"Hey, you okay?"

A soft voice made Willow jump. She straightened quickly and looked up.

This time, it was Scottie. Of course she would walk in just in time to witness Willow's moment of weakness.

"I'm fine," Willow answered automatically.

Scottie regarded her. "Friends, remember? You could tell me if you're not fine. I wouldn't blame you after the morning you had. Things seemed pretty tense when I walked in earlier."

Crap. Scottie clearly expected more than small talk about the Thorns or the constant drizzle. Willow opened her mouth to change the topic or assure her once again that she was fine but then realized she didn't want to brush her off. She snapped her mouth shut.

That was a first. She never felt the need to unload with colleagues. She kept her problems and worries to herself or shared them only with her sister.

But under Scottie's open, nonjudgmental gaze, she found herself saying, "Celeste just told me she thinks I'm ready for more responsibility."

"You are," Scottie replied immediately, as if there wasn't a doubt in her mind. "The way you handled the situation earlier proves it. Even Celeste was impressed—and so was I."

Heat rose to Willow's cheeks. Scottie's praise felt different from Celeste's. Her voice was warmer, tinged with admiration, and there was no assessing look in her eyes. Unlike Celeste, she wasn't testing Willow, measuring her performance. Willow fidgeted with a stack of sticky notes, not sure what to say.

"Seriously," Scottie added, "you're really good at improvising. You seem to have a backup plan for everything."

Willow emphatically shook her head. "Not everything. Some things you can't prepare for."

She wasn't talking about what had happened in the elevator, but as the words lingered in the silence between them, they seemed to take on a new, deeper meaning.

"Anyway," Willow said quickly, "Celeste wants me to take over Barb's workload, and Barb's just going to shadow me for her last few weeks at Kudos. I admit it's a little intimidating."

"I know it's a lot of responsibility, but Celeste wouldn't give it to you if she didn't think you were ready," Scottie said softly.

It wasn't the responsibility that scared Willow. She could handle that. She also didn't mind working longer hours. What she struggled with was the creeping fear that the added stress would be like pouring gasoline on the smoldering embers of her weird effect on tech. But she couldn't tell Scottie that.

Scottie watched her closely, her head tilted to one side in a way that Willow was starting to recognize as typical for her.

"It's fine. I'm just a little nervous." Willow forced a smile. "But I'm sure I'll manage. Like you just said, I'm good at improvising."

Scottie studied her for a moment longer as if sensing there was more. But she didn't press. Instead, she answered Willow's half-hearted smile with a more genuine one. "You are. But if you run into any trouble, there are people at this company who'll have your back." She searched Willow's eyes. "Okay?"

"Okay," Willow whispered around the lump in her throat. But as she gathered her sticky notes and slipped from the conference room, leaving Scottie to deal with the smart board, she already knew that if the real trouble happened, there wasn't a single person at Kudos she could trust with it—not even Scottie.

Chapter 17

If there was one thing Willow hated more than tech glitches, it was parties.

She'd been sitting in her car with the engine off for the past five minutes, hands clenched around the steering wheel.

The street was lined with cars, so she'd had to park half a block away from Barb's house. At least that meant her colleagues wouldn't see her sitting in the dark, trying to talk herself into going in.

She wished she could have stayed home and curled up with a book and a mug of hot chocolate. But not showing up hadn't been an option.

While there would be an official, company-organized farewell party at work on her actual last day, Barb had also wanted a more personal, relaxed celebration, so she had invited over the colleagues she was friendly with.

After everything Barb had done for her, teaching her all the tricks, processes, and office politics at Kudos, attending her retirement party was the least Willow could do.

Sighing, Willow grabbed her gift—a scratch-off world map for Barb's cruise, shoved the door open, got out, and locked her car.

Every house on the block seemed dark except for Barb's. Knowing Barb, she had invited all her neighbors to the party too—which meant more strangers Willow would be forced to interact with.

Willow ducked her head and tugged up the collar of her coat against the drizzle as she hurried toward Barb's craftsman-style home.

The driveway was crowded with cars. A warm glow spilled from the house onto the wide front porch, and a string of fairy lights curled around the railing.

Silhouettes moved past the curtained windows, and a burst of laughter drifted through the front door as Willow climbed the steps.

The party already seemed to be in full swing. Hopefully, she wouldn't be the last one to arrive, drawing attention to herself.

Willow paused in front of the door to brace herself.

Before she could bring herself to knock, the door swung open, and Barb stood there, beaming. "Willow! I'm so glad you could make it! Come on in."

Willow let herself be ushered inside, shrugged out of her wet coat, and took off her shoes, adding them to the footwear already lining the hallway. "Uh, here. I brought you something." She held out the gift-wrapped cardboard tube that held the scratch-off map.

Barb's smile grew even wider. "Ooh! That's so thoughtful of you!"

"It's just something small," Willow said. "For your travels once you retire."

"Thank you. I'll open it once everyone is here." Barb gave her a warm, one-armed hug, making Willow stiffen as she braced for a jolt of electricity.

Thankfully, there wasn't one. Maybe the damp air outside was working in her favor, or it was the fact that Barb's house had hardwood floors instead of carpet. At least she wouldn't be zapping half of the guests.

Barb released her, lightly gripped her elbow, and led her farther inside. "Come meet my husband and our brood."

The hum of conversation, the clinking of glasses, and the scent of freshly baked rolls drifted over as they entered the living room. A big banner reading *Happy retirement* stretched above the couch. Clusters of helium-filled balloons in gold and silver floated against the ceiling.

A tall man with steel-gray hair and brows like furry caterpillars set aside his glass and came over.

Barb slipped her arm through his and leaned in to him with a fond smile. "This is my husband, George." She gestured to a woman who looked like a younger version of her. "And this is our youngest, Erin. She and her brother don't live at home anymore, but they flew in just for the party."

"What can I say?" Erin chuckled. "I could never resist free food."

Willow shook their hands, relieved when she didn't zap them either.

"I heard a lot about you from Barb," George said. "Don't worry—all good things. You made it much easier on Barb to retire, knowing Kudos will be in good hands."

Aww, had Barb really said that? She flicked her gaze at Barb, who smiled and nodded.

"I know you'll keep the Operations crew in line and keep the office from descending into chaos," Barb said.

Before Willow could think of how to respond, a man in his mid-thirties walked up to them, a laptop tucked under one arm. "Can anyone help me with the HDMI connection? I can't get Mom's slideshow to play on the TV."

"Here comes my other offspring, Daniel," Barb said.

"Hi." He switched the laptop to the other arm to shake Willow's hand. "You must be the miracle-working Willow. You wouldn't happen to know how to set this up by any chance?"

Barb's eyes widened. "No! Not Willow. Ask someone else. Anyone else."

A flush heated Willow's chilled cheeks.

Daniel gave his mother a puzzled look.

"I've never met anyone who has such bad luck with tech," Barb explained. "But that might be a blessing in disguise. Unlucky with gadgets, lucky in love." She winked at Willow and pressed a glass of champagne into her hand. "Here. You go mingle. I'll help my son with the slideshow before he throws the laptop out the window."

Willow gripped the stem of her glass. *Unlucky with gadgets, lucky in love? Yeah, right.* She didn't believe it for a second but forced a small smile. At least Barb had given her an excuse to walk away instead of leaving her behind to make awkward small talk with her husband and daughter. She gave them a friendly nod and stepped past them farther into the living room.

Clusters of her co-workers gathered everywhere, most of them near the buffet, sampling the appetizers. She only recognized about half of them. Either Barb had also invited a few people from other departments, or some of them were her friends or neighbors.

Celeste stood by the window, talking to their supply chain analyst and the logistics coordinator. In a tailored blazer and sleek slacks, she stood out from the rest of the guests, who had clearly dressed for comfort. She radiated the same commanding presence as she did at work.

When Celeste looked up from her conversation, Willow quickly turned away so she wouldn't be expected to join them. She had no idea what to say to her boss outside of the office.

Willow took a sip of champagne and scanned the room in search of a quiet corner.

Her gaze froze on someone across the room. *Scottie.* Her pulse gave a jolt, and she nearly choked on her champagne. She hadn't known Barb had invited her.

Clearly, Scottie didn't share Willow's hatred of parties. In dark-blue jeans and an emerald-green sweater that set off her blonde hair, she looked relaxed and comfortable. She was gesturing animatedly while chatting with two Kudos employees whose names Willow had forgotten.

Their laughter drifted over.

Then Scottie looked up and seemed to catch sight of her. She stopped mid-sentence, and a welcoming smile curved up her lips. "Hey," she mouthed across the room.

Willow hesitated. Should she go over and say hi? It would be better than making small talk with strangers, right?

Before she could decide, Scottie excused herself and crossed the room toward her.

"Hi," Willow said. "I didn't know you'd be here." *Ugh.* Not exactly a great conversation starter.

"Barb insisted. You know how she is—saying no was not an option." Scottie tilted her head. A line formed between her eyebrows as she studied Willow. "You don't exactly look thrilled to see me."

"Oh, no, no, it's not you."

Willow's answer made both of them wince. Why did she keep saying that to Scottie?

"It's…this," she quickly added and gestured at the room full of people. "Parties aren't my strong suit. I'm more of a hiding-in-the-corner person."

The line on Scottie's forehead smoothed out as she grinned. "Ah. Let me know if you want me to run interference."

Willow didn't like being a damsel in distress who had to be rescued. Her weird effect on tech put her in that position at work too often already.

But Scottie didn't look at her with pity. Her tone had been completely neutral, as if Willow's dislike for parties was as normal as her own enjoyment of them. She'd merely put the offer out there, without any pressure.

"Maybe you could hang around for a few minutes," Willow heard herself say. *What the hell…?* She stared at the glass of champagne in her hand. Was it already affecting her after barely two sips? "I mean, just so people don't see me standing here by myself and come over to rescue me."

"Right." Scottie's smile crinkled the corners of her eyes. "Just pretend to hang on my every word so people don't pull you into endless small talk."

Willow nodded. "Good plan. I'm not a great actress, but I'll do my best to make it believable."

It didn't take long for Willow to realize she didn't have to do any acting. Her laughter and the easy flow of their conversation wasn't a performance at all. That didn't really surprise her, but she hadn't thought Scottie would be able to make her feel this at ease in a room full of strangers.

Scottie effortlessly entertained her with a story about an employee from the marketing department who'd submitted a ticket regarding a frozen laptop.

"I told him to try to reboot it, but he said that wouldn't help. Turns out the laptop was literally frozen—like encased in a thin sheet of ice from condensation."

Willow laughed. "What?"

"Yep. He had left it in his car all weekend, thinking, 'This is Portland; it won't get that cold.' But that weekend, a rare cold snap hit us—and voilà, frozen laptop."

"Oh my God." Even Willow had never managed something like that. "Did the laptop survive?"

"By some miracle, it did," Scottie replied. "But I had to thaw it out before I could work on fixing it."

Two of their colleagues wandered over, drawn in by Scottie's dramatic gestures and their laughter.

Scottie immediately involved them in the conversation, while Willow nibbled on an appetizer—a tiny pastry stuffed with spinach and feta. She even threw in a comment every now and then. Now that Scottie did most of the talking, her participation was an option, not an obligation. That took the pressure off and allowed her to relax for the first time since she'd arrived.

It seemed as if barely any time had passed when Barb clapped her hands together. "All right, folks, time to dig in!" She gestured at the buffet table, where steaming platters of food were arranged.

Their colleagues immediately lost interest in the conversation and hurried toward the buffet.

Only Scottie and Willow stayed behind.

"You holding up okay?" Scottie asked her quietly.

Willow nodded. Amazingly, she hadn't even glanced at the clock on the wall once to see how much longer she'd have to stay before she could leave without appearing rude.

"Good." Scottie gently nudged her. "Then let's grab some food before it all disappears."

They loaded up their plates with salmon in lemon-dill cream sauce, mashed potatoes, roasted butternut squash, and mixed greens salad with pears and walnuts.

Once they had their food, Scottie steered Willow toward a pair of empty chairs and a small, round table by a window. Rain streaked the glass, and blurred fairy lights twinkled in the backyard.

"Is this okay?" Scottie asked as she set her plate down.

"It's perfect," Willow replied. "Prime real estate."

"Yep. Great view and an easy escape route in case we have to make a break for it." Scottie gestured at the French doors two steps away from their table.

Willow gave her a skeptical look. "I doubt you've ever run from a party. You actually enjoy them, don't you?"

Scottie leaned back in her chair, the picture of ease. "Of course. What's not to enjoy? It's so interesting meeting new people. Everyone's got a story to tell, if you're willing to listen." She discreetly nodded toward a guy who carefully carried two heaping plates across the room. "He just spent two weeks in Sweden and took a selfie with a moose."

An image of a moose grinning into the camera rose in front of Willow's mind's eye, making her laugh.

"And she"—Scottie pointed at a woman with huge, dangling earrings—"has written three mystery novels and is plotting her fourth as we speak."

"Oh, so it's entirely possible that some poor fictional murder victim will be poisoned at a retirement party?" Willow asked.

"Wouldn't rule it out." Scottie gestured with her fork at the only guy wearing a tie. "He's got the best story, though. He used to be a magician as a weekend side hustle, mostly working children's birthday parties. Gave it up after a dove escaped and dive-bombed the birthday girl."

Willow nearly choked on a bite of salmon. "You're making that up!"

"No, I swear. He showed me pictures."

Willow continued to stare at her. "How did you find out all these things? We've been here for less than an hour, and you could write the biography of half of Barb's guests!"

Scottie shrugged and speared a piece of squash with her fork. "Guess it's a talent."

"Yeah, it most certainly is." Willow shook her head. "I don't know if I should admire you, despise you, or volunteer you for the CIA."

"I'd make a horrible spy. I would probably blow my cover in the first five minutes, so I vote for admiring me." Scottie popped the roasted butternut squash into her mouth and chewed enthusiastically.

Willow did admire her. But before she could decide whether she should admit that, Barb's husband rose and tapped his glass.

He gave a short but heartfelt speech, expressing his excitement at finally getting Barb all to himself and at how much he looked forward to traveling the world with her.

When he sat back down, Barb dabbed her eyes and kissed him gently.

Apparently, some relationships did last.

Then Celeste followed, thanking Barb for thirty years of tireless work and dedication to the company. "Kudos won't be nearly as efficient without you," she finally finished. That was the biggest praise in her book.

Willow tried not to think about how large Barb's shoes would be to fill.

When the applause subsided and everyone continued their conversation, she excused herself and headed to the nearby beverages table.

The scent of cinnamon and baked apples rose from a Crock-Pot.

Willow took a mug and used a ladle to fill it with hot apple cider. When she picked it up to carry it back to the table, pain shot through her fingertips. She flinched, nearly dropping the mug.

Scottie was at her side in an instant. "Did you burn yourself?"

"No, no, I'm fine." Willow waved her away and flexed her fingers. "It's just that...my fingers are sore."

Scottie arched her eyebrows. "Oh?" Her voice dropped an octave.

Heat rushed into Willow's cheeks. "Not from what you are thinking."

A teasing grin spread over Scottie's face. "I'm not thinking what you're thinking. Apparently, you're the one whose mind is in the gutter."

Willow ignored the comment and carefully carried the mug back to the table.

Scottie followed. She sat across the table from Willow, her grin now replaced by a concerned look. "Okay, all teasing aside. What happened to your fingers?"

"I've been messing around with my bass lately, but I haven't touched it in years, so I haven't built up my calluses yet. The strings are tough on my fingers. Not as bad as a guitar, but still. That's why my fingertips are sore."

Scottie reached across the table, took Willow's hand, and gently turned it over so she could inspect her fingertips.

The contact sent a small jolt through Willow. She was about to apologize for zapping Scottie again when she realized it hadn't hurt, nor had there been the faint crackle or spark that usually happened from static. While her skin still tingled where Scottie's hand lingered, Scottie hadn't flinched or reacted in any way. Maybe the jolt had been only in her imagination because she had expected it to happen.

When Willow stared at their hands, Scottie quickly let go and withdrew to her side of the table as if only now realizing she'd been touching her. "Sorry," she said, her gaze directed at her plate.

"It's okay. Like I said, they're just sore." Willow flexed her fingers once more. They felt weirdly cold now that Scottie had let go.

Scottie picked up her fork. "So you're playing the bass again?"

Willow nodded and went back to eating too.

"Oh, Willow! That's fantastic!" Scottie beamed at her as if she'd said she had solved world hunger.

Her reaction made Willow feel warm all over, but it also stunned her. Scottie seemed happy for her on a level she hadn't expected. None of the friends she had made in the past ever seemed to care that much about her accomplishments. She ducked her head. "Not sure my sister or the cats would agree. I'm beyond rusty. Just plucking some strings, hoping it sounds remotely like music. It's nothing, really."

"It's not nothing," Scottie said firmly.

Willow looked up and met her gaze.

Scottie's eyes seemed to glow with intensity.

Finally, Willow nodded in acknowledgment.

"How did it feel?" Scottie leaned forward, closer to Willow, apparently not wanting to miss a single word.

"Weird," Willow said. "Like something I've done in another life. But also like getting back a part of me."

Scottie's fingers twitched as if she wanted to reach across the table and take Willow's hand a second time. But she didn't. "I'm really glad you picked it back up, then."

"Me too." Willow busied herself with a forkful of salmon and swallowed down the lump in her throat. "How about you?"

"I've got no plans to take up playing bass. I need all my fingers in full working order." Scottie waited for a beat, then added with a grin, "To fix computers."

"Of course." Willow reached for the apple cider, hoping Scottie would blame any redness on her cheeks on the hot beverage, not the vivid mental images of Scottie's fingers doing things that had nothing to do with computers. "No, I mean... Will you hold up your end of the deal and go out on a date with someone?"

She told herself she was just making conversation to pass the time. But the knot in her stomach said otherwise. Truth be told, talking to Scottie had never been merely a filler, even when they'd been stuck in the elevator, waiting to be rescued. Within minutes, Willow had started asking questions because she wanted to know the answer, and now wasn't an exception.

The teasing grin faded from Scottie's face. She swirled her fork through the mashed potatoes on her plate. "It's not that I don't want to hold up my end of the deal, but I'm not sure I'm ready. I haven't been on a date in more than ten years. Talk about being rusty." She let out a self-deprecating huff of laughter. "I'd probably panic, forget how to flirt, and compliment her Wi-Fi speed, then politely shake her hand at the end of the night or something."

Willow laughed but shook her head. She couldn't imagine that. In her mind, Scottie would be the most charming date ever.

Before she could reply, a shadow fell over their table.

Barb appeared beside them, cheeks flushed. She studied them with a knowing look, as if she'd heard every word. "Oh, if only we knew a single, queer woman who could give you a trial run!"

Willow nearly dropped her fork. "What?"

"A practice date." Barb gestured impatiently with the empty champagne glass she was holding. "With someone kind and understanding—someone who's willing to put up with Scottie's rust until her dating skills are shining again. You should volunteer."

Absolutely not. What she should do was to keep her distance and make sure things between them stayed safe and platonic.

"No," Scottie and Willow said at the same time.

"Why not?" Barb asked.

"Because…" Willow faltered. She didn't have an answer. At least not one that she could say out loud. She sent Scottie an imploring gaze, silently asking her to jump in.

"Well," Scottie said, "because…" She waved her fork. "Because we're friends."

"So?" Barb glanced back and forth between them. "If you're friends, why wouldn't you want to help each other out?"

"Because…" They traded helpless looks.

"Since you can't give me a straight answer…no pun intended, let's settle this another way," Barb said. "With a planking contest."

Willow's fork clattered onto her plate. "A planking contest?" Her voice came out in a high-pitched squeak that only bats would be able to appreciate.

"Yeah, you know." Barb mimed dropping to the floor. "That exercise where you put your forearms and toes on the floor and try to hold your body in a straight line for as long as you can. If you win, I'll shut up about it forever. If I win, you'll help Scottie knock the rust off."

Willow continued to stare at her. Barb couldn't be serious. How many glasses of champagne had she had? She wasn't slurring, but her grin was a little too broad and her voice a bit too loud.

"That's not a good idea," Scottie said. "We're not even done with dinner yet. Do you really want the salmon to make a reappearance while we're planking?"

Barb shrugged. "We'll wait an hour for the food to settle."

"You're not thinking clearly, Barb," Willow said. "This is your retirement party. It wouldn't be fair."

"Excuse me?" Barb clutched her chest in fake offense. "Are you calling me old?"

"What? No! I meant..." Willow lowered her voice and gestured at the empty flute dangling from Barb's fingers. "Clearly, you've been enjoying your party."

"So I've had a glass of bubbly...or three. It's a planking contest, not brain surgery." Barb squinted at them. "What are you so concerned about? You're not afraid to lose to little old me in front of all of my guests, are you? Or are you nervous you'll enjoy the practice date a little too much?"

"Of course not," Scottie said quickly.

Willow huffed in confirmation. "We're not nervous."

"So?" Barb drawled. "If you're not nervous, what's stopping you?"

They looked at each other.

This was ridiculous. They weren't considering doing this...were they?

Scottie tilted her head in a silent question, which Willow, to her surprise, could read without a problem. *Do you think we can beat her?*

Willow gave her the tiniest nod. *Of course we can. She's twice our age and a little tipsy.*

So? Scottie's facial expression seemed to ask. *Are we doing this?*

It was silly. But Barb was an incorrigible matchmaker. She would spend her last two weeks at Kudos trying to get them to go on this ridiculous practice date. The thought of making her shut up about it forever was tempting. Willow blew out a breath and nodded.

Scottie nodded back.

They turned back around to face Barb.

"Okay," Willow said. "We're in."

Barb triumphantly waved her empty glass. "I'll be back for planking in an hour. Prepare to be anihi...annila...um, totally crushed!"

Chapter 18

An hour later, everyone had finished dinner, and, as promised, Barb returned. The flush from earlier had faded, and the empty champagne glass was nowhere to be seen.

Chairs scraped across the hardwood floor as the guests helped make space in the living room. Two of their colleagues shoved the beverages table against the wall.

"Wait!" Barb's daughter said. "You'll bruise your elbows on the hardwood floor!" She hurried off and returned with yoga mats that she spread out on the floor.

Some of the guests gave them incredulous stares, while others leaned forward eagerly, not wanting to miss a second of this unusual spectacle.

Celeste stood at the edge of the cleared space, arms crossed, brows knitted together. "I'm not sure I should be allowing this."

Barb's husband patted her arm and whispered something to her.

"I can't believe we agreed to this," Willow murmured out of the corner of her mouth.

"Yeah, me neither." Guilt pricked at Scottie. She felt bad about humiliating Barb at her retirement party. "Are you sure about this?" she asked Barb. "It's not too late to back out."

Barb firmly shook her head. "Oh, no, I'm not backing out. Are you?"

Scottie looked at Willow.

"It's just one practice date, right?" Willow asked.

"Well," Barb replied, "I'd say as many as Scottie needs to feel confident she's knocked the rust off."

"One is fine," Scottie said quickly. "That's all I need. I'm a fast learner. Besides, we'll win this."

Willow nodded. "Right. Let's do this."

Scottie lowered herself to the floor while Willow gracefully slid onto the mat opposite of hers.

Barb eased herself down with unexpected limberness.

"Ready?" Barb's husband, George, asked. "On my count. Three... Two... One... Go!"

Scottie tensed her belly muscles and pushed up into the planking position. God, she hadn't done this in ages. Ironically, she was as rusty at planking as she was at dating! She peered at Willow.

Willow's form was a work of art. Her planking form, of course. She looked as if she belonged on the cover of a fitness magazine. It took all of Scottie's willpower not to stare.

Focus!

Seconds dragged by painfully slowly.

"Thirty seconds!" George shouted.

Not bad. At least she'd made it this far. But she was starting to struggle. Her shoulders and core muscles burned. The others had to feel it too, right? She peeked at Willow again.

Willow's fair face was slowly turning red. Her jaw was tight.

Scottie sent her an encouraging smile—that probably looked more like a grimace—and glanced to her left.

Barb held her position perfectly. Her breathing was even and her arms steady.

What the hell? Scottie's own arms were starting to quiver. Her abs burned. Her shoulders screamed.

"Forty-five seconds!" George shouted.

Their colleagues cheered and clapped. "Barb! Barb! Barb!"

Traitors. Scottie didn't have the strength to glare at them. Her hips dipped, but she fought her body back up. She risked another glance at Barb.

The damn woman was smirking!

"Shit," Scottie mouthed to Willow, who nodded weakly.

Her arms were trembling too.

At least Scottie wasn't the only one struggling. She gritted her teeth and tried to hang on, not wanting to embarrass herself in front of Willow.

But it was a losing battle. Just as George shouted, "One minute," Scottie's arms gave out, and she collapsed onto her belly with a muffled curse.

A second later, Willow landed on the floor too.

Breathing hard, Scottie rolled onto her back and stared up at the helium balloons.

The room erupted in cheers.

Finally, Scottie sat up.

Barb rose to her feet in one smooth motion and triumphantly raised her arms in the air, to the applause of their colleagues. Her cheeks were flushed, but her eyes sparkled. "I still hold the planking record down at the rec center. Did I forget to mention that?"

"Yep, you sure did." Scottie got up and shook out her arms.

Willow was already standing. Several strands of hair had escaped the loose twist pinned to the back of her head, and a few fine wisps curled at her damp temples. Somehow, she still managed to look graceful, though. She gave Scottie an incredulous stare. "What happened?"

"We were played," Scottie replied.

"Nah." Barb laughed. "I won fair and square. Guess that means you two will go on a date."

Scottie's stomach flipped. Her mouth went so dry that she longed to stick her entire head in the pitcher of iced tea on the beverages table. She had been so sure they'd win against their sixty-something colleague that she hadn't let herself think about what it would mean if they lost.

She would have to go on a date with Willow Greene.

Not that it was an awful thought. In fact, it wasn't awful at all, and that was part of the problem.

As Willow had reaffirmed in the staircase last month, she wasn't into dating or relationships, and Scottie's heart was still healing and would bruise easily. This was not a good idea.

But beneath the dread, an undeniable spark of excitement flickered to life at the thought of taking Willow out.

Scottie smothered it mercilessly. It would be a practice date, not the real deal.

"Practice date," Willow corrected as if she'd been thinking along the same lines.

Barb waved her hand. "Tomayto, tomahto. Now, who's ready for some cake? I burned a lot of calories!"

The last of the guests filed out of Barb's home, laughing and waving. Scottie and Willow brought up the rear.

The rain had stopped, but the pavement still glistened under the streetlights. Scottie paused at the edge of the porch and breathed in the damp air.

"Wow," Willow said as she joined her. "I don't think I've ever been the last to leave a party!"

Scottie smiled. She liked to believe that she had something to do with making the party more bearable—maybe even enjoyable—and that Willow hadn't stayed just for the food. "Well, there's a first time for everything. Who knows, maybe you'll even start to like parties."

"I highly doubt it." Willow stepped off the porch, and Scottie followed.

"Where did you park?"

Willow gestured vaguely down the street. "A couple of blocks that way."

It was darker in that direction, just a few old streetlights casting a weak glow onto the wet sidewalk.

"I'll walk you to your car," Scottie said.

"You don't have to."

"I know."

They set off down the street side by side. Their footsteps splashed through shallow puddles, but otherwise, the neighborhood lay in silence.

Willow hunched her shoulders against the damp chill. Under an old maple tree, she finally stopped and pulled a set of keys from her coat pocket.

"Wait, this is your car?" Scottie pointed at the fire-engine-red, boxy Honda, which was older than either of them. She had caught a glimpse of it the night of their elevator ordeal, but she hadn't gotten a good look at it then—maybe because her head had still been spinning from their short kiss.

Now she cupped her hands around the driver's side window to peer inside. Were those vinyl seats and a stick shift jutting out from the floor? It was too dark to be sure.

Willow shifted her weight beside her. "Don't laugh. I know it's old, but it's very reliable."

"I'm not laughing," Scottie said. "And it's not old—it's retro, just like your Nokia. It has personality. Kind of like—" She stopped herself before she could compare Willow to an old car. "Anyway, I love classic cars and would never laugh at a '78 Civic. That's what it is, right?"

Willow blinked. "Yes. How did you know?"

"My dad loves old cars. I grew up tinkering with them."

"Oh, that's cool," Willow said, sounding as if she meant it.

Silence settled between them, interrupted only by the distant splash of tires cutting through a puddle.

Scottie shoved her hands into her pockets. "So...should we swap numbers so we can figure out when and where for our practice date?" She pulled out her phone and held it out so Willow could enter her number.

Willow hesitated. She kept her hands buried in her coat pockets. "Um..."

Did she regret accepting Barb's challenge and having to go on a date? Scottie bit her lip. "Look. I know you're not dating. If this practice date thing makes you uncomfortable, I could talk to Barb and—"

"No," Willow said quickly. "It's fine. We're both on the same page. We know it's not real. It's just a trial run. Besides, I still owe you a coffee."

"Coffee?" Scottie asked. "Is that what you want to do for our date... practice date? Go get coffee?"

Willow shrugged. "I don't know. You're the local. Why don't you pick something? I'm fine with anything."

"Okay." Scottie's mind was already flipping through options. She wanted something fun that Willow would enjoy yet that didn't scream *Date* with a capital D. A candlelit dinner or a romantic stroll through the Lan Su Chinese Garden were out. "I'll think of something and surprise you."

"All right." Willow pulled out a small notepad from her ever-present giant purse, wrote something down, and tore off the sheet before handing it to Scottie, careful not to brush her hand in the process.

Scottie stared at the neat row of digits. "Is that your phone number? Why didn't you just type it into my phone?" Did she have a problem with germs and thought Scottie's screen was greasy? But Willow had sat on the elevator floor and had shared a mini picnic with her—not something a germaphobe would do.

Willow shuffled her feet. "Maybe I'm retro too." The tiny sheepish grin she gave Scottie was incredibly charming.

Scottie smiled back. Willow remained an enigma. Unfortunately, that only made her more interesting to Scottie. "Okay. I can respect that." She tucked the note with Willow's number into her pocket. "I'll text you when I've come up with something fun."

"Great," Willow said.

They lingered next to the Civic for another few moments.

Finally, Willow unlocked her car. "Well, I'll see you soon, then."

Scottie nodded. "Drive safely, and enjoy the rest of your weekend."

"You too." Willow opened the driver's side door and climbed in.

A few seconds later, the old car started up.

Scottie stepped back and watched it disappear down the road. When she couldn't make out the taillights anymore, she stared into the night for a few moments longer. She was going on a practice date with Willow Greene, and she didn't want to examine too closely how she felt about that.

Sometimes, life really took strange turns.

Chapter 19

"Willow?" Fiona called through the door on Saturday morning, then—without waiting for a reply—stuck her head into Willow's room. "Hey, Jessie, Ali, and I are going to Suki's for karaoke tonight. Want to come?"

Getting up onstage with Fiona and her equally outgoing friends was Willow's personal nightmare, so she was happy to have an excuse. "Sorry, I can't. I have plans today, and I don't know when I'll be back."

"Plans?" Fiona squinted at her. "You never have plans." Her gaze went to the bed, and her eyes widened as she took in the skirts, sweaters, jeans, tops, and slacks covering every inch of the surface. "Do you have a date?"

"No, it's n—"

"Oh my God, you have a date!" Fiona screeched. "Why didn't you tell me? Who is she? Where did you meet? How did she manage to convince you to go out with her? And where are you going?"

Willow threw a blouse at her. "Whoa, calm down! I said it's not a date. It's just a practice date."

"A…what?"

Willow scratched her head. How could she explain that one? "At Barb's retirement party, Scottie mentioned that she hadn't been on a date in years, so Barb suggested we do a no-pressure trial run to knock the rust off."

Fiona stared at her as if Willow had told her she was training for a one-way mission to Mars.

Okay, it sounded ridiculous when you said it out loud.

"Let me get this straight." Fiona waved the blouse Willow had tossed at her. "The woman you kissed in an elevator and then told 'never mind, I don't date' is looking for someone to trial-date, so naturally, you volunteered."

"I didn't volunteer. Barb, uh, challenged us to a planking contest…and we lost." Not one of her finer moments; Willow had to admit that.

Fiona burst out laughing. "A planking contest? At a retirement party?" She shook her head. "When you moved in, I promised that you wouldn't get bored anytime soon. Who knew that *you* would be the one keeping *me* entertained!"

"Glad to be of service," Willow mumbled and snatched the blouse away from her sister.

"So…if it's not a real date, why does your bed look like you're auditioning for a fashion show?" Fiona pointed at the battlefield that used to be Willow's bed.

"Because Scottie texted to say I should wear something comfy yet not so over-the-top casual that it would get us kicked out of a restaurant."

"Right. And you had to dig deep into your closet to find something like that." Fiona smirked. "Because comfy yet presentable is not your usual style at all."

Willow opened her mouth, then closed it. Okay, maybe she had gone a bit overboard. "I'm a little nervous, okay? Scottie isn't the only one who's rusty."

"Aww." Fiona gave her a gentle bump with her shoulder. "Well, maybe you two can knock off some of that rust together." She made it sound like a double entendre.

Willow gave her a stern look. "I'm quite happy with my layer of rust, thanks. It's Scottie who wants to start dating again, not me."

"Right." Fiona nodded, still grinning in that annoying-big-sister way. She walked over to the bed, picked up an emerald-green sweater, and held it against Willow's shoulders. "This one. It brings out the green in your eyes. Pair it with some skinny jeans and those boots we got when I visited you last fall. They'll make your legs look like a supermodel's."

Willow pulled the sweater from her sister's grasp and tossed it back onto the pile. "I don't care what my eyes or my legs look like. It's not like I'm trying to impress anyone."

"Uh-huh. Keep telling yourself that." Fiona sauntered to the door. "Have fun at your practice session, Rusty."

Scottie climbed into the driver's seat and tugged the seat belt across her chest, careful not to wrinkle her corduroy shirt.

Just as she was about to start the engine, her phone rang in her pocket.

Her heartbeat spiked. Maybe it was Willow. Was she calling to back out? She'd had a week to reconsider since Barb's party.

Quickly, Scottie fished her phone from her pocket and glanced at the screen.

It wasn't Willow. It was Kassidy.

So Willow wasn't backing out.

Scottie didn't allow herself to pause and examine how she felt about that. She swiped her thumb across the screen. "Hey, what's up?"

"Not my Internet," Kassidy grumbled without preamble or even a hello. "My browser won't load half the pages."

"Ah. It's probably because you set the tracker blocking to maximum security."

"I have no idea," Kassidy replied. "Can you come over and fix it? I'll order that should-be-illegal pizza you like."

Scottie let out a dramatic gasp. "Illegal? If anything, bad-mouthing Hawaiian pizza should be a crime." Her mouth watered reflexively. "As tempting as it sounds, I can't come over. I'm on my way to pick up Willow."

Silence stretched long enough for Scottie to imagine her friend arching her eyebrows.

"I thought you said you decided to just be friends?" Kassidy finally asked.

"We did," Scottie said. "We're not going on a date. I mean, not really."

"Not really?" Kassidy repeated. "Isn't dating a little like being pregnant? You either are or you aren't."

"I'm not."

"Pregnant?"

Scottie stared up at the roof of her car. "Going on a date with Willow!"

"Right. That's why you got a haircut yesterday."

Scottie ran a hand through her admittedly trimmed hair. "What? Now I can't get a trim without you suspecting I'm going on a date? My bangs were getting in my eyes; that's all."

"Okay," Kassidy said. "If you're sure it's not a date, I believe you."

Damn. Now Scottie felt as if she was lying to her because she hadn't told her the full truth. "Willow and I...we're meeting up because..." Okay, this was embarrassing to admit, but she forged on. "Because our colleague Barb overheard me saying that I'm a little rusty when it comes to dating, and she suggested finding a safe person to practice with. So Willow and I are doing a trial run to knock the rust off."

This time, the silence lasted so long that Scottie started to suspect Kassidy had dropped the phone.

"Do you really think Willow is?" Kassidy finally asked, her voice very quiet and serious. "A safe person to practice with, I mean."

"Of course she is," Scottie bristled. "She would never judge me for being hopelessly out of the dating loop."

"That's not what I meant," Kassidy said. "But if Willow had asked you out last month after your adventure in the elevator, instead of reaffirming that she's not looking for a relationship, you probably would have said yes. Which means you're going on a trial date with someone you wanted to go on a real date with. Sounds like a fantastic idea. What could possibly go wrong?"

"Nothing will go wrong." But deep down, Scottie knew Kassidy might have a point. She forced a light laugh. "You make it sound as if I was about to propose to Willow! I accepted that nothing will ever happen between us. We're friends, and I'm happy with that."

"Are you sure?" Kassidy asked with an uncharacteristic softness. "This entire thing sounds like you're staging some elaborate self-sabotage."

Scottie shook her head even though Kassidy couldn't see it. "It's harmless. No need to worry. Listen, I'd better go, or I'll start my practice date by being late."

"All right. Talk later."

Scottie said goodbye and was about to tap the screen to end the conversation when she remembered why her friend had called. "Oh, wait! Go into the browser settings and turn the tracker and ads blocking from strict to standard. The sites should load just fine once you've done that."

"Thanks," Kassidy replied. "Guess I owe you some of that disgusting pizza after all."

"I'll hold you to that. Take care." Scottie ended the call, dropped the phone onto the passenger seat, and started the car. As she drove toward Willow's house, Kassidy's question echoed through her mind: *What could possibly go wrong?*

Chapter 20

It was exactly ten a.m. when Scottie eased her car to a stop at the curb and double-checked the address.

The purple house across the street didn't seem to fit Willow, but a glance at the text Willow had sent her confirmed she was at the right place. With its bold color and the two dormer windows sticking out from a steep roof, it looked like something out of a fairy tale.

Scottie got out, locked the car, and made her way toward the white front door. *This is just practice,* she told herself. *Not the real deal.* There was no need for her heart to beat in this ridiculously fast rhythm. She ignored her damp hands, rang the doorbell, and put on a smile that she hoped appeared casual.

The woman who opened the door wasn't Willow, but she beamed at Scottie as if they were old acquaintances. Long, brown hair streaked with purple tumbled onto her shoulders in tousled waves. Purple-framed glasses perched on her broad nose, and bold eyeliner made her green eyes pop. She wasn't tall, but she radiated energy and confidence as she leaned in the doorway and gave Scottie a thorough once-over. "You must be Scottie," she said with a warm grin.

"That's me."

"I'm Fiona, Willow's sister. Come on in." Fiona stepped aside with a flourish.

Scottie had known that Willow lived with her sister, but Fiona wasn't what she had expected. She wasn't even sure now what she had pictured—probably someone introverted and cautious, who tried to fit in, like Willow. Definitely not someone wearing wide-legged lounge pants in a bold floral pattern and a slouchy, off-the-shoulder T-shirt with paint spatters.

She followed Fiona through a short hall and into the living room, where mismatched armchairs warred for space with a scarred wooden coffee table and a huge couch piled with colorful pillows. An abstract piece of art in scarlet red took up most of one wall, while a more realistic painting of a gnarled tree hung over the fireplace. Tendrils of two Pothos plants cascaded from small pots on either end of the mantle. Nothing really seemed to match, yet it formed a cozy, lived-in harmony.

A glimpse through an arched doorway revealed a dining area and a kitchen beyond that. Each room had an accent wall painted as boldly as the house's exterior: burgundy in the living room, teal in the dining room, and sunflower yellow in the kitchen.

A chunky white cat slept curled up into a ball on one end of the sofa. A tortoiseshell strode into the room and hopped up onto the coffee table to inspect the intruder invading her territory.

"Spice!" Fiona scooped up the cat before it could scatter the pieces of what looked like a dissembled typewriter on the coffee table.

Scottie leaned closer to check it out.

The top of its pale green metal casing had been taken off, revealing a tangle of grimy type bars.

"The newest addition to Willow's collection," Fiona said. "She's not yet done with this one."

"That's cool. Is she restoring them?"

Before Fiona could answer, the stairs creaked, then footsteps approached.

Scottie turned and—for a second—forgot how to breathe.

Willow appeared in the doorway. At work, she always tied her hair into a ponytail or tucked it behind her ears, but now it cascaded freely over her shoulders. She wore a formfitting, emerald-green sweater that made the green in her hazel eyes stand out brighter than Scottie had ever seen. Its V-neck dipped just low enough to reveal the elegant line of her collarbones and the delicate hollow of her throat. Knee-high, chocolate-brown boots and dark-blue jeans did dangerous things for her legs—and to Scottie's pulse. It was a simple, casual outfit, yet it hit Scottie harder than a flashy gown would have.

Not the real deal, she reminded herself and tried to play it cool, very aware that Willow's sister was watching her. "Good morning."

"Hi," Willow said, her gaze on Scottie's hair. "You're right on time."

"Of course I am. It's been a while, but even I know that showing up late on a first date is a big no-no." Scottie ran her hand through the soft layers that were still long enough to push back. She tried not to wonder whether Willow liked the new haircut.

Willow lifted her index finger. "*Practice* date." She emphasized the first word.

"Right," Scottie said. "Are you ready to head out?"

Willow nodded and led the way. As she walked toward the door, she grabbed her jacket from a hook next to it.

"Have fun," Fiona shouted after them. "And remember that practice does make perfect."

"Ignore her," Willow muttered.

"So she knows it's just practice and we're not going out for real?" Scottie asked as she followed her out of the house.

"Yes. She knows I don't date, so I had to tell her the whole story, including our embarrassing planking failure." Willow tried to steer Scottie toward the left. "Let's take my car."

Scottie squinted over at her. Her own car was parked at the curb only a few steps away. Why wouldn't they take it? "What?" she asked in a teasing tone. "Is my Subaru too much of a lesbian stereotype for you?"

A chuckle escaped Willow. "No. I just...um..."

"I'd love to take a closer look at your car sometime, but for today, I think we should stick with mine," Scottie said. "I'm not sure how your retro ride would handle where we are going."

Willow followed her to the Subaru. "Where are we going?"

Scottie opened the passenger-side door and held it for her. "Get in and find out."

As Willow settled into the passenger seat of Scottie's Subaru, her gaze landed on the dashboard—and the clear plastic bag sitting there. It was full of zip ties. "Uh, should I be worried?"

Scottie looked over from where she had clicked her seat belt into place and grinned. "Only if you're afraid of trolls."

"Trolls?" Willow had no idea what she was talking about.

"You'll see," was all Scottie said as she started the car.

When Scottie pulled out onto the road and was distracted by traffic, Willow took a moment to study her.

Scottie had gotten a haircut. For a moment, Willow missed the rebellious, slightly too long strands that had always made her fingers itch with the need to reach out and brush them back. But she had to admit the new style looked good too. Scottie's hair was now cropped short in the back. The soft waves still framed her face in an easygoing style but no longer fell into her eyes.

She wore black jeans and a corduroy button-down in a warm shade of sienna, worn untucked and open over a plain black T-shirt. The look suited her—neat but relaxed.

Scottie glanced over. "What?"

"Nothing. Just... You cut your hair."

Scottie brushed a hand through it. "Yeah. I got tired of having it in my eyes all the time."

"It looks good."

"Thanks. You look great too."

"Thank you." Warmth filled Willow's chest. Was Scottie just practicing her dating skills, or did she mean it? Probably the former, she told herself. Not that it mattered.

Scottie competently merged onto the on-ramp that led to the upper deck of the Fremont Bridge.

The white steel arch of the bridge stretched in front of them. Beneath them, the river glinted in the morning sun, and an amazing view of downtown Portland opened up.

To the right, the Willamette ran north, while, to the left, Willow could make out the mid- and high-rise buildings of the Pearl District and the West Hills beyond that.

Minutes later, downtown was behind them, and they made their way north on Highway 30, following the river.

Slowly, the landscape began to change. The city faded away and was replaced by wooded hills to their left and scattered industrial buildings and the river to their right.

"So," Willow said after a while, "where are you taking me?"

"Not telling," Scottie replied. "It's a surprise."

"I'm not sure that's a good answer. What if the person you'll date for real doesn't like surprises?"

Scottie flashed her a grin. "Thanks for the touching concern for my future date. I'm sure it has nothing to do with your own curiosity."

Willow gave a regal nod. "Of course not. I'm just taking my duties as your practice partner and dating adviser seriously."

Scottie gave her an amused look. "Oh, now you're my dating adviser? How did you get promoted? I thought you hadn't been on a date in ages either."

Willow smiled and shrugged. "You know what they say: Those who can't do teach. And as your teacher, I'm making you aware of the fact that not all women like surprises."

"Duly noted," Scottie said. "I'm still not telling you where we're going."

"Fine. I'll make sure to warn your future date to expect the unexpected."

For a while, they drove in silence. Finally, even the warehouses and rail yards thinned as they continued deeper into the woods.

Willow peered through the windshield. "I haven't been this far north since moving here."

"So your sister kept your adventures confined to goat yoga, the vacuum cleaner museum, pear-and-blue-cheese ice cream, and other explorations within city limits?" Scottie asked.

Willow stared at her. It had been seven weeks since she had mentioned that, and Scottie still remembered the ice cream flavor she had tried? If she was always that attentive, she wouldn't need a lot of dating practice. "It's not Fiona's fault. If it were up to her, she'd drag me to the North Pole and back. She's the adventurous type."

"But you aren't?" Scottie asked.

"I like exploring a little, but right now, I'm learning so many new things at Kudos during the week that by the time the weekend comes around, my brain is ready to hide at home and decompress with an audiobook and—"

"An old typewriter?" Scottie asked.

A flush crept into Willow's cheeks. "You saw that?"

Scottie nodded. "Was I not supposed to?"

"No, it's fine. It's just…a little geeky."

Scottie's laughter filled the car. "Remember who you're talking to. Geeky is hot." She paused. "Uh, I mean…"

The heat in Willow's cheek increased to furnace level. "It's fine. You're practicing your complimenting skills for your future date."

"Right. Like your sister said: Practice makes perfect." Scottie cleared her throat. "So...you collect typewriters?"

"Not on purpose," Willow said. "It all started a few years ago, when my parents gave me an old typewriter as a gag gift. It was battered but beautiful. I watched a lot of YouTube videos and taught myself how to restore it so I could sell it. But by the time it looked as good as new, I couldn't bear to part with it."

Scottie chuckled. "Ah, a foster fail."

"You could say that. The first of many."

"How many do you have?" Scottie asked. There was no judgment in her voice.

"Twelve," Willow said, again flushing a little. "Whenever I see one at a flea market or a yard sale, I can't resist rescuing it. My bedroom looks like a typewriter museum."

Scottie let out a whistle. "I'd love to see it sometime. Uh, the typewriter museum. Not your bedroom."

"Of course." By now, even the tips of Willow's ears were burning. *It's just a practice date,* she told herself for the thousandth time. There was no reason to blush at Scottie's innocent slips of the tongue.

She had a feeling she would tell herself that a few thousand times more before this date was over.

They had been driving for forty-five minutes when Scottie turned left onto a narrow, curvy road that led uphill through the forest.

Now Willow understood why Scottie hadn't wanted to take her car.

Behind a bend in the road, Scottie eased the Subaru into a small gravel pullout to the right. "We're here." She grabbed the bag of zip ties and got out.

Willow followed and looked around.

Not that there was much to see, other than trees, ferns that were still glistening with raindrops from the night before, and a rickety old train trestle.

"We're deep in the woods, in the middle of nowhere, and you're carrying a bag of zip ties. If that's your idea of a date, you might need more help than even I as a highly qualified dating adviser can offer." But despite her joking comment, she felt safe with Scottie, even in the middle of nowhere.

Scottie laughed. "Okay, I admit it's starting to look like something out of a true crime podcast. But you'll see in a second."

They walked a few steps uphill to where the old, disused railroad bridge stretched across the narrow road.

Scottie stopped and spread her arms wide. "Welcome to the Troll Bridge."

Willow furrowed her brow. "Toll bridge?"

"Troll," Scottie repeated and gestured at the bridge.

Willow took a closer look.

Dozens of little trolls dangled from the weathered beams and poles, some of them thirty feet up. Even more were pinned to a wooden wall at the bottom of the structure.

Every kind of troll known to mankind seemed to be present: plastic trolls, stuffed trolls, a handmade felt troll, and even trolls painted directly onto the boards. There was a Santa Claus troll, a Dracula troll, an armed-to-the-teeth soldier troll, and a troll in a bikini.

Their big tufts of neon-pink, blue, yellow, and orange hair stood out against the brown and green of the forest.

It was the last thing Willow had expected. Not a place that she would have picked for a first date—and maybe that was the point. The less this felt like a real date, the better, so Willow was grateful for Scottie's choice. She turned in a slow circle to take it all in. "What on earth is this?"

"One of Portland's lovable oddities," Scottie said with a proud grin. "No one knows for sure how it started, but legend has it that a family hung the first troll twenty years ago. They probably told their kids about trolls living under bridges and put one of the little guys there to surprise them."

"Aww, that's cute."

Scottie nodded. "And then people kept adding their own trolls. The population goes up and down. The last time I went, most of them had gotten stolen, but people always replace them."

Willow raised her brows. "People really steal them?"

"Yeah. Even though it's bad luck to remove a troll."

They stood side by side on the narrow road and admired the trolls.

"Which one is your favorite?" Scottie asked.

Willow scanned the colorful trolls on the wooden wall until one choice jumped out at her. "Ooh, this one!" She pointed at a plastic troll with a bass.

Scottie laughed. "It rocks."

"Yours?" Willow asked.

"This one." Scottie pointed without hesitation at a tiny yellow troll someone had placed in a knothole.

"Aww. Cute."

A car rounded the bend and approached slowly. The road was barely wide enough for one vehicle, so they stepped closer to the wall of trolls to let the car pass behind them.

Their shoulders brushed, and Willow was hyperaware of how close they stood. The clean cedar scent of Scottie's shampoo filled her senses.

When the car had passed, Scottie shifted so that their shoulders no longer touched.

Willow missed the contact immediately—just because it was cool beneath the bridge, where the sun couldn't reach them.

Scottie pulled something from her pocket and held it out to her. "I brought two little friends so we can pay the troll toll."

Willow glanced down.

On Scottie's palm rested two little plastic trolls with shocks of rainbow-colored hair sticking up above their heads.

"So if removing a troll is considered back luck, does leaving one behind mean good luck?" Willow asked.

"I'd like to think so."

"How do we fix them to the bridge?" Willow scanned the other trolls. Some had screws through their bellies, while others had been nailed to the boards. "We're not going to drill a hole through our poor little rainbow trolls, are we?"

"No. That's where these come in." Triumphantly, Scottie held up her bag of zip ties.

"Ah. So that's what they were for."

"Yep. It's a completely harmless non-murdery zip tie situation."

"I can see that now, but as your dating adviser, I've got to advise you to instead bring flowers to your real first date." An image flashed through Willow's mind—Scottie handing over a dozen long-stemmed red roses to a woman who buried her face in the bouquet to smell them, then looked up at Scottie with a smile.

"Got it. No zip ties on a first date." Scottie nodded. "I hear you. No need to frown—I promise to heed your sage advice."

Frown? She wasn't frowning, was she? Willow made an effort to smooth out her brow...and chased away the image of the flower-receiving woman.

They fastened their trolls to a beam with the zip ties, then lingered for a few minutes longer, pointing out the oddest trolls to each other.

Scottie laughed at a giraffe troll. The sound of it echoed through the trees, making Willow smile.

Among the trolls, she spotted a small wooden sign that read: *Love is the bridge that connects earth to heaven.*

Maybe she had been wrong about the Troll Bridge not being a good place for a first date. There was a little romance here after all.

Finally, Scottie checked her wristwatch. "We should head back. I got us a table at Screen Door."

"Screen Door?"

"One of the best brunch spots in Portland," Scottie said. "They have the yummiest bananas Foster French toast, and their buttermilk-battered fried chicken and waffles are to die for. Does that sound okay?"

Willow's stomach rumbled an enthusiastic reply.

Scottie chuckled. "Guess that's a yes."

Chapter 21

"Oh, wait!" Scottie had taken two steps back toward the car when something occurred to her. "We should take a picture of us in front of the bridge before we leave."

They returned to the wall of trolls, and Scottie pulled her phone from her pocket. "Could you?" She held it out to Willow. "Your arms are longer; you can get us and our rainbow trolls in the frame more easily."

Instead of taking the phone, Willow hid her hands in her jacket pockets. "Oh, no. You should do it. I'm terrible at selfies."

Scottie studied her.

Willow's face, which had been so open and full of laughter earlier, now seemed as careful and reserved as it usually was at work. She was avoiding Scottie's eyes.

Why was Willow acting as if Scottie had asked her to hold a rattlesnake? It was the second time she had refused to take her phone. What was up with that?

Suddenly, Willow was back to being unreadable, and Scottie hated it. She wanted to reach over, nudge her gently, and ask what was going on. But the tense set of Willow's shoulders told her that was not a good idea, so she decided to let it go. The last thing she wanted was to make Willow uncomfortable for any reason.

"Okay. I'll take it. But fair warning: I might end up cutting off your head—in the non-murdery way, of course."

It had been the right thing to say. Willow's tense posture softened, and she stepped closer until their shoulders once again brushed, filling Scottie with warmth.

She flipped the camera around, raised her phone, and stretched her arm out as far as possible. "Ready? Okay, troll squad, say cheese!"

Willow leaned closer. "Cheese."

"One more." Scottie put on a dramatic expression, eyes wide, mouth forming an O as if a few dozen angry trolls had been chasing her through the forest.

Willow snorted but played along, putting on her best date-in-a-haunted-place face.

Scottie snapped another picture. "Perfect. If that doesn't convince Barb that I'm ready to go on a date, nothing will."

When Willow laughed, Scottie quickly took another photo before lowering the phone.

Side by side, they strolled down the narrow road, back toward the car.

A man walked toward them, a large black dog trotting beside him.

Scottie couldn't help tensing, but only for a second. *It's leashed and not interested in you.* She forced herself to relax.

Thankfully, the dog didn't pay them any attention. Its ears were pricked, tail wagging, as it focused on something deeper in the forest.

Right before they passed the man and his dog, Willow moved around to Scottie's other side without a word.

Scottie stared at her. "What was that?"

"You said you're scared of dogs and that your body tenses up when you see one coming toward you," Willow said quietly.

She had put herself between Scottie and the dog because she had remembered what Scottie had told her in the elevator! Scottie swallowed against the sudden lump in her throat.

"I thought maybe it would help." Willow peered at her. "Does it?"

Not really—because now Willow was closer to the sharp canines, and the thought of the dog lunging at Willow was as scary as if it were attacking her. Still, the way Willow had tried to protect her was deeply touching.

"A little," Scottie replied, her voice hoarse. "Thank you."

"Don't worry. If we come across a butterfly, you can be the one to rescue me."

Scottie burst out laughing, startling the dog and making it bark.

She jumped and held back more laughter.

Clearly, Willow thought Scottie's butch pride would take a hit because she had needed to be protected. But truth be told, she didn't mind—not when it was Willow doing the protecting. Scottie wasn't afraid to show her vulnerability in front of her because she sensed that Willow would still take her seriously, no matter what.

They were both smiling as they climbed into the Subaru.

Willow clicked her seat belt into place. "That was fun."

Scottie looked at her. "Yeah?"

Willow nodded.

"Good." She was glad Willow thought so. It shouldn't matter because this was just a trial run, with no second date on the line. But she still wanted Willow to have a good time. Smiling, she put the key in the ignition and turned it.

A series of rapid clicks came from beneath the hood, but the engine refused to start.

Scottie's smile faded. She tried again.

Click-click-click-click. The dashboard lights flickered weakly, then went dark. Not even a wheeze came from the engine.

Shit. Her car had never refused to start before. While it was nearly ten years old, it had always been reliable. Why did it have to happen now of all times? "You didn't kidnap a troll when I wasn't looking, did you?" Scottie asked to lighten the mood.

"No." Willow's features were tight with tension. "That sounded like it's the battery, didn't it?"

"Yeah." Scottie sighed, popped the hood, and got out of the car.

Willow followed.

Scottie opened the hood, and they both peered into the engine bay.

No sign of corrosion on the battery. Scottie traced her fingers over the connections. Nothing seemed loose.

She closed the hood with a thump. "Looks like the battery is dead. We need someone to jump-start it." She glanced toward where she had last seen the guy with the dog, but he was gone. "Who thought I would ever wish the guy with the dog back?"

Willow sank against the hood. "What now?"

"Now I summon a roadside troll." Scottie pulled her phone from her pocket, grateful to see two solid bars of LTE service, and opened the AAA app. She hit *Request Roadside Assistance,* confirmed their location on a map, and chose *battery issue* from a list of options.

A few seconds later, a message popped up.

Scottie's shoulders slumped. "AAA is sending help. But it'll take them an hour and fifteen minutes to get here. By the time we make it back to the city, our brunch reservation will be gone. Heck, Screen Door might even be closed by then." This wasn't how she'd wanted their date…practice date…to go.

"I'm sorry," they both said at the same time.

Scottie glanced at Willow. "Why are you apologizing? It's not like it's your fault."

"Not like it's yours either."

"Yeah, but it's my car, and I know you're hungry, and—"

"Exactly. So come on." Willow pulled open the passenger-side door and nodded toward Scottie's side. "I'll treat you to brunch."

"You know it won't start, right?"

"Trust me and get in."

Scottie shrugged and got in.

"We really seem to be making a habit out of this." Scottie gestured at the center console, where half the contents of Willow's purse were spread out between them.

Willow nibbled on a slice of dried mango. "Well, it might not be chicken and waffles, but at least we're not starving."

"And we're not stuck in an elevator." Scottie popped a honey-roasted almond into her mouth. "That's progress, right?"

Willow chuckled. "Right."

Rays of sunlight drifted through the canopy above them, painting patterns on the dashboard.

They had left the doors slightly open, so pine-scented air and birdsong surrounded them, making it feel like a picnic in the forest.

Scottie leaned back against the driver's seat and felt strangely at peace. She wasn't even tempted to check the app for an update on the roadside technician's arrival time. This wasn't how she had thought their practice date would go, but she would take it.

She watched Willow wrestle with the wrapper of a granola bar. "No Oreos this time?" she asked with a teasing grin.

Willow pressed a hand to her chest. "Oh my God, how could I? Excuse my horrible oversight. I'll make sure to rectify my grave mistake next time."

"Please make sure you do, or I'll have to report you to the dating adviser headquarters." Then Scottie remembered that there wouldn't be a next time. This was a one-off practice date only. But maybe, if they both had fun, they could hang out as friends sometime.

Willow broke the granola bar into two equal halves and held out one.

"Thanks." Scottie took it. Her finger brushed Willow's, and a spark of static electricity passed between them.

They both pulled back with a startled "ouch!"

Scottie rubbed her tingling fingertips together. "Wow. That keeps happening. You're like a walking lightning rod!"

Willow shoved her hand beneath her thigh. "I'm sorry," she said quietly.

Scottie turned in the driver's seat as much as she could to study her. "Hey, you know I was just teasing, right?"

Willow nodded but didn't look at her.

Tapping her arm or knee to get her attention was probably not a good idea. "Willow? Look at me, please."

Slowly, Willow turned her head and made eye contact.

"I was really only teasing," Scottie said. "But—"

"I know. It's fine."

Scottie shook her head. "No, it's obviously not. I can tell what I just said wasn't merely a fun comment to you, so I won't say it anymore, okay?"

Willow looked as startled as if she'd received a second jolt.

"If you ever want to talk about it and explain why that hurt you, I'd be happy to listen," Scottie said softly. "But if you don't, that's okay too." While she didn't fully understand what was going on, she didn't have to. She would do whatever was necessary to avoid hurting Willow again.

Willow stared through the windshield into the forest beyond. Finally, she said, "You dropped your half of the granola bar."

Scottie peered into the gap between her seat and the center console but couldn't see it. She'd have to fish it out later, but for now, she didn't care. "That's okay. At least it wasn't an Oreo."

That got her a twitch of a smile from Willow. "I was bullied in high school," she said after a while, her voice so quiet that Scottie barely heard it over the birdsong surrounding them. "One of the things they called me was lightning rod. Because I was tall and thin, I guess, and because…" She curled her fingers into a fist. "They didn't need much of a reason. They just called me any mean thing that got a reaction out of me."

Scottie imagined a younger, even more vulnerable Willow being surrounded by half a dozen teens shouting mean nicknames at her. Every muscle in her body stiffened. "I'm sorry. That sucks. Couldn't your parents or teachers do anything to stop the little assholes?"

Willow shook her head and glanced out the windshield again. "I never told them."

"What?" Scottie asked, sharper than intended. She gentled her voice. "Why not?"

Willow shrugged. "I didn't want to cause even more trouble."

Even more? Scottie couldn't imagine Willow as a troublemaker. "You weren't the one causing trouble! They were!"

The hint of a smile returned to Willow's face, and this time, it spread until it reached Willow's eyes.

"Uh, why are you smiling?" Scottie rubbed her mouth with the back of her hand. "Do I have pieces of almonds or mango stuck to my face?"

"No. It's just...funny to see you get so worked up about it, more than fifteen years after it happened." Willow directed her gaze to the center console. "It's kind of nice."

Scottie's cheeks went hot. Admittedly, she had harbored fantasies of kicking the asses of Willow's bullies. "Well, yeah. If we ever run into one of them, let me know. I have some zip ties left. We could chain them to the dumpster behind a fish restaurant until they apologize."

Then she realized that her statement included an assumption that they would keep spending time together. They both kept making references to future activities.

Her phone buzzed in her pocket before either of them could say anything.

Scottie pulled it out and checked the new message. "It's an update from AAA. Our technician is now an hour away."

Willow dug into her giant purse and pulled out a battered deck of UNO cards. "Just enough time to beat you at UNO."

Scottie laughed. "You brought a deck of UNO cards to our practice date? Were you afraid we'd get stuck in an elevator again, or is that in the official dating adviser handbook?"

"Of course it is—right there on page twenty-two," Willow shot back.

"Let me guess: right between 'always bring snacks' and 'never admit to a geeky hobby unless they do it first'?"

Willow shuffled the worn cards. "No. Snacks are on page three, and regarding geeky hobbies, it says to own it with confidence." She cleared the center console of snacks and dealt the cards with practiced flicks. "All right. House rules: The Reverse card means the next person loses their turn, and if you forget to yell 'uno,' you lose a gummy bear."

Chapter 22

By the time they made it back to Portland, it was after two p.m. and Screen Door had closed for the day.

Willow bit her lip. She couldn't believe that she had killed Scottie's battery. That was exactly why she had wanted to take her own car—and why she didn't date.

The Troll Bridge and Scottie's easygoing company had been so much fun that she had nearly forgotten that sooner or later, something always went wrong, messing up the date.

But being stranded in the forest and having to call AAA didn't seem to bother Scottie. She hadn't let it destroy her good mood. Even when she had kept losing at UNO, she hadn't stopped laughing.

Willow admired her positive attitude but couldn't trust it to last should they spend more time together. Even an easygoing person like Scottie could only take so many tech mishaps before she lost her patience.

Maybe her prediction would become true sooner than she had thought because once they'd made their way back across the Fremont Bridge, Scottie grew increasingly tense and restless.

Her grip on the steering wheel was tight, and her gaze darted back and forth between the dashboard clock and the establishments to the left and right.

"Hey, you okay?" Willow asked quietly.

"Oh, yeah, I'm fine. Just looking for somewhere to take you. It's too late for lunch but too early for dinner that comes with cloth napkins, so I admit I'm at a loss." She watched the road like a hunter looking for prey.

"Scottie," Willow said. "Relax, okay? I'm not the queen, and this is just a practice date. It doesn't matter where you take me."

"It matters to me," Scottie replied quietly. "I want you to have a good time, even if it's just a practice run."

Willow held her tongue before she could confess that playing cards in Scottie's Subaru had been more fun than she usually had on dates. "Okay, let's try it this way: Where would you go if you were out and about in this part of Portland on a Saturday afternoon and found yourself getting hungry?"

"Potato Champion," Scottie said without hesitation. "But that's not an option."

"Why not?" Willow asked.

"Well, because...it's a food cart. Not exactly haute cuisine."

Willow clapped her hands. "Great, because I'm not an haute cuisine kind of woman. Let's go!"

Scottie hesitated. "Are you sure? What will Barb say if she hears I took you to Potato Champion?"

Willow leaned toward her and whispered, "How about we just don't tell her?"

"Deal." Grinning, Scottie stepped on the gas.

In what felt like no time at all, they pulled into a spot on a side street just off Hawthorne and got out of the car.

Scottie locked the Subaru and led Willow around the corner, to the pod of eight food carts that were set up around a large white tent with wooden tables, benches, and several firepits placed between them. Strings of lights stretched across the outdoor seating area; they would add to the cozy atmosphere once it got dark. The scents of melted cheese, sizzling carne asada, and fried potatoes mingled, making Scottie's mouth water.

Willow's steps faltered as she took in the carts.

"Are you sure this is okay?" Scottie asked. "We can go someplace else if you'd rather—"

"What? No! I was just trying to figure out which one we'll eat at. It all smells so good!" Willow stuck her nose in the air. "Which one is Potato Champion?"

"Over here." Scottie steered them to a metal trailer with jagged mountain peaks and pine trees painted on it. She watched Willow as they got in line behind a couple of other customers. Was Willow really fine with eating at a food cart instead of going to a fancier place?

Willow studied the large black chalkboard above the cart with the same rapt attention she would probably give the menu in a restaurant. "I can't decide. What do you usually get?"

"Depends on my mood. Their palak paneer fries are amazing, and I haven't seen them anywhere else. If I want something simple, I usually get the fries with the rosemary truffle ketchup, and if I'm up for an adventure, I go for the PBJ fries."

"PBJ?" Willow echoed. "They put peanut butter and jelly on fries?"

Scottie laughed at her skeptical face. "Yep. It's a peanut satay sauce with smoky chipotle raspberry jelly. It's unusual, but really, really good."

"Hmm." Willow scratched her nose. "I'd love to try it, but what if I don't like it?"

"You'll never find out if you don't try it," Scottie said.

It was Willow's turn to order, and the guy inside the food cart gave her an expectant look.

Willow hesitated for only a second longer, then nodded decisively. "All right. I'll take the PBJ fries and a Coke, please."

Scottie playfully pumped her fist. "You won't regret it. And if you do, I'll share my palak paneer fries." She ordered her food and a ginger ale.

The vendor twisted the caps off their bottles and slid them across the counter.

They found an empty table nearby and took a seat while they waited for their order to be done. The warmth from a firepit directly next to them warded off the cool November air.

Their table wobbled a little, but Scottie quickly fixed it by sliding a folded napkin under one leg.

Willow gave her a grateful nod. "You're always fixing something, aren't you?"

Scottie didn't know why it was, but somehow, a subtext seemed to hide in Willow's comment. "Not always," she replied. "Some things don't need fixing." Like today, for example. Despite all the mishaps, it had been perfect for her.

That seemed to be the right answer to give because a smile spread across Willow's face. Before she could answer, their number was called.

Scottie stared at the food cart. "That was fast. Stay. I'll get it." Within a minute, she carried two paper boats full of hand-cut, golden fries back to their table.

Hers were smothered in spinach-based sauce and squares of paneer cheese, while Willow's were topped with peanut sauce and raspberry jelly.

"Oh wow," Willow said as Scottie set the food down on the table, "that looks like it could get messy."

Scottie nodded. "That's half the fun."

Despite her comment, Willow dug right in. She eagerly pierced a fry with her plastic fork and took a big bite. Her eyes widened. "Oh my God," she mumbled around her mouthful of PBJ fry, "this is really good."

Scottie laughed and relaxed. "I told you so!" She speared a cube of paneer cheese and a couple of fries and popped them into her mouth. A gentle kick of spice spread along her tongue, making her hum. She slid her paper boat toward Willow. "Here. Try mine."

Willow did while offering Scottie a few PBJ fries in return. She chewed with the same enthusiasm as before and let out a low moan that warmed Scottie's body more than the firepit.

Scottie quickly shoved a couple of fries into her mouth to distract herself.

"Yum," Willow said when she had swallowed. "They're great too. I can understand why this is your comfort food."

Scottie took her time swallowing the PBJ fries, enjoying the salty-sweet-smoky mix of flavors. "It used to be," she said quietly. "I haven't been here since Tanya and I split up. I couldn't bear it."

Willow paused with another fry halfway to her mouth. "You used to come here with her?"

Scottie nodded.

"Oh, Scottie. Why didn't you say so? We could have gone somewhere else." Willow let go of her plastic fork and moved her hand across the table.

For a moment, Scottie thought she would take her hand, but then Willow paused and curled her fingers around her bottle of Coke.

"Tanya and I were together for ten years, and we lived in Portland for all of them. If I avoided every place she and I have ever been to, I'd have to either leave the city or spend my life sitting at home." Scottie tilted her head and gave her a crooked smile. "Which, admittedly, was what I did the first few months after the breakup. A smaller apartment opened up in my building, so I moved and holed up there."

"I'm sorry," Willow said in a near whisper. Her hand tightened on her Coke. "I can't even imagine what that must have been like."

"It sucked," Scottie replied, not feeling the need to sugarcoat things around Willow. "But now I'm ready to make those places mine. This"—she waved her hand back and forth between them—"really helps to not make it feel like hers anymore."

"Good." Willow gave a firm nod. She dipped a fry in jelly and held it up as if for a toast. "To making things yours again."

Scottie grinned, thoroughly charmed that Willow would toast new beginnings with fries even though their beverages were right there. She picked up a palak-sauce-covered fry and touched it to Willow's as if they were clinking glasses. "And to trial runs that don't go according to plan but work out for the best."

They let their fries rest against each other for a moment while looking deeply into each other's eyes. The buzz of conversation from neighboring tables and the sizzle of the food cart friers seemed to fade away.

Then they popped their fries into their mouths.

The spinach-and-curry aroma from Scottie's dish mingled with the peanut-and-raspberry from Willow's. The mix of flavors shouldn't have worked, but strangely, it did.

Willow laughed at the ridiculousness of it all, a low, easy sound that wrapped around Scottie like a warm hug.

She watched Willow across the table. A tiny dab of peanut sauce clung to the corner of her mouth. For once, she seemed entirely at ease. The afternoon sun cast an orange glow across her face, making her skin appear impossibly soft.

Scottie leaned back and let herself soak it in. She nodded to herself. *Yeah, this trial date is definitely working out for the best.*

Scottie brought the Subaru to a stop in front of Willow's house and shut off the engine.

For a moment, they sat in silence.

"In case I haven't said it before, this place is really cute," Scottie finally said. "Is it Fiona's?"

"Are you saying I wouldn't pick a cute house?" Willow jutted out her bottom lip in a playful pout. Then she caught herself. *What are you doing? You're not flirting with her, are you?*

"I'm saying you wouldn't pick a purple house," Scottie replied.

How confidently she'd said that! As if she knew Willow that well already. And, of course, she was right.

"Plus your sister was wearing purple frames and has purple streaks in her hair. Kind of gave it away." Scottie grinned. "I'll walk you to the door. It's a practice date, after all. Gotta hone my dating skills."

They got out and walked the few yards to the house together. At the small, recessed entryway built into the front of the house instead of a porch, they paused and turned to face each other.

The sun was setting, giving Scottie's hair a golden sheen. Willow couldn't tear her gaze away. She tucked her hands into her jacket pockets so she wouldn't be tempted to reach out and brush the soft waves back.

"So," Scottie said, shuffling her feet, "what's the verdict? If this had been a real date, would you consider a second one?"

Willow froze. The answer should have been an easy one. But was Scottie's question really entirely hypothetical?

Scottie chuckled as if to fill the silence between them. She lowered her gaze to her feet. "You don't need to answer. Considering we were stuck in the woods and lost our brunch reservation, I bet that would probably be a big, fat no."

Willow's stomach clenched. She realized too late that her hesitation had made Scottie doubt herself. For Christ's sake, she was supposed to help her, not undermine her confidence in her dating skills! Scottie had a hard enough time starting to date again after her ten-year relationship had failed. She didn't need Willow to make it harder.

The worst part was that if she had been the dating kind and this had been a real date, she would have wanted to see Scottie again. The thought of never repeating a day like this made her unexpectedly sad.

But it was safer that way.

She cleared her throat. "I had a great time. If it had been a real date, I would have asked you out on a second one."

Scottie's head came up. Her eyes gleamed with something warm and hopeful. "Yeah?"

Willow nodded, her throat too tight to speak.

Scottie studied her, gaze soft yet questioning. "You know, if you—"

The door swung open, and Fiona stepped out of the house in a sequined deep-red top, bell-bottom jeans, and platform boots. "Oh, hey. You're back just in time for karaoke. Want to come?" She looked back and forth between them, making it clear the invitation extended to both of them.

Scottie glanced at Willow, as if taking her cue from her. Whatever she read in Willow's expression made her shake her head. "No, thanks. I think we had enough of an adventure for a day."

"Yeah," Willow said. "I'm going to pass too."

Fiona gave them a curious look yet didn't ask.

But Willow knew her restraint would only last until Scottie was gone. Then she would put Willow through her version of the Spanish Inquisition.

Scottie turned back to Willow. "Thank you for today. For helping me knock the rust off. If you ever get tired of spreadsheets and production schedules, there's a career as a dating adviser waiting for you. I'd write a raving testimonial."

Laughter bubbled up from deep within Willow's chest. "Oh God, no. I think I'd better stick to my spreadsheets."

They smiled at each other.

"Good night, Willow," Scottie said.

"Good night." She watched as Scottie walked down the path to her car, climbed in, and slowly drove off, waving until she disappeared down the street.

Fiona leaned against the metal railing. "Practice date, huh? I have to admit the way she looked at you didn't appear like practice at all. That looked like the real deal."

"You're imagining things." Willow tightened her grip on her keys and considered rushing past her sister, escaping into the house. But Fiona would never let her hear the end of it. "We had a really nice time; that's all."

"What did you do?" Fiona asked.

"She took me to see the Troll Bridge—dozens of little toy trolls that people hung on an old train trestle—and she had reserved a table at Screen Door for brunch. But then her car wouldn't start. We ended up stranded in the woods for nearly two hours, waiting for AAA, so we lost the brunch reservation."

Fiona exhaled heavily. "Oof! What a disaster!"

"You'd think so, right?" Willow said, her thoughts still on the day she'd had. "But somehow it wasn't. We played UNO and went to a food cart instead, and she introduced me to PBJ fries."

"Ooh, I've had those! They're amazing. But I didn't think I'd ever get you to try them, or I would have taken you there myself."

"Hey, I let you talk me into giving pear-and-blue-cheese ice cream a try."

"Yeah, that only took me three lifetimes of begging and bribery," Fiona replied.

Willow shrugged. Her sister was exaggerating, of course, but she might not be totally wrong. Maybe Willow was a little more adventurous when she was around Scottie, but she didn't want to admit that.

"So, let me get this straight..." Fiona tapped her chin. "You had to deal with car trouble in the woods, lost your brunch spot, and braved PBJ fries...and yet you're standing here, smiling like you had the time of your life?"

"It was really nice." Defensiveness crept into Willow's tone. "But it's not something I should get used to."

"Why not?" Fiona asked. "She clearly likes you. And as much as you try to deny it, I think you like her too. So why the hell shouldn't you go out with her again—on a real date?"

Willow sent her a dark look. "We've been over this. You know why."

"Oh, come on. What's the worst that could happen?"

"Another dead battery. Scottie becoming suspicious. The date being a complete disaster." Willow ticked them off on her fingers, then mentally added, *The date being wonderful.* She held up her hand before Fiona could cut in. "You know I'm right. Every time I try to be normal, it ends the same way. I'm fairly sure it was me who caused her car battery to die. There won't be a happy ending for me with this weird tech affliction." Scottie had handled one dead battery with good humor, but how long until she either grew suspicious or her patience ran out? Besides, Scottie had been through a lot lately. She deserved someone who could help her heal, not someone she had to fix.

"Fine, I'll let you be. Just don't be surprised if Scottie refuses to let you hide."

Before Willow could even open her mouth to protest, Fiona brushed past her and sauntered toward her car.

Chapter 23

When Willow got off the elevator and entered the operations department on Monday morning, the bullpen was already buzzing with phones ringing and keyboards clacking.

Willow weaved her way through the maze of desks until she got to her own. She hadn't even set down her purse or turned on her computer yet when a crown of silver hair popped up over the low divider.

"Well?" Barb drawled. "How did the date go?"

"*Practice* date." Willow dropped onto her chair and directed a slightly exaggerated beaming smile at her colleague. "Good morning to you too, Barb! I hope your last week at Kudos is off to a good start."

"It would be if my protégé didn't leave me in suspense," Barb muttered. "Come on; tell me how it went."

Willow shoved her purse beneath her desk. "There's not much to tell. We never even made it to brunch."

Barb's eyes went wide. "Ooh! You skipped brunch and went straight to dessert?" She bounced her silver eyebrows suggestively.

"Barbara Peisner!" Willow's cheeks burned. She glanced around to see if anyone had overheard Barb's insinuation.

Luckily, Celeste was nowhere to be seen, and their co-workers were busy at their desks. No one seemed to be listening in on their conversation.

Exhaling, Willow turned back toward Barb. "Nothing like that. Her car didn't start, so we got stuck for a while, waiting for AAA, and didn't make it back to the city in time. We ended up having PBJ fries instead of brunch."

"PBJ fries?" Barb repeated as if Willow had confessed to dipping sardines into caramel sauce.

Crap. She hadn't meant to let that slip. "Don't judge them till you've tried them. They're amazingly good."

"That might be, but they are not what we would have called a romantic meal in my day." Barb shook her head. "Clearly, Scottie needs to knock a lot more rust off if that's her idea of romancing a woman."

Willow opened her mouth to defend Scottie, but Barb didn't give her a chance. She kept talking.

"Which means"—Barb paused like a magician about to pull a rabbit from her top hat—"you two need a second practice date!"

"No," Willow said firmly. "Absolutely not."

"Why not?" Barb asked, innocence personified.

Willow waved her hand. "Well, for one thing, Thanksgiving is this week, and then I'll be taking over for you. We're both busy."

But Barb didn't seem convinced. "So go out once you've recovered from the turkey coma and you've made it through your first week without me. December is the perfect time for romance."

Willow picked up a pen and fiddled with it. "I'm not looking for romance."

"I'm not asking you to marry her. Just go on a second date and have some fun."

Willow hesitated. For a moment, she allowed herself to imagine spending another day around Scottie and her easy, calm energy. Admittedly, she didn't hate the idea—quite the opposite.

She had kept people at arm's length for so long. She had always told herself she was better off by herself, never letting herself think about all the things she was missing—friendship, companionship…love.

But Saturday had cracked something open, and now she had a hard time closing that door again. The loneliness she'd suppressed for years began to bubble up. She had spent the rest of the weekend bustling around the house, cleaning out the fridge and doing her sister's laundry, just for something to do while Fiona was out with friends. For the first time ever, the silence had bothered her.

"Come on," Barb said. "This is my last week. Three days and I'm outta here, sipping piña coladas at the cruise ship bar. Do you really want our last hours together to be tense because we're arguing over your refusal to go on a second date?"

No, of course Willow didn't want that. Barb had trained her well and had been her champion during her first two months at Kudos. "You're fighting dirty."

"One of my many skills," Barb said with a grin. "So?"

Willow sighed. "Fine."

Barb lit up like a Christmas tree. "Fine?"

"Fine," Willow repeated. "That is...provided Scottie wants to go on a second date...practice date with me. It's not just up to me, you know? Maybe Scottie doesn't want a second trial run. Maybe she feels she's knocked off enough rust and would rather go on a real date with someone else."

"So ask her," Barb said as if that were the simplest thing in the world.

"I will."

When Barb's head disappeared behind the divider, Willow slumped against the back of her office chair and stared at her still-dark screen. The black rectangle showed a wide-eyed reflection of herself.

Ask her. Barb's words echoed through her mind. Barb had said it casually, as if it were as easy as picking up a carton of milk on her way home. But for Willow, it was anything but.

Oh God. What had she just agreed to? Her pulse thudded in her ears, and her stomach rotated like a carousel at the thought of asking Scottie out.

Her nervous system didn't seem to get that it was only a practice date.

"Oh crap," she whispered. She got up to make herself some tea. She knew better than to turn on her computer right now, when she was this out of sorts.

It would probably crash before she could even open her email, and having to call IT was the last thing she wanted to deal with right now.

Chapter 24

On Wednesday afternoon, the operations department had been transformed into a party zone. It was the day before Thanksgiving and Barb's last day at the company, and Kudos Entertainment was pulling out all the stops for her.

The scents of lime and cilantro greeted Scottie as she entered Operations. A taco bar—Barb's favorite—stretched along the counter in the break room, trays piled high with all kinds of taco toppings. A sheet cake sat on the table, ready for cutting.

Colorful streamers dangled down from the ceiling, and a large banner proclaimed, *Happy retirement, Barb!*

Employees mingled in small groups in the bullpen and the break room, plates and paper cups in hand. Barb wasn't hard to find; her laughter rang out over the hum of conversation.

Scottie made her way over to Barb to wish her all the best.

"Scottie!" Barb immediately pulled her into a hug. "Thanks so much for coming by! I wasn't sure I'd get to see you before I left."

"I wouldn't dream of not saying goodbye. And I wanted to give you this." Scottie held out a framed photo with a red ribbon, showing Barb as Kudos's Santa Claus a few years ago, complete with a fake belly and a long, white beard.

Barb laughed. "I didn't think there were any pictures of that."

"I'm in IT," Scottie said with a grin. "If any data ever existed, I can retrieve it." She glanced over Barb's shoulder and let her gaze drift over the employees.

"She's over there," Barb said with a knowing smile.

Scottie looked in the direction Barb was discreetly pointing.

Somehow, she wasn't surprised to see that Willow had found a corner to hide out in. She had retreated to a quiet spot in the break room, tucked between the lime wedges and the recycling bins, both hands wrapped around a paper cup, trying not to talk to anyone.

Scottie chuckled quietly. Somewhere in the dictionary entry about introverts and parties, there had to be a picture looking exactly like this.

"Why don't you go over and say hi?" Barb said. "I think there's something she wanted to ask you anyway."

Scottie didn't need much convincing. "All right. Take good care of yourself, and enjoy every minute of your much-deserved retirement." She gave Barb another hug.

"Will do," Barb replied. "Don't be a stranger, okay? I think you have my number. I expect updates on…well, everything."

Scottie playfully saluted. "I'll keep you posted on how Kudos is faring without you." She weaved through the clusters of chatting employees and made her way over to Willow.

"Still hiding out in a corner?" She kept her voice soft so she wouldn't startle her.

Willow swiveled her head around. The relief in her eyes filled Scottie with warmth. "I told you I highly doubt I'll ever start to enjoy parties."

"That you did," Scottie said with a smile. "Want me to hang out for a few minutes so no one tries to come over and rescue you?"

"Well, it worked last time, so…yes, please."

Scottie stepped closer and took a moment to study her.

In a lavender blouse and a gray pencil skirt, Willow looked as lovely as ever. Even the way she fiddled with her paper cup seemed graceful. A few wisps of dark-brown hair had slipped free from her low ponytail, as if wanting to escape as much as Willow did. It softened her careful composure and framed her fair face.

Scottie realized she'd gone quiet, staring in silence for longer than reasonable. She quickly cleared her throat. "So…Barb's last day is finally here. Are you still nervous about taking over?"

Willow glanced left and right as if not wanting any of her colleagues to overhear. "I'll be fine."

Scottie continued to look at her. "I know. But that's not what I asked."

Willow stared down at her paper cup and circled the rim with one long finger. "Can I be honest?"

Scottie tore her gaze away from the unexpectedly sensual sight. "Always."

"I am a little nervous," Willow said quietly.

"I get it. Barb is a force to be reckoned with. But so are you. You braved PBJ fries; you can handle Kudos."

"It's not that I doubt my ability to do the job, but..." Willow waved her hand around the room. "Barb knows everyone. She knows how to handle people—who she needs to get tough with and who needs a gentle hand."

Scottie tilted her head. "True. But she had thirty years to learn the ins and outs of people at Kudos. She knew most of us since we were wet-behind-our-ears baby employees."

They chuckled together.

"Besides, don't sell yourself short," Scottie added. "You're better with people than you think."

Willow sent her a look that was part skeptical, part hopeful. "How so?"

"Rumor has it you got stuck in an elevator with Kudos's near-claustrophobic IT support person and managed to calm her down."

"Hmm. I guess I did."

Scottie nodded. "See? You've got Barb-level people skills after all."

"I wouldn't go that far. It's different with you."

The words lingered between them, carrying more meaning than Willow might have intended.

Scottie's mouth went dry, and she struggled to swallow.

Before she could think of something to say, Willow dropped her gaze. "So, what are your plans for Thanksgiving?"

"Going home," Scottie answered. "My folks live in Corvallis, less than two hours from here, so I'll be eating way too much, watching football, and dodging my parents' advice on my love life or lack thereof. You?"

"I'm staying in Portland, spending it with my sister."

"Is it going to be just the two of you?" Scottie asked.

Willow shook her head. "Fiona usually invites every friend and neighbor who's single and doesn't have family in the area, and it turns into a loud, chaotic potluck."

"So basically another party?"

Willow put on a dramatically pathetic face. "Unfortunately, yes. But at least this one will come with pumpkin pie."

Both went quiet for a few moments, then Scottie said, "Barb mentioned there's something you wanted to ask me?"

Tension returned to Willow's posture. She sent a dismayed look in Barb's direction, then fixed her gaze on a spot above Scottie's shoulder. She twisted the empty paper cup between her fingers.

Scottie wanted to reach out and cover Willow's hands with her own, calming her, but she reined herself in. One practice date didn't give her the right to do that. Now that their trial run was over, they were back to being friendly work acquaintances—even though Willow didn't feel like any of her other co-workers at all. "You look like you're about to ask me for a kidney."

Willow crumpled the paper cup and tossed it into a nearby garbage can, still not making eye contact. "No. I promise your organs are safe. It's just..."

"Hey, I hope you know you can ask me anything."

Finally, Willow looked at her. The hint of vulnerability in her eyes took Scottie's breath away. "Barb cornered me on Monday morning as soon as I walked in."

Scottie had expected that. "Let me guess. She wanted a full report on Saturday."

Willow nodded. "Barb thinks we need a do-over. According to her, waiting for AAA and eating PBJ fries isn't considered the pinnacle of romance. She insists you need more dating practice."

Barb, ever the matchmaker, even now that she was about to retire.

"Didn't we agree not to tell Barb about Potato Champion?"

Willow hung her head. "I know. I'm sorry. It slipped out."

"It's okay." Scottie didn't care what Barb thought. As long as Willow had enjoyed their not-a-real-date date, that was all that mattered to her. She studied Willow. "So Barb thinks we need a second practice date. What do you think?" She would have expected Willow to shoot down Barb's suggestion right away. Why hadn't she?

"I don't know," Willow murmured. "I mean, it's Thanksgiving tomorrow, so obviously not right away. But if you still feel a little out of practice, we could..."

"Could...what?" Scottie prompted. She wanted to hear it from Willow.

Willow pulled her shoulders back and looked into Scottie's eyes. "Would you want to go on another date with me?"

A spark of elation flared through Scottie. *She doesn't mean a real date,* she cautioned herself.

"Uh, practice date, of course," Willow quickly added.

Of course. Scottie had known that's what she'd meant. But it would be great to spend more time with Willow anyway. "Why not?" She struggled to keep her voice even and casual. "I'd be up for it if you are. Are you?"

"Well," Willow said, "if it helps you knock the rest of the rust off, I'd take one for the team."

"Wow," Scottie mumbled. "High praise for my dating skills." Was that really how Willow viewed the time they spent together? Just some kind of charity? The thought started a dull ache beneath her ribs.

Then she saw the humorous twinkle in Willow's eyes, and the ache in her chest disappeared.

"Seriously, your dating skills are just fine," Willow said. "In my expert opinion, you don't need to knock more rust off, no matter what Barb thinks. All you need is a little polishing."

"Polishing, hm?" Scottie couldn't help smiling.

Willow nodded.

"I can live with that," Scottie said. "So, do you want me to plan something for our polishing session?"

"Actually, if you don't mind, I'd like to plan it this time."

"Oh, really?" Scottie hadn't seen that coming, but she liked the idea of Willow taking the initiative.

"Yes, really." Willow gave a decisive nod. "What if your date—the next woman you'll actually go out with—wants to be the one to plan something? As your dating adviser, I think you need to learn how to let your date take the reins every now and then."

Scottie grinned and leaned in slightly, closer to Willow's ear. "Who says I have problems in that department?" The line came out flirtier than she had intended.

A flash of heat seemed to sear through Willow's eyes, making Scottie's pulse skip.

Mercifully, Celeste tapped her fork against her plate, the sharp clank cutting through the moment. "If I could have everyone's attention, please. I'd like to say a few words to honor Barbara."

As the chatter around them stopped, they turned away from each other and faced the front of the room. The temperature seemed to drop a few degrees, and Scottie could breathe again.

Jesus, Scottie. She tugged on her collar. *If you're really planning to go on another practice date with her, you'd better get a hold of yourself. Willow's made it clear she doesn't want to date for real, and the last thing you need is another crash and burn. Not when you're only just getting your feet back under you.*

She would head to Corvallis tomorrow and use Thanksgiving and her family's company as a reminder that she needed stability right now, not another tangle of chaotic feelings. After that, she would be ready for a second practice date and for friendship with Willow.

Chapter 25

Fiona's house smelled as if every single container from the supermarket's spice aisle had collided. Sage, thyme, and rosemary warred for dominance with curry, chili, and lemongrass.

The mix of aromas from the Thanksgiving potluck Fiona was hosting reminded Willow of eating at the pod of food carts with Scottie. She wished she were back there instead of in Fiona's full house.

The living room, dining area, and kitchen were packed with guests. Fiona fluttered from one group to the next like the social butterfly she was, while Willow had volunteered to act as a bartender. At least pouring wine and mixing cocktails kept her busy and gave her an excuse to stay at the edge of the party instead of being drawn into the center.

Fiona's cats seemed as unamused by all the visitors as Willow was. Sugar had escaped upstairs to hide under Fiona's bed as soon as the first guests had arrived. Spice perched on top of the fridge somewhere behind and above Willow, ears back, and glared down at the chaos.

"Same, girl," Willow muttered. "Same."

Someone walked up to the kitchen island that served as a makeshift bar.

Willow turned and gave the woman—Melissa? Marissa?—a polite smile.

"Hi," the stranger said. "I heard you were the woman to talk to for the good drinks."

"What can I get you?" Willow asked, ignoring the flirty tone.

"Why don't you surprise me?" Melissa or Marissa answered. "I trust you."

Willow lifted her brows. "A risky thing to say to an amateur bartender."

Melissa/Marissa flashed her a grin and leaned one elbow on the counter. "Maybe I like risky."

Ah. She had to be the colleague Fiona had mentioned—the one who was queer, single, and looking. Willow had a feeling her sister had invited her in the hopes they would hit it off. Melissa/Marissa seemed nice enough, but Willow wasn't interested.

She put on her professional bartender expression. The flirty colleague probably hoped for a Sex on the Beach or another cocktail with a suggestive name, but Willow made her a simple gin and tonic—a drink without any hidden messages. She garnished the glass with a slice of cucumber, then slid it across the counter.

Melissa/Marissa took a sip. "Ooh, you're hired! Best drink ever!"

"Glad you like it." Willow gave her a weak smile, then turned away under the pretense of having to cut more lemons.

After a moment, Melissa/Marissa gave up her attempts to flirt with her and drifted back into the living room.

Spice sent a hiss after her from on top of the fridge.

"Yeah, I know," Willow murmured. "That was beyond awkward."

Nothing like her interactions with Scottie at all. She kept picturing Scottie and the easy way she would navigate a crowd like this. No doubt she would charm everyone effortlessly, leaving them bent over with laughter. Willow didn't want to admit how much she wished Scottie was there to "rescue" her, as she had during Barb's two retirement parties.

Was Scottie having fun at her parents' house?

Willow pulled out her phone. Should she text Scottie to tell her happy Thanksgiving?

She hesitated.

Scottie was with her family, and Willow didn't want to interrupt. But then again, a two-word message wouldn't be much of an interruption, right? It would be just a polite text between friends.

The thought of reaching out and connecting with Scottie proved too much to resist. She typed a quick message—merely saying *Happy Thanksgiving*—and then spent much too long debating whether to add an emoji. Finally, she decided on a turkey emoji, hoping to make her text appear less boring but not too personal either.

She stared at it for a second, then hit *send* before she could talk herself out of it.

Scottie leaned against the counter in her parents' kitchen, dish towel at the ready.

Her dad stood at the sink with his sleeves rolled up and his arms up to his elbows in suds. He rinsed off a casserole dish and handed it to Scottie to dry.

Ben and Hazel, two of her almost siblings, waited behind her, passing plates and glasses down the line until her cousin Noah put them away.

They fell into a comfortable rhythm, honed by years of practice.

The scent of roasted turkey and sweet potato casserole still hung in the air.

Laughter and shouts drifted over from the living room, where the rest of the clan had crowded onto couches and armchairs to watch the football game. Her mother was the loudest, trading playful barbs with Uncle Dave about the score.

Scottie wondered how Willow would fare with her noisy family. Would she hide in a corner, or would she relax and let them draw her into a conversation, the way she did with Scottie?

Her phone buzzed on the kitchen counter.

Scottie wiped her hands on the dish towel and checked her messages.

Probably another meme from Kassidy, who had sent her a picture of two turkeys earlier, one of them asking, *What are you thankful for?* And the other one replying: *Vegans.*

But it was a text, not a meme, and it wasn't from Kassidy—it was from Willow. The message simply read: *Happy Thanksgiving.* Willow had added a turkey emoji.

Just a short line, but it brought a smile to Scottie's face. She hadn't expected to hear from Willow today, and knowing Willow was thinking about her on Thanksgiving—even for a second—felt special.

Scottie tossed the dish towel at Ben, who caught it neatly. "Take over for a minute, would you?" Without waiting for his answer, she typed a reply.

Happy Thanksgiving to you too. Are you surviving your sister's party so far?

Willow's reply appeared almost instantly. *Barely.*

The noise in the Prescott household faded away as Scottie and Willow typed back and forth.

No one there to rescue you from others coming over to make small talk? Scottie added a winking smiley face.

Not a single soul, Willow replied. *I had to answer questions about how I like the Portland weather half a dozen times.*

It wasn't exactly an *I miss you,* but Scottie would take it.

How are things at Casa Prescott? Willow asked.

Instead of explaining, Scottie lifted her phone, took a snapshot of the living room, and sent it to Willow: Her mom, uncles, aunts, and cousins involved in heated discussions about football, the now-adult daycare kids sitting with their backs against the couch the way they had when they'd been little, and her cousins' offspring rushing around on a sugar high from the pie.

Willow sent a wide-eyed emoji. *Wow. Big family! I had no idea you had so many siblings!*

Well, technically, I don't, Scottie replied. *Just a couple of cousins. But my mom ran a daycare out of our house when I was growing up. There were always kids around, so I never felt like an only child. Some of them became almost like foster siblings and are still part of the family.*

That explains it, Willow texted back.

Explains what? Scottie asked.

Why you're so good with people.

Willow's compliment warmed Scottie more than the food in her belly.

"What's got you grinning like that?" Her father's voice brought her back to the kitchen. "Or should I say who? Haven't seen you glued to your phone like that since you were sixteen and had your first girlfriend."

Heat rose to her cheeks. She shoved the phone into her back pocket.

Within seconds, several of Scottie's cousins and almost siblings crowded around her.

"Ooh! Scottie's got a new girlfriend!" Ben said in a singsong voice.

Scottie took the dish towel from him and gave him a playful snap with it. "There is no girlfriend."

"Why didn't you bring her?" her mother called from the living room.

Scottie grimaced. Figures that her mom would hear that one sentence even over the noise from the TV. She cupped her hands around her mouth, forming a makeshift megaphone, to make sure the entire family heard her. "I repeat: I do not have a new girlfriend."

Her mother made a sound of disappointment and returned her attention to the football game.

But Ben, Hazel, and Noah weren't as easily deterred.

"If there's no girlfriend, why are you blushing?" Hazel asked.

"Because I'm embarrassed for you lot," Scottie shot back.

"Okay, that's enough. Out!" Her father flicked suds at them. "All of you."

Reluctantly, they trooped out of the kitchen.

When Scottie wanted to follow her cousin and the daycare alumni, her dad held on to the back of her sweater. "Not you. Sit and tell me what had you grinning at your phone like that." He pulled out one of the barstools from the kitchen island.

Scottie climbed up and dangled her feet the way she had as a kid. It was comforting to see that some things never changed.

Her father calmly looked at her, waiting for her to explain without pressuring her.

"It's not what you're thinking," she finally said. "It's...complicated."

He nodded. "I can imagine. After what Tanya did to you, it's only natural that the next relationship would feel a little complicated."

"No, Dad. That's not it. There is no relationship. I was texting a friend; that's all."

He studied her for a while. "Okay. But if you ever want to talk—about that friend or anything else, I'm here." He moved to clean the sink, giving her space.

"Thanks, Dad," Scottie said hoarsely. She wanted to tell him about Willow, about how she could make being stuck in an elevator or waiting for AAA fun. But how could she explain their practice dates? How could she tell him more about the situation, when she didn't know what "more" was there to tell?

Sighing, she folded the dish towel and joined the rest of the family in the living room.

Chapter 26

On the first Thursday of December, at six thirty, Willow parked her Civic across the street from Scottie's apartment building and grabbed her phone from the passenger seat. *I'm here,* she texted.

Scottie's answer arrived immediately. *Want to come up for a minute? I usually don't let women see my apartment until the third date, but I'll make an exception for you.*

Willow hesitated. But truth be told, she was curious and wanted to see Scottie's home. *Okay. On my way,* she texted back.

She climbed out of the car, locked it, and crossed the street.

The neighborhood was still bustling, people cutting through an alley with shopping bags. The first floor of Scottie's building was made of concrete and had large glass storefronts housing a grocery store, while the four upper floors were clad in orange metal panels.

She rang the doorbell, and Scottie buzzed her in. Willow pulled open the glass door and crossed the modern lobby. She took the elevator up to the third floor and found unit 318.

The door was propped open, and Scottie stood just inside the apartment, greeting her with a warm smile.

She wore a light-blue sweatshirt with a polo-style collar, two buttons left undone, and a pair of black khakis. Golden waves of hair fell onto her forehead, and her brown eyes crinkled at the corners. "Hi. Come on in." She opened the door wider to let Willow enter.

Scottie's one-bedroom apartment was small, but the tall windows made it feel bigger.

The first thing Willow noticed were the plants. They were everywhere—potted ferns on the windowsill, a poinsettia on the coffee table, and an ivy plant dangling down from a macramé hanger in a corner. All of them were thriving, their leaves a healthy green. Clearly, Scottie was taking good care of them.

Scottie had already put up her Christmas tree. It was decorated with red and silver ornaments and cute little figurines like a cow wearing a Santa hat. Huge googly eyes stared back at her from branches near the top.

A loud laugh burst out of her, surprising even Willow. God, she loved Scottie's goofiness. It made her relax for a change. "Um, your Christmas tree is looking at me. Why does it have eyes?"

Scottie chuckled. "I saw them in a craft store, and it seemed like a fun idea—and I think it was. I got a few good laughs out of my friends."

Did Scottie count her among them?

Willow pushed the thought away and continued to look around. Her gaze drifted to the wooden contraption next to the poinsettia. It was a half-finished 3D puzzle that would be a marble run once it was done. Its tracks twisted and turned like a wooden roller coaster.

She nearly commented, saying that she loved 3D puzzles too and that maybe they could do one together next time. Then she reminded herself that there wouldn't be a next time. This was their final practice date.

Scottie stood next to her in silence, as if waiting for her verdict. Finally, she raised her brows.

Willow usually wasn't a person who openly voiced her thoughts, but with Scottie, she felt comfortable to do so. "It's not what I expected."

"Better or worse?" Scottie asked.

"Different," Willow replied. "I thought it would be more…I don't know…high-tech. Not like this." She pointed at the plants, the wooden puzzle, and the goofy Christmas tree.

"I've got a small desk with a computer in my bedroom, but I try not to take work home with me," Scottie said. "This is what I like in my spare time."

"It's wonderful." Willow could imagine curling up on the couch with a book, relaxing without fear of destroying an expensive electronic gadget. She immediately chased the mental image away. "Ready to go?"

"Yep." Scottie grabbed her jacket and keys. "Lead the way."

The Civic was parked beneath a streetlight. When Scottie saw the car, she made a beeline for it and trailed a hand over the hood in a gesture so tender, it sent a shiver through Willow. "Are we taking her or my car?"

"Her?" Willow repeated with a smile.

"Of course." Scottie playfully put her hands on her hips. "Don't tell me you gave her a male name."

"Who says she has a name?"

Scottie merely raised her eyebrows.

"Okay, okay. Her name is Ruby—because of her color. And yes, we're taking her."

"Cool," Scottie said. "Ruby really looks great for her age. I can tell you're taking good care of her."

In a few areas, the paint was starting to bubble, and the black vinyl seats were a bit worn, but otherwise, Ruby had held up well. "I'm only the second owner. She belonged to an older gentleman who rarely drove her."

"Can I drive?" Scottie directed a hopeful look at her.

"Can you even drive a stick?"

Scottie flashed her an exuberant grin. "Get in and find out!"

Willow hesitated. No one but her had ever driven Ruby, but faced with Scottie's eager smile, she couldn't say no. She tossed her the keys.

Scottie caught them, looking like a kid who'd been given the keys to a candy store. She nearly skipped over to the driver's side and climbed behind the wheel.

Willow laughed at her antics.

Scottie trailed her fingers over the wood-grain veneer running across the top of the dashboard.

Jesus. Willow's mouth went dry. Did Scottie have to keep fondling the car in such a sensual way?

Scottie tested the hand crank on the door, rolling down the driver's side window, then rolling it back up, the biggest grin on her face.

"It doesn't have power steering, and the radio doesn't work," Willow told her, "but everything else does." Truth be told, she hadn't replaced the radio on purpose—one fewer piece of electronics that could fail. She drove an old car with minimal electronic components for that very reason.

Scottie turned the key in the ignition. When the engine rumbled to life, she beamed. "Listen to her! She started without a hitch!"

Willow smiled back and watched her from the passenger seat. She marveled at the way Scottie found so much joy in small things like getting to drive a classic car. Maybe she should try to be more like that—at least for this one night. She promised herself that she would enjoy this practice date without thinking of the fact that it would be their last one.

Scottie slid the gear stick into first, let the clutch out slowly, and added a little gas, smoothly easing the car into the crawl of traffic down SE 11th Avenue.

"You have driven a stick," Willow said.

Scottie nodded. "My dad wouldn't have let me move out until I had learned how."

"Is he a mechanic?" Willow asked.

Scottie's chuckle filled the car. "No. He's a high school physics teacher. This is his last year in the classroom, but he'll keep mentoring the robotics club, and my mom is converting the garage into a workshop to keep him busy once he's home full-time."

"Smart woman," Willow said. "My parents got divorced within a year of retiring. Their careers kept them busy, but once they stopped working and spent more time around each other, they realized they had nothing in common anymore."

"I'm so sorry." Scottie stopped at a traffic light and glanced over with a look of compassion.

"It's okay. They split up on good terms." Willow fell silent. She was stunned at the way she kept telling Scottie personal stuff, even things she didn't like to talk about.

"Where to?" Scottie asked, not trying to pressure her into telling her more.

"Take a right here," Willow replied.

Scottie did. Her hands were steady on the steering wheel, and she handled the little car as if she'd been driving it for years. She hummed as she guided the Civic along Southeast Belmont Street.

Neon lights flashed, and music drifted out of bars and restaurants as they passed them.

"This is fun!" Scottie said. "It's amazingly easy to drive."

The pure, unadulterated joy on Scottie's face took Willow's breath away. She almost wished the ride wasn't so short so she could watch her a little longer.

But all too soon, they reached their destination. Willow directed her into a small parking lot, where Scottie eased the car into the last open space.

Scottie shut off the engine, then turned toward her and made eye contact. "Thank you for letting me drive."

"You're very welcome." If Scottie got so much joy out of it, she would even let her drive back.

They got out, and Willow led her toward the small, seventies-themed bar, tucked between a Vietnamese restaurant and a vintage clothing store. This time, she was the one who held the door open for Scottie before following her in.

Plush olive-colored velvet booths and orange plastic chairs lined the walls to the left and right. Hanging lamps cast an amber glow onto square wooden tables. At the end of the long, narrow room stretched a bar. Curved wood shelves undulated behind it, reaching from floor to ceiling. Rows of bottles glinted in the warm light.

Willow halfway expected a disco ball to hang from the ceiling, but instead, a large, illuminated potted palm took up the center of the room.

ABBA was playing in the background.

A tiny knot twisted in her belly as she watched Scottie take it all in. What if she didn't like it?

Scottie glanced around and laughed. "Trust you to take me somewhere retro!"

"Tonight is Drag Bingo night," Willow said softly, watching Scottie's reaction. "I thought it might be fun."

"Ooh, I bet it is!" Scottie seemed as delighted as she'd been getting to drive the Civic. "Come on, let's grab a table before they're gone."

The knot in Willow's stomach unraveled.

Scottie lightly placed her hand on the small of Willow's back as she guided her past several busy tables. The gesture was casual, but the warm weight of Scottie's hand still made Willow's heart beat faster.

Was Scottie just practicing her dating skills, or was it an instinctive, entirely unconscious touch?

Scottie gestured at a booth, letting her slide in first.

Willow took a seat, and Scottie slid in next to her.

A laminated menu was tucked into a holder in the middle of the table. Scottie pulled it out, opened it, and angled it so Willow could see it too.

Willow leaned closer and was acutely aware of the warmth of Scottie's thigh pressed against her own.

But neither of them shifted away.

A waiter came to take their order before Willow's distracted brain had a chance to process the offerings, so she ordered the first thing that came to mind. "I'll have a cheeseburger, fries, and a Coke."

Scottie grinned. "Can't go wrong with the classics." She glanced up at the waiter. "I'll have what she's having."

The performance started just as their food arrived.

An elegant drag queen in a sequined dress, towering heels, and a platinum-blonde wig sashayed onto the tiny stage and lip-synced to "Dancing Queen." Her flawless makeup was a work of art.

Scottie nodded her head to the beat and held her cheeseburger with both hands, chewing happily as she followed every move onstage.

Willow found herself watching Scottie as much as she watched the performer, again fascinated by the enthusiasm Scottie put into everything she did. She tried to focus on the show, but the awareness of Scottie's thigh against her own never left her.

Once the notes of the last song faded away, the audience clapped and whistled.

Scottie let out a "whoop" and didn't seem at all bothered that she was clapping more loudly than everyone else.

Willow glanced around to see if anyone was staring but then stopped herself. She had wanted to take a page from Scottie's book, and now she would. Holding her head up high, she clapped louder too.

Grinning, Scottie bumped her with her shoulder.

"Thank you, beautiful people!" the drag queen said into her microphone. "I'm your host. and mistress of the bingo cage, the incomparable Sissy O'Sass. Are you ready for Drag Bingo?"

The audience cheered.

"For all of you Drag Bingo virgins, the rules are simple—it's like regular bingo, just with more sass. If I call a number you have, you take your little dauber and give it a good spank. If you get five in a line, scream 'Bingo!' at the top of your lungs. But I'll warn you: If you scream it and don't have it, I get to spank you." Sissy O'Sass turned, bent at the waist, and mimed spanking herself before swiveling back around. "And here's my favorite rule: If two people have bingo at the same time, they get to come up onstage and have a dance-off!"

Get to? Willow shuddered. Having to dance onstage was a scenario straight from her nightmares.

"You okay?" Scottie asked.

Willow nodded.

Scottie gave her a soft smile. "You're picturing having to do a dance-off, aren't you?"

It was wonderful and scary to realize how well Scottie knew her already. She nodded again.

"Don't worry," Scottie said. "I'd grab your card and pretend it's mine."

Willow stared at her. Scottie was almost too good to be true.

A server interrupted by stepping up to their table and handing out bingo cards and daubers.

Scottie studied the five-by-five grid of her card. "Have you ever played before?"

"Of course," Willow replied. "Everyone's played bingo."

"Not me," Scottie said. "I know, I know. I must be the only person in North America who never played bingo at school as a kid."

"No worries. It's really easy." Willow leaned closer. It was unexpectedly wonderful to be the one to teach Scottie something, even if it was just bingo. "See how the columns are labeled B, I, N, G, and O? If the hostess calls N-11, for example, you look for the number eleven under the N column. If you have it, you mark it with the dauber."

"Got it." Scottie grabbed her dauber like a sprinter getting ready for the big race.

Sissy O'Sass spun the bingo cage. The white balls rattled inside. Then she plucked one out and held it up. "B-7!"

Scottie trailed her finger down the B column. "Ooh! I have it!" She opened her dauber and enthusiastically smashed it down on the B-7 square.

Willow didn't pay a lot of attention to her own card. Her gaze was on Scottie, who focused so intently that her tongue poked out of the corner of her mouth. She was completely unselfconscious, and it was the cutest thing ever.

Anticipation rose as their hostess called out more numbers and people kept marking their cards, probably coming close to a bingo.

Sissy O'Sass pulled another ball from the cage and held it up. "O-66!"

Scottie marked her card, raised it high in the air, and yelled, "Bingo!"

Two tables down, a man in a Hawaiian shirt shouted "Bingo" too, but Willow barely noticed because Scottie threw her arms around her for an exuberant hug.

Willow stiffened for a second, but no zap followed. Her eyes fluttered shut as she sank against Scottie. God, she smelled so good, and she felt even better. Willow fought the urge to bury her nose against Scottie's neck.

"Ooh, gentlefolks, we've got a tie!" Sissy O'Sass's voice cut into Willow's cocoon. "You know what that means: a dance-off! Come on up, darlings, and show us what you've got!"

The audience cheered and clapped.

Scottie let go and slid out of the booth.

Willow's stomach dipped with nervousness for her.

But Scottie didn't seem to have any stage fright. She sauntered to the stage, jogged up the two steps, and took up position next to her competition as if she did this every day.

The music started, and Willow recognized "Hot Stuff" by Donna Summer. She half laughed, half choked. Clearly, the Drag Bingo organizers were out to kill her.

Scottie began to dance. She moved with playful confidence, clearly not caring at all that an entire bar full of people was watching as she shimmied and twirled her body to the music. Her disco dance moves should have looked cheesy. It was obvious that she wasn't a professional dancer, but Scottie's abandon more than made up for it. She pointed at complete strangers in the audience, drawing them in. Every time the chorus hit, she swayed her hips in a sensual rhythm.

Willow grabbed her Coke without looking away from the stage and took a big gulp. She found herself swaying in the booth, caught up in the music…or maybe in Scottie.

When the song ended, Sissy O'Sass asked for applause for the guy in the Hawaiian shirt first.

Admittedly, Willow had no idea how Scottie's competition had done. She hadn't spared him a single glance.

Then the drag queen asked for applause for Scottie.

Willow clapped, stomped, and whistled. She knew she was drowning out everyone else, but she didn't care.

Across several tables, her gaze met Scottie's, who flashed her a wide grin.

"Looks like she brought her fan club." Sissy laughed. She grabbed Scottie's hand and raised it. "Gentlefolks, we have a winner!"

Scottie bowed playfully and accepted the envelope with her prize.

The audience cheered again.

A minute later, Scottie slid back into the booth with flushed cheeks. The velvet dipped beneath her, making their thighs touch again. With a flourish, she handed Willow the envelope. "Open it and see what we won."

"We?" Willow repeated. "You won the dance-off. If I had been up onstage, they would have laughed me out of here."

"I wouldn't have laughed," Scottie said quietly. "Open it."

Willow did.

A gift certificate for two fell out.

The universe seemed determined to sabotage her resolution to limit the time she spent with Scottie. But it wasn't just any gift certificate; it was a class at a local pottery studio.

"Oh, cool," Scottie said. "I've always wanted to try that."

Willow nodded weakly. All she could think of was the sapphic romance novel she'd read this past weekend. It contained a scene in which the two main characters used a pottery wheel together...ending with a heated make-out session.

Images of clay-smeared fingers sliding over bare skin flashed through Willow's mind, but the hands in her mind didn't belong to the characters from the book. They looked suspiciously like Scottie's.

Willow quickly slid the gift certificate back into its envelope and raised her hand, desperately signaling to the waiter. She needed another drink—an ice-cold one, preferably.

Once Drag Bingo ended, they sat in the booth, finishing their drinks, while "Jolene" by Dolly Parton drifted through the bar's speakers. Every now and then, they commented on something—the music, the drag queen's earlier performance, the other patrons. Mostly, they sat in companionable silence, though. It didn't feel tense or uneasy; it felt as if they had become comfortable with each other and didn't need to fill every second with chatter.

Scottie leaned back in the velvet booth and nursed her second Coke. Warmth still buzzed through her, not just from the adrenaline kick of the dance-off but mostly from Willow's closeness. She wasn't eager to leave, and Willow didn't seem to be in any hurry either. She swirled the half-melted ice cubes left at the bottom of her glass and appeared to be deep in thought.

Was Willow thinking about what would happen after tonight too?

Then Scottie froze, her hand still on her glass.

A familiar figure rose from a table across the room.

For a moment, Scottie thought she must be imagining it, but the auburn hair and confident posture were unmistakable, even in the low light.

It was Tanya.

They hadn't seen each other in more than eight months, not since that night Tanya had sat her down and told her she didn't love her anymore and wanted more from life than spending it with her.

Scottie hadn't gotten any warning then—just like now. Tanya was suddenly there, right across the room.

Her hair was a tiny bit longer, falling in stylish layers around her face, but otherwise, she hadn't changed at all. Scottie wasn't sure what she had expected—maybe for their breakup to have had an effect on Tanya too. But she looked as polished as ever in a fitted blazer, completely unaffected, as if neither their ten-year relationship nor their breakup had ever happened.

A rush of memories swept over Scottie, overwhelming her.

Tanya's gaze was on her. She didn't seem surprised. Perhaps she'd seen Scottie onstage earlier. She bent and whispered something to the woman sharing a table with her—possibly her new girlfriend. Then she crossed the room, heading straight for Scottie.

Scottie's pulse thundered in her ears as she tracked Tanya's path toward them.

"You okay?" Willow's gentle voice cut through the haze.

"Yeah. No. Shit. Tanya's here. She's coming over."

Willow's head swiveled around. She stared toward the approaching figure. Her jaw tensed, and an emotion Scottie couldn't read flickered across her face.

They both sat stiffly, watching Tanya walk toward them.

"Hi," Tanya said when she reached the table. The familiar scent of her expensive perfume filled Scottie's nose. "I saw you onstage earlier and thought I'd come over and say hi."

Something soft touched Scottie's hand on the table.

Scottie looked down, and it took her a second to understand that Willow had reached over, slid her hand over Scottie's, and laced their fingers together.

The gentle contact and the softness of Willow's skin against her own derailed Scottie's thoughts. She nearly forgot about Tanya as all of her senses locked onto Willow. A tingle rushed up her arm, then spread through the rest of her body, and she was fairly sure it wasn't due to static electricity this time.

"Tanya," Scottie finally managed to get out. "Hi."

Willow gave her hand a reassuring squeeze. "Hi, I'm Willow." A polite smile curved her lips, very different from the genuine one she'd given Scottie earlier, when she'd returned from the dance-off. She held Tanya's gaze as if she belonged by Scottie's side. "Scottie's girlfriend."

Willow's fingers flexed around hers, as if she'd shocked even herself.

She had certainly stunned Scottie, who struggled to keep her expression neutral and not give them away.

Tanya's gaze darted to Willow, then to their intertwined hands on the table.

Willow stroked her thumb across Scottie's knuckles.

Scottie lost her breath. A swarm of butterflies took flight in her belly.

A shadow darted across Tanya's face. "Nice to meet you, Willow," she said, but it sounded like a polite string of words that had slipped out automatically. She smoothed a hand down her blazer. "I'll let you two get back to your evening." She turned toward Scottie. "It was good to see you. You're looking well."

Scottie mumbled something that she hoped was "You too."

Tanya lingered next to the table for a moment longer, and then, with one final nod, she turned and walked away.

Scottie sat frozen. She stared at Tanya's retreating back, her fingers still laced with Willow's. *What just happened?* She tore her gaze away from Tanya and directed it at their intertwined fingers. "What was that?"

"I have no idea." Willow was still staring after Tanya. "She just waltzed over here and told you you're looking well, like she still has every right to compliment you after what she did!"

What? Scottie's head was spinning, so it took her a moment to figure out Willow was talking about Tanya. "No, I mean...this." She nodded down at their hands.

Willow's cheeks flushed a deep red. "I...I don't know." She started to withdraw, but Scottie held on.

"In case Tanya is still watching," she said hastily.

"Right." Willow left her hand where it was.

"Why did you tell her you were my girlfriend?" Scottie asked, trying not to get distracted by the way Willow's skin felt against hers.

"I'm so sorry. I shouldn't have done that." Willow covered her face with her free hand. "That was completely inappropriate."

Scottie softly pulled her fingers down. "I wasn't complaining. I just wanted to know why."

"I only had a second to think of something. I guess I reacted on instinct."

Scottie couldn't help arching her brows. Holding her hand and telling her ex they were a couple was an instinctive reaction?

"I didn't want her to think you were sitting here, crying into your beer, waiting for her to take you back or something," Willow added. "I wanted her to realize you've moved on. That you're over it."

Willow continued to ramble and apologize for a minute or two. Then she fell silent and directed a pleading look at Scottie. "Say something."

Scottie didn't know what to say. She was still stunned on so many levels—by Tanya's sudden appearance, by Willow's quick thinking and her uncharacteristically impulsive action. But most of all, she was stunned by the effect Willow's simple touch had on her. As soon as Willow had intertwined their fingers, she'd been focused on the feel of Willow's hand in hers, not on Tanya.

"I'm not," Scottie finally said.

"Not what?"

"Not completely over it."

"Oh," Willow whispered and tried again to withdraw her hand.

Scottie tightened her grip. "The breakup really shook me. It tore my life apart without warning, and I'm still in the process of putting the pieces back together. But I just realized that while I'm not over *it*, I'm over *her*."

"Really?" Willow asked quietly. "You seemed pretty shaken when you came face-to-face with her."

"Oh yeah, I was. I've been dreading this moment for months—running into her somewhere. Maybe even seeing her with someone new." She gestured toward the woman at the table with Tanya. "Seeing her caught me off guard, but it didn't shatter me, nor does the thought of her with someone else." The tidal wave of grief and longing she'd expected had been more like a trickle of sadness. "I don't want her back."

What she wanted was to keep holding Willow's hand.

Willow licked her lips. "Good. I mean, it's good that you're healing and aren't considering taking her back after what she did to you."

"Not an option," Scottie said firmly. "Not that she would want me back."

"Oh, I think she has a regret or two."

"No, she doesn't. She was the one who broke up with me."

Willow snorted. "Did you see the way she looked at you…and at me, when I introduced myself as your girlfriend?"

"No, I didn't," Scottie said. "Truth be told, I was too busy staring at you." She smiled and shook her head. "You're full of surprises."

Willow lowered her gaze to the tiny slivers of ice left in her otherwise empty glass. "I'm sorry."

"I didn't say that was a bad thing."

Willow peeked up. "No?"

"Definitely not." Scottie softly squeezed her hand. "Come on. Let's order another drink. And this time, I need something stronger than soda."

"God, yes," Willow murmured.

Scottie signaled the waiter, careful to leave her other hand in Willow's—just in case Tanya was still watching, of course.

Willow was glad that Scottie had asked if she could drive again. She was still in a daze. For a change, no tech glitch had interrupted this date…practice date. This time, Willow had been the one who had glitched. She couldn't believe she had taken Scottie's hand, pretending they were a couple!

As if by an unspoken agreement, they had kept holding hands all the way back to the car—just in case Tanya was watching them. At least that was what Willow had told herself. But deep down, she knew that wasn't the true reason. The truth was she hadn't wanted to let go. Holding Scottie's hand had felt so right—as if they were connected, a unit, them against the world. She had missed that feeling, and she hadn't been quite ready to lose it.

When they had reached Scottie's neighborhood, Willow had insisted on walking her to the door. The walk from the car to Scottie's apartment building felt both much too short and impossibly long. They weren't holding hands now, and the lack of contact between them felt strange… wrong, somehow.

They paused at the glass entrance door and turned to face each other. Willow wanted to reach out and run her fingers through the soft waves framing Scottie's face.

What was wrong with her? She had never been a physically affectionate person.

The soft light above the front door cast a pale circle around them, illuminating Scottie's broad, open features.

"I had a really good time," Willow said. The words felt too clichéd, too inadequate after the wonderful yet complicated evening they'd had.

Scottie gave her a look that seemed as intimate as intertwining their fingers. "Me too. Thank you for planning this. It was perfect."

Willow nodded and shifted her weight.

If this were a real date, this would be the moment where one of them would lean in and they'd kiss.

She wasn't supposed to think about that. Of course that wouldn't happen. This wasn't a real date, no matter how much it had felt like one. The terms were clear: They were friends, and this was just a drill.

Still, the quiet between them stretched on. There was more to say. Finally, Willow couldn't stand it anymore. She needed to break the tension. "So…how do you feel?" she asked and immediately regretted it.

The question was too open and could be misunderstood. Scottie might think she was asking how she felt about her. Before Scottie could even open her mouth, Willow rushed to add, "After running into your ex."

Scottie directed her gaze upward as if thinking about it for a moment. "Free." The word came out like an exhale. "I thought seeing her would reopen all my wounds so that I'd be back to square one and take another eight months to recover. But it didn't. I'm fine. I can really start over now."

Warmth filled Willow's chest. She was truly happy for Scottie.

"Thank you for helping me shake off not just the rust but some of that burden too," Scottie said.

Before Willow could find the right words to respond, Scottie leaned in.

Oh my God! Is she going to—?

Scottie brushed her lips against Willow's cheek. It was just a barely there touch, short and impossibly tender.

But Willow's entire body reacted as if Scottie had captured her mouth in a passionate lip-lock. A dizzying wave of heat spiraled down her body, spreading all the way to her toes. Her knees went weak. Her skin burned where Scottie's lips had touched her cheek. Her pulse thrummed. She was swaying on her feet and realized she had reached past Scottie and gripped the metal door handle next to her—which was probably what had stopped her from zapping Scottie again.

She had always thought swooning heroines who got weak in the knees were a silly, over-the-top Hollywood thing, not something that happened to real people. Definitely not something that happened to her.

But here she was, swaying on her feet, all because of a chaste, completely platonic kiss to the cheek.

She managed to get out a strangled, "Uh, good night." She had no idea if that was the right response or what Scottie had said last.

"Good night," Scottie answered, sounding as if she had lost track too.

Willow gave a quick, clumsy wave, then turned and fled to the car as fast as she could without breaking into a run. Somehow, she managed not to stumble and fall over her own feet. Her hands shook, so it took her a moment to unlock the driver's side door.

She started the engine and drove away without allowing herself to look back.

Her heart was still racing by the time she parked in front of her own house. She turned off the engine but kept sitting in the dark, gripping the steering wheel.

The warmth of Scottie's hand in hers and the gentle brush of her lips against Willow's cheek lingered as if carved into her skin forever.

Images from tonight flashed through her mind: the joy on Scottie's face when she had gotten to drive the Civic, the gentle touch on the small of her back, Scottie's sensual dance moves on the stage, holding her hand, then her heartfelt thank-you and that tender kiss on the cheek.

Their second practice date had changed a lot of things for both of them.

Even though she was usually great at controlling and denying her feelings, Willow could no longer pretend Scottie was just a colleague she was friendly with. At least to herself, she could admit that if circumstances were different, she would want to date Scottie for real.

But while a lot had changed, one thing had remained the same. Scottie might feel free now, but Willow was still stuck. She would never be free of her weird effect on electronic devices.

What was she supposed to do now?

Chapter 27

"Willow."

At the voice suddenly next to her, Willow looked up from the inventory database she'd been updating with incoming supply information.

Celeste stood in front of her desk, tablet in hand.

Willow jumped. "If this is about the shredder..."

Her boss's brow creased. "What's wrong with the shredder?"

So it wasn't about that...or, most likely, about the printer she had managed to jam three times this week, all because Willow's emotions had been completely out of whack. She had tried to fix the devices herself rather than submit a ticket to IT, not yet ready to face Scottie. "Oh, nothing," she said quickly. "What can I do for you?"

"I noticed you still haven't hung your snowflake."

Willow blinked. "Pardon me?"

"The snowflake for the tree in the lobby." Celeste gestured at the still-blank paper snowflake on Willow's desk. "It might not seem like the most effective use of your time or serve any obvious purpose, but we've been hanging snowflakes every holiday season for several years now, and following tradition builds company culture and is good for cohesion."

Willow bit back a smile. Leave it to her boss to make hanging a paper snowflake seem like a reasonable strategy to increase productivity. "Oh, right. I've been meaning to hang it."

"Please make sure it's up by the end of the workday," Celeste said. "Our management team expects the tree to be finished before the holiday party tomorrow."

"Of course. I'll do it right away."

Celeste gave her a crisp nod and strode back to her desk.

Willow picked up the snowflake and turned it over in her hands. The paper caught against the new calluses on her fingertips. One side shimmered silver, while the other was made of white paper. Every employee was supposed to write a wish for the next year on the snowflake and hang it on the company Christmas tree in the lobby.

She grabbed a pen, then hesitated. Truth be told, she hadn't forgotten to hang her snowflake; she had been avoiding it all week, while her colleagues added their wishes to the tree.

What was she supposed to write? There was only one thing she could think of, but she could never have it, even if she filled out an entire avalanche of snowflakes.

She'd always tried to be content with her life the way it was and not wish for impossible things.

But lately, that resolve had started to waver. Ever since her second practice date with Scottie last week, stray what-if thoughts had kept slipping through the cracks.

What if she and Scottie would go on a third date—a real one?

What if she could take Scottie's hand again—this time, without letting go once they were alone, no longer being observed?

And what if Scottie leaned in at the door again, not for a brush of lips on her cheek but for a kiss that left Willow dizzy and made her forget the reason she'd kept a careful distance?

The snowflake with its empty paper side had taunted her all week because deep down, she knew exactly what she longed to wish for. What she wanted most was more time with Scottie, more moments where they were laughing together, holding hands, more kisses to her cheek...her lips...every inch of her body.

Heat swirled through her, and she roughly shook her head, chasing off the very much not work-appropriate thoughts. She couldn't write any of that on a piece of paper that would be hung on the company Christmas tree. Scottie's name couldn't appear anywhere because Scottie might be reading it.

Other than Scottie, what else did she want?

What she wanted most of all was to stop feeling as if she was too much, as if her life was always about to go off the rails, as if she destroyed everything she touched—devices and relationships.

Her pen hovered over the paper side of the snowflake. Then, without allowing herself time to reconsider, she scribbled *Be normal.*

She stared at the two words on her snowflake. She wanted to crumple it up and ask Celeste for a blank one, but she knew it would only call attention to her.

Be normal. Okay, that was generic enough that no one would know what it was really about—or that it was her wish.

She would sneak down to the lobby, hang her snowflake, and get back to her desk before anyone even noticed she'd been gone. Willow grabbed the piece of paper and made her way to the lobby to hang her impossible wish.

When Scottie stepped off the elevator, the scent of pine greeted her.

The company Christmas tree towered in the center of the lobby. Strings of lights in red and blue—Kudos's brand colors—twinkled on its branches. Dozens of paper snowflakes added a homemade charm to the corporate display. At the very top, a large star made of faceted acrylic caught the light and scattered it in tiny rainbows across the polished floor. After the incident a few years ago—when the crystal tree topper had fallen off and hit their former COO on the head—they had opted for something shatterproof.

Scottie walked up to the tree, still not sure what to put on her snowflake.

Six months ago, she would have filled the blank space without hesitation. Her wish would have been obvious: heal—start over after Tanya had torn her life apart and figure out who she was after her ten-year relationship had gone up in flames.

But that had been then. Now that ache in her chest was barely noticeable anymore. She had seen Tanya at the bar, and it hadn't gutted her the way she had feared it would. The shards of her life had begun to fuse back together.

Which left her in need of a different wish.

She scanned the snowflakes on the tree for some inspiration.

A new car.

Buy a house.

Go to Bali.

Receive a raise.

Run a marathon.

Have a baby.

All good wishes, but none of them fit her.

If she was being honest, she knew what she wanted to write. She could sum up her wish in six letters: Willow.

She wanted to date her for real.

But did she have a right to wish for that when it was obviously not what Willow wanted?

It had been a week since Willow had bolted from her front door and disappeared into the night. Scottie hadn't heard from her since then—no texts, no accidental run-ins in the elevator or the coffee shop, not even an IT ticket.

Scottie had been tempted to reach out at least a dozen times every day, but she had stopped herself, not wanting to pressure Willow. The next move had to be Willow's. But she hadn't contacted Scottie.

Had Scottie overstepped a boundary? The thought made her stomach churn.

Scottie hadn't planned the kiss on the cheek that had made Willow run. She had been so full of gratitude that a simple thank-you hadn't seemed like enough. Because Willow was a huge part of why she was starting to heal. She'd made her feel as if she was enough after all. Scottie even believed her now when Willow said her reluctance to date had nothing to do with Scottie. It wasn't that she was lacking anything, even if Tanya thought differently.

So she'd leaned in and brushed her lips against Willow's cheek.

Even a week later, Scottie could still feel Willow's warm skin and the heat emanating from her as Willow blushed.

But then cold had rushed in when Willow had fled.

Scottie sighed. She wouldn't solve this problem standing in the middle of the lobby. Maybe she needed to text Willow anyway.

But first, she had to fill out her snowflake before her manager kicked her ass for putting it off again.

She walked over to the reception desk, borrowed a pen from the receptionist, and twirled it between her fingers for a few moments. Then she wrote *Be enough* on her snowflake.

Not enough to make Willow want a relationship with her…even though, truth be told, she still wanted that.

But she needed to believe that even if she was single, she was not the discarded half of a couple. She was whole by herself, just as she was.

After adding an exclamation mark, she handed the pen back and returned to the tree. She had just raised herself up on her tiptoes to reach the branch she wanted when the elevator chimed behind her.

Scottie glanced over her shoulder—and sank back onto her heels.

Willow got out of the elevator. In a black midi skirt, tights, a formfitting burgundy turtleneck, and ankle boots, she looked as beautiful as ever. She clutched a snowflake of her own.

Their gazes met across the lobby.

For a moment, Willow's steps faltered, as if she wanted to retreat into the elevator. Then she pulled back her shoulders, gave Scottie a faint smile, and walked toward her.

❦

Willow barely made it out of the elevator before stumbling to a stop.

Scottie stood in the middle of the lobby, staring at her from in front of the Christmas tree.

The acrylic star that topped the tree painted a rainbow of lights across her hair.

God, she looked good in a long-sleeved black company polo, the sleeves casually pushed up to her elbows. Maybe a little tired, as if she had slept as badly the past few days as Willow had.

Willow slowly walked toward her, not yet sure what she would say once she reached her.

After she'd realized she wanted to date Scottie for real, the earlier ease between them was gone.

"Hi," they both said at the same time.

Scottie shifted her weight and nodded at Willow's paper snowflake, then at the one she held. "Guess I'm not the only one who's running late on this."

Willow wanted so badly to see what Scottie had written. Did her wish have anything to do with her?

But if she glanced at Scottie's snowflake, it was an invitation for Scottie to look at hers. The urge to find out what Scottie had wished for was strong, yet the need to protect her own secret was even stronger.

For a moment, they both stood still, neither making a move to hang her snowflake while the other was watching. Then, as if by an unspoken agreement, they circled to opposite sides of the tree to give each other privacy.

Willow scanned her part of the tree for a hidden spot, then slid her snowflake behind a branch, where it was almost completely hidden by someone's wish for a lifetime supply of snickerdoodles. She reached around and gave hers one last nudge to make sure the paper side faced inward.

Scottie emerged from her side of the tree, her hands now empty. She shoved them into her pants pockets.

Tension tightened Willow's chest. She tried to act all cool and casual. *Be normal,* she reminded herself. But she had no idea what to say. Small talk was beyond her capabilities right now.

"I was wondering," Scottie said, each word slow and hesitant, "do we need to talk?"

Willow sucked in a breath. Leave it to Scottie to address the elephant in the room.

"I think we do," Scottie added before Willow could assure her they were fine and there was no need to talk. "But maybe this isn't the best place for it." She gestured discreetly toward the reception desk and to the employees crossing the lobby.

Willow nodded. This wasn't where she wanted to have that conversation. Not that she wanted to have it at all.

"Have you had lunch yet?" Scottie asked. "We could go to Bistro Elysium and grab something to eat while we talk."

"Sorry, I don't have time for lunch. With Barb gone, it's chaos up there. I've been eating lunch at my desk while putting out fires all week." It was the truth, but she was secretly also glad to have a reason to avoid the conversation and the complicated feelings Scottie stirred in her.

Scottie's face fell, and her shoulders drooped. "Oh. Okay. I get it. December is one hell of a time to be thrown in at the deep end."

Willow bit the inside of her cheek. She couldn't handle the crushed expression on Scottie's face. "We could grab a quick coffee, if you want." She forced a small smile. "I still owe you one anyway."

God help her, she was hopeless when it came to this woman. One sad look from Scottie and all her good intentions to stay away melted faster than snow in Portland.

Scottie's eyes lit up. "Coffee sounds great."

"Let me get my purse and coat," Willow said. "I'll meet you outside in five minutes."

When Scottie nodded, Willow hurried toward the elevator, glad to have a few moments alone to steady her nerves and brace herself for the conversation ahead.

Willow guided Scottie toward a coffee shop two blocks away, not the one closest to the office, where she had accidentally outed herself to Scottie. It felt like ages ago now.

This one accepted cash. Her insides were a knot of tension. No way would she risk touching the payment system and making it glitch, especially not with Scottie watching.

The sidewalks were still wet from the morning drizzle, and the air felt cool on Willow's overheated cheeks. A thick blanket of gray clouds seemed to press down on her, matching her mood.

Neither said much until they entered the coffee shop.

Thankfully, the line was short.

They ordered a latte and a chai latte, and Willow pulled a twenty-dollar bill from her wallet to pay for them both.

The barista frowned at the cash, but Willow pretended she didn't notice.

When their beverages came, Scottie pointed to a small table by the window. "We could sit over there."

"Mind if we walk?" Willow asked. "I need some air."

"Sure."

They left the coffee shop and walked in silence for a few steps.

Scottie kept some distance between them, carefully avoiding letting their shoulders brush. It was a stark contrast to their practice dates, when she had guided Willow with a hand on the small of her back.

Had those little gestures just been Scottie practicing her dating skills, so now that she'd knocked the rust off, she no longer wanted that contact? The thought stung, but Willow shoved it away and told herself it didn't matter.

Willow lifted her cup and took a sip, mostly to cover up the silence.

"I've been trying to figure out what I did wrong the other night... when you just took off. It was the kiss on the cheek, wasn't it?" Scottie's question cut through the heavy silence. "If it was, I'm really sorry. I never meant to cross a line or make you uncomfortable."

Oh my God, was that what Scottie thought? Had she been carrying this worry around all week, chewing on it ever since Willow had bolted from her front door?

She stopped walking to stare at Scottie.

The expression on Scottie's face nearly undid her. She looked so earnest, so torn up over something that wasn't her fault, that it broke Willow's heart.

The kiss hadn't been the problem; the feelings it had evoked in Willow were. That innocent kiss had cracked something open deep inside of her, a door she'd kept carefully locked and bolted for years.

While she couldn't tell Scottie that, she had to reassure her.

"No," she croaked out through a tight throat. "You have no reason to apologize. You didn't do anything wrong." She wanted to take Scottie's hand to drive her message home, but her fingers were shaking and would betray her emotions, so she kept them wrapped tightly around her paper cup.

Scottie searched her face, clearly wanting to believe yet not sure she should. "I need you to know I wasn't trying to push anything, and I hope you didn't think I was using you to knock off some rust in the kissing department too. I respect you too much for that. I just wanted you to know how much you'd helped me and how grateful I was, and words didn't seem like enough."

A sharp pang flared through Willow's chest as she watched Scottie twist herself into knots over a heartfelt gesture. Scottie was open, sincere, and genuine—everything Willow wasn't...or couldn't be. Willow hated that she was hurting this kind, wonderful woman. "I know that, Scottie. You were just thanking me. I never thought it was anything else. Really, we're fine. At least I hope we are." She searched Scottie's eyes.

"Of course we are." The set of Scottie's shoulders loosened, but the tension didn't fully leave her face. She fiddled with the lid of her paper cup. "If kissing you on the cheek was fine, why did you run away?"

Crap. She had hoped Scottie would leave it at that and not ask.

Willow started walking again. She looked at the pavement, unable to face Scottie, but she could still feel Scottie's gaze on her. "Our practice dates brought up a lot of stuff for me. Stuff I wasn't expecting."

That was as honest as she could be without revealing too much. She didn't want to lie; Scottie deserved better.

"I get it," Scottie said softly.

Willow swallowed. "You do?"

"Of course. My relationship with Tanya left some scars, and I assume you've got some relationship baggage too. Of course some of that would get dredged up on the first dates you've been on since, even if you were just helping me practice."

The emotions their practice dates and the kiss on the cheek had brought up had nothing to do with any of her exes, but Willow decided not to correct Scottie's assumption. "Yeah, I guess you're right."

They walked on in silence that was less tense than before.

When they reached the little plaza in front of the Kudos Entertainment building, Scottie paused. "I'm really glad we talked and cleared that up.

But if I ever do something that makes you uncomfortable, please tell me. Your friendship has come to mean a lot to me, and I don't want to screw it up."

Friendship... The word settled on Willow heavier than it should have. Was that what Scottie wanted—being friends?

"You're not screwing up anything." Willow was. She fought to keep her voice from cracking. "But okay, I promise...if you promise me something in return."

"Anything," Scottie said immediately, even though her gaze was a little wary.

"I appreciate how genuine and open you are. It's something I really admire about you, and I don't want you to change because of me or second-guess everything you do or say around me. Promise me you'll always be yourself."

A smile spread across Scottie's face—the first real, unguarded Scottie grin Willow had seen that day. "I promise." She held out her paper cup.

It took Willow a moment to understand she wanted to seal the promise by tapping their cups together. The gesture was so typically Scottie that she couldn't help smiling. She touched her cup to Scottie's.

Unfortunately, she couldn't make the same promise and was relieved Scottie hadn't asked her to. She couldn't allow herself to be fully open... or could she?

No, of course not. Telling Scottie the whole story would be too much. No one would believe that, not even someone as understanding as Scottie.

But if she wanted to keep Scottie in her life, even as a friend, she might have to tell her something eventually. Maybe she could admit to having a string of bad luck with electronics.

It felt like a big risk—like opening the Pandora's box that Scottie's innocent kiss had cracked open even farther.

All her instincts shouted at her to slam that box shut forever.

She wasn't sure if she could, though. Part of her didn't want to. She wanted to throw the lid wide open and let herself feel everything.

Yet, at the same time, she was scared of what would happen if she did. Whenever she'd let someone get close, it had always ended the same way—and this time, she wouldn't leave only a string of broken devices scattered in her wake.

For once, it might be her heart that broke.

Chapter 28

"Is it unsalvageable?" Fiona asked from where she was sitting cross-legged on the floor, wrapping Christmas presents.

When her sister's voice cut into her thoughts, Willow nearly dropped the cotton swab she held. She sighed. "I think so."

"Really? It doesn't look that bad." Fiona pointed at the machine on the coffee table in front of Willow.

"Oh. The typewriter. No, it's fine, just a little grimy." Willow dipped the cotton swab in rubbing alcohol and ran it along the slender arm of a type bar, removing dust and ink.

Usually, she found restoring a typewriter comforting, almost like a form of meditation, but tonight, it wasn't working. Her thoughts were still going in circles. Every time she tried to focus on cleaning the type bars, her mind dragged her back to this morning's conversation with Scottie and the upcoming holiday party.

Would Scottie be going—and would she be going alone? She'd said she was over Tanya, so maybe she would bring a plus one.

Fiona lifted her brows. "Yeah, of course the typewriter. What did you think I was talking about?"

"Nothing," Willow said quickly. "I was just deep in thought, not really listening. Sorry."

"Yeah, I noticed. You've been sitting there, staring at it for the past ten minutes. I haven't seen you this checked out since you got your wisdom teeth removed."

Willow grimaced. "We don't talk about that. Ever."

"Okay, then tell me what you were thinking about right now." Fiona warningly held up her pair of scissors. "And don't say 'nothing'!"

Willow snapped her mouth shut, then opened it again. "Our office holiday party," she finally said. "It's tomorrow."

"Ah." Fiona sent her a knowing grin. "You were trying to come up with an excuse to get out of it. How about your go-to—a last-minute stomach bug?"

Willow let out a long sigh. "Honestly, I thought about it. But I have to go. Even Barb's coming, and she just retired. I can't get away with skipping it my first year with the company."

"So if that's already decided, what's the problem?" Fiona studied her. "It's who else will be there, isn't it? Are you still avoiding Scottie?"

Willow softly pressed a key to test whether the type bar moved smoothly—and to have a reason to look away. "I wasn't avoiding her," she murmured without raising her gaze from the typewriter.

"Right."

"I wasn't. We actually talked today. There was"—she gestured with a cotton swab—"a little misunderstanding, but we cleared it up. We're all good."

"Then what's the problem?"

Willow hesitated, not sure she wanted to say it out loud because that would make it real. As long as she kept it to herself, she could pretend it was no big deal.

"Ah," Fiona said in that all-knowing tone. "It's not about whether she'll show up to the party—it's about whether she'll show up alone. Maybe now that you've helped her knock the rust off, she'll bring a date."

Willow groaned. "I hate it when you do that."

Fiona plopped a bow onto a box. "Do what?"

"Guess what I'm thinking," Willow muttered.

"It's really not hard in this case." Fiona waved a piece of ribbon at her. "You, dear sister, have a typewriter situation on your hands."

Willow glanced at the half-dismantled machine in front of her. "Um, yeah. That's why I'm working on it."

"Not that one. I'm talking about your favorite IT person. Scottie is like one of your typewriters. You discover them by coincidence when you aren't even looking for another one and then tell yourself you'll fix them up for someone else to enjoy. But by the time you've lovingly removed the rust and restored them to their old glory, you're attached to them and can't bear to give them away. Does that sound like your situation with Scottie at all?"

The cotton swab slid from Willow's hand. *Oh crap.* "I hate that even more."

"What?"

"When you are right." The thought of Scottie walking into the hotel ballroom with another woman on her arm was like a sharp punch to the ribs. Willow struggled to breathe.

Fiona put the wrapping paper and her pair of scissors down. "I didn't think you'd admit it. So why don't you do what you always end up doing with the typewriters—keep them? Or, in this case, keep the woman?"

"Because typewriters don't run." The answer tore out of Willow in a burst of anger, frustration, and sadness. "They don't give me that look when I tell them the truth about what happens to electronic devices around me. They don't stare at me like I'm some kind of digital virus when their thermostat starts blasting heat in the middle of July. They don't get angry when I can't afford to go on vacation with them because I just had to replace my washing machine. They don't hate me when I accidentally break the camera that—"

"Okay, okay!" Fiona held up both hands. "I get it. I know you've been through a lot. Had your heart broken by your shitty exes again and again."

That was the thing—she hadn't. Well, not since Mia, who wasn't even an ex. Willow had always held back a part of herself, never getting fully invested. But with Scottie, she wasn't sure she could do that if they ever got involved.

"But how do you know Scottie would run, stare at you in that judgmental way, or do any of the other things?" Fiona asked when Willow remained silent. "Just because all of your shitty friends and exes did doesn't mean she would."

"I know," Willow got out through a dry throat. "I don't want to assume she'll act like everyone else did. She's"—she waved a small brush, trying to find the right word to describe Scottie—"incredible. Kind and patient and easygoing."

Fiona threw a crumpled-up piece of gift wrap in her direction. "Then what are you waiting for? Grab that woman and hold on to her with both hands, tech affliction be damned!"

Willow sighed. "I wish I could. But it's not that easy."

"Maybe it is," Fiona countered. "Maybe you're making it more difficult than it has to be."

Was she? Willow desperately wanted to believe it.

Scottie hadn't let the drained car battery spoil their practice date. She hadn't laughed at Willow's old car—quite the opposite—and she never treated Willow as if she were a bother or incompetent, no matter how many support tickets she submitted.

Even her teasing about the Nokia phone had been gentle, done in a way that allowed Willow to laugh with her instead of ducking her head in shame.

When Scottie had called her a walking lightning rod and Willow had winced, she had immediately promised to never say it again, even before Willow had told her about the bullying she'd had to endure.

"I don't know," she murmured. "She's wonderful and patient now. But what if it doesn't last?" All of her girlfriends—not that there had been that many—had started out patient, then became increasingly confused before their feelings turned into resentment. She couldn't bear if that happened with Scottie.

Fiona shrugged. "You'll never find out if you don't try it."

The words echoed through Willow's mind, but it wasn't Fiona's voice she heard; it was Scottie's. That had been exactly what Scottie had said during their first practice date, when Willow hadn't been sure she should risk trying the PBJ fries.

And Scottie had been right—she hadn't regretted it.

But a relationship wasn't the same as an order of unusual fries.

Her phone buzzed next to her on the coffee table, snapping Willow out of her thoughts.

It was a text from Scottie.

Willow's heart started beating faster, and her stomach did a traitorous flip. She pushed back the cotton swabs and small brushes to unlock the device and read the message.

Hey, Scottie had written, *will you be braving the holiday party tomorrow?*

So Scottie had been thinking about the office holiday party too.

Willow re-read the text three times, trying to figure out the tone. Was Scottie just making casual conversation? Was she simply curious? Or was there more behind that question? Was she, too, wondering if Willow would bring a plus one?

Finally, Willow gave herself a mental kick and replied: *Yeah, I'm going. You?*

Yup, Scottie answered. *I've got to represent IT since Mateo is out sick and Gordon's pretending to be sick so he can dodge the party.*

I can empathize, Willow typed back. *To be honest, I was thinking of getting "sick" too. But then I figured it's my first year at Kudos, so I'd better show up.*

Good, Scottie replied.

Three dots appeared, indicating that Scottie was typing more.

Then they vanished.

Willow frowned, willing them to reappear, but they didn't.

"What's wrong?" Fiona asked.

"Nothing," Willow murmured, still watching her screen. "Scottie was typing something. But she didn't send it."

Fiona clapped her hands. "Ooh, Scottie! Speak of the devil! Is she going to the party?"

Willow nodded.

"Ask her if she's bringing someone," Fiona said.

Willow made a face. "No. I can't ask her that. It would look desperate. Or jealous. Or like I'm trying to ask her out."

"Ask her," Fiona repeated more firmly. "You need to prepare emotionally in case she's showing up with someone else."

Crap. Her sister was right. If Scottie planned to walk in with another woman, she needed to brace herself. She could just ask, pretending she was making small talk. "All right. Fine. I'll ask."

It took a minute to draft a short text, then a few more to rewrite it half a dozen times.

"Christ, it took my ex less time to sign the divorce papers than it's taking you to send this text—and that's saying something!" Fiona muttered.

Willow glared at her, but Fiona pretended she didn't notice and went back to wrapping presents.

Finally, Willow settled on: *Are you bringing a plus one?*

A casual, totally normal question. Right?

She hesitated, her finger hovering over the screen before she finally hit *send*.

Instead of sending the message, her phone froze.

"Not now!" Willow aimed a pleading look at the device.

The text went out with the familiar *whoosh*.

"Phew."

Another whoosh echoed through the living room.

Then again. And again.

"No, no, no, no, no!" Willow tapped the phone, desperately trying to stop the succession of repeat messages, but the text was sent out a fifth time.

Then, finally, everything went quiet.

It was too late to undo it; Scottie had probably already seen them.

Groaning, Willow covered her face with her free hand. *Great.* Now she looked as if she really, urgently wanted to find out if Scottie would bring someone to the party. Which, of course, she did.

Fiona looked up from the present she was wrapping. "What? Is she bringing a date?"

"Don't know yet." Lips pressed into a tight line, Willow held out the phone, showing Fiona the five identical messages.

"Wow!" Fiona chuckled. "Someone's a little eager to find out!"

"I didn't send all of them! My phone glitched! It sent out the same text five times, and now I seem like an obsessed stalker!"

It was another reminder why dating Scottie for real was not a good idea. She spread digital chaos wherever she went. Nobody wanted to deal with that for long.

Willow fumbled with the phone, then typed: *Sorry! My phone is being weird. I only sent it once, I swear.*

No worries, Scottie replied. *And to answer your question, I'll be flying solo this year.*

It was a silly office holiday party, not a not-guilty verdict being handed down by a jury. She shouldn't have been so relieved.

"You're beaming," Fiona said with a grin of her own. "Let me guess: She's not bringing anyone."

"No, she's not." Willow tried to sound cool, calm, and collected but knew she was failing spectacularly.

With a triumphant "whoop," Fiona grabbed a handful of ribbons and tossed them into the air like confetti. "Ask her if she wants to go together!"

Another text from Scottie arrived, so Willow ignored her sister.

You? Scottie had asked.

Was she waiting with bated breath, hoping for a negative response too? Willow wasn't sure and didn't want to read too much into it.

Flying solo too, she typed. Then, with her gaze glued to the small screen, she waited. And waited.

Fiona's off-key humming and the crinkling of wrapping paper sounded overly loud.

Spice stalked in, sniffed the wrapped boxes, and batted at a dangling ribbon, but Willow kept her attention on the phone.

What was taking so long?

Several minutes ticked by without another text from Scottie. Was that the end of the conversation for her?

Just as Willow was about to give up and go back to her typewriter, her phone buzzed again.

So neither of us is bringing someone, Scottie's message said. *Do you want to go together?*

Willow froze. She waited for a second text bubble to arrive. One that said: Just as friends, of course. Or maybe: So I can save you from the evils of small talk again.

But no such message came.

Did Scottie think adding an explanation wasn't necessary because it should be obvious after she had told Willow this morning how much she valued their friendship? Or had she not added anything because she wanted it to be a date, not two single friends hanging out at an office party?

A spiraling sensation started in Willow's head, then spun down her chest and into her belly. What was she supposed to answer?

She wanted to go to the party with Scottie; that much was clear.

But if she said yes, what would she be agreeing to? After kissing Scottie in the elevator two months ago, she had promised herself to stop sending mixed signals.

If she went with Scottie, she had to be open to whatever it would mean.

Was she?

Or, of course, she could be the one to clarify and add a "just as friends" or make a joke about needing to bring Scottie as a human shield to keep away their chatty colleagues.

But when she tried to type something like that, her thumbs refused to move.

No, that wasn't what she wanted. Scottie was so much more to her than a human shield. But did she have the courage to admit it?

"You're doing that thing again," Fiona said. "That overthinking thing."

Willow didn't look at her. She stared at Scottie's last message until the words blurred before her eyes.

But they still echoed through her mind. *Do you want to go together?*

Her heart thudded. *I'd love to,* she typed, then froze with her thumb hovering over the *send* button.

Don't, a voice in the back of her mind screamed. It wouldn't work. It never did.

But maybe it would with Scottie. Or maybe Scottie really meant it only as going together as friends. Either way, she would never find out if she didn't try.

Before she could chicken out, she pressed her thumb down.

The whoosh sound of the message sending filled the living room.

Another one followed. Then a third one.

With wide eyes, she watched as three identical text bubbles appeared in a row.

I'd love to.

I'd love to.

I'd love to.

Willow groaned. "Oh come on! Not again!"

"Not what again?" Fiona asked.

Willow's phone buzzed with another message from Scottie.

"Give me a minute," Willow murmured, all her attention focused on the device.

Great, Scottie had written, followed by three beaming emojis—probably one for each of Willow's texts. *Want to pick me up?*

Despite her tension, Willow couldn't help laughing. *You're just suggesting that because you hope I'll let you drive my car again,* she replied.

Well, there's that, Scottie answered.

Okay, I'll pick you up tomorrow at six thirty. At least if Willow picked her up, Scottie wouldn't run into Fiona again. Her sister couldn't be trusted to keep her mouth shut. Plus if Willow drove, Scottie wouldn't end up with another dead car battery.

"Willow?" Fiona waved to get her attention. "What's happening?"

She looked up from her phone, no doubt with a stunned expression on her face. "We're going to the party together."

"Yes!" Fiona threw herself backward onto the floor and flailed her arms and legs with a triumphant squeal.

Spice let out an indignant hiss and darted from the room, her tail puffed up like a bottlebrush.

"That's so amazing!" Fiona kicked her leg in the air again. "I'm so proud of you!"

"Hey, I didn't say it's a date," Willow protested.

Fiona grinned. "But you also didn't say it wasn't."

Willow slumped against the back of the couch and clutched the phone to her chest. *Oh God.* She might be going on a date with Scottie—and if she was, this time, it would be a real one!

Chapter 29

Scottie stood at the curb in front of her apartment building and tugged her coat tighter around herself, shivering in the damp air that had a December bite to it.

She fought the urge to check her watch again and instead fidgeted with the knot of her tie.

Shouldn't Willow be here by now? Scottie had gone downstairs as soon as Willow had texted to say she was on her way to pick her up.

Just as Scottie was about to check her phone, Willow's by-now familiar retro car turned onto her street.

Play it cool, Scottie told herself as the Civic came to a stop. Willow probably assumed they were just two friends attending an office holiday party together. She wouldn't have agreed if she'd known how much Scottie wanted it to be a date…or would she?

The driver's side door opened, and Willow got out.

And just like that, "cool" went out the window. Scottie could barely breathe, much less appear calm and collected as she took Willow in.

Willow had left her wool coat unbuttoned on the drive over, so Scottie could see what she wore beneath. Scottie thought Willow looked beautiful in her everyday office attire—pencil skirts, pastel-toned blouses, and unassuming cardigans—but nothing had prepared her for the sight of Willow in an emerald-green cocktail dress.

Its '50s-inspired style was perfect for Willow, elegant without being flashy. The sweetheart neckline was office-party-appropriate yet sexy, revealing the graceful curve of her collarbone. The snug-fitting bodice hugged her slim waist. From there, the full skirt flared out and ended mid-calf, giving just a hint of her long legs.

Her shiny brown hair fell softly onto her shoulders. Either the cool air or excitement painted her cheeks pink.

Before Scottie could make her mouth—or her brain—work, Willow said: "Sorry I'm late. It took me a few minutes to coax the heater into working without making weird whale noises."

"Totally worth the wait," Scottie said before she could stop herself. "You look amazing."

The color of Willow's cheeks deepened. "Thank you. From what little I can see, you clean up pretty well yourself."

Scottie unbuttoned her coat and opened it with a dramatic flair, as if she were doing a striptease.

Despite the cool air, her body warmed as Willow's gaze trailed down her suit.

"You probably can't tell in this light, but the suit isn't black; it's a dark green, so we're matching." *Shit.* She was babbling. Scottie snapped her mouth shut.

"Oh, I can tell," Willow murmured. "I like the tie."

"I thought I'd lean into the holiday spirit." Scottie smoothed her fingers over the little red Santa hats and the tiny silver snowflakes on her green tie.

Willow's gaze seemed to track the movement of Scottie's fingers. "Good choice."

They stood next to the car for several moments, looking at each other.

Finally, Willow cleared her throat. "We should get going. Do you want to drive?" She held up the keys.

Scottie nodded, glad for the distraction that focusing on traffic would provide. "Absolutely." She took the keys.

Both of them were careful not to let their fingers brush. But it didn't matter. The space between them felt charged with electricity anyway, making Scottie's skin prickle.

She escorted Willow around the car and opened the passenger door for her.

"Thank you." Willow gracefully climbed inside and tucked her dress in as she sat.

"My pleasure," Scottie replied, meaning it. It felt special to be the one who got to open doors for Willow—as if this really were a date. She closed the door, careful not to catch the hem. Once she was settled behind the wheel and had put on her seat belt, she glanced over to make sure Willow was buckled in too.

Willow looked over and gave her a small smile—a little nervous but genuine. Her dress shimmered in the dashboard light, making the green flecks in her hazel eyes stand out.

Scottie's breath caught again. God, if she kept spending time with Willow, she really needed a firewall around her heart. Despite her best intentions not to get involved with anyone after her big breakup, she was starting to become smitten with Willow—and she wasn't sure there was anything she could do to stop it.

The lobby of the Rosebud Hotel looked like the set of a Hallmark holiday movie.

A massive Christmas tree stretched nearly to the chandelier on the ceiling. A garland dotted with pine cones and red berries ran along the length of the reception desk, and a pair of nutcracker statues flanked the elevators.

Willow's heels clicked on the polished marble as she followed Scottie to the coat check.

Scottie helped her out of her coat, then handed it to the attendant, along with her own.

While Scottie was busy pocketing the claim ticket, Willow took the opportunity to look her over in better light. The dark-green suit jacket was tailored close at the waist, giving her an athletic silhouette. Her black leather dress shoes were polished to a shine, reflecting the fairy lights running along the edge of the coat check counter. She looked effortlessly dapper, yet the tie with the tiny Santa hats added a bit of her typical playfulness and her goofy charm.

When Scottie turned toward her, Willow quickly tore her gaze away.

A sign saying *Kudos Entertainment holiday party* guided them toward the ballroom the company had rented.

Scottie paused at its double doors that stood open. "Ready to brave the party?"

"No," Willow said honestly.

Scottie gave her an encouraging smile. "Don't worry. I'll be your emotional support IT tech." She crooked her arm in a gesture that was equally playful and chivalrous. "Shall we?"

Willow slipped her hand onto the bend of Scottie's arm. The contact sent a subtle buzz through her body, but she knew it had nothing to do with static. The fabric of Scottie's suit jacket was smooth beneath her fingers, and the warmth of Scottie's skin filtered through. She took a deep breath and followed Scottie in.

The sound of the party hit her first. A live band that took up one side of the stage played a jazzy version of "Let It Snow." Animated conversations, laughter, and the clinking of glasses reverberated through the large space.

Round tables draped with white linen and folded red napkins took up most of the room, each with a centerpiece of holly and flickering LED candles. Strings of fairy lights trailed down the ballroom's columns, looking like falling snow.

A buffet stretched along one wall, and a dessert station with a chocolate fountain had been set up in the corner. The open bar next to it was a hive of activity. The scent of pine mixed with roasted herbs and spiced cider.

When Scottie and Willow entered, several of their colleagues paused their conversations and looked over.

Willow gripped Scottie's arm more tightly. "Did I mention I hate parties? Everyone's staring!"

Scottie leaned closer. "If they're staring, it's only because you look stunning," she whispered, her breath warm on Willow's ear.

Heat rose to Willow's cheeks.

Most of their colleagues were staring at Scottie, though, probably because she was wearing a suit and tie.

Willow held her head up high. She admired Scottie for walking into a company event, where their CEO, COO, and all the VPs would be present, in a suit, totally at ease with who she was and not caring what anyone else thought.

A waiter walked past with a tray of champagne flutes, and Scottie snagged two glasses. "Or did you want something from the bar?"

"Champagne is fine, thanks." Willow took the glass Scottie held out.

Scottie clinked her glass to Willow's. "To you—for making it through your first quarter at Kudos and the busiest time of year."

Especially without ruining every single electronic device in Operations. She did deserve some champagne for that. Willow took a sip.

Scottie pointed across the room to a quiet spot near one wall. "Think we can claim it before anyone else does?"

"Ooh, let's try."

As they made their way toward it, people greeted Scottie with warm smiles.

Scottie introduced Willow to anyone she didn't already know, but she didn't pause long enough for them to be sucked into small talk.

Finally, they reached their quiet spot, and Willow relaxed as they people-watched.

After a while, they went to the buffet. Scottie piled her plate high with a little bit of everything, while Willow took a tiny quiche and a fig jam crostini, mostly so she'd have something to do with her hands.

Scottie eyed her plate. "You'd better load up. Mr. Haggerty likes to give a presentation of every company event throughout the year. We'll be here for a while."

Willow added some mashed potatoes, prime rib, and roasted veggies to her plate. "Does this look like I'll survive the night?"

Scottie chuckled. "Your chances just went up."

They found a table at the back of the room. Scottie pulled out a chair for her and waited for Willow to sit before taking a seat too.

The attention warmed Willow to the core. Was Scottie this chivalrous with all her female friends, or was she treating the office party as a date?

Just as Willow reached for her cutlery, footsteps approached their table. "Willow! Scottie!" A familiar voice cut through the background noise.

When Willow looked up, Barb was making her way toward them, beaming broadly, her husband in tow.

They stood to hug her.

"It's great to see you." Willow gave her former colleague a tight squeeze. "How's retirement treating you?"

"Blissfully! I get to sleep in every day!"

"And by 'sleep in,' she means getting up at seven," George threw in.

They all laughed.

Barb hugged Scottie too, then moved back a step to take them both in. "Aww, you two look so cute together!"

Together? Did she assume they were a couple, just because they were both wearing green?

Neither of them corrected her, though.

She really needed to find out if this was a date. But what if it wasn't? Asking would make things awkward.

Barb pointed at the two empty chairs. "Do you mind if we sit with you? Unless we'd be crashing your date," she added and looked back and forth between them with a knowing smirk.

Scottie flashed her a smile. "There's always room for you, Barb." Again, she didn't correct Barb's assumption. She steadied Willow's chair with one hand and waited for her to take a seat before she settled next to her.

Barb caught Willow's gaze with a broad grin and waggled her eyebrows.

Willow spread her napkin across her lap and pretended not to see it. *Oh God.* She was trapped at a table with the company's biggest matchmaker, at the office holiday party that might just be a date.

Half an hour later, not a scrap of food remained on Scottie's plate. She leaned back in her chair, letting the hum of chatter in the ballroom wash over her while stealing glances at Willow.

The flickering LED candles at the center of their table threw a golden glow across her fair features and made the satiny fabric of her dress shimmer. Now that she was no longer wearing her coat, the capped sleeves revealed her slim, graceful arms.

"Go on, you two. Don't let us old folks stop you." Barb's voice pulled Scottie from her near trance.

Scottie turned her head. "Stop us from what?"

The older woman gestured toward the dance floor.

Only now did Scottie realize the band had eased into a softer, slower song, and couples were getting up to dance.

Scottie was as rusty at dancing as she was at dating. Aside from that dance-off at bingo night, she hadn't danced in ages. But she longed to hold Willow close, even if it was only for the length of one song. This might be the only chance she would ever get. She tilted her head and gave her a questioning look, trying hard not to appear too eager. "What do you think? Would you like to dance?"

Willow hesitated just long enough to make Scottie's heart sink. "I'm not a great dancer."

"Perfect," Scottie said. "Neither am I. We can be awkward together."

Willow gave her a reluctant smile. "All right. Lead the way, then."

Scottie rose, her heartbeat quickening. She tried to keep her cool as she placed her hand in the small of Willow's back and guided her past the other tables. It was just a dance at an office party. Willow hadn't corrected Barb's assumption that they were on a date, though. Did that mean she really considered it one? Or had she decided that it was simply easier to let Barb think whatever she wanted?

The dance floor wasn't crowded, only a handful of couples moving in a slow rhythm.

Scottie held out her hand.

Willow hesitated. She glanced around as if searching for something but didn't seem to find it.

Scottie gave her a quizzical look, still offering her hand.

Finally, Willow placed her fingers on top.

A zap shot through Scottie's palm, and a visible arc of light crackled between their clasped hands.

"I'm so sorry!" Willow tried to pull back, but Scottie held on.

"It's okay. I'm getting used to your electric personality." Scottie sent her a gentle smile. Was that what Willow had been looking for—something to ground herself so she wouldn't zap her?

Willow stared at her for a moment, then her fingers relaxed in Scottie's steady grip.

Tentatively, Scottie pulled her closer. A rare moment of insecurity overcame her as she worried about stepping on Willow's toes and where to put her hand, not wanting to make Willow uncomfortable.

Then Willow settled her hand onto Scottie's shoulder, and everything seemed to fall into place.

Scottie eased her hand onto the small of Willow's back. The soft fabric warmed beneath her fingers, as if Willow's body was reacting to her touch.

They found their rhythm immediately. Willow moved with elegant grace, guiding Scottie along with subtle shifts of her body as if she were the one leading.

"You lied," Scottie murmured.

Willow looked at her with wide eyes. "What?"

"About not being a great dancer."

Color returned to Willow's cheeks. "You're not so bad yourself."

Scottie knew she was clumsy compared to Willow's elegance, but Willow didn't seem to mind at all.

They didn't try any fancy moves, no polished steps, because Scottie hadn't danced in years. But she also hadn't felt so alive in just as long.

The hem of Willow's dress swirled around them, the fabric rustling against Scottie's legs with every turn.

She deeply breathed in the scent of something apricot. A strand of Willow's hair tickled Scottie's cheek, and she realized they had moved closer, barely two inches between them now. Willow fit against her so naturally, it made Scottie's head spin. The brush of Willow's leg against her own sent heat spiraling through her. Every nerve in her body was attuned to Willow's closeness, the warmth of her hand on Scottie's shoulder, the slide of the silky fabric beneath her fingers.

The other couples and the ballroom seemed to disappear as they slowly swayed together.

Scottie had no idea how long they danced like that. One song? Two? Maybe three?

Every now and then, Willow's hand slid down a little, from her shoulder to her arm, then back up again, almost as if in an unconscious caress. Scottie had left her suit jacket at the table, and with only the thin fabric of her dress shirt between them, it was as if Willow's fingertips were trailing over her bare skin.

She swallowed hard. Her pulse beat faster than the music. Her eyes fell shut, and she struggled not to press her cheek against Willow's—or her mouth to the tempting curve of her lips.

Abruptly, the bright stage lights came up, and the band stopped playing.

"All right, everyone!" Mr. Haggerty's voice cut through the haze in Scottie's mind. He tapped the microphone. "It's time for the Secret Santa gifts! Please head over to the Secret Santa table and open your present."

Willow's hand slipped from Scottie's shoulder, leaving behind a lingering tingle.

Reluctantly, Scottie let go of Willow's hand. Their moment of closeness was over, and it was all she could do not to stumble on unsteady legs as she followed Willow across the room.

The rustle of gift wrap and the excited squeals of her colleagues seemed to come from a great distance. Willow tried to tell herself it was the glass of champagne or the wine she'd had with dinner that was making her head spin, but she knew it was Scottie's intoxicating closeness.

Dancing with Scottie, being held close, had made her feel safe, beautiful, and electrified all at once. For the first time in her life, the latter didn't seem like a bad thing.

Maybe she really could learn not to hate parties.

The stray thought of her overstimulated brain made her chuckle.

Scottie smiled as if by reflex. "What?"

"Oh, nothing," Willow said quickly. "Just looking forward to opening my gift."

Scottie nodded. "There's mine." She pulled a small gift bag with her name on it from the pile of presents.

Willow's gaze was focused on Scottie's broad hands, the strong fingers that had rested on her back just a minute ago. It took her a few moments to shift her attention to the object Scottie pulled from the bag.

It was a miniature arcade machine, a six-inch retro-style cabinet with tiny buttons and the smallest joystick Willow had ever seen.

"Ooh, that's cool!" Scottie studied it from all sides.

Willow laughed. "Aww, that's adorable!"

Scottie held it out to her. "Here. You love retro stuff. Want it?"

Willow stared at her, touched that Scottie would offer it to her. But she couldn't accept it. She would find a way to make it short-circuit before the new year. "No, no, you keep it. I have a present of my own." She finally spied her name on one of the tags and pulled a small, wrapped box from the pile.

Carefully, Willow peeled back the paper and opened the lid.

Inside, nestled on a velvet cushion, was a wristwatch. With its white face and a chocolate-brown leather strap, it was elegant but understated. Something that Willow could have seen herself wear—if she had been able to wear a watch.

She had tried as a teen, but it had always started to lose time immediately, then stopped working altogether within a week. After trying half a dozen different watches, she had finally given up.

"Nice," Scottie said. "You don't have one, do you?"

Willow bit her lip. "No."

"It's perfect, then."

"Yeah." Willow forced a small smile and tried to shake off the gloomy thoughts about draining batteries and tech disasters. All she wanted was to enjoy this evening with Scottie—and maybe to dance with her again.

But apparently, their CEO had other plans. As soon as each employee had opened their Secret Santa gift and everyone had returned to their tables, he reached for the microphone again, launched into a speech, and presented a slideshow of important company milestones throughout the year. Photos from product launches, anniversaries, the company BBQ, and even Barb's retirement party flashed across the big screen above the stage.

"And now," Mr. Haggerty drew out the words dramatically, "it's time for the coveted Kudos Entertainment company awards! First up: the Golden Headset Award, awarded for bravely fielding the most ridiculous call from a customer. It goes to"—he nodded at the band to play a drum roll—"Brent Walters from Customer Support!"

A bearded guy rose from one of the tables and bowed. Under the cheers of his colleagues, he went up onstage and accepted the award.

After handing out several other awards for "accomplishments" like holding the longest Zoom meeting, killing most office plants, and having the densest sticky note jungle along their screen, Mr. Haggerty finally made it to the last award on his list. "Last but certainly not least, it's my honor to present the award for causing most paper jams and other tech glitches!"

The band played another dramatic drum roll.

"And the award goes to...Willow Greene from Operations!"

Laughter erupted around Willow. Her colleagues clapped, cheered, and whistled.

Willow sat frozen, the noise roaring through her ears.

"Where is she?" Mr. Haggerty looked around, shading his eyes with his hand. "Come on up and accept your prize!"

Barb gave her a nudge that finally made Willow rise.

She caught a glimpse of Scottie, who gave her a look of sympathy as Willow stepped away from the table.

The walk to the stage felt as if she were caught in one of her nightmares. Cheeks burning with humiliation, she stumbled up the three steps. Her thundering heartbeat almost managed to drown out the cheering of her colleagues.

The CEO held up a small bronze plaque shaped like a printer with smoke rising from it. "We appreciate your valiant battle against technology." He stuck out his free hand, clearly expecting her to shake it as if she had really won a coveted award.

Willow's gaze darted around. Just like earlier, on the dance floor, there were no metal objects in sight. Unless she wanted to rip the microphone from his other hand, there was nothing for her to ground herself on.

Mr. Haggerty stuck out his free hand a little farther.

She had no choice. Hoping for the best, she reached for it.

A painful jolt raced up her arm.

"Ah!" He yelped and jerked back, looking at her as if she had kicked him in the shin. The microphone squealed with feedback.

More laughter rippled through the ballroom.

Even Willow's ears were burning now. She grabbed the plaque, mumbled an apology, and fled from the stage.

The faces around her blurred as she rushed past them. She caught glimpses of laughing expressions and clapping hands.

Someone from Operations patted her back as she passed.

Then one face swam into focus—Celeste. She wasn't clapping or cheering. Willow's boss sat ramrod straight at one of the tables, her perfectly glossed lips pressed into a thin line and her arms crossed over her elegant dress. Her gaze zeroed in on the plaque in Willow's hands as if it were a personal affront to her and her entire department.

A few tables over, the COO sat with the other higher-ups of the company. He wasn't clapping either. He squinted at her from beneath pinched brows.

Willow ducked her head and hurried past, back to the relative safety of her table.

"Hey, you okay?" Scottie whispered as Willow sank onto her seat. She rested one arm along the back of Willow's chair, as if wanting to engulf her in an embrace.

Willow couldn't even look at her. She didn't want to see the expression of pity or the curious questions on Scottie's face. "Yeah. I just need some air." She couldn't stay here for even one second longer, so she grabbed her clutch and jumped to her feet.

"Wait! Let me—"

But Willow was already rushing toward the exit, eyes burning with the tears she struggled to hold back.

Chapter 30

Willow didn't pause to collect her coat from the attendant. The cold air outside hit her like a wall, but she didn't stop. She was halfway across the parking lot when she remembered that she had picked up Scottie and couldn't just leave her behind.

Her steps slowed as she tried to think. What was she supposed to do now? She couldn't go back inside.

By the time she'd reached her car, she still didn't have an answer. Her hand hovered over the door handle, then dropped to her side.

The streetlights cast dim pools of light across the asphalt, and the faint hum of cars in the distance filled her ears as she tried to slow her racing heartbeat.

She realized she was still clutching the bronze plaque of the jammed printer, its edges digging into her skin.

Before she could hurl it across the parking lot, hurried footsteps approached.

"Willow?" Scottie's breathless voice came from behind her.

Reluctantly, Willow turned. "I'm here."

Scottie jogged toward her, Willow's coat clutched in one hand. She held it out to her.

"Thank you." Willow shrugged into the coat without making eye contact and stuffed the damn plaque into one of its deep pockets, never wanting to see it again.

"Are you okay?" Scottie asked softly.

"Yeah. Just a little queasy. Probably drank too much." Willow pulled her car key from her clutch. "Why don't you take my car home? I'll order an Uber. Please tell Barb and George I wasn't feeling well."

But when she tried to press the key into Scottie's hand, Scottie refused to take it. "No. I'm not letting you go home alone when you're clearly upset. Talk to me. Please. What's going on?"

"Nothing's going on," Willow said, still unable to look at her. "I just had a bit too much champagne."

"Bullshit." Scottie's tone managed to be gentle yet no-nonsense at the same time. "This isn't about the champagne. It's about the award, isn't it?"

Willow stared at her feet.

"Oh, Willow." Scottie reached out as if about to squeeze her arm but then stopped. "Forget about Mr. Haggerty's silly award. No one takes them seriously. A couple of years back, I got a medal for most coffee being consumed in a single workday. It's just a joke."

A rush of emotions swept over Willow—anger, frustration, and the raw ache of no one understanding, not even Scottie. Her gaze jerked up, and she glared at Scottie with burning eyes. "It's not just a joke to me! This is my life!" She slammed her fist against her own chest. "Printers jamming, batteries draining, computers glitching..."

"Yeah, I know you had a string of bad luck with tech lately, but—"

"No! You don't understand. It's not just lately, and it's not just bad luck!" Then she realized what she'd blurted out and snapped her mouth shut.

"What do you mean?" Scottie took a step closer and reached for Willow's hand, even when she tried to withdraw, afraid of zapping her again.

When the expected jolt went through them, Scottie held on, never even flinching.

"Please," she said softly. She tilted her head in that characteristic Scottie way, ready to listen. "Talk to me. I want to understand."

Her words broke down every barrier Willow had erected. She was so tired of hiding her secret, of carrying its burden alone. Her shoulders slumped, and she hung on to Scottie's hand as if for dear life. "I break things," she whispered. "Electronics. Computers, printers, cash registers, TVs...anything."

"You mean...by zapping them?"

"No. Yes. I mean, that's part of it. I seem to build up more static electricity than other people, but it's more than that. Devices just start glitching whenever I'm around, especially when I'm anxious or upset—

sometimes without me even touching them. Something inside me drains their batteries or fries their parts, and I can't stop it. I'm like a walking, talking electromagnetic pulse, destroying everything in my path."

And now she had likely destroyed whatever it was that was growing between them too. Scottie probably thought she was making things up.

Silence stretched between them. Scottie didn't say anything for several moments.

"Jesus," Scottie finally whispered.

Willow's heart plummeted. God, how naive had she been—to think, even for a second, that Scottie might believe her? That she could do this... date Scottie for real? She ducked her head and tried to pull away.

But Scottie held on.

"I know how ridiculous that sounds," Willow said without looking at her. "Like an episode of *The X-Files* or something."

"Hey." Scottie squeezed her hand. "I love *The X-Files*."

Willow slowly raised her gaze. A spark of hope grew in her, despite her half-hearted attempts to smother it. "You do?"

"Yeah, of course. I mean...Gillian Anderson...hello!" Scottie let out a playful whistle.

"No, I mean... You believe me? You don't think it's weird...that *I'm* weird or—"

Scottie stopped her with another squeeze of her hand. "Of course I believe you. Why would you make something like that up? And if you're weird, that just means you're a perfect fit. Um, for Portland, I mean."

A raw sound escaped Willow, and even she couldn't tell if it was a laugh, a sob, or an attempt to whisper Scottie's name. She covered her mouth with her free hand, trying to hold everything inside, but it was useless. The tears she'd been fighting broke free and ran down her chilled cheeks in hot tracks.

Scottie pulled her close by their joined hands, then let go and wrapped her arms around Willow in a protective embrace, shielding her from the world.

Willow's clutch slipped from her fingers and hit the pavement. She clung to Scottie with both hands, pressed against her solid form, and buried her face against Scottie's dress shirt. Little broken noises tore from her throat as she sobbed against Scottie's shoulder—first at the pain and loneliness of hiding all her life, then at the relief of Scottie believing her, of being accepted…of being made to feel normal.

The damp warmth of Willow's tears soaked through the fabric at Scottie's shoulder, but she didn't care about what it did to her dress shirt. She only cared about Willow.

A lump formed in her throat as she held her close. The pain bubbling up from deep inside Willow made her want to cry right along with her.

Willow trembled against her and pressed her face harder against Scottie's shoulder.

Scottie tightened her hold. She wanted to shield her from everything that had hurt her, but she knew all she could do was be there for her now.

Gasping sobs shook Willow as years of held-in pain and shame seemed to pour out.

Scottie rubbed her back in slow, soothing circles. "It's okay," she whispered softly. "You're okay."

God, she couldn't imagine what Willow must have been through over the years. As she held Willow close, Scottie's mind began fitting pieces together like a puzzle. So many things about Willow made sense now:

Her second, old-school phone. The desk drawer full of spare batteries. Her classic car with the bare minimum of electronics. Her reluctance to take a selfie with Scottie's phone. Her habit of touching metal objects and always trying to pay in cash. Why Scottie had gotten zapped when she'd touched her…or kissed her in the elevator.

Suddenly, it all became clear.

After a while, Willow stilled against her. Her shoulders stopped heaving, and the heart-wrenching sobs faded into uneven breathing. Finally, she pulled back and wiped at her cheeks with the back of her hands. In the parking lot light, her eyes were red and her face blotchy, yet to Scottie, she was still beautiful.

"Sorry," Willow mumbled without looking at her. "I didn't mean to do that. I don't know what's wrong with me."

"Nothing." Scottie gently touched her fingers to Willow's chin and lifted it so Willow would make eye contact. "Absolutely nothing."

Willow stared at her. Her lower lip started to tremble, and then the tears came again, softer this time.

Scottie drew her close once more.

When Willow finally raised her head off Scottie's shoulder, Scottie dug through her coat pockets and offered her a clean tissue.

"Thanks." Willow's voice was hoarse. She blew her nose and wiped her cheeks again.

"You held that in for a long time, didn't you?"

Willow nodded. "My entire life."

"Oh Willow." Scottie resisted the urge to pull her close again, not sure if it was what Willow wanted. Instead, she bent, picked up the clutch that had tumbled to the ground earlier, and handed it back. "So you've always been that way?"

"Pretty much. We think it runs in the family. After my grandmother died, we found a drawer full of dead watches. I instantly knew why. I can't wear a watch either."

So Willow's grandmother had lived her entire life without telling anyone, not even her family? Scottie couldn't imagine how lonely that must have been. While Willow hadn't quite chosen that route, she had kept people at arm's length too—and now Scottie understood why. "Thank you for telling me. I know that took a lot of courage. I just wish you'd have told me sooner. I could have helped."

Willow shoved the tissue into her coat pocket as if deciding she was done with the tears. She adamantly shook her head. "No. I don't want your help." Her voice became stronger, more urgent. "I don't want to be a problem you have to fix."

"You're not! You're so much more to me." The admission tore out of Scottie before she could stop it, and her tone left no doubt about how she meant it.

The words hung between them in the cool, damp air.

Willow stared at her, eyes wide, lips parted.

Oh shit. Scottie had no clue how to take it back. Truth be told, she didn't want to. But this was also not the moment to burden Willow with her feelings, which she likely didn't return. "Sorry. I shouldn't have said that."

Willow kept staring at her. "But...did you mean it?"

Scottie's throat was too tight to speak, so she just nodded.

"You're really special to me too," Willow confessed in a whisper. "But I'm not sure I can do this." She gestured back and forth between them. "I'm as bad with relationships as I am with electronics. I never managed to make either last—and this time, with you, I really want to."

Scottie's heart leaped hard against her ribs. She gave Willow a tremulous smile. "You're in luck. I've been told I'm great at both. At least that's what I thought before Tanya sat me down and—"

"Forget Tanya!" Willow said, a fierce fire in her red-rimmed eyes. "She was a fool for letting you go. I don't want to hurt you like she did, but I'm not sure what would end up hurting you more: not even trying or investing your heart and it not working out."

"I think you know me well enough by now to have a good idea what option I'd choose, right?" Scottie asked softly.

Willow nodded. She drew a shaky breath and raised her gaze to meet Scottie's. "Then we should...maybe give it a try?"

Wild hope swirled through Scottie, but she needed to be sure they were on the same page. "You're not just talking about another trial date, are you?"

Willow shook her head. "No. I'm talking about a real one."

Everything around them went very still. The distant hum of traffic seemed to fade away.

Scottie's pulse tripped, her heart hammering, wild and full of wonder. The corners of her mouth lifted into a beaming smile. "I'd love that."

"Me too," Willow whispered.

They stood in the middle of the hotel parking lot and smiled at each other. The same emotions spinning through Scottie were reflected on Willow's face: disbelief, nervousness, but mostly joy.

Scottie lifted a hand and tenderly brushed away a tear that still clung to Willow's cheek.

Willow's lashes fluttered, and she leaned into the touch.

"I know this isn't how it's supposed to go," Scottie murmured, still drinking in the delicate curve of Willow's cheekbones, the vulnerability in her eyes, and the fullness of her lips. "I mean, people don't usually kiss *before* the first date, but..." She realized she was rambling and cut herself off. "May I kiss you?"

"No!"

Oh. Scottie's shoulders slumped.

"I mean, yes! Yes! But wait! First, I have to…" Willow put her hand on the Civic.

Scottie blinked and tried to grasp what Willow meant, even though her brain felt a bit hazy. "But I touched you already." She gestured at the soft cheek she had cradled a moment ago. "No one got zapped, so I think we can skip that step."

"Oh. Right." Willow's brain didn't seem to be in full working order either. "Well, can't be too safe. I really don't want to hurt you."

"You won't," Scottie whispered, sensing that Willow wasn't just talking about a little zap. She leaned in slowly, her gaze fixed on Willow's face, taking in the way her pupils widened and her breathing sped up as the distance between them narrowed to a mere inch.

Warm puffs teased Scottie's mouth, increasing her anticipation. The air around them felt charged, but not with static.

Their lips met, gentle and tentative at first.

This time, there was no painful jolt. Just the softness of Willow's mouth beneath hers.

Scottie lifted one hand to rest it in the small of Willow's back and pull her closer as she deepened the kiss.

Willow parted her lips. A tiny noise escaped her. She slid one hand up the front of Scottie's coat and curled her fingers into the lapel.

Their bodies fit together as perfectly as they had on the dance floor.

Scottie touched her tongue to Willow's, then—at Willow's enthusiastic response—caressed it with sensual strokes. Willow tasted faintly of champagne, chocolate from the dessert station, and something intoxicating that made Scottie's head spin.

When they finally broke apart, Willow's face was flushed, but this time, it wasn't from crying. Her red-rimmed eyes shone bright, and her lips curved into a happy grin.

Scottie immediately wanted to kiss her again.

But before she could, rain began to fall in a steady stream, soaking them both.

"Damn. I think that's our cue to stop." Scottie nodded toward the hotel. "Do you want to go back inside?"

Willow shook her head, her gaze not on the sky but on Scottie. "I want to stay right here and kiss you again."

Scottie didn't hesitate for a second. She cupped Willow's face, cradling it tenderly between her palms, leaned forward, and kissed her again, rain be damned.

By the time Willow made it home an hour later, she was soaked to the bone. Her wool coat clung to her like wet seaweed; her hair was plastered to her skull in dripping strands, and her pumps made little *squelch-squelch* sounds with every step as she entered the house.

She barely managed to kick them off before Fiona appeared at the end of the hall in her pajamas. "Hey. I was starting to worry. You don't usually stay at an office party this lo—" Then she took a closer look at Willow and stopped dead. "Oh my God! What happened?"

"It's called rain," Willow replied. She wasn't yet ready to share the details of her evening, not even with her sister. Not before she'd had the time to sort through the whirlwind of emotions twirling through her. Most of what had happened tonight was so completely out of character for her—breaking down and crying in Scottie's arms, telling her about her weird effect on tech, throwing caution to the wind and suggesting a real date, and kissing her in the middle of a hotel parking lot…and then again…and again at Scottie's front door.

"Ever heard of umbrellas?" Fiona looked her up and down. "And why did the rain smear your lipstick and make your lips all puffy?"

Heat shot into Willow's chilled cheeks. "Uh, I… I'll explain in a minute. But first, I need a hot shower." Or maybe a cold one. She slipped past Fiona and headed down the hall toward the bathroom.

Fiona rushed after her. "Oh no. I'm not letting you escape before you tell me what happened." She followed her into the bathroom and sat on the closed toilet lid while Willow stripped off her dripping coat. "Tell me everything. Start from the beginning. How was the party?"

Willow peeled off the rest of her clothes and stepped beneath the hot spray, buying herself a few seconds. "A disaster. They gave me an award for causing the most paper jams."

"What? Who would do that?"

"Our CEO. He thought it was funny, and so did everyone else." Willow's cheeks burned at the memory, and she knew it wasn't from the hot water. "I left."

"Oh, Will." Fiona sounded seconds away from pushing back the shower curtain and climbing in to give her a hug.

Quickly, Willow added, "Scottie followed me out. I told her everything. About me. My tech thing."

Fiona let out a loud gasp. "You told her? Wow. Did she freak out? Give you a rational, sciencey IT explanation?"

"No. She just...believed me." Willow still marveled at it. Scottie hadn't doubted her, hadn't provided alternative explanations for the weird phenomenon, hadn't even asked a ton of questions. She had simply accepted it as if it were the most normal thing in the world. "She said there's nothing wrong with me. And I just...I completely lost it. I cried all over her like a big, snotty mess."

For a moment, Fiona was uncharacteristically quiet. "You...you cried? On her shoulder?"

Willow could barely believe it herself. "Literally."

"How did she react?" Fiona asked.

"She was wonderful. Just held me." Willow could still feel Scottie's strong arms around her and her warm shoulder against her face. "And she said I'm so much more to her than a problem she has to fix."

Fiona sucked in an audible breath. "Ooh, this is getting good."

"Fi!"

"Don't Fi me! Tell me what happened next!"

"She... We... We kissed."

Fiona squealed. "Yes! Yes! Yes! How was it?"

Willow shut off the water and reached for a towel while she searched for the right words. "It was...everything. Unexpected. Tender. Hot. Wonderful." She swallowed. "Right."

But another word came to mind too: *terrifying*. Because if their very first real kiss already felt like this, how was she supposed to ever recover if things didn't work out?

A shiver went through her. She wrapped herself in her fluffy towel and stepped out of the shower.

Fiona paused in the middle of her victory dance. "What happened then? You didn't run, did you?"

"No. We talked, and I drove her home." Willow reached for a second towel and wrapped it around her wet hair.

Fiona studied her through the steam that filled the bathroom. "How do you feel?"

"Remember when you took me bungee jumping for my twenty-first birthday?" Willow asked.

"Of course I remember." Fiona laughed. "You stood on the platform forever, nearly peeing your pants, and then screamed the entire way down, but afterward, you admitted it was fun."

"I didn't scream," Willow said in mock offense. "Okay, maybe a little. I feel kinda like that now. Like I'm stepping off the edge, loving the rush, but not entirely sure the cord is going to hold."

"Oh, Willow. You're falling, aren't you?"

They both knew she wasn't talking about bungee jumping anymore.

Willow swallowed heavily. "I could…if I let myself. She's really special, Fi."

"I figured. Otherwise, you never would have told her about the tech thing. I still can't believe you did."

A shaky laugh escaped Willow. "Me neither."

Fiona gently grasped Willow's bare shoulders and gave her an earnest big-sister look. "Please don't run from this. Give your hot IT lady a chance."

Willow no longer protested Fiona calling Scottie that. After all, Scottie was hot—and if her tech affliction didn't mess things up, maybe she really would be Willow's. "I'm trying to. We're going on a date tomorrow—a real one."

Another squeal from Fiona nearly pierced Willow's eardrums.

"That is, if I don't lose my hearing before that," Willow muttered.

Fiona squeezed her shoulders. "I'm so happy for you!"

"Hey, I said *date*, not *wedding*!"

"Still, it's a big deal."

Yeah, it really was. She hadn't been on a date in ages, and the last one she'd been on had been a disaster. "Any sage advice?"

"Just one thing." Fiona squeezed her shoulders one last time, then let go and sauntered to the door. "Stop worrying about the bungee cord and just enjoy the fall."

Chapter 31

Scottie had slept like a baby after company-wide system crashes and executives screaming about lost data, but she'd been up for most of the previous night, mentally replaying their kiss in the parking lot…and each one after.

But her mind had also shown her flashes of Willow's tear-streaked face and the broken little noises that had escaped her when she had cried in her arms. Scottie's insides still clenched whenever she thought about it.

Today, she wanted Willow to be able to forget about that. She didn't want her to have to worry about tech glitches or draining batteries even for a second, so she had paced her apartment for hours, trying to come up with the perfect fully analog date—no screens, no Internet, no digital devices; just them.

When Willow stopped in the middle of the Memory Den parking lot, her lips forming an excited "ooh," Scottie had a feeling her hours of thinking and searching had paid off.

The two-story former warehouse spanned an entire city block. Its pale gray facade didn't look like much. A spray-painted mural of a giant tomato, a cucumber, and a corn cob stretched around its side, indicating its beginnings as a produce distribution center in the 1930s.

But above the narrow flight of metal stairs was a sign that read *Memory Den – Vintage Mall*, and Willow stared up at it as if she was about to enter a cathedral or another place of worship.

"A vintage mall?" She glanced back at Scottie.

Scottie nodded. "An entire place full of retro stuff. I thought we could go on a treasure hunt together."

"Let's go!" Willow was already heading up the stairs.

Laughing, Scottie followed her inside.

The space was huge! Hundreds of vendor booths were lined up along wide aisles.

The air smelled faintly of old leather and mothballs, but Willow didn't even seem to notice.

She turned in a slow circle, taking it all in. Her face held an expression of childlike wonder as she scanned racks of vintage clothing and shelves full of porcelain figurines, rotary phones, dolls, leather-bound books, and lamps with tasseled shades.

Each booth was a world of its own, carefully curated by its owner. Some looked like museum displays, while others were a chaotic mix of knickknacks.

There was even a fully equipped kitchen from the 1950s, with a checkered floor, vinyl chairs, mint-green Formica countertops, and a white fridge.

They wandered around and browsed the stalls for an hour, then realized there was another level with even more displays upstairs.

"Imagine the stories each item in here could tell," Willow murmured, entirely immersed. She traced the delicate purple flowers on a teapot with her fingertip.

Goose bumps prickled up Scottie's arms. Who knew browsing a vintage mall could be so sensual! She tore her gaze away and tried to focus on the interesting items around her.

One jumped out at her, its neon color screaming for attention.

"Ooh, look! I found your Christmas present!" Grinning, Scottie pointed at a lime-green polyester tracksuit.

Laughter burst from Willow. The clear, bright sound cut through the background chatter of other vintage treasure hunters.

Scottie watched her, completely captivated. Making Willow laugh was quickly becoming her favorite pastime.

Willow's often reserved face was unguarded, and her usually tense shoulders had relaxed. "Don't you dare buy that!" She grabbed Scottie's hand and dragged her away from the ugly tracksuit.

There was no spark this time, at least not the electric kind. But the feel of Willow's soft skin and the graceful fingers she had trustingly slipped into her grasp set off a warm buzz that hummed through Scottie's body.

Scottie stared at her for a moment, then continued on to the next display like that, fingers intertwined, pretending it was no big deal when her racing heart said it definitely was.

After a few steps, Willow seemed to become aware that she was still holding on to Scottie's hand—or maybe that she had touched Scottie without zapping her.

"It's okay," Scottie said before Willow could let go. "Looks like today isn't a high-static day. But even if it was, I wouldn't care. I don't want you to ever hesitate to touch me just because of a little zap. Unless, of course, you would rather not get zapped yourself."

"Me?" Willow laughed. It sounded a little shaky. "No. I'm used to it."

"But you're also used to not touching people, aren't you? I don't want you to constantly rein yourself in around me."

Willow swallowed. "I don't want that either, but it'll take some getting used to."

"Well, we have plenty of opportunity to practice here." Scottie waved at one of the many stalls filled with vintage clothes. She took a silk scarf and looped it around Willow's neck, letting her fingers brush against warm skin.

Willow's pulse jumped under her fingertips, but she didn't pull away. "Practice. Right."

They moved on to the next stall.

Willow stopped in front of a display of hats. "Hold still." When Scottie did, she placed a fedora on her head and adjusted the brim, her expression fully focused, as if it were of the utmost importance that she get the angle just right.

Scottie grinned at how cute she was.

"There." Willow swiped a strand of hair off Scottie's forehead, her knuckle lightly grazing skin. She was holding her breath, then exhaled when no zap happened.

Scottie knew a lifetime of not touching people couldn't be overcome in one afternoon, but maybe this could be a start.

Willow led her over to a rack of clothes and pulled out a tan suede jacket. As she did, she slid her fingers along the metal bar, discharging any static that might have built up.

Scottie doubted Willow even realized she'd done it. It had probably become an ingrained habit over the years.

"Ooh, you'd look good in this." Willow held out the jacket. "Try it on."

"It probably won't fit," Scottie said yet put it on anyway. The suede was butter-soft, even though the fabric bunched a little around her shoulders.

"Here." Willow stepped close, adjusted the collar, and smoothed her hands over the suede.

Scottie suddenly felt as warm as if she were wearing a fur coat. "It's a little small." Her voice came out hoarse.

"Yeah. But it looks great anyway. Check it out." Willow directed her around, toward a gilded mirror leaning against the wall.

"Mm-hmm. Looks wonderful." Scottie's gaze wasn't on the jacket, though; it was on their reflection, framed by the golden edges of the mirror. Willow stood next to her, so close that their bodies were touching from shoulder to hip. She held on to Scottie's arm with one hand.

A flush rose up Willow's neck in the mirror. "I'm practicing, okay?"

"I know. I'm really enjoying it."

Willow blushed again, then bumped Scottie with her hip. "Come on, you. Let's see if we can find any *Star Trek* memorabilia." She helped Scottie take off the jacket, then immediately reached for her hand again.

Smiling, Scottie followed her down the aisle.

By the time they made it back to the car, Willow's feet ached, and it had gotten dark outside. Somehow, they had managed to spend three hours inside the vintage mall!

Her cheeks ached as much as her feet—from laughing and smiling so much. Never before had a date felt so easy, playful, and unguarded. She'd had to be careful for so long, always on the lookout for the next zap or tech glitch, that she'd nearly forgotten what it felt like to relax around someone who wasn't Fiona.

At first, she'd grounded herself any chance she got, but after a while, she had caught herself touching Scottie without brushing her knuckles against a metal rack or shelf beforehand. Still, there hadn't been a single zap.

Was it just luck, or was it because she felt so comfortable around Scottie?

In any case, it was the best date she'd ever been on.

Neither of them had bought much. Willow had admired a portable Underwood typewriter from the 1930s, but with a glance at the price tag, she had moved on. Scottie had bought a fun UFO planter for her succulents, while

Willow had found a denim jumpsuit that would be perfect as a Christmas gift for her sister.

She sank into the passenger seat with a relieved sigh, grateful to be off her feet. "Will I ever get to drive my own car again?"

It wasn't an honest complaint. She enjoyed the blissful grin on Scottie's face too much as she navigated the Civic northward.

Scottie chuckled. "Probably not." With a light, sure grip on the steering wheel, she drove through the dark streets.

Rain began to drum against the windshield. Instantly, memories of kissing Scottie in the hotel parking lot flooded back, and Willow wondered if it would happen every time it rained.

She thought she knew where they were going—probably to Le Pigeon or one of the other restaurants on East Burnside—but Scottie kept driving, weaving through streets Willow didn't recognize.

"Are you sure we're going the right way?" Willow asked after a while, squinting through the rain-splattered windshield. "Sorry my car has no GPS. Feel free to use your phone."

"Don't need it," Scottie said. "I know exactly where I'm going."

Finally, she pulled into a small, empty parking lot on a street that seemed mostly deserted.

Several low structures sat in the darkness beyond, but none of them looked like a restaurant.

"This is where we'll have dinner?" Willow asked.

Scottie chuckled at her puzzled expression. "Yep. Just trust me, okay?"

They got out of the car, and Willow brushed her knuckles against the door to get rid of any static. Scottie had told her she would rather risk getting zapped than not being touched at all, and Willow wholeheartedly agreed. But while it was nice to not have to be so vigilant all the time, she still thought a jolt-free touch was the best alternative of all.

Scottie came over to her side, opened an umbrella, and put Willow's hand on the bend of her arm. "Close your eyes and hold on to me."

That kind of trust had never come easy for Willow, but she forced her eyes closed, allowing Scottie to guide her.

Wet gravel crunched beneath their feet.

Somewhere, a wind chime tinkled, and the rain drummed down on their umbrella.

"Almost there." Scottie gave Willow's hand holding on to her arm a soft squeeze. Then she paused, and the warmth of her hand disappeared.

A door creaked open, and Scottie carefully led her inside.

Humid air hit Willow, carrying the scent of earth and herbs. Where were they?

"Okay, you can look now," Scottie said.

Willow opened her eyes and found herself in a greenhouse.

Strings of fairy lights wound over the metal rafters and through shelving racks, casting a soft glow over hanging baskets of blooming Christmas cacti, trays of herbs, and rows of terracotta pots.

Raindrops beaded on the glass walls, which shimmered in the warm lights. The patter on the roof created a soothing melody.

Farther into the greenhouse, in the middle of the walkway, a small table had been set up among the greenery. A wicker basket and two large thermoses waited in the center.

It was as magical as the rest of their date had been.

Willow stood there for several seconds and absorbed everything.

"Is this okay?" Scottie asked quietly.

Willow whirled around to face her. "Okay? It's wonderful!" Tears stung her eyes. She really had to stop with all the crying. No one wanted to date a crybaby. But all the effort and thought Scottie had put into planning their first real date touched her deeply.

She tugged her hand free, cupped Scottie's face, and kissed her, moving her lips against Scottie's in a tender caress.

Scottie made a sound of pleasure deep in her throat and instantly returned the kiss. Her hands came up and gripped Willow's hips, steadying her, and Willow realized she'd been swaying.

God, the things kissing Scottie did to her.

"Thank you," she whispered against Scottie's mouth.

"My pleasure. Literally." Scottie smiled, then kissed her again before taking her hand and leading her to the table. She pulled the chair out for Willow, who gratefully sank onto it.

"What is this place?" Willow looked around again.

"It's a plant nursery. A friend of mine works here."

Willow grinned up at her as Scottie circled the table. "Do you always take your dates to your friends' workplaces?"

"Not usually." Scottie took a seat across from her. "But a few years ago, I was invited to a wedding that rented out a large greenhouse located on an urban farm that doubled as an event space. It was super romantic, but I knew I wouldn't be able to book something like that for our date on such short notice. So I begged my friend to let us use one of their greenhouses for a couple of hours tonight."

"Whatever you had to promise them in return, I think it was worth it," Willow said.

Scottie looked at her with a dramatically miserable expression. "I'll have to forgo Hawaiian pizza for a month. My friend hates it with a passion."

Willow gasped. "Oh my God. However will you survive?"

"Well, maybe like this..." With a flourish, Scottie flipped back the lid of the wicker basket and unpacked its contents, placing containers of cheese cubes, cherry tomatoes, grapes, slices of salami, veggie sticks, and a loaf of fresh bread on the table. She poured them each a bowl of pumpkin soup from one of the thermoses.

Willow's mouth watered. "Wow. You really went all out. This is perfect."

They ate surrounded by greenery while the rain tapped on the roof. The glass panes around them had fogged up from the humid air, leaving them in an intimate little world of their own.

Once they had fed each other the last grape and the last bit of cheese, Scottie handed her a mug of hot chocolate, which she had poured from the second thermos.

Willow studied her across the rim of her cup. "I know what you're doing."

"Spoiling you for anyone else?" Scottie flashed her a grin. "Yes, that's my evil plan."

Willow chuckled. "That too. But that wasn't what I meant. This whole date, the vintage mall, this place... You're creating a no-tech date, aren't you?" Scottie hadn't even pulled out her phone to take a picture of the wall full of vintage radios, and she had paid in cash. And now she had surprised her with a picnic in a greenhouse instead of taking her to a restaurant where Willow might make the credit card reader glitch.

"Well, more like low-tech." Almost apologetically, Scottie pointed at the fairy lights and the LED candles on the table. "My friend said using real candles in the greenhouse was a no-no, so I had to use these. I brought replacement batteries, though, just in case."

Warmth filled Willow's chest, and she swallowed down the lump in her throat so she could speak. "You're very sweet, and I really appreciate it. But I want you to know that I don't expect it for every date. You don't have to go to all the trouble to keep me from anything digital." She gave Scottie a serious look. "It's not going to last."

Scottie stilled.

"Creating a tech-free zone, I mean," Willow quickly added. "It's not like I can avoid electronics forever. On Monday, I'll be back in the office, surrounded by computers, screens, and printers."

"I know," Scottie said. "It's not about avoiding it forever. I just wanted you to have a break. One night where you don't need to worry about a thing."

The sincere look on Scottie's face, the pure uncomplicated affection pierced all of Willow's defenses.

Her eyes burned. "You really have to stop making me cry," she got out, her voice choked with a mix of both laughter and tears.

Scottie reached across the table.

Willow took her hand, keeping the other one on the metal table.

"I'll try," Scottie said. "I much prefer to make you smile."

"Oh, I know a way to achieve that," Willow replied, trying to lighten the mood. She let her gaze flick from Scottie's eyes to her lips.

"Getting ice cream on the way home?" Scottie asked innocently. But she was looking at Willow's mouth too.

"I wouldn't say no to that, but I was actually thinking of something"—Willow leaned forward—"even sweeter." She tugged on Scottie's hand until she was leaning across the table too, only inches separating them now. Her hot breath brushed Willow's face.

Scottie's pupils widened. Her tongue darted out and licked her lips.

"And something warmer," Willow added. "Much, much w—"

Scottie surged forward and kissed her until Willow forgot about ice cream, tech glitches, and everything else.

Chapter 32

On Monday morning, Willow turned into the Kudos employee parking lot, her tires splashing through puddles.

The Portland sky was as gray as the surrounding office buildings, and she was about to start a long, busy workday, but for once, Willow didn't care. She still carried that wonderful lightness from the weekend.

If she focused, she could still hear their laughter drift through the greenhouse and feel the warmth of Scottie's lips on her own.

With a smile, she slung her bag over her shoulder, got out of the car, and locked it.

Before she could take a step toward the building, her phone rang. She fished it from her purse.

Scottie's name flashed across the small screen.

The way her heartbeat sped up was ridiculous. She fumbled to accept the call before it could go to voicemail. "Hey," she said, trying to sound casual.

"Hey." Scottie's voice, warm and low, rumbled through her ear. "What are you wearing?"

Willow nearly stumbled into a puddle. Her ankle boots squeaked to a halt on the wet pavement, and her face went hot despite the chill in the air. "Uh..."

Scottie laughed. "Sorry to disappoint, but this isn't that kind of call. I didn't mean it like that. I'm just trying to figure something out."

Willow rubbed her burning cheek with her free hand. "How to make my heart rate skyrocket?"

"No. But good to know that does it for you."

You. You do it for me. Willow bit her lip before she could voice the thought. As Scottie had said, this wasn't that kind of call. "So what are you trying to figure out this early on a Monday? Shouldn't you be at work?"

"I'm about to head out, but I just thought of this while I was getting dressed and didn't want to forget to ask you about it."

Images of Scottie getting dressed flared through Willow's mind—Scottie slowly sliding her pants up her legs, her chest still bare in the soft morning light. She suppressed a strangled noise.

What on earth was up with her libido? She had never reacted like this to anyone else.

Willow cleared her throat. "Ask me about what?"

"What you're wearing," Scottie replied. "What materials, I mean. Cotton, wool, polyester?"

"Oh. You could have led with that."

"I know." Scottie chuckled. "But what would be the fun in that? So?"

"Uh, mostly cotton, I guess." Willow slowly made her way toward the Kudos Entertainment building, dodging puddles left and right. "Why's that important?"

"Because of the friction," Scottie answered.

The way Scottie said *friction* did things to Willow's brain—and her body—that she wasn't ready for on a Monday morning, in the middle of the company parking lot.

"For example," Scottie continued, "when you wear a wool sweater and you rub up against the back of your chair all day, you're building up static that could make your tech issues worse."

Willow suppressed a sigh. The heat dissipated from her body.

Scottie didn't seem to notice her sudden silence. "Synthetics like nylon and polyester are bad too. They're like little lightning factories. And rubber-soled shoes can trap the charge instead of letting it discharge naturally. Have you thought about trying leather soles or buying an antistatic wristband? I sometimes wear one of those when I'm working on a highly sensi—"

"Stop," Willow said, more sharply than intended.

Scottie instantly fell silent.

Crap. Willow took a deep breath. "I'm sorry, but...can we please slow down?"

"S-slow down?" Scottie sounded so small, so confused that Willow instantly regretted her words.

She shifted her bag higher on her shoulder and glanced left and right to make sure no colleague could overhear her. This wasn't a great place for this discussion, but she needed to say it now. "I told you I don't want you to fix me."

"That's not what I'm doing," Scottie replied, a hint of defensiveness creeping into her tone. "I'm only trying to help."

A sigh escaped Willow this time. "I know. You mean well. But I've been living with this my entire life. If there were any easy solutions, don't you think I would have found them by now? I've done all the research, worn all the right fabrics, tried all the tricks. And some of them help a little, but nothing I do can get rid of it. Believe me; I've tried." She was talking fast and loud, but she couldn't stop herself. Years of frustration were leaking out. "When you start suggesting solutions, it makes me feel stupid—like you assume I haven't thought of it already or I haven't tried hard enough."

"What? No, I—" Scottie stopped herself and took several audible breaths. "I don't think that for a second. You're smart and resourceful, and I'm sorry if I made you feel otherwise. I guess it's a reflex. When I see a problem, I try to fix it. It's the default mode in my job."

"But I don't want to be a job to you," Willow whispered.

"You're not," Scottie said firmly. "Yes, I want to make your work life easier and help with the tech glitches, but I admit it's for unprofessional reasons."

A tiny smile snuck onto Willow's face, and her tension eased. "Unprofessional, hm?"

"*Very* unprofessional," Scottie said. "But you're right. I'll try to rein it in, okay? No more tech advice—unless you ask for it. And I really hope you will because I want us to be a team."

"I want that too." Willow's voice was scratchy, and she struggled to keep it steady.

Her phone beeped with a low-battery warning, even though she had charged it before leaving home.

"My battery is about to die. If we get cut off, don't think I hung up on you."

"Thanks for the warning. I really need to get going too. Do you want to grab lunch together later?" Scottie asked quickly. "We could go to your lunch spot in the park if you'd rather avoid the cafeteria."

"I'd love that," Willow said.

They lingered for a moment, neither ending the call, even though Willow's phone beeped again and she had long since reached the entrance to the Kudos building.

"Scottie?"

"Yeah?"

"I'm sorry for coming down on you so harshly. It's just that this is really important to me. My entire life, as soon as people found out, they've reduced me to this one thing. I'm always either the liar who's making stuff up to get attention or the weirdo who stops watches and crashes computers. The person you have to fix."

Scottie sucked in a sharp breath. "That's not who you are to me. I know you're telling the truth, and I don't see you as someone to fix—because you aren't broken."

The words landed somewhere deep in Willow's chest, where she had tucked away all the shame, the pain, and the frustration over the years. She pressed her trembling hand to her breastbone. "You're making me cry again," she said with a shaky laugh.

"I wasn't trying to do that either," Scottie replied. "I just wanted to make your life easier."

"You are." Scottie probably had no idea how much what she had just said was helping. "This...us...is still very new. I guess we'll both have to learn how to navigate my tech quirks and all the issues that come with them."

"We will," Scottie said, her usual confidence back in her voice.

Willow had never wanted to believe something so much. "Yeah," she got out through the lump in her throat. "We will."

Her phone beeped another warning.

"I really have to go," Willow said. "See you at noon, okay?"

"Can't wait. Oh, and Willow?" Scottie's voice dipped lower. "If I ever call to ask you what you're wearing again, it *will be* one of those calls."

Heat shot up Willow's neck and into her cheeks. A low groan escaped her. "You say things like that and expect me to focus on work?"

Scottie chuckled and ended the call.

Willow stood there for a few seconds longer, phone pressed to her ear. Then she put it away with a quiet laugh. Scottie really was one of a kind. She was the only person Willow knew who could make her feel so many emotions in such a short time, taking her from anger and frustration to hope, joy, arousal, and that startling sense of being seen and appreciated for exactly who she was.

With a determined tug, she pulled the glass door open, already looking forward to her lunch break.

Willow barely had time to stow her bag beneath her desk before Celeste strode over to her cubicle.

"Mr. Sorensen wants to see you."

Willow swallowed. "Now?"

Celeste gave a curt nod. "As soon as you get in, he said."

"Oh." That didn't sound good. "Did he say what this is about?"

"He'll let you know." Her boss's tone was clipped and her expression as composed as ever, giving nothing away. Only a slight tightening around her jaw didn't match her calm.

"Okay. I guess I'll head upstairs, then." Willow tried to sound as if being called to the fifteenth floor, where all the executive offices were, was an everyday occurrence, but her voice wobbled.

Celeste's gaze softened for a moment, betraying something like sympathy or concern. "It's the corner office to the right." She looked as if she wanted to add something, maybe *good luck,* but then she gave Willow a curt nod, turned, and walked away with measured strides.

Willow stood frozen for a second. Then she grabbed her ID badge and made her way to the elevator.

Her hand shook as she pressed the call button. A static jolt snapped through her fingertip, stinging hard enough to make her flinch.

Once the elevator arrived, she stepped inside and carefully used her knuckles to tap the button for the fifteenth floor.

For once in her life, she prayed for a tech glitch—something that would make the elevator get stuck again. But, of course, the damn thing behaved perfectly today.

When the metal doors slid open on the top floor, the scent of lime polish and expensive cologne greeted her.

Her thoughts raced as she headed down the hall. What could Mr. Sorensen want? She had met him only once so far, and she doubted he even remembered her—which was the way she preferred it.

Flying under the radar of her bosses had always been her best strategy. But now something had drawn his attention. Had it been that ridiculous paper jam award she'd received on Friday? She remembered the grim expression on his face as she'd walked past his table with the plaque in her hand.

Thick burgundy carpet muffled her steps as she entered the outer office.

Mr. Sorensen's executive assistant looked up from her monitor.

Willow forced a smile. "Good morning. I'm Willow Greene."

"Ah." The EA gave her a knowing nod. "Go right in. Mr. Sorensen is expecting you."

Willow crossed the plush carpet on shaky legs and smoothed her clammy palms down her slacks, trying to make herself look more composed than she felt before she knocked on the door.

"Yes?" a deep, muffled voice drifted through the wood.

She sucked in a deep, steadying breath, then slowly opened the door and entered the corner office.

Mr. Sorensen sat behind his massive desk. A floor-to-ceiling window stretched behind him, showing downtown Portland and the gray sky. He was barely older than her, but his hairline had already begun to recede. His suit screamed money, and his shave was as perfect as the knot on his tie.

"Good morning, Mr. Sorensen," Willow said, trying hard to keep her tone friendly but professional, without a hint of a tremor. "Ms. Covey said you wanted to see me?"

He nodded. "Have a seat."

Willow sank onto the low-backed visitor's chair. Her heart raced. She felt the way she had back in high school, when the principal had called her into his office after she'd fried the second computer in a year.

He leaned back in his executive leather chair, folded his arms behind his head, and studied her, making her sweat. "How long have you been with Kudos now?"

Surely he knew the answer to that question. "Two and a half months."

"Two and a half months," he repeated, stroking his clean-shaven chin. "And in that time, you've filed about a dozen separate IT tickets."

Her mouth went dry. So this was about the tech glitches. She pressed her palms to her thighs and fought to quell her rising panic. "I know that sounds like a lot, but if you read IT's reports, you'll see that—"

"It *is* a lot," he said, his gaze steely. "Maybe your previous employer didn't think so, but at Kudos, we pride ourselves on hiring tech-savvy people so we can keep our IT team lean and our processes running smoothly."

Willow dug her nails into her thighs. She wanted to argue and defend herself, but what could she say? Compared to glitch-free veterans like Barb, she did generate a lot of tickets. It wouldn't matter to Mr. Sorensen that she'd resolved three times as many tech issues on her own, without bothering to contact IT, and stayed late nearly every day to make up for lost time.

"I spoke with our CIO and the IT manager, and we'd all like to get to the bottom of this," Mr. Sorensen continued. "So, from now on, I want you to document everything—every software crash, every printer jam, every time your computer hiccups. CC me on all correspondence with IT. If there's a systemic problem, I want to see where the breakdown is."

Willow's head bobbed too fast. "Yes, absolutely. I'll do that."

"Good."

Was that it? Could she go? She shifted her weight forward, ready to jump up and escape the stifling office and his attention.

But he kept studying her across the desk. "I also spoke with Ms. Covey. About you."

Every muscle in Willow's body locked up tightly. Did Celeste have any complaints about her, other than the tech issues? She still couldn't read her immediate supervisor or guess what she thought of her.

"She seems impressed with your resourcefulness and your work ethic," Mr. Sorensen said.

Oh. Willow slumped against the back of the chair.

"Since she appears to think so highly of you, I've decided to give you a chance to prove yourself."

The tension crept back into Willow's muscles. What did he want her to do?

"We've got an important presentation for a licensing deal with Unicorn Pictures coming up in January," Mr. Sorensen said. "You've probably heard the name."

Willow nodded. Everyone at Kudos had. Unicorn Pictures was a major film studio, and Kudos was trying to get the exclusive global rights to design, manufacture, and sell a range of toys based on their latest franchise.

"I'll be presenting the proposal to the guys from Unicorn myself, and I want you to assist me. You'll help me prepare the presentation deck, gather any material I might need, handle logistics in the room that day, and make sure the AV setup runs without a hitch."

Oh please no. Of all the things to assign to her, why did it have to be that? She could handle preparing the presentation deck and gathering material, but making her responsible for the tech setup was like asking the family klutz to carry the wedding cake up a flight of stairs.

"I want you in the conference suite an hour early to set up for the presentation and make sure everything's ready to go."

"Our conference suite?" She tried to sound calm. "So we're not flying down to their studio in LA for this?"

"No. They requested to come here. They want to see our design studio in person and get a feel for how we operate. So the entire building will be under a microscope. We need to be at our absolute best to impress them."

Willow didn't get it. If he was so desperate to impress the Unicorn Pictures team, why would he assign her of all people to set up the conference room?

When she didn't say anything, he gave her an imploring look. "Can you do that?"

"Of course," Willow said, hoping her voice didn't betray her rising panic. "I won't let you down. Thank you for the opportunity, Mr. Sorensen."

"Very good. I'll have my EA send you the details later this week." He turned back toward his sleek laptop, dismissing her.

On shaky legs, Willow slipped out of the room and fled to the elevator.

The moment the metal doors closed behind her, she slumped against the mirrored wall.

Despite what he'd said, this wasn't a chance to prove herself. It was her *last* chance. He was testing her. Either she pulled this off smoothly, or he would get rid of her.

In her mind, she could already see it: the laptop refusing to boot or the PowerPoint presentation freezing mid-slide.

Her stomach churned. *This is it. I'll be fired.*

Her days at Kudos would be over, just when she'd finally started to feel like she belonged there—at the company, in Portland, and in Scottie's life. And now, one spark, one little tech glitch could send it all crashing.

Chapter 33

Shortly before noon that day, Scottie had volunteered to handle a ticket up on the thirteenth floor, where an Operations employee struggled with network connectivity issues.

She resolved them quickly, managing to glance across the bullpen to Willow's desk only every now and then.

When she was done, it was time for lunch. *Perfect timing.*

Grinning, she crossed the room toward Willow, her coat draped over her arm, ready to head to lunch.

Willow wasn't at her desk; she was in the next cubicle, discussing something with the co-worker who had taken over Barb's workspace. Willow pointed at the screen, then leaned forward and reached around him for his mouse to show him something.

"Oh no!" Quickly, he slid it out of her reach. "You're not touching my mouse! I need it to survive the day."

Willow's cheeks flushed crimson. "Okay, fine, I'll keep my wisdom to myself and won't show you the magic button."

Her light, teasing tone didn't fool Scottie. She could hear the hurt behind it.

Willow must have sensed her watching because she looked up. Her face softened, and her tightly held shoulders loosened a little.

Scottie lifted her hand in greeting. "Hey. Ready for lunch, or do you need a few minutes to wrap things up?"

The co-worker—Tony? Toby?—looked back and forth between them with a curious expression, probably trying to figure out if they were friends…or more.

At some point, they would have to talk about how to handle their relationship while they were at work. Did Willow want to keep it out of the office, or was she fine with her colleagues knowing that they were dating? Maybe they could talk about it over lunch.

"I'm ready," Willow said immediately, as if she couldn't wait to get out of there. She circled the divider and grabbed her purse and jacket from the back of her chair. "See you later, Toby."

As they crossed the bullpen, Scottie could feel the tension radiating off Willow.

Was this about Toby and his attempt to hide the mouse from her? Clearly, Willow was starting to get a reputation among her colleagues as a person who broke devices.

That wasn't good, but Scottie hoped it wouldn't last.

Kudos Entertainment had always been the kind of workplace where the only thing faster than the Internet connection was the spread of gossip. If someone from the executive floor started an affair with the receptionist or a new intern was caught taking reams of paper from the building, the rumor mill would move on and forget about Willow's "tech jinx."

When they got into the elevator and Willow pressed the button for the lobby, every single floor button lit up.

Luckily, no one else was with them. Scottie raised her brows but didn't say anything until they'd left the building. She had the sneaking suspicion that this was about more than just Toby.

Willow wasn't still angry with her, was she? Scottie had thought they had resolved their first argument and ended the phone call on good terms.

Outside, the rain had stopped, but the clouds still hung low and heavy.

"Hey," Scottie said quietly as they crossed the street toward Willow's lunch spot. "You okay?"

A shaky breath escaped Willow. "Yes. No. I'm having a horrible day."

"I'm sorry. Is this about…us? Our argument this morning?"

"Argument?" Willow repeated as if it had no longer been on her radar at all. "No! We're fine. I promise."

"Then what's wrong? And don't even try to tell me it's nothing."

"It's not nothing. It's *everything,*" Willow whispered. "It feels like my entire world is about to crash."

Scottie pulled her over to a bench in the park and used her coat sleeve to wipe away a few raindrops clinging to the wood before directing Willow to take a seat. "What happened?"

She sat beside her, leaving a bit of space, just in case Willow wasn't ready for closeness after the morning she'd had.

But Willow inched toward her almost immediately. Her fingers twisted around the strap of her purse until the leather creaked. "As soon as I got to my desk this morning, Celeste came over. Said the COO wanted to see me."

"Sorensen?" Scottie frowned. He didn't usually get involved with day-to-day stuff in Operations. "What did he want?"

Willow bit her lip. "He called me on the carpet because of my tech issues. He wants me to document every little hiccup and CC him on all IT requests from now on so he can track where the breakdown is happening."

Scottie bunched her hands into fists. "That's rich!"

The words burst out of her, startling a crow into flight that had been pecking at a discarded sandwich.

"He's lecturing you about your tech mishaps? He calls IT for all kinds of ridiculous bullshit, like accidentally deleting his desktop shortcuts and wanting us to reinstall the programs that he thinks he uninstalled. Track the breakdown! Ha!" Scottie snorted. "That guy couldn't troubleshoot his way out of a login screen! The only reason he's COO is because he's engaged to Mr. Haggerty's daughter! Everyone knows it's really Celeste, not him, who keeps Operations running smoothly!"

Willow blinked as if stunned by her outburst.

Scottie slumped against the back of the bench. "Sorry. It's just... It makes me furious when admin—especially women—are criticized for every little misstep, while the men higher up in the corporate hierarchy mess up all the time and still get fat bonuses at the end of the year."

That was true, of course, but if Scottie was completely honest, she had to admit that her protective reaction hadn't been so much about admin in general and more about how he had treated Willow in particular.

"Yeah, but unfortunately, that's not all." Willow stared at a cluster of bare trees next to their bench. "He wants me to assist him with the licensing proposal presentation for Unicorn Pictures."

"Wow." Scottie hadn't expected that. "That's an important project." At first glance, getting to work on that seemed great. But then why was Willow so anxious?

It dawned on her after a moment. "He wants you to set up the laptop for the presentation."

Willow nodded miserably. "The Unicorn Pictures team is coming here instead of us going to LA, and Mr. Sorensen wants me to set up the conference suite. I just don't get it. If this deal is that important, why risk having me of all people do the tech setup? Why not ask his EA? I bet she's done it a hundred times without any glitches."

His motivation finally became clear to Scottie. She gritted her teeth until her jaw hurt. "Because he needs someone to blame if the proposal tanks."

"What?" Willow shook her head. "But why would he assume it'll tank? Is he sabotaging it on purpose by assigning employees he thinks are incompetent?"

"No," Scottie replied. "He probably figures his chances of landing the deal are slim—and for once, I agree with him. Unicorn Pictures hasn't signed with Kudos since Sorensen took over. They were really happy to work with Ms. Saunders, his predecessor, but have always gone with the competition since he became COO. If they're coming here instead of having Sorensen go to LA, they want to vet our team culture and production capabilities. They're not sure we can handle a global launch under his leadership. He's under pressure, and he needs a scapegoat in case things go south."

"Oh crap," Willow whispered. "This isn't just a test, is it? He's setting me up to take the fall."

Scottie nodded grimly.

"And there's nothing I can do about it. I can't refuse, and I can't call in sick the day of the presentation. Anything I do would end up getting me fired." Willow's shoulders hunched. She didn't look angry, just defeated.

A fist seemed to tighten around Scottie's stomach. She opened her mouth to suggest that she do the tech setup for Willow.

But then she snapped her mouth shut. She had promised not to offer more unsolicited tech advice or to try to fix Willow's problems for her. And she wanted to keep that promise, but watching Willow sit there, pale and anxious, made it almost unbearable. She couldn't just stay put and do nothing.

Was getting HR involved an option?

But what would they tell them? That Sorensen had assigned her this task because she kept causing tech issues?

No, that definitely wouldn't help Willow's case.

"I really hoped this time would be different," Willow whispered.

"What do you mean?"

"This"—Willow waved toward the Kudos office building across the street—"is exactly what happened at my last job."

Scottie turned fully toward her. When they'd been trapped in the elevator together, Willow had told her that she'd been fired from her last job, but she hadn't revealed the reason—or at least not all of it. "They set you up to take the fall for management too?"

"No, not that part. They let me go because I kept having tech issues. They never said it outright, but I could tell. I was too expensive as an employee. Too much trouble."

Scottie reached over and took her hand. A jolt zapped through her fingers and raced up her arm. Even the scars on her scalp seemed to ache from leftover static. *Ouch.* That had been stronger than ever before, probably reflecting the turmoil inside Willow.

Willow tried to pull back, but Scottie refused to let go. "You're not trouble." She emphasized every word. "You're hardworking, smart, and resourceful. Any employer worth their salt should be happy to have you."

Willow tried a smile, but it ended up looking more like a grimace. "You say that now. Wait until all the IT tickets start to pop up as my anxiety rises in the weeks leading up to the presentation." She pressed her lips together. "Even if the presentation itself goes smoothly, Mr. Sorensen might end up firing me for the string of tech disasters."

Scottie's protective instincts roared to life again, and this time, she couldn't contain them. "Please, Willow. Let me help. I'm not trying to take over and fix your problems for you, but maybe I can offer a helping hand every now and then."

"But it wouldn't be just every now and then." Willow ran her free hand through her hair, smoothing back the tangled strands. "You haven't seen how bad it can get if I'm stressed and panicking. I can't ask you to clean up all my messes."

"You're not asking. I'm offering. I like helping you, and I don't care how often it happens." Scottie's cheeks warmed at the confession. "Being the superheroine with the toolbox who gets to swoop in and rescue you... Not that I think of you as a damsel in distress, but...having you trust me to help makes me feel like maybe I am enough. Like I have something to offer."

"You do," Willow said firmly. "And you are enough."

"I believe that now—because of you. Early on, when we were stuck in that elevator—you told me I didn't need to change to deserve love. So if anything, *you* were the one who fixed *me*, not the other way around."

Willow stared at her with tears gleaming in her eyes.

Scottie tightened her grip on Willow's hand. "Now let me return the favor. Let me help. If we work together, I'm sure we can find a way to save your job."

Willow hesitated, clearly wrestling with old demons. Finally, she nodded. "Okay," she whispered.

The rush of relief sweeping over Scottie was so intense that she swayed. "Thank you."

"Don't thank me yet," Willow said with a bitter chuckle. "You might regret it once all the IT tickets start to come in."

"Never. If your tech acts up, don't even bother filing a ticket. Text me directly. I might be able to tell you how to fix it yourself so we can avoid leaving a paper trail. Or at least you can jump the queue and get help faster so you don't fall behind on your work." Or maybe she could resolve Willow's IT issues without documenting anything. If there were no tickets in the system, Mr. Sorensen wouldn't find out. It was a risk; Scottie knew that, but she was willing to take it.

Willow searched her face. "Are you sure it's okay for me to get special treatment?"

"Of course it's okay." Scottie tried to put a bit of levity into her tone. "As my girlfriend, you should get the special VIP tech support package."

Willow sat very still. "Girlfriend?" she repeated barely above a whisper.

Scottie froze, only now realizing what she'd said. *Oh hell.* "Ugh. Too much, too soon, right? I know we've been on only one date…unless you count our practice dates, which you probably don't, so I realize I'm going much too fast. I really didn't mean to… Well, I did, but—"

Scottie was still rambling, tripping over her words, when Willow leaned in and kissed her.

The words instantly trailed off, and so did Scottie's scrambled thoughts except for *mmm* and *so soft* and *don't ever stop.* She melted against Willow's warm lips.

Emotions seemed to flow back and forth between them.

Willow wrapped one arm around Scottie, pulling her close. Her fingers tangled in the fabric of Scottie's coat as if she never wanted to let go again.

Scottie lifted her free hand and cupped Willow's face, stroking her cheek with one finger, while their mouths continued to caress each other.

When they broke the kiss and moved back a little, Willow smiled for the first time since Scottie had picked her up for lunch.

Scottie traced her curving lips with her fingertips. "So you're okay with me calling you my girlfriend? You don't think we're going too fast?"

"Well..." Willow pressed a kiss to Scottie's fingers. "Us dating might be new, but let's be honest. We've been dancing around this for a couple of months now. I tried to forget about that kiss in the elevator..."

"But I'm hard to forget and even harder to resist," Scottie finished the sentence with a grin.

"That you are."

"Okay, then. VIP girlfriend support package officially activated." Scottie made a *beep-beep-boop* noise, like a program coming online. "All systems ready."

Willow's laughter wrapped around her like a warm hug. "What does that VIP girlfriend support package include?"

"Unlimited priority troubleshooting. Faster response times. Full confidentiality." Scottie ticked off each benefit on her fingers. "And as many kisses as you want."

Willow leaned against her shoulder. "I accept."

Scottie chuckled happily. While their tone was playful and lighthearted, she knew how hard it was for Willow to accept her help. "It was throwing in the kisses that convinced you, wasn't it?"

"Totally."

Their lips came together again, and the kiss only ended once Willow's stomach let out a fierce growl.

They pulled back, laughing.

"That support package wouldn't also include lunch, would it?" Willow asked. "I forgot mine upstairs."

Scottie stood and pulled her up from the bench. "Come on. Let's go find a food cart and see if they accept your VIP girlfriend badge."

"Ooh, there's a badge?"

"No." Scottie flashed her a grin. "I just wanted to have a reason to call you my girlfriend again."

Willow's gaze went soft. "You can call me that anytime."

Scottie's heart felt as if it could barely contain all the emotions she felt. "Yeah?"

"Yeah." Willow intertwined their fingers. "But I still want that badge."

Laughing, they walked toward the food carts at the corner, still hand in hand.

Chapter 34

On Friday morning, Mateo gestured wildly as they entered the Kudos building together, nearly spilling some of his coffee—or maybe Gordon's. "Did you see that all-company email fiasco yesterday?"

"No." Scottie had been away from her desk for most of the afternoon, setting up a new computer in HR and then helping Willow with an Outlook glitch. "What happened?"

"Someone in Sales accidentally hit *reply all* on a department-wide email and told everyone in great detail about needing a mental health day off to recover from a disastrous Bumble date."

Scottie groaned. "You're kidding."

"That's not even the best part. As soon as they noticed their mistake, they panicked and sent a follow-up email."

"Let me guess," Scottie said. "The classic *please disregard my previous email.*"

"Yep." Mateo rolled his eyes. "Which, of course, made people curious, so by the time their manager contacted us, wanting us to delete it from everyone's inbox, almost the entire department had opened it."

He fell silent as they squeezed into the nearly full elevator.

Katia, Mr. Sorensen's executive assistant, stood near the back, scrolling through her phone. A couple of people from Marketing huddled in the middle.

The doors began to glide shut when hurried footsteps echoed across the lobby.

Since Mateo had his hands full with two paper cups, Scottie stuck hers out and caught the doors before they could close.

They slid open again.

Willow stood in the opening, taking in the crowded elevator. Her hair was damp from the light drizzle outside, the ends curling around her green scarf that brought out the greenish flecks in her hazel eyes. Her gaze instantly connected with Scottie's. "Thank you."

Mateo shifted to the side, making space for Willow between him and Scottie.

"Good morning," Willow said, her voice low and intimate in the small space.

Several employees echoed Willow's greeting, even though Scottie knew Willow had been talking mostly to her.

"Morning," Scottie replied. She wanted to say so much more: *How did you sleep? Did Mr. Sorensen send you his presentation draft? Want to come over to my place after work?*

But a dozen Kudos employees would be listening to their every word.

Willow had said she was okay with being called her girlfriend anytime, but did that mean she was ready to reveal their relationship to their colleagues? With all the tech glitches that had happened this week, they hadn't gotten around to talking about it.

Telling Gordon and Mateo about them would probably be fine. Willow knew they were more than co-workers to Scottie; they were almost like family.

But Mr. Sorensen's EA was just two feet away. If she found out they were a couple and let her boss know, he might start to keep an eye on Scottie too—and find out she hadn't filed a ticket or documented any of the tech glitches Willow had been dealing with since Monday.

So it was better to play it cool and act all professional.

But as the elevator started its ascent, Willow shifted her weight.

They were now so close that their coat sleeves brushed, and Scottie could feel the heat emanating from Willow. The faint scent of Willow's apricot shampoo filled her nostrils.

Scottie struggled against the urge to lean toward her. Willow's hand was barely an inch from her own. Scottie ached to extend her pinkie and make contact with Willow's. Having her so close yet still not being able to touch her was torture.

In the crowded elevator, no one would notice...or if they did, they would assume it was an accidental contact.

But the risk of setting off a spark and drawing everyone's attention was too great. So Scottie kept her hands to herself and her gaze fixed to the floor numbers above the door.

She could feel Willow peering at her out of the corner of her eye, though. Very likely, she was just as insecure about how to act around her in front of their co-workers.

Finally, the elevator stopped on the tenth floor.

Scottie let Mateo get out first. When she followed him out, she glanced back over her shoulder and caught a glimpse of Willow, who gave her a tiny smile.

Then the door closed between them.

Sighing, Scottie turned and caught up with Mateo.

He regarded her the way he would a server that kept crashing for no discernible reason. "Damn, that was painful to watch. You've really got no game. Zero riz."

"What?"

He gestured back toward the elevator with the paper cup in his right hand. "Didn't you notice? She was giving you those secret looks. Like she was trying to act chill, but her face was basically saying: 'Ask me out already!' You had the perfect opportunity right there, and you just stood there like a damn statue, missing all the signals!"

Scottie bit the inside of her cheek to keep from grinning. If only he knew he was giving her flirting advice about her actual girlfriend! But it was good to hear that she hadn't been the only one who'd been fighting her yearning. "Maybe I was just being professional."

He snorted. "Yeah, right. Try being a chickenshit!"

They reached their office, and Scottie pulled the door open.

Mateo strode past her, still shaking his head. "Seriously. You need lessons, my friend."

Gordon was already at his computer. He reached for the paper cup Mateo held out to him like a man dying of thirst. "Lessons in what?"

Mateo flopped onto his chair. "Asking out women. We ran into Willow in the elevator, and genius here didn't even try to flirt or ask for her number."

"Willow?" Gordon asked. He was hopeless with names…or faces…or anything to do with people.

"Yeah. Willow Greene, her girlfriend from Ops."

"Ah."

Scottie lifted her hand to intervene. This was getting ridiculous. "Guys—"

Mateo cut her off with a wave. "Yeah, yeah, we know. She's not your girlfriend. You're not interested in more heartbreak, yada, yada."

Okay, she had to tell them now. Otherwise, she'd be lying to them, even if only by omission. She cleared her throat. "Actually… She is."

"Interested?" Mateo asked. "Yeah, that's what I've been trying to tell you!"

Scottie stretched across her screens to turn on the tiny Christmas lights on the bonsai above her desk. She took her time turning back around before she said: "My girlfriend."

They both whirled toward her and stared.

"What?" Mateo asked. "Seriously?"

"How did that happen? And when?" Gordon added.

Scottie smiled. When had it happened? She thought back to every encounter she'd had with Willow, from the moment she had first spied her behind and her shapely calves sticking out from under her desk.

"I guess during the practice dates Barb talked us into, we both realized we didn't want to practice for dating other people," she said, skipping over the kiss they had shared when they had gotten stuck in the elevator. "We wanted to date each other. It just took us a while to admit it. I finally asked her to go to the office holiday party together—and she said yes."

Mateo leaned over and slapped her shoulder. "Smooth move! Real slick. Maybe you've got some game after all."

"Thanks, I guess."

Gordon raised his brows. "So you've been dating her for a week and didn't say anything? Oh, wait! That's why you spent so much time in Operations this week! Outlook issues!" He painted quotation marks in the air with his fingers. "Is that what they're calling it these days?"

Scottie faced their teasing with a good-natured smile. "She really had Outlook issues." And printer issues. And SAP issues. Not that she would ever tell them that now that she had to protect Willow's secret. "But I admit I didn't mind that it gave me a reason to see her. I really like her."

Gordon and Mateo fell silent and traded a long look.

Scottie sobered too. "But please keep it quiet for now, okay? Now that Mr. Sorensen is breathing down her neck because she's assisting with his presentation, she doesn't need more gossip about her."

Gordon nodded right away, all teasing gone. "Of course. No one will hear it from us. Right, Mateo?"

Mateo mimed zipping his lips. "Promise. But I gotta say, I did not have you starting an office romance on my bingo card! I thought you'd stay single forever."

"Yeah," Scottie said. "So did I. Guess my heart rebooted faster than I expected."

Her phone buzzed. It was a message from Willow. *Hey. Sorry if things were a bit awkward in the elevator. I wasn't sure what to do.*

Me neither, Scottie texted back.

I'm fine with telling people about us if you are, came Willow's next message. *I have enough secrets. I don't want you to be one of them.*

Warmth filled Scottie. Willow was pretty reserved, always keeping people at arm's length, never revealing much about herself—and, of course, Scottie now understood why. She hadn't expected her to be so open about their relationship, but it came as a wonderful surprise.

"Ooh, judging by that grin on her face, the girlfriend just texted!" Mateo said.

"None of your business," Scottie replied without looking up from her phone.

"That's a yes," Gordon said.

Scottie ignored them and typed, *If it were up to me, we'd shout it from the rooftops. But maybe we should wait until after the presentation. You don't need any extra attention on you right now.*

After a short pause, another text from Willow popped up. *You're right. And so thoughtful it's unfair.*

Scottie's mouth curved into a grin. *Unfair?*

Yes, Willow replied. *Because keeping our relationship quiet for now probably means no more kisses on our lunch break.*

Ugh. Scottie grimaced. Willow was right. Sharing kisses on a bench across the street from Kudos was not exactly discreet. She slumped against the back of her chair and replied with a string of crying emojis, then added a broken heart, hoping the dramatic flair would make Willow smile.

When Willow sent back a hugging emoji, Scottie countered with a hamburger.

A string of question marks popped up a few moments later.

Want to head over to Lloyd Center for lunch? Scottie typed. *If we can't have kisses, we can at least have burgers.*

Burgers it is, Willow replied.

Scottie hesitated only a moment before sending her next text. *Just so you know, I told Gordon and Mateo about us. Hope that's okay. Don't worry, they won't say a word.*

Of course it's okay, Willow answered. *I figured you'd tell them. You spend half of your life with those two after all.*

Jealous? Scottie shot back teasingly, then winced. Jesus, she had to slow down. Yes, they were officially together now, but maybe it was too soon to talk about spending half their lives together—even though what Scottie really wanted was to spend her entire life with Willow.

Three dots appeared. They seemed to hover on her screen for ages before Willow's message finally popped up. *Maybe.*

Scottie grinned. She could live with *maybe.* For now.

Gordon glanced over. "Everything good?"

Scottie sent a quick *Talk later,* then finally turned toward her work. "Yes," she said, unable to hide the smile tugging at her lips. "Everything's great."

Chapter 35

"Mmm. This is exactly what I needed after the week I had." Willow cradled her mug of apple cider-caramel latte and nodded down at the bag full of books next to their table. "Books and coffee—best combination ever."

They had browsed Powell's City of Books for hours, and Scottie had to admit it was the perfect way to spend a rainy Sunday afternoon. She had followed Willow through the aisles, arms full of the books Willow kept handing her, and watched as Willow brushed her fingers along the spines with a happy smile on her face. It was the first time she'd seen Willow fully relax all week.

Neither of them was in a hurry to leave the bookstore or the cozy café tucked into one corner of its first floor.

Bleacher-style elevated seating stretched along one end of the space, but they had managed to snag one of the small wooden tables. Bookshelves surrounded them, and a mural along one wall and the central column depicted scenes from *The Princess Bride* but in a Portland setting, like a pirate ship sailing beneath the Steel Bridge. A tiny Pride flag stuck out of one of the potted plants on a shelf behind the coffee counter, making Scottie feel even more at home.

She took a sip of her own beverage—a s'mores mocha—and hummed at the chocolatey taste. "I thought you didn't like coffee, or at least preferred tea?"

"I like both, but I usually drink tea at home because…" Willow picked a few flakes of the almond croissant they had shared off her sweater. "Well, the coffee machine and I aren't exactly friends."

"Ah." Now that they spent more time together, Scottie was starting to realize how many small—and not so small—things in Willow's life were influenced by the effect she had on tech. "They can be temperamental little divas."

Willow laughed. "Right." A bit of powdered sugar dusted the corner of her mouth.

Scottie reached over and wiped it off with her thumb, just to have an excuse to touch her. Luckily, there hadn't been a single zap all afternoon. "So, how are you spending Christmas? Are you and your sister hosting a big dinner for half of Portland's singles again?"

Willow shook her head. "We were supposed to have a few of Fiona's friends over, but Fi woke up with a sore throat earlier this week. She took a COVID test." She grimaced. "It was positive. Sorry I forgot to tell you. I was in survival mode all week after finding out Mr. Sorensen wants me to do the tech setup for the presentation."

"Totally understandable," Scottie replied. "How's Fiona holding up?"

"She's fine, just exhausted, achy, and grumpy about being quarantined in her room. We had to uninvite everyone. She's really bummed out."

"And you?" Scottie asked.

Willow shrugged. "I've kept my distance, constantly spray the house down with Lysol, and tested myself twice, just to be safe. Both tests came back negative, or I never would have met up with you."

"No, I meant...are you bummed out too about having to cancel your Christmas plans?"

"You know me and parties. I'll be fine by myself. I'll just stay in my room and read. Maybe do some work on the presentation and format the slides for Mr. Sorensen." Willow snorted into the foam of her latte. "They looked like a fifth grader made them using PowerPoint 2010—including clip art."

Scottie studied her across the table. "You're not going to see your parents over the holidays, especially now that you won't get to spend it with your sister?"

Willow toyed with the handle of her mug. "No, not this year."

"Why not?" Scottie asked, raising her voice a little to be heard over the hiss of the espresso machine. "Where do they live?"

"My mom is still in Sacramento, and my dad just moved to Eugene. But I don't see them much these days."

Scottie sent her a questioning look. Eugene was barely two hours away, and there were direct flights from Portland to Sacramento.

Willow gave an awkward shrug. "After they divorced last year, they each got their own place and had to buy everything new—TVs, microwaves, dishwashers, dryers, the whole lot. So they aren't exactly eager to invite me over."

Scottie stared at her. For a moment, she struggled to grasp what Willow was telling her. Then it hit her, sharper than a jolt to the heart. A stinging burn shot up her chest. Her pulse spiked so fast, she had to grip the edge of the table with one hand to keep her balance—or maybe to keep herself from jumping up and hurling curses. "What?" She spat out the word. "They're putting the toaster oven over their own daughter? That's awful!"

"No, it's fine. I get it. Appliances are expensive." Willow's tone was calm, as if this wasn't new to her. She swiped a few crumbs off the table, eyes downcast, her long, dark lashes standing out against pale cheeks.

How often had she brushed off things like this, acting as if it didn't bother her? No wonder Willow had never trusted anyone with her secret if this was how even her own parents reacted to it!

Her heart ached for Willow. She reached across the table and cupped her hands around Willow's, which clutched her mug as if it were a lifeline.

A strong zap stung Scottie's fingers and raced up her arms, but she didn't flinch back. Softly, she squeezed Willow's hands. "They're your parents. They should care about you, not about the price tag on their appliances. I'm sorry."

Willow looked up and gave her a smile before lowering her gaze to their hands. "It's okay," she said. "Really."

But Scottie's fingertips were still smarting, proving that her parents' behavior upset Willow more than she wanted to admit. She hoped that one day, Willow wouldn't feel the need to hide or downplay her emotions in front of her anymore.

"Come home with me."

Willow's head snapped up. She stared at Scottie. "What?"

The words had burst out of Scottie before she had thought them through, but she had meant them. No one should have to sit alone with just a messy PowerPoint presentation for company on Christmas—especially not Willow. She squared her shoulders and repeated: "Come home with me for Christmas. My mom cooks too much food anyway, and I know everyone would love to meet you."

A hint of uncertainty crossed Willow's face. "I, um, don't know if that's a good idea."

"I don't have to introduce you as my girlfriend if you're not ready for that. You can be just Willow. Whatever makes you most comfortable." She caressed Willow's knuckles with her thumb.

"No, that's not it." Willow set the mug down and took Scottie's hands in both of hers. "I wouldn't mind being introduced as your girlfriend. I like being just Willow—but I like being your girlfriend even more."

When usually reserved Willow said romantic things like that, it short-circuited Scottie's brain until she had no words. All she could do was give her a happy smile. "What is it, then?" she asked when she could speak again.

Willow licked her lips. "The thought of meeting your family makes me really nervous. And whenever I get nervous..."

It finally dawned on Scottie. Willow wasn't just having meeting-the-family jitters. "You're scared to cause any tech glitches."

Willow hung her head and nodded. "What if...?" She swallowed audibly. "What if I break something important?" Her whisper was so quiet that Scottie could barely hear her.

The agony in her voice made Scottie wonder if something like that had happened in the past. She squeezed Willow's hands. "Nothing in my parents' house is more important than having you there."

Willow looked up and into her eyes as if searching for the truth there.

Scottie held her gaze, showing her how much she meant every word.

"I'm not sure your parents will see it the same way," Willow finally said.

"They will," Scottie said firmly. "They've been asking to meet you ever since I first mentioned you."

"But how would we explain it if the TV suddenly turns off or the Christmas lights start to flicker?" Willow asked.

Scottie shrugged. "We never turn on the TV on Christmas. And if anything else glitches, we'll just roll with it. Laugh it off or something." She paused, then added gently, "Or we could tell them the truth. My family would never make fun of you or—"

"No!" Willow cut her off, then stroked Scottie's fingers as if silently apologizing. "You knowing is one thing. But telling anyone else..." A visible shiver went through her. "I can't cope with that. Not right now."

"Okay," Scottie said. "Then I'll cover for you."

Willow firmly shook her head. "I don't want you to have to do that. You should just enjoy Christmas and the time with your family."

"And I will. I'll enjoy it even more if my wonderful girlfriend is with me." She gave Willow her best puppy dog look. "Please. Come with me."

Willow drew her shoulders up, then let them drop with a big exhale. "Okay. I'll come."

"Yes!"

The word slipped out so loudly that people at the surrounding tables stared at them.

Scottie didn't care. She drew Willow's fingers to her mouth and kissed them. "Thank you. I promise you won't regret it."

Willow gave her a doubtful look.

"Just think of all the perks of spending Christmas with my folks. My dad makes the best eggnog you have ever tasted—and you'll get to wake up with me on Christmas morning."

When Willow's eyes widened, Scottie realized she had failed to explain a few things.

"Um, that is, if you are okay sharing a bed with me," she added quickly. "My cousin Noah and his kids are already taking the guest room, so my parents will probably assume you'll sleep with me. I mean, sleep in my old room. But if you're not comfortable with that, you get the bed, and I can bring an air mattress for me. No pressure whatso—"

Willow tugged her forward by their joined hands and stopped her with a quick kiss. "No air mattress. I'd love to wake up with you on Christmas morning."

"Oh. Great." Scottie gave her a grin that probably looked a little dopey. "See? It's already shaping up to become the best Christmas ever."

Chapter 36

Just before noon on Christmas Eve, Willow glanced through the Civic's passenger-side window and watched the road signs flash by.

Corvallis – 12 miles, one of them read.

Not long now. The closer they got to Scottie's family home, the worse Willow's nerves became.

She tried to tell herself the trip to Corvallis would be good for her. It would be a nice distraction from all the problems at her job. In fact, it was already working: Instead of panicking about the upcoming presentation, she was now worrying about meeting Scottie's family.

Willow grimaced. *Great.* It was like a nesting doll of anxiety, with one worry tucked inside another.

Scottie glanced over. She was navigating the holiday traffic with a constant grin on her face, either because Willow had let her drive the Civic again or because she was about to see her family. Her hair was tousled from the knit cap she'd worn earlier, and Willow hadn't said anything because she secretly loved the look. "You doing okay over there?"

"Yeah. Just..."

"Nervous," Scottie finished when Willow hesitated to admit it.

Willow sighed. "A little. Okay, a lot."

Her phone buzzed, and she fished it out of her purse. "Sorry. It's Fiona. I told her to check in when she wakes up."

"Tell her I hope she feels better soon," Scottie said.

"Will do." Willow checked what her sister had written.

I'm up. Kinda. Did you make it to Corvallis?

Hey, sleepyhead, Willow answered. *Not yet. Still in the car. How are you feeling?* Fiona had been asleep when they had left, and Willow hadn't wanted to wake her just to say goodbye.

Like I have a bad case of the Christmas Plague, Fiona replied.

I'm really sorry, Willow texted back. *But at least you won't starve to death. If you get hungry, there's lasagna in the fridge, soup in the freezer, and a loaf of the cranberry bread you love on the counter. And your gifts are under the tree.*

Gifts, plural? Fiona replied. *I thought we agreed to stick to just one this year?*

The smaller one is from Scottie. She says hi and hopes you feel better soon.

There was a longer pause before Fiona's next text popped up. *Scottie got me a gift? Wow. She's a keeper! If you don't want her, I'll take her.*

Not a chance. I want her. Willow hit *send,* then froze and stared at what she'd written.

It was true.

She wanted Scottie.

Not just for however long it lasted before it fizzled out or Scottie got fed up with the glitches. She wanted them, together, until the end of time. This was it for her.

The realization hit her with the force of a lightning strike. She clutched her phone, heart racing. How the hell had this happened? How had she gone, in the span of only a few months, maybe even weeks, from denying herself a single date with Scottie to wanting a lifetime with her?

But while she had no idea how it had happened, there was no denying that it had. She was in love for the very first time in her adult life, and it scared the hell out of her because she'd always believed that relationships didn't last.

Would this one?

She desperately wanted it to.

Her battery level dropped from eighty percent to fourteen.

She typed a quick message to Fiona, then threw the phone onto the back seat, as far away from her turbulent emotions as possible.

Scottie glanced over, a worried look on her face. "Everything okay with Fiona?"

"Hmm? Oh. Yes. She was really impressed that you got her a gift." Willow forced a smile and shoved her fears and hopes to the back of her mind, not ready to deal with them—or talk about them with Scottie.

Scottie grinned. "What can I say? I've always been good at charming the families of my girlfriends."

"Lucky you," Willow murmured, trying not to think of Scottie with any of her exes and their families. "I'm terrible at it."

"I have a really hard time believing that."

"I've never even met a girlfriend's family before." Her relationships had always ended before they could reach the point of holiday invitations or meeting the parents.

"Then how do you know you're terrible at it?" Scottie asked. "If you let them see what I see, you'll do just fine."

Willow studied her strong profile. "What do you see?"

Scottie turned her head for a second to make eye contact, then redirected her attention to the road ahead. "Someone worth bringing home," she said quietly.

In the sudden silence, the squeak of the windshield wipers against the misty glass sounded overly loud.

A burning sensation swirled up Willow's sinuses. "God, you're so charming it's dangerous," she got out, caught between laughing and crying.

"I know." Scottie gave her a smile. "But that wasn't just a charming line."

"That's what makes it so dangerous."

The radio came on, playing "All I Want for Christmas Is You."

They both stared at it.

Scottie arched her brows. "I thought the radio doesn't work?"

"It doesn't. Didn't—even before I bought the car. Its previous owner said it hasn't worked in decades."

Scottie reached over and took her hand. Her warm grip settled Willow's nerves in a way nothing else ever had. "Let's take it as a good omen for this trip."

Mariah Carey's high, bright voice filled the car as the song hit its chorus.

Scottie started to sing along, so off-key that Willow thought for a moment she was doing it on purpose to make her laugh.

Then it hit her. No, Scottie wasn't trying to cheer her up; she really couldn't sing to save her life.

Laughter bubbled up Willow's chest.

"What?" Scottie asked.

"Nothing, nothing," Willow answered but continued to chuckle. "It's just good to know there's one thing you're not perfect at."

Scottie playfully clutched her chest with one hand. "Are you implying I can't sing?"

"Let's just say if I cause a glitch at your parents' house and we need a distraction, you could break into song."

"Ha! Wait until you hear the rest of the family sing—I'm the most talented one of the bunch!"

They rode the last few miles laughing and singing.

Willow tried to slow her breathing as she followed Scottie up the walkway toward her parents' house. Passing out wouldn't make for a great first impression.

Three steps led to a covered porch and a white, slightly weathered front door. A cluster of colorful ceramic pots to the right held violas and pansies. Some of them looked as if they'd seen better days, and the garland wrapped around the porch rail was a bit crooked.

Willow found it strangely comforting. It meant things didn't need to be perfect in the Prescotts' home; they were allowed to go wrong—and they probably soon would.

The muffled sounds of chaos drifted through the door—laughter, loud voices, and the squeal of a child.

Scottie shifted her overnight bag to her left hand and lifted her right, about to grab the doorknob. "Ready?"

Willow hesitated, clutching her own bag with both hands. "You told them you're bringing me, right?"

"Of course. You're pretty much the only thing I've been talking about ever since the office holiday party."

Scottie's emotional openness still stunned her. She swallowed heavily.

"Hey." Scottie reached over and rubbed the small of her back, finding the spot that held most tension almost as if by instinct. "Relax and just be yourself. I guarantee they'll love you."

Just be yourself. Willow wasn't sure that was good advice. Being her was what broke things. She tried to smile. "Okay, let's—"

"They're here!" a child's voice shouted from inside.

The door flew open, and the noise level exploded.

A little boy of maybe five launched himself into Scottie's arms.

"This is Logan, my cousin Noah's youngest." Laughing, she swung him around, then set him down and pulled Willow into the house.

The hallway was crammed with boots and coats, and Willow followed Scottie's example, adding her shoes to the pile.

A man in his sixties, dressed in a ruby-red, ugly Christmas sweater, climbed over the mountain of winter gear to get to them.

Scottie dropped her bag and engulfed him in a bear hug.

He was taller and leaner than Scottie, but Willow instantly knew he was her father, even before Scottie said, "Merry Christmas, Dad."

"Merry Christmas, honey." Finally, he pulled back and regarded Willow. He had the same kind brown eyes as his daughter. "You must be Willow. Glad you could make it." He readily offered his hand. "Come on in and feel right at home."

"It's so nice to meet you, Mr. Prescott." Willow kept one hand on the doorknob behind her as she returned his warm handshake.

He chuckled. "Oh please. Call me Rick. If you call me Mr. Prescott, I feel like I need to start taking attendance and handing out a pop quiz."

Willow smiled. His easygoing personality reminded her so much of Scottie that she finally relaxed the tiniest bit.

"Where's Mom?" Scottie asked.

"Can't you hear her?" Her father gestured to the left, where the noise of a whirring kitchen appliance was coming from. "In the kitchen, torturing the broccoli."

Willow set her bag down next to Scottie's and followed her into the kitchen.

It was a large space, with cream-colored cabinets that looked a little worn and a giant stainless-steel fridge that, by contrast, appeared brand-new. A wide archway led to the dining area, which flowed into the living room.

Scottie's mother stood at the large wooden center island, pureeing broccoli with an immersion blender, so she hadn't heard them enter yet. She was on the shorter side, but her frame wasn't fragile at all. She looked as if she could bench-press her husband. Her blonde hair—a shade darker than Scottie's—held a few traces of gray. She was humming a Christmas song, maybe "Last Christmas," but Willow wasn't sure.

Even over the noise of the blender, Willow could hear that she sounded as off-key as Scottie.

Scottie nudged Willow with her elbow and mouthed, "See?"

The blender let out a high-pitched whine, then shut off abruptly.

Willow froze. *Oh crap. Was that me?*

Scottie's mother lightly shook the blender, but it refused to work. "Oh come on! There's no going on strike on Christmas!"

"Hi, Mom. We're here! Merry Christmas!" Scottie quickly crossed the kitchen and folded her mother into a tight hug, providing the perfect distraction.

"Scottie!" Blender forgotten, her mom returned the hug.

Willow stayed back, kept her hands at her sides, and tried not to touch anything.

After a few seconds, Scottie let go of her mother and turned toward Willow. "This is my mom, Carol. Mom, this is Willow—my girlfriend." Happiness seemed to light up Scottie's features from within.

God, she was too cute. Willow dragged her gaze away from Scottie and directed it toward her mother. "Merry Christmas. Thanks so much for having me." She extended her hand and reached for the metal handle of a drawer with the other.

But before she could make contact, Carol closed the distance between them, ignoring Willow's outstretched hand and pulling her into a warm embrace.

Willow stood very still for a second, then hesitantly put her arms around her in a loose hug, careful not to touch any spot not covered by Carol's sweater or apron.

As Carol let go and pulled back, her wrist brushed Willow's fingers.

An audible crack of static snapped between them, and a painful little jolt zapped up Willow's arm.

Scottie's mother flinched and rubbed her wrist.

Oh, no, no, no! Willow backed up several steps. "I'm so sorry. It's my sweater!"

"It must be her socks," Scottie said at the same time.

Carol looked back and forth between them, then grinned the same charming way Scottie often did. "Don't worry about it," she said to Willow. "I gave birth to this one." She patted Scottie's arm. "I'll survive a little zap."

Scottie groaned. "Oh God, Mom, please. Not the sixteen-hours-of-labor story!"

"Seventeen," her mother said. "And she weighed a whopping—"

Quickly, Scottie covered her mom's mouth with one hand. "No one wants to know that, Mom."

"I do." Willow wanted to hear everything there was to know about Scottie.

"Eight pounds, fourteen ounces," someone shouted from the living room.

Willow glanced toward the archway that led to the dining area and the living room beyond.

A sea of unfamiliar faces peered back at her with open curiosity.

"Great, thanks, Uncle Dave. Now that we've got that out of the way, let's go meet the clan." Scottie took Willow's hand and led her over to the living room.

She pointed out uncles, aunts, cousins, and her cousins' kids until Willow lost track of faces and names. Then she gestured to a group of people—two men and two women—lounging on the floor with their backs against the couch. "And these are my mom's former charges, the infamous daycare alumni."

"You mean *legendary*," a brunette woman quipped. She smiled up at Willow. "Hi, I'm Hazel."

Willow gave them a wave, glad that no one got up to shake hands or hug her. "Hi, everyone. I'm Willow." She hesitated, then added, "Equally legendary."

That earned her a round of chuckles.

Scottie wrapped one arm around her hips and beamed.

"Want to keep me company while I cook?" Scottie's mother called from the kitchen. "You could tell me all about how the two of you met."

The thought of being around so many appliances made Willow nervous, but she didn't know how to decline, so she followed Scottie back to the kitchen.

Scottie gave her mother an apologetic look. "Actually, Mom, that story will have to wait. I promised Willow a quick tour of Corvallis."

Willow nearly sank against the counter as a wave of relief washed over her.

"We'll be back before dinner," Scottie added. "Need us to grab anything while we're out?"

Her mother waved her off. "No, we've got everything we need. Have fun, you two."

"Ooh, tour of Corvallis!" One of Scottie's cousins—a curly-haired, blond guy—let out a whistle. "Is that what it's called now?"

Scottie grabbed a roll of paper towels off the counter and threw it at him.

It sailed across the dining area and the living room and landed squarely on his chest.

Before he could launch a counterattack, Scottie directed Willow down the hall. They climbed over the pile of boots and escaped onto the porch, leaving the noise and the chaotic interactions behind.

A sharp breath whooshed out of Willow.

"Sorry." Scottie took her hand and rubbed it. "I know they can be a lot. But it'll only be like this today. Tomorrow, the daycare alumni will be with their own families, and most of my cousins will go see their in-laws, so it'll be just the core crew."

Willow shook her head. "It's not them. They seem wonderful."

"What is it, then?"

"Are you sure this is a good idea?" Willow gestured back at the house. "Maybe I shouldn't be here."

Scottie's grip on her hand tightened. "Don't say that. I think it's going really well."

"Well?" The word burst out of Willow. "Within thirty seconds of walking in, I killed the blender and basically assaulted your mother with a jolt of static!"

"Nah, it's not dead, just a bit dazed. And you heard Mom. What's a little zap for the woman who made it through sixteen hours of labor?"

"Seventeen," Willow said automatically.

"See?" Scottie gave her a gentle bump with her shoulder. "You'll fit right in. Just give it a chance. Give *yourself* a chance to settle in."

"Okay. I promise I'll give it my best." Willow took a deep breath and tried to shake off her tension. "So, someone promised me a tour of the town."

"Yeah." Scottie led her back toward the car, which they had parked halfway down the street because the driveway was full. "Brace yourself. Major landmarks ahead. Riverfront Park, the OSU campus, and the playground where I broke my arm trying to impress a girl on the monkey bars."

Willow chuckled, and it sounded only a little shaky. "Did it work?"

"Nope. But maybe this time, it will." Scottie reached out to open the passenger-side door for her.

Willow stopped her with a quick touch. She curled her fingers into the lapels of Scottie's coat and pulled her in for a kiss. "It already did," she whispered against her lips.

Chapter 37

Willow sat at the Prescotts' long dining table, surrounded by chaos.

One of the kids spilled soup all over himself, two of the daycare alumni tossed pieces of bread at each other, and everyone talked over each other at the volume of a group of kindergartners at recess—not because they were arguing but because they were excited to be together.

Scottie was clearly in her element. She gestured animatedly as she told her dad all about Willow's classic car, cracked jokes with her almost siblings, and gave a pep talk to her youngest cousin, whose girlfriend had just broken up with him. When she rose to get the salt from the kitchen for Uncle Dave, she touched her mother's shoulder as she squeezed past her chair.

Once she returned, she set a small, moose-shaped glass of eggnog down next to Willow's plate. "In case you need it," she whispered into Willow's ear, then dove back into the conversation with her cousin.

Willow smoothed her finger over the antler-shaped handle of the glass but didn't pick it up. Alcohol and family gatherings didn't mix well for her. If she wanted to make a good impression, she couldn't afford to lose control.

Instead, she slowly ate spoonfuls of the tasty broccoli-cheese soup and observed Scottie with her family.

It was fascinating to discover new facets of the woman she was falling in love with. Or maybe it wasn't really a new side of Scottie. She was the same Scottie she'd known all along, just amplified.

What would Scottie think if she ever got to meet Willow's own family? She would probably love Fiona once they got to know each other better, but Willow wasn't so sure about her parents.

Carol slid the bread basket toward her. "You doing okay, hon?"

Willow nodded quickly. "Yes, thank you. The soup is delicious."

"Thank you. We keep it simple on Christmas Eve"—Carol waved at the three giant steaming pots of soup and chili on the table—"to leave room for the big feast tomorrow."

Finally, once every plate was empty and every piece of bread had disappeared, Rick slapped the table and rose. "All right, kitchen crew! Let's roll!"

Scottie, Ben, Hazel, Noah, and the other cousins and daycare siblings jumped up and began to stack plates.

Willow got up to help.

Scottie's mother stopped her with a decisive wave. "Rick and the kids have their system all worked out. You'd only get in the way. Stay and let us get to know you."

Willow sank back onto her chair.

As Scottie followed her dad out, she sent a reassuring look back over her shoulder.

"So, Willow." Scottie's great-aunt Dorothy, a tiny woman in her eighties with startling blue eyes, turned toward her. "How did you meet our Sarah?"

"Um, Sarah?" Willow's overwhelmed brain needed a few seconds to remember it was Scottie's legal name. "Oh, you mean Scottie."

The matriarch nodded. "How did you two lovebirds meet?"

For the first time, the chatter around the table stopped as everyone's attention turned to Willow. They leaned toward her, eager to hear her answer—and Scottie wasn't there to run interference.

Willow's throat went bone-dry. She took a careful sip of the eggnog, buying herself a few seconds. "We, um, met at work."

"Do you work in IT too?" one of Scottie's aunts asked.

"Oh God, no."

Everyone chuckled at Willow's outburst, then regarded her with expectant gazes, obviously wanting to hear more.

Willow hesitated. Her mind raced. How could she tell them their story without revealing that her constant technological disasters had brought them together?

Even if they wouldn't suspect that she had caused all the glitches, she wanted them to think she was someone worthy of kind, extraordinary Scottie, not some incompetent ditz who couldn't even turn on a computer without help.

The Christmas lights on the tree flickered, and the smart speaker, playing soft Christmas music in the background, abruptly cut out, leaving an awkward silence.

Everything around Willow seemed to stop.

Her pulse thudded in her ears. *Don't panic. Whatever you do, don't panic.* That would make everything worse, causing more devices to glitch. Scottie's family would then realize what an electrical hazard she was.

Willow held her breath, waiting for the disgruntled curses, the suspicious looks her way, the frantic attempts to fix the speaker or fiddle with the lights.

But no one batted an eye.

"I keep telling Rick they don't accept expired coupons for the power bill," Carol quipped. "He has to actually pay."

Everyone laughed and moved on.

"Oh yeah, remember the year Rick—genius physics teacher that he is—was competing with the neighbors for the best holiday decorations and accidentally fried half the extension cords?" Aunt Pam threw in.

More laughter rippled through the living room.

The lights steadied, but the speaker stayed off.

No one seemed to care—or even notice. They were too busy teasing each other and telling stories about past holidays, their easy chatter replacing the music.

Willow stared at them. She was starting to understand a lot about Scottie now that she had met her family.

Scottie could be the goofy, upbeat, outgoing person that she was because she'd never been asked to be anything else—never been told to be careful, to not touch anything, to rein in her emotions so she wouldn't cause a short circuit.

"Everything okay in here?" Scottie strode into the room and began to gather unused paper napkins, but Willow knew it was just an excuse to check on her. "Are you all being nice to Willow?"

"If you haven't scared her off yet, I'm sure we won't manage," her great-aunt said. "Now shoo! She was about to tell us how you two met!"

Scottie hesitated, lingering behind Willow.

Willow leaned back until her head brushed Scottie's chest. "It's okay."

Scottie softly squeezed her shoulder, then walked out, but not before giving everyone at the table a warning look.

"So?" Great-Aunt Dorothy said.

Willow took a steadying breath and fought down her anxiety. In this unflappable chaos of a family, maybe you could break the blender and would still be welcomed with a hug.

"I started as an admin at Kudos—the company Scottie works for—in October, and during the first few weeks, I needed IT's help a lot. Scottie was usually the one who showed up to fix my messes."

"I bet she volunteered," Scottie's mother said with a knowing grin.

No one asked why she'd needed so much help from IT. Maybe they assumed she had fabricated those tech emergencies so she would get to talk to Scottie.

Willow exhaled and lowered her tense shoulders. "Hm, I never found out if she actually did. I thought maybe she just kept drawing the short straw. It took us getting stuck in an elevator to make me realize she was interested too."

Chairs scraped over the hardwood floor as everyone slid closer, hanging on her every word.

"You got stuck in an elevator together?" Great-Aunt Dorothy's blue eyes widened. "Tell us more!"

So Willow did.

It was close to midnight when Scottie's mother shoved the decks of cards to the middle of the table and got up. "All right, everyone. I'm calling it a night. I have to get up early to get the turkey in the oven."

A round of groans and protests rose, but everyone stood anyway.

Chaos broke out as they all hugged, cracked one last joke, and tried to determine whose car had to pull out first to clear the tangle in the driveway.

Scottie kept an eye on Willow, making sure she was doing okay with being hugged and squeezed by every aunt, uncle, cousin, and almost sibling. At least no zaps happened this time.

Willow had seemed to relax the tiniest bit after dinner and had held her own during the card game. In fact, when the time came to add up the scores, everyone had been surprised to find Willow had come out on top.

Everyone but Scottie. She'd seen it coming. Willow was a good observer who watched others closely, and she was quick to adjust her play whenever necessary.

Scottie tried to keep her proud grin in check but knew it was hopeless. Her chest puffed up at how damn clever her girlfriend was—and how hard she'd tried to fit in with her boisterous family.

Her father wrenched Scottie from her thoughts by engulfing her in an embrace. "It's good to have you home—and to see you so happy." He gave her a hearty pat on the back and nodded in Willow's direction. "I like her, even though she won half my retirement fund."

Warmth filled her at his easy acceptance, even as she protested: "We weren't even playing for money, Dad."

"Good thing," he said before Scottie's mom dragged him upstairs.

Finally, it was just Scottie and Willow in the living room.

"Come on, card shark. Let's go to bed." Scottie took her hand and led her up the creaking stairs.

The quiet of Scottie's old bedroom settled around them like a cozy blanket.

Willow looked around, and Scottie tried to see her childhood sanctuary through Willow's eyes.

They both took in the narrow bookcase crammed full of battered comic books, the sleek model of the *Star Trek: Voyager* spaceship dangling from the ceiling, and a signed soccer jersey pinned next to the faded poster of a band that she had only hung up because she'd had a crush on their pretty lead singer.

It was a little strange to have Willow in this space, but she realized she wasn't embarrassed to give her a glimpse of teenage Scottie.

"Very cute," Willow said with a smile.

"Not half as cute as you." Scottie swiped a strand of hair behind Willow's ear and studied her. "How are you holding up? Really."

Willow had been an absolute trooper all night, chatting with Hazel, holding her own even against Uncle Dave in the card game, and bearing the good-natured arguments that had broken out at the table with a patient smile.

Scottie had to bite her lip a few times to keep from laughing at the look on Willow's face—as if she were watching a documentary about an animal species that was fascinating but possibly about to eat her alive.

"I'm okay," Willow said. "I mean, you know how I am about parties."

"It's not a party; it's family," Scottie corrected with a grin.

Willow huffed. "Any gathering of more than two people for social reasons is a party. But I admit this one wasn't too bad. Your mom and dad…everyone, really…they were all very nice and went out of their way to make me feel welcome. I still can't believe they didn't care when the lights started to flicker and the smart speaker cut out."

Scottie shrugged. "That's just how we roll. We've always been the go-with-the-flow type of family." She shifted a little closer and lowered her voice. "Are you sure you don't want to tell them the truth? If you did, I promise they'd take it in stride."

Willow's entire body went still, and her expression shuttered as if she'd closed a door somewhere inside of herself. "I thought we already talked about this. I'm not comfortable with anyone but you knowing."

"I just hate to see how much pressure keeping it a secret puts on you," Scottie answered quietly. "That has to be exhausting."

"It is. But what are the options?" Willow held up her hand before Scottie could say anything. "It's very important to me to make a good first impression on your family. I don't want them to think I'm weird or making stuff up to appear more interesting than I really am."

Scottie could tell there was a lot of painful history packed into that one sentence. Clearly, that was exactly what had happened in the past. Someone—a friend, a family member, or a lover—had dismissed Willow's effect on tech as an attention-seeking lie or something that only happened in fantasy movies.

She wrestled down her anger at that person—or, more likely, multiple people—from Willow's past. "All right. It's totally up to you. I won't tell them anything if you're not comfortable with it, and I won't bring it up again. I just want you to know that I'm here for you, no matter what." Slowly, she reached out, keeping her gaze on Willow's face so she could retreat if Willow's body language told her she didn't want to be touched.

When Willow's expression invited the contact, she put one hand on her hip and gently tugged her closer. "Okay?"

Willow's tension seemed to drain away beneath her touch. "Okay," she whispered and leaned her forehead against Scottie's shoulder.

Scottie closed her arms around Willow and held her tightly.

Willow's arms wrapped around her too, and she sank against Scottie with her full weight, obviously trusting her to keep them from pitching backward.

They stood there for a while until Scottie's eyes drifted closed.

"Come on." She gently rubbed Willow's back. "Let's go to bed before we fall asleep standing up."

They took turns getting ready for bed in the small attached bathroom.

The sight of Willow's toothbrush in the cupholder next to hers brought a smile to Scottie's face. She gave the frosted glass a gentle tap. This was what she wanted in the long term. The thought made her roll her eyes at herself. *God, such a U-Haul lesbian!*

Quickly, she changed into her favorite pajama bottoms and a white T-shirt, then held the bathroom door open for Willow. "All yours."

A few minutes later, when Willow emerged, Scottie nearly lost her ability to form a coherent thought.

Willow was wearing an oversized gray cotton sleep shirt with a cartoon reindeer on the front. The hem ended mid-thigh, leaving an expanse of long, elegant legs exposed. The wide neckline had slipped off one shoulder, revealing the elegant arc of her collarbone and a stretch of fair, soft-looking skin. Her effortless grace took Scottie's breath away.

"Wow," she murmured through a dry mouth. "I didn't think you'd bring the sexy sleepwear on a family visit!" She was only half-joking.

A lovely deep pink flooded Willow's cheeks. She glanced down at the shirt, then at Scottie, giving her an incredulous look. "You think Rudolph the Red-Nosed Reindeer is sexy?" She pointed at the cartoon character plastered across the front of her sleep shirt.

"No," Scottie murmured, and for a second, she allowed her gaze to sweep down those endless-looking legs. "I think *you* are sexy."

Willow's blush deepened. "Scottie." Her groan sounded like a mix between an admonishment and a plea for more. "I don't know if tonight… if I'm…"

"Relax. I promise to be on my best behavior. It's been a long day for both of us, and knowing you, you're totally depleted from being around so many people."

Willow blinked. She looked caught between being deeply touched that Scottie understood this fundamental part of her and terrified that Scottie already knew her so well and could effortlessly see through her armor.

A faint pink rose in Willow's cheeks again, but then she met Scottie's gaze, and one corner of her mouth lifted into a grin. "You're right. We're both tired, so I'll try my best to keep my hands to myself too."

"Damn," Scottie said with a playful pout. She walked to the bed and pulled back the comforter. "Which side do you prefer?"

"I don't really have a side since I sleep alone."

Scottie paused. "But you have slept...stayed the night with someone before, right?"

"Yes, of course," Willow said. "Just never long enough to have a side."

Scottie cleared her throat, not sure what to say to that. "Well, you'll have one now. You get to pick." She searched Willow's face. "If you want to."

Willow caught her lower lip between her teeth in a gesture that looked much too sexy. Finally, she nodded. She glanced back and forth between both sides of the bed, then pointed to the right one.

Scottie had assumed she'd go for the other side, where the bedside table with the lamp was, so she could turn on the light if she had to get up during the night.

Then she understood. Willow had avoided that side for exactly that reason—because it was where the lamp and the small digital clock were.

She made a mental note to remove all electronics from her bedroom at home. "Right side it is." She walked around to the left.

As they slid beneath the covers, Scottie's heart raced, but she reminded herself that nothing would happen tonight. She wasn't going to have their first time be a rushed thing in her childhood bedroom, with her nosy cousin and her parents right next door. She wanted a chance to worship Willow all night, take her time, and see if she could make her let go of her reserve and cry out her name.

Dammit. She mentally slapped herself. Now was not the time to think about that, not with Willow in bed next to her, so close they were almost touching.

She reached out and turned off the bedside lamp.

Darkness enveloped them. Only a streetlight and the neighborhood's Christmas decorations cast a faint glow on the bed.

Scottie lay still, intensely aware of Willow's warm presence mere inches away. Was Willow a cuddler? Would she allow Scottie to spoon her while they fell asleep?

She didn't ask, not wanting to pressure Willow into something she might not be comfortable with.

They lay next to each other in silence for a few seconds.

The sheets rustled as Willow rolled over to face her. "Scottie?"

Scottie tried to make out her expression in the faint light. If she wasn't mistaken, Willow looked tense, her teeth tugging on her lower lip. "Yes?"

"Can I ask you something?"

"Of course," Scottie said without hesitation.

"When you were a kid, did you ever mess up?" Willow asked, her voice lowered to a whisper. "I mean, really mess up?"

Scottie wasn't sure what she had expected her to ask, but not that. She sensed that this question wasn't just a way to get to know her better. This might not even be about her.

"Ever?" She forced a chuckle. "Try all the time. My daycare siblings got me in trouble a lot. Of course, if you ask them, they'll say it was the other way around. But it wasn't anything mean or overly dangerous, just silly stuff."

"Like what?" Willow asked.

"As a kid, I thought tattoos were the coolest thing ever. So one Christmas, when I was about six, I asked for one. But when Christmas morning came and my parents didn't gift me with a visit to a tattoo studio, I locked myself in the bathroom and tattooed myself with a permanent marker until I looked like a tiny little biker. Even put one on my forehead."

Willow laughed so hard, the bed shook. Then she sobered. "What did your parents do?"

"Oh, they were big into letting me experience the natural consequences of my actions. The next day, they sent me outside to play covered in Sharpie tattoos, knowing the neighborhood kids would tease me. Another time, Hazel, Jen, and I were playing with the Barbie house, and I insisted Barbie needed to mow the lawn. I got my mom's sewing scissors and cut off an inch of the flokati rug around the dollhouse."

Willow laughed again, and the carefree sound made the entire flokati debacle worth it. "Nooo!"

"Yes." Scottie nodded gravely.

"What did your parents do about that one?" Willow asked.

"Nothing," Scottie said. "They left the carpet that way for the next five years. Every time a new daycare kid arrived, I had to explain why the carpet had a bald spot. That consequences-of-your-own-actions thing really worked on me. By the time I hit puberty, I was the best-behaved kid ever."

"Meaning you didn't get a tattoo, even later?"

Scottie chuckled. "Nope. No tattoos." She was silent for a few moments. "How about you?"

"No tattoos either," Willow replied. "I considered it once, but I was too afraid the tattoo machine would turn off when the tattoo artist approached me with an inked-up needle."

"No, I meant..." Scottie tried to remember Willow's exact words. "Did you ever mess up when you were a kid?"

Willow's entire body went rigid next to her. "I did. Really badly."

Scottie held her breath. "What happened?"

"When I was little, we always visited my grandparents—my dad's folks—on Christmas Day. My grandpa was really into model trains. He had an entire miniature town set up in the basement, with little stations, tunnels, and bridges. It was beautiful." She let out a wistful sigh. "One year, he got a new engine for Christmas, and he proudly took Fi and me downstairs to show it off. We watched the train go around and around, and I don't know why I did it, but...I reached out and touched it. There was a flash and smoke. Or maybe I just remember it that way. All I know is that none of the trains worked afterward."

"Oh, Willow." Scottie ached to pull her close, to wrap her arms around her and shelter her from that painful memory, but she sensed that Willow was too full of reproach for herself to allow it right now.

"My parents didn't talk to me the entire two-hour ride home. After that, we stopped going to my grandparents' for Christmas." In the dim light, Willow's lips formed a tight line. "Natural consequences, right?"

"What? Oh my God, no! Willow, that's not the same!" Scottie sat up in bed. "You didn't do anything wrong. Of course you touched the train! You were a kid! That's how kids learn. By touching things, exploring, and—"

"But I'd already learned! Or at least I should have. My parents had told me a thousand times not to touch other people's stuff."

"You think my parents didn't tell me to stay away from my mom's scissors?" The words poured out of Scottie, and she couldn't make herself stop—didn't want to make herself stop. "But when I didn't listen, they didn't punish me by refusing to talk to me, taking away the dollhouse, or forbidding me from ever playing with Jen and Hazel again."

"Of course they didn't," Willow said.

"Yeah, but that's basically what your parents did to you!" Scottie cut in before Willow could say anything else, too agitated to stay quiet. If she ever got to meet Willow's parents, she'd have to use up all her self-control so she wouldn't yell at them until they understood what they had done to their daughter. "Giving you the cold-shoulder treatment and taking away visits with your grandparents... That's just cruel! You didn't deserve that!"

"But I touched the engine," Willow said, as if stuck on that one thought. "I destroyed it."

"Did you mean to?" Scottie asked, already knowing the answer.

Willow wildly shook her head. "N-no, of course not. It was just so fascinating, and I wanted to see...to...to..." Her voice broke.

Scottie let herself sink back onto the mattress until her face was right in front of Willow's and she could make out her eyes in the dim light. "Willow, you weren't the one who messed up that day. Your parents were. Big-time."

"It's not their fault. They were overwhelmed. Didn't know how to handle things," Willow got out. "Handle me."

"It wasn't your fault either. You didn't choose this." Scottie made a helpless gesture, indicating the glitches and jolts. "So why the hell were they treating you like you were Darth Vader with a jackhammer?"

Laughter exploded from Willow. Then, within a heartbeat, it turned into sobs. She pressed her hands to her mouth to muffle them, but the raw, heart-wrenching sounds slipped past her fingers.

Scottie's heart ached for her. She understood. This wasn't about the model train. It was about the people Willow had lost because of her tech quirk, the bonds she'd never been able to make. Finally, she couldn't stand it anymore. "Willow, please... Can I hold you?"

"You'll get zapped," Willow choked out.

"I don't care if you don't."

Scottie opened her arms, and when Willow crawled into them, she braced for a painful jolt.

A faint spark arced between them, visible in the dark, but instead of the sharp sting she'd expected, it felt more like a tickle, as if Willow's body and mind were too exhausted to build up a more powerful charge.

Willow burrowed into her, face pressed to the spot where Scottie's neck met her shoulder.

The hot breath on her skin sent a rush of sensations down Scottie's body, but the fierce protectiveness she felt was the stronger emotion.

She trailed her hands up and down Willow's back in a slow, soothing rhythm. "You did nothing wrong," she whispered again and again. "You didn't deserve that."

Every now and then, a shudder ran through Willow, as if decades-old tensions were draining from her body. Her breath came in shaky gulps, but no tears dripped onto Scottie's shoulder. That little bit of reserve made Scottie ache for her even more.

She held her close until Willow's breathing finally started to calm and the stiffness in her shoulders melted away in their tight embrace.

"You did nothing wrong," Scottie whispered one last time. "It was never your fault. Never. Do you get that?"

Willow didn't answer.

For a moment, Scottie thought she was still reprimanding herself, struggling to believe that she hadn't deserved her parents' punishment. But then she realized that Willow had fallen asleep in her arms.

A feeling she couldn't name swept over her. It wasn't just that she was falling deeper in love with Willow every day, though she knew that was happening too.

But Willow—reserved Willow, who kept her heart behind a firewall—letting Scottie see her so vulnerable, allowing herself to be held, dropping off to sleep in sheer exhaustion half on top of her...

It took Scottie's breath away and humbled her in a way nothing ever had.

Scottie stayed awake a little while longer, holding Willow close, listening to her soft breathing in the darkness.

When her eyelids grew heavy and her muscles twitched, at the edge of sleep, she pressed a gentle kiss to the top of Willow's head. "Sweet dreams."

Willow murmured something unintelligible, clearly still sound asleep.

Scottie settled the covers more comfortably around Willow's shoulders. Then she closed her eyes and drifted off to sleep with one final thought: Was it too late to switch out the paper snowflake she'd hung on the corporate tree? If she got just one wish for Christmas, it would be for Willow to finally be at peace with herself.

Chapter 38

Willow drifted awake in a bubble of warmth and comfort. She blinked, trying to orient herself in the unfamiliar bedroom. Something soft yet solid pressed against her side and pinned her to the mattress. It took her sleep-dazed brain a few moments to realize what—or rather who—it was.

Scottie was sprawled half on top of her, one arm draped over Willow's waist, one leg slung across her thigh as if claiming Willow in her sleep. Her face was tucked against the curve of Willow's neck. Warm breath washed over Willow's skin while soft strands tickled her collarbone.

Sometime during the night, they had apparently traded places. Now Willow was lying on her back, with Scottie nestled against her like a big, floppy, lovable golden retriever puppy.

A contented hum vibrated through Scottie, and she snuggled even closer, her leg tightening around Willow's own, as if trying to prevent her from going anywhere.

Tenderness flooded Willow. She lay very still, hoping to make this moment last forever.

But all too soon, other, less pleasant memories of the night before crept in.

God, she couldn't believe she'd fallen asleep on Scottie and, worse, cried all over her...again! She really had to stop doing that. But being here with Scottie's family had stirred up a lot of stuff for her—things she hadn't even been aware were still bothering her.

She remembered the last words she'd heard before she'd drifted off to sleep. "You did nothing wrong," Scottie had said in a soothing yet fierce whisper. "You didn't deserve that."

Lying here, with Scottie's warmth covering her, a tiny part of her started to believe it.

She'd been just a curious kid. What she'd done was no worse than Scottie cutting inches off her parents' flokati rug. The mental image of little Scottie—Barbie in one hand, a pair of scissors in the other—proudly showing off the "freshly mowed lawn" made her chuckle.

Compared to that, was touching her grandfather's engine really so bad?

Scottie twitched. Her eyes fluttered open, still hazy with sleep. She yawned and stretched luxuriously, her strong body sliding against Willow's in ways that suddenly made her wide-awake.

"Morning." Scottie's husky voice rumbled through her, sending a ripple of goose bumps up Willow's spine. She lifted her head off Willow's shoulder, and a soft smile spread over her face as she glanced down at her. With her hair a disheveled mess, she somehow managed to look both adorable and sexy at the same time. "How do you feel?"

"Good," Willow said and was amazed to find that it was true. "Lighter." She reached up and smoothed back a few of Scottie's wild strands. "I'm really sorry about last night. I didn't mean to—"

Scottie stopped her with a soft touch to her cheek. "Don't apologize. I suspect your parents probably told you the opposite, but with me, you're allowed to have feelings."

"I do," Willow whispered. "Have them."

Scottie raised herself up on one elbow, leaning over her.

Their gazes locked.

Slowly, without looking away, Scottie traced the curve of Willow's lower lip with the pad of her thumb. "Yeah?"

Before Willow could decide whether this was the moment to confess her love or lean up and kiss her, the door burst open.

"Auntie Scottie! Willow!" Logan shouted. "Get up! Santa came!" He charged into the room, followed by his sister, Lily, both still in pajamas.

Groaning, Scottie rolled onto her back, away from Willow. "Hey, you're supposed to knock first, remember, buddy?"

Logan skidded to a stop next to the bed. "Oh. Sorry. But Santa came! You have to come downstairs!"

"Um, can we have five more minutes?"

"No! It's time for presents!" He pulled on Scottie's arm.

"Auntie Carol said to tell you there's coffee," Lily announced with all the seriousness of an eight-year-old on an important mission.

Willow gave her bedmate an amused look. "Your mom's got your number."

"Nah." Scottie pressed a quick kiss to her cheek and whispered into her ear, "You do."

When Willow blushed, Scottie grinned and bounced out of bed. "We'll be right down. Go and make sure your dad doesn't drink all the coffee."

When Willow followed Scottie downstairs, the house looked as if everyone had been up for hours already. The heavenly scent of roasting turkey drifted over from the kitchen, and the smart speaker apparently worked again, playing soft Christmas music.

Scottie's parents, her great-aunt, several aunts and uncles, and one remaining cousin—Noah—were in the living room, gathered around the tree.

Willow and Scottie squeezed onto the large, L-shaped couch between Rick and Carol and watched the kids dive into their piles of presents.

Once their excited squeals had calmed down, Willow placed the first of her presents on Scottie's lap.

Scottie tore off the wrapping paper with the same enthusiasm as her cousin's kids. "Ooh, a hoodie!" She pulled it out and traced the little cartoon character—a witch brandishing a sparkling wand—and the letters that read *Tech Witch.* "Perfect!" She pulled it on over her T-shirt right then and there, wearing it proudly as she opened the second gift Willow had gotten her.

When the paper fell away, Scottie stared down at leather straps and metal buckles that were clearly meant to go around her hips. Instead of showing off her gift to the rest of the family, she peered at Willow with raised eyebrows.

Willow burst out laughing and gave her an it's-not-what-you're-thinking look. "It's a gardening tool belt, with leather holsters for your pruner and all the other gardening tools."

"Oh. Right." Scottie fully pulled it free of the paper and touched the smooth leather. "Exactly what I assumed it was."

"Right." Willow chuckled, enjoying that, for once, she'd been the one to make Scottie blush.

Scottie playfully dug her elbow into her side. "Thank you. Now I'll look really badass while I plant tomatoes."

"Yes," Willow murmured, already imagining it. "You definitely will."

"Hey, you two, stop it!" Scottie's father called over to them.

Willow froze. So far, the Prescotts had seemed completely at ease with any displays of affection from them. Had she misjudged them, and they weren't fine with it after all?

But Rick was grinning as he nodded down at the weather station he had just unboxed. He had immediately set up his new toy, but something didn't seem quite right with it—the display insisted the temperature inside the house was 105 degrees. "You're messing with the sensors."

A flutter of panic raced through Willow. *Oh God. He knows! He knows it's me causing all the glitches!*

Rick tapped the screen, and the displayed temperature ticked up to 106. "Those heated looks definitely have to stop, you two." His tone was teasing.

Oh. Ohh. So that was what he'd meant. He was neither homophobic, nor did he suspect that her energy was messing with his weather station. Willow slumped against the back of the couch.

Scottie softly rubbed her knee, and Willow leaned against her side, trying to slow her racing heart.

"Here." Scottie set a heavy package onto her lap, probably to distract her. "Open it."

Willow hoped no one noticed that her fingers were trembling as she carefully removed the paper—or if they did, they would think it was just excitement.

When she lifted the lid, she forgot about the weather station.

On her lap, with a red satin bow wrapped around it, sat the beautiful old typewriter she'd admired at the Memory Den!

Willow lovingly trailed her fingers over the keys. "Scottie," she whispered. "You didn't!"

"Totally did." Scottie beamed as if she were the one receiving this incredible gift. "I saw the way you looked at it, so I went back and got it as soon as they opened the next day."

Willow swallowed. "You spent way too much, but…thank you. It'll get a special place of honor in my collection."

The Prescotts leaned closer, oohing and aahing over the typewriter.

Only Great-Aunt Dorothy seemed unimpressed. "What's so special about that thing?" The lines on her forehead became more pronounced as she squinted at it. "I had one just like it when I first started at Oakley and McLanders."

The rest of the family burst out laughing, which only deepened Dorothy's frown.

When Willow wanted to set the typewriter back in its box, Scottie stopped her with a touch to her arm. "There's something else inside."

Willow peeked into the box.

It was a laminated badge, dangling from a rainbow lanyard. A photo of herself stared back at Willow, and she recognized it as one of the pictures Scottie had taken beneath the Troll Bridge.

Below the photo, bold letters read: *VIP girlfriend badge.*

Laughter rose up Willow's chest, replacing part of her anxiety.

"Well," Scottie said, a crooked grin playing around her lips, "you said you wanted one."

Willow nodded. "Thank you." She lifted it from the box and slipped the rainbow lanyard around her neck. While she loved the typewriter, the badge might be her favorite gift ever.

In the meantime, the Prescotts had opened more of their own gifts.

Carol held a digital photo frame and watched with a happy smile as the screen cycled through pictures of her loved ones. "Oh, that's so cute! Look, that's Scottie as a five-year-old!" She pressed the frame into Willow's hands.

The rotation of photos halted, frozen on little Scottie's adorable gap-toothed grin.

Willow's stomach twisted into a knot. *Oh, no, no, no. Not again!*

"Hey, at least it's got good taste," Scottie said, probably trying to laugh it off. "It could have stopped on a picture of Noah."

Noah threw a crumpled-up ball of wrapping paper at her.

"Let me see." Rick took the frame from Willow's trembling hands, and it immediately started working again.

It wasn't broken, and neither was the weather station, Willow tried to tell herself. They were just glitching and would start to work again once she left. All she had to do was stay calm for the rest of the visit so she wouldn't affect anything else.

"Uh, Auntie Carol?" Lily's voice came from the kitchen. Apparently, she had gotten bored at the slow pace at which the adults opened their presents, so she had wandered into the kitchen, maybe hoping to sneak some candy. "Is the turkey supposed to look like this?"

Everyone jumped up and rushed into the kitchen.

Carol hurried to the oven and yanked the door open.

Smoke curled up.

Quickly, Scottie crossed the kitchen and opened a window before the smoke alarm could go off.

When the smoke cleared, Willow caught a glimpse of the turkey. The once magnificent twenty-pound bird was now a black heap.

"What happened?" Rick asked. "Did you set it to the wrong temperature?"

Carol helplessly fanned the turkey, as if that would make any difference. "No. It's at 325 degrees."

Rick turned off the oven and peered inside, then immediately jerked back. "Damn, the heating element is running full blast! I'd bet money the temperature sensor malfunctioned." He grinned at Scottie and Willow. "I told you two to stop messing with the sensors!"

It was a joke, but it pierced Willow's paper-thin defenses. Nausea gripped her. She had done this, and this time, it wasn't just a little glitch. She had ruined Christmas for Scottie's kind, welcoming family!

The need to escape—to leave before she could cause any more disasters—overwhelmed her. She had to get away before she turned the rest of dinner into a smoldering heap of ash too or destroyed Carol's brand-new fridge.

Don't cry! Don't you dare cry again. Not in front of them.

Before anyone could see the tears burning in her eyes, she pushed past Uncle Dave and stumbled through the obstacle course of boots in the hall.

The screen door closed behind her with a thud.

Cold air stung her overheated cheeks. It seeped through her socks, and she realized too late she hadn't even paused to put on shoes. She gripped the railing and stared out across the yard without seeing anything. Maybe her parents had been right after all. She should have stayed home.

The door creaked open behind her.

Willow straightened and pressed the heels of her palms to her eyes but didn't turn around. "I'm okay, Scottie. Go back inside. I just need a minute."

But instead of leaving, footsteps crossed the porch toward her.

When she turned, it wasn't Scottie; it was her parents.

Without saying a word, Carol walked over and gently wrapped a coat—her husband's, judging by the size—around Willow's shoulders. Rick followed and set a pair of slippers on the porch beside her.

Their kindness nearly undid her. Her eyes started to prickle again, and she kept her gaze on the slippers as she shoved her feet inside so they wouldn't see her tears.

They studied her, their expressions a mixture of genuine concern and confusion.

"What happened, honey?" Carol asked. "Did you and Scottie have a fight?"

"No," Willow croaked out, not wanting them to think for even a second Scottie was to blame for this mess in any way. "Scottie had nothing to do with it. I was the one who ruined dinner."

Carol gently rubbed Willow's coat-covered arm. "Nonsense. How could you have ruined anything? You weren't even in the kitchen!"

The door opened again, and Scottie slipped out onto the porch. "Mom! Dad! I told you to give her a minute!"

Her parents didn't look at her. Their questioning gazes remained fixed on Willow.

"What's going on?" Rick asked.

Scottie stepped next to Willow but didn't answer for her or try to take over.

Willow knew it was her decision, even if it was one she didn't want to make. But even less, she wanted to keep lying. The Prescotts deserved better.

She looked at Scottie, and a slight glimmer of hope flickered alive inside of her. Maybe, like Scottie, her family would believe her. Maybe they wouldn't laugh or whisper behind her back or start treating her like a menace.

She gripped the railing with one hand, digging her nails into the painted wood while clutching the VIP girlfriend badge around her neck with the other. "It's me. I zap people, and I do things to anything electronic. I make devices glitch or the batteries drain, and it gets worse when I'm nervous or stressed. I was the one who made the blender stop working, the speaker cut out, the photo frame freeze, and the weather station go haywire. And I torched the turkey." She wrapped the coat more tightly around herself, unable to look at them, afraid to see their reactions. "I'm sorry I ruined your Christmas. So, so sorry."

"You didn't ruin anything," Rick said.

Slowly, Willow dared to glance up.

"Yes, some people build up more static than others, and discharges can damage microchips if you're handling them directly, but studies show that human electromagnetic fields simply aren't strong enough to—"

"Forget the studies, Dad," Scottie sharply cut in. She wrapped one arm around Willow's shoulders. "This isn't high school physics. I've seen it happen, and so have you!" She gestured toward the house with her free hand. "What more proof do you need? Just trust what Willow is telling you!"

Rick scratched his head and studied Willow for what felt like a long time. "What you're describing shouldn't be possible."

"Dad!" Scottie growled out, heat in her eyes.

"Actually, I know a guy like that," Noah piped up from the screen door. "Barry from accounting can never get his key card to work. Sometimes, even his car doesn't unlock."

Willow squeezed her eyes shut. *Wonderful.* The entire family had witnessed her confession.

"Would you let me finish?" Rick raised his voice to be heard over the commotion. He turned toward Willow. "What I was going to say is this... I've been teaching physics for nearly thirty-five years. I admit my mind is reeling right now, trying to pick this apart and prove it's not possible."

Willow leaned more heavily against Scottie's side. She couldn't blame him, even though his disbelief stung.

"But then again, back in spring, I didn't think it would be possible to have Scottie home for Christmas, happy and smiling, instead of holed up in Portland, brooding over the woman whose name shall not be mentioned. Yet here she is." He smiled at his daughter. "So clearly, I don't know everything about what's possible."

His wife elbowed him. "Yeah, honey. That's what I keep telling you. There are more things in heaven and earth than your physics books know." She turned toward Willow. "Don't worry about the turkey. So what if it's a little, uh, crispy?"

An incredulous giggle bubbled up Willow's chest before she could stop it. She stared at Scottie's mom. "It's not just a little crispy; it's incinerated! I turned it into a twenty-pound lump of charcoal!"

"We don't care about the damn turkey," Carol responded.

"Or that photo frame or the weather station or any of that newfangled stuff," Great-Aunt Dorothy called from inside the house.

Carol nodded. "What we care about is seeing Scottie happy. Right?"

"Right," the entire family chorused.

"And you seem to make her happy. So..." Carol pulled open the door and gestured for Willow to step back inside.

Willow hesitated, still not fully trusting that it was a good idea. "But dinner—"

Scottie squeezed her gently. "We still have the ham, the mashed potatoes, the green beans, the sweet potato casserole, and enough pie to feed an army. We're fine."

Uncle Dave stepped onto the porch. "What's everyone doing out here? Can we finally get the food on the table? I'm starving!"

Rick's booming laughter echoed down the street.

His wife joined in, and soon the entire family was laughing, even though Willow suspected one or two of them might still have no clue what was going on.

Willow wasn't sure she had fully grasped it either. How could the Prescotts just shrug and ask her back inside now that they knew what was really going on with her? Did they honestly not care about the string of malfunctioning devices she left in her wake?

The entire clan trooped back into the house.

For a few seconds, Willow stared after them, still not able to wrap her mind around it. Then she stumbled after them on shaky legs, with Scottie half pulling, half steadying her.

Noah closed the door after them. "Next year, we'll skip the turkey and order Chinese takeout. I've wanted that for years."

"And everyone is getting socks," Carol added with a playful grin. "No electronics."

The teasing continued as everyone helped get the food on the table, but Willow didn't hear any of it because Noah's words kept echoing through her brain. *Next year!*

She gave Scottie a wide-eyed look. Despite everything—all of the glitches and the things they wouldn't be able to have with her around—they wanted her back next Christmas, when even her own family hadn't welcomed her into their homes?

Scottie gave her a soft, understanding smile. "That's decided, then. Hope you like egg rolls."

Willow laughed, and the tears she'd been fighting for the last half hour finally slipped down her cheeks. She quickly wiped them away. "Love them," she croaked out.

Holding tightly to Scottie's hand, she followed her into the kitchen.

Chapter 39

Scottie was grateful her mom had sent them home with enough food to feed both Greene sisters for a week because Willow hadn't had time to breathe, much less cook, since they'd returned.

Willow was struggling to keep up with her usual workload while also preparing for the looming presentation, plus trying to make up for the time she lost whenever her computer or software acted up.

As a result, Scottie hadn't seen her outside of the office since they'd returned from Corvallis.

Finally, for New Year's Eve, they'd made plans to spend the evening together, and Scottie couldn't wait.

By three o'clock, she was itching to leave work. Mateo had already clocked out early, and Gordon was only delaying going home because his in-laws were visiting.

Just as she shut down her computer and shouldered her laptop bag, her phone buzzed with a text.

It was from Willow.

I'm so sorry! I know we wanted to go see the drone show at the square, but I'm still stuck in the middle of a thousand things. PowerPoint nuked every single transition, and I'll have to redo all of them. I'm going to be here until at least eight.

That would be cutting it pretty close since the drone show started at nine, and she didn't want Willow to get there totally exhausted. *We could go to the later one, at midnight,* Scottie texted back. *Or we could order Chinese and stay in. Let's see how you feel once you make it out of here.*

Three little dots appeared, then disappeared, as if Willow wasn't sure she should accept the offer. Finally, her reply popped up. *Are you sure you really don't mind? I feel awful about changing our plans last-minute.*

Scottie sent back a hugging emoji. *As long as I get to kiss you at midnight, I'm up for anything.*

I can promise you that, Willow answered right away. *I'll be with you at the stroke of midnight, even if I have to threaten PowerPoint with a stapler.*

Scottie chuckled and was about to reply when the door swung open.

Miles Donnelly, her direct supervisor, stood in the doorway. "Scottie. Can I talk to you for a minute before you leave?"

"Sure." Scottie pocketed her phone, slid the laptop bag off her shoulder, and followed him to his office, ignoring the what-the-hell-did-you-do-now look Gordon sent after her.

Miles closed the door behind them, which was not a good sign.

He settled into his leather chair and gestured at her to take a seat.

With growing tension, she sank onto the visitor's chair.

He leaned forward, resting his forearms on his desk, and regarded her with a serious expression. "You might remember the conversation we had back in October."

"Uh, which one?" Scottie asked. The one that immediately came to mind was, hopefully, not the one he was talking about.

"I asked you what the heck was going on with Willow Greene up in Operations because she'd already submitted a string of tickets not even two weeks into the job."

Scottie's stomach tightened, and she struggled to keep a neutral expression in place. "I remember." Somehow, she managed to keep her voice even.

"You assured me she wasn't sabotaging her devices," Miles said, "just having a bit of bad luck."

Scottie nodded tersely. "And that's still my assessment."

"I told you to keep an eye on her," Miles continued as if she hadn't said anything.

"I did." *Oh yeah. I really did.* She was looking at Willow any chance she got, watching the way she scrunched up her nose when she focused hard, tracing the elegant line of Willow's collarbone, admiring every graceful movement. But, of course, she wasn't going to tell her boss that.

Miles's gaze didn't soften. "I talked to her supervisor, Ms. Covey, this morning, and she mentioned Ms. Greene having some issues with Outlook before Christmas. So I checked the system to see if we'd managed to resolve the problem."

Alarm bells went off in Scottie's mind. She knew what he had found—or rather: what he *hadn't* found.

"Imagine my surprise when I couldn't find a single ticket for it." He let the words hang in the air.

Scottie's stomach seemed to plunge to her ankles.

That wasn't the only ticket missing in the system. At least a handful of times, she had slipped upstairs after five, when almost everyone was gone, or had casually dropped by during lunch, pretending to do a quick update when she had really fixed Willow's latest glitch. Plus she'd helped her on the phone nearly every day, all without official documentation.

She waited for him to bring up the other incidents, but he didn't.

Apparently, he didn't know the full extent of her VIP girlfriend support. He only seemed aware of the Outlook problems, not all the other glitches that had occurred since Mr. Sorensen had told Willow he wanted her to assist him with his important presentation.

Scottie's mind raced, scrambling for an excuse. "Sorry, boss, you're right! Totally my mistake! I happened to be upstairs, in Operations, when Outlook started acting up, so I fixed it on-site right away. I was going to create a ticket later, but it must've slipped my mind. With the new year approaching, I was focused on wrapping up the backlog instead of documenting an already resolved routine incident."

There, that sounded halfway reasonable while also downplaying the Outlook snafu.

Miles squinted at her, his bearded face a wall of disapproval. "Documentation isn't optional; you know that. You need to create a ticket for every problem you work on, even if you fix it in two minutes. What if it reoccurs? Or it turns out it's part of a network-wide, bigger problem? We'll never find out if it's not in the system." He tapped a pen against his desk as if to drive home his point. "From now on, you need to document every single issue, especially for an employee like Willow Greene."

An employee like Willow? What the hell was that supposed to mean? Scottie clenched her jaw. She wanted to snap at him, but, of course, she knew she couldn't. A confrontation would help neither her nor Willow.

With a herculean effort, she swallowed down an angry reply. "Of course. You're absolutely right. Won't happen again."

He gave her a terse nod. "See that it doesn't."

Stiffly, she rose and walked to the door.

"Oh, and Scottie?"

She turned, her tension skyrocketing.

"Enjoy your New Year's."

She nodded and murmured something—hopefully "happy New Year to you too" and not "screw you!" Her head spun so fast that she wasn't sure.

Then the office door closed behind her, and she slumped against the wall. *Shit.* That had been close. Too close.

She stumbled back to her office on shaky legs.

Gordon immediately looked up from his screens. "What did he want?"

"He reamed me a new one for not documenting Willow's Outlook issues," Scottie muttered.

He swiveled his chair around to face her fully. "I take it he doesn't know about her SAP issues, the Teams glitches, or her ongoing feud with the printer?"

Shit. Scottie stared at him. "You know about that?"

"Please. You might be able to fool Mateo and even Miles, but I've been around since people thought floppy disks were high tech!"

She should have known. For someone who rarely left his desk, he had eyes everywhere.

"She's not tanking her devices on purpose just so she can see you, is she?" His question didn't sound like an accusation…or even really like a question.

Scottie didn't want to lie to him, but neither could she explain the full truth, so she just said: "No."

He nodded as if he'd already known that too.

She waited for the expected interrogation—for him to dig for the real reason Willow was experiencing so many tech disasters.

Instead, he just asked, "So, what's your plan?"

Scottie rubbed her hands over her face. "I don't really have one. I'll have to be more careful, I guess, but I won't stop helping her, and I can't create a new ticket every time one of Willow's devices glitches. She's already under scrutiny, and I can't let her lose her job."

He adjusted his wire-frame glasses and gave her a somber look. "If you're not careful, you're going to lose yours."

His quiet words hit her like a punch to the gut. She had willingly stepped onto a ledge, and now Gordon had pointed out how steep the drop would be. "I know. Trust me, I know. But what can I do? I'm not going to let her fend for herself."

"Does she know you're not creating tickets for any of her issues?" Gordon asked.

Scottie hesitated. "She...might."

"What's that supposed to mean?"

"It means we didn't talk about it. She didn't ask if I'd document her problems, and I didn't tell her I wouldn't."

"Christ on a bike." He dragged his hand through his graying hair, disheveling the perfectly styled strands. "You've got your very own don't-ask-don't-tell situation. Sounds like it's getting really messy. How long do you think you can keep that up?"

"No idea." Scottie sighed. "As long as I have to. At least until Sorensen's presentation. After that, things should ease up a little."

When he opened his mouth, she held up her hand. She didn't want him to ask her what she would do if things didn't ease up or escalated before the presentation. Right now, she had no answers.

"I'd better get going." She slung her laptop bag over her shoulder and walked to the door but then paused and glanced back. "You won't mention this to anyone, will you?"

He gave her a blank look. "Mention what?"

"Right." She tipped an imaginary hat. "Thanks. And now go home before Lin files a missing person report."

"Nah. She knows exactly where I am—and why. I'm not keeping secrets from my wife."

Was that supposed to be a dig at her for not telling Willow she wasn't documenting her tech issues?

Maybe she was just imagining things because her nerves were raw.

She gave him a short wave, then walked out into the hallway and toward the elevator, relying on muscle memory to guide her because her head felt weirdly hollow.

Her thoughts were too slow and too fast at the same time, and yet they didn't come up with one useful solution.

She forced herself to focus on the one positive thing: She would see Willow tonight.

Whatever awaited her in the new year, she would worry about it later.

Chapter 40

Willow pulled into the nearly empty Kudos employee parking lot a little before nine on New Year's Day.

She'd barely managed to drag herself out of bed because she hadn't gotten home from watching the drone show with Scottie until two.

But she knew this was the perfect opportunity to catch up on the work she'd had to put aside while rebuilding that cursed PowerPoint presentation. There would be no interruptions from colleagues today and no witnesses around if any tech glitches happened, so she had gotten Celeste's permission to get into the otherwise closed building.

Suppressing a yawn, she climbed out of the car and locked it.

Two men were crossing the parking lot ahead of her.

She recognized one of them. With his dark, curly hair, Mateo was unmistakable even from behind. The man beside him was older and looked perfectly put together in a crisp suit and coat, his graying hair neatly parted.

Maybe he was IT management or one of the higher-ups from Finance or Sales.

Should she call out a greeting?

Before she could decide, Mateo's voice carried back to her. "I'm starting to feel like a CIA agent on a secret mission. Will you finally tell me why we have to do this today? We could've upgraded Marketing's monitors tomorrow."

"Self-preservation," the older man replied. "My mother-in-law has been visiting since Christmas."

So he wasn't Scottie's boss. He must be Gordon, the elusive third member of IT support.

"And why did *I* have to come?" Mateo grumbled.

"I wanted to talk to you without Scottie being around. I'm worried about her." Gordon kept his voice low, but it carried in the unusually still air.

Willow nearly crashed into a parked car. Her heart hammered against her ribs. Why was he worried about Scottie? What was going on?

"Me too." Mateo sighed. "It won't be long before Miles finds out what she's been doing—or rather: what she *hasn't* been doing. If she's not careful, she'll be the one they kick out the door."

Gordon stared at the younger man. "You know about that?"

Mateo huffed. "Please. Of course I know. It wasn't exactly hard to see when you're expecting it. You know Scottie. Loyal to a fault."

"Yeah. And that's why she's not going to stop. We'll have to find a way to—"

The rest of Gordon's words cut off as he used his badge to get them into the building, and the glass door closed behind them.

Willow stood rooted to the asphalt for a second, then darted after them.

It took her three tries before the card reader finally recognized her badge. When she burst into the building, Gordon and Mateo had already reached the elevator.

She sprinted across the lobby, her ankle boots squeaking on the travertine.

The two men entered the elevator, then turned, probably to see who was making such a ruckus.

Her heart raced as she jumped in after them.

Mateo froze with his hand still on the button for their floor. "Uh, hi, Willow. Happy New Year!"

Willow bit her lip. "Happy New Year."

"Willow?" Gordon echoed. Through his wire-frame glasses, his gaze flicked to her ID badge. "Oh. You're Scottie's Willow."

"Yes, I am." She tapped the button for the thirteenth floor with her knuckles, ignoring the sharp zap, then waited impatiently until the doors closed. "Sorry, but…I couldn't help overhearing your conversation. Is Scottie in trouble?"

Mateo mumbled something that sounded like a Spanish swear word. He and Gordon looked at each other and hesitated.

"Please. If something's wrong and she needs help, I have to know. What's going on?"

Gordon raked his fingers through his neatly combed hair. "Scottie would kill me if she knew I told you, but she's like a little sister to me, and I don't want her to lose her job."

Willow gripped the railing that ran along the metal wall. "Why would she lose her job? She's great at it!"

"She is. But she didn't log a ticket for your Outlook problems, and our boss noticed. Luckily, he doesn't know about any of the other issues you had lately, which she didn't document either. But if he ever finds out..."

A dozen different thoughts rushed through Willow's mind, all of them panicked. Scottie was in trouble with her boss—because of her. And Scottie's colleagues knew about her issues. Had Scottie told them?

No. She wouldn't do that. She'd protected Willow's secret from the moment she'd found out about it. Apparently, she had even gone so far as to not document any of her tech glitches.

Gordon and Mateo traded another look.

"You didn't know, did you?" Gordon asked quietly.

Willow shook her head, unable to speak. She had assumed Scottie wouldn't document the times she'd helped her on the phone, because, technically, it had been Willow who'd resolved the problem. Or maybe that she would downplay things in her reports. But she had assumed Scottie would at least open a ticket whenever she'd actually shown up at her desk to fix an issue.

Scottie hadn't filed anything at all, protecting Willow's job, even at the risk of losing her own.

Of course that's what loyal-to-the-bone Scottie had done. Willow should have suspected sooner. Instead of asking Scottie to make sure she wasn't endangering her career, she had simply let her handle it, and that was so out of character for her! She had never allowed herself to depend on anyone.

The elevator chimed, and the metal doors slid apart on the tenth floor.

Mateo stepped between them so they wouldn't close, while Gordon kept facing her. "I don't know what exactly is going on, but is there anything you can do to—?"

"Yes," she said before Gordon could even finish his question. "Don't worry. I'm not going to let her take the fall for me. Thank you for telling me."

He gave her a tense nod.

Mateo stepped back, and Gordon followed him out into the hallway.

Before any of them could think of something else to say, the doors closed between them.

Willow slumped against the elevator wall. The steel was cool against her back, but that was nothing compared to the coldness that gripped her inside at the thought of Scottie losing her job—because of her.

No! She would not let that happen.

Willow had spent her entire life dealing with her own messes. It was only recently that Scottie had made her believe that letting someone in was okay. That allowing someone to help wouldn't end in disaster.

She had started to rely on Scottie to an extent that, now that she thought about it, was as shocking as it was scary. It was outright dangerous—not just for her, but for Scottie too!

Under no circumstances would she allow her goddamn tech jinx to get Scottie fired. She had to put a stop to it, starting right now.

No more texts to Scottie whenever her software glitched. No more calling her for help with the printer. No more running to her superheroine with the IT toolbox whenever her computer acted up.

From now on, she would go back to fixing her own problems. She would learn work-arounds, sneak in replacement devices, or watch hours of YouTube tutorials to figure things out herself. She had done it for years, and she could do it again. And if she had to admit defeat because nothing she tried was working, she would go through official channels and submit a ticket to IT. If that got her into her boss's crosshairs, so be it.

The elevator dinged, and the doors opened on the thirteenth floor.

Mind still reeling, Willow walked toward the frosted glass door leading to the Operations bullpen.

Everything was dark behind it, and the door was still locked. Not even Celeste had come in today.

Willow gripped her ID card and tapped it against the door's sensor.

A red light flashed, and the card reader responded with a protesting beep, denying her access.

Two more tries yielded the same result.

Willow let out a sharp breath. "Okay." No texting Scottie. She was faced with the first tech problem of the day, and she would deal with it on her own.

No more VIP girlfriend IT support. The thought made her ache, but she knew it was necessary.

She fixed her gaze on the stubborn card reader and tried to come up with a way to outsmart it.

Chapter 41

Scottie gripped the warm paper bag containing Willow's favorite Chinese takeout and walked out of the elevator.

Silence greeted her on the usually busy thirteenth floor. Everyone had probably long since gone home, just Willow was still here, working late for the third time this week to make up for time she had lost dealing with tech glitches.

Willow truly was the hardest-working person Scottie had ever met. She knew how much it stung that some people in the company assumed she was lazy or incompetent. That couldn't have been further from the truth.

The frosted glass door leading to the bullpen stood open, and Scottie slipped inside.

Most of the overhead lights were turned off. Only one corner of the room was lit: the area around Willow's desk. Darkness had fallen outside, and raindrops clung to the floor-to-ceiling windows, blurring the lights from surrounding buildings and the MAX stop across the street.

Scottie's gaze veered across rows of empty desks and immediately zeroed in on Willow.

They hadn't seen each other since Sunday. Seventy-two long hours without a single glance at her, so Scottie paused at the edge of the cubicle labyrinth to drink her in.

Willow sat at her desk, shoulders hunched, her attention firmly locked onto her two-monitor setup. She hadn't noticed Scottie yet. Her normally neat ponytail was coming loose, as if she'd tugged at her hair in frustration. Faint shadows lingered under her eyes. Clearly, she wasn't sleeping enough.

Scottie worried that she was running herself ragged, but Willow had brushed off her concern, saying she just had to make it one more week, until the big presentation.

Of course, Scottie worried anyway—hence the takeout delivery.

The only good thing was that the tech hiccups had been surprisingly rare lately. Willow hadn't texted or called with an emergency in at least a week. No Outlook tantrums, no paper jams, not a single corrupted file... which was great, of course, but it also meant they hadn't gotten to spend any time together at work.

Wait a minute! If the glitches were taking a break, why was Willow working late to make up for lost time? And why had the tech disasters stopped? Shouldn't the pressure of the approaching presentation make them happen more frequently, not less often?

Something wasn't adding up.

"You trash heap of an ERP system," Willow muttered. "And here I thought German engineering was supposed to be efficient, not whatever the hell this is."

Ah. Scottie bit back a smile. Even annoyed, Willow managed to sound adorable. Clearly, she was wrestling with SAP. So the tech glitches hadn't stopped after all.

Scottie crossed the bullpen. "Hey, you."

Willow jumped. She snatched her hands away from the keyboard as if she'd been caught in the middle of hacking a government website. "Scottie!" She pressed her fingers to her chest. "You scared me half to death! I didn't hear you come in."

"Sorry. You were so focused on your work, I doubt you would have noticed a marching band walking in."

A tired smile darted across Willow's face. "I much prefer you to a marching band."

"Yeah, especially since the marching band wouldn't have brought you this." Scottie held up the bag, then set it down on the corner of Willow's desk. "Sesame chicken noodles, dumplings, and spring rolls. I hope this makes up for scaring you."

Willow's stomach let out an appreciative rumble. "That's so sweet of you. Thank you! I'll eat as soon as I finish this."

Scottie leaned a hip against the desk. "Something giving you trouble?"

Willow waved her hand. "Oh, just SAP being SAP."

"Why don't I take a look while you eat?" Scottie nudged the food toward her.

"It's fine. I've got this."

Scottie studied her for several moments. Something was wrong. Not with SAP but with Willow. She could almost see Willow's walls snapping back into place, and she didn't understand why she was suddenly being shut out. "What's going on?"

"Nothing," Willow said, but she didn't meet Scottie's gaze.

"Why won't you let me help you?" Scottie couldn't stop the frustration from leaking into her tone. "I thought we were past this whole one-woman army thing, where you think you have to solve every problem by yourself."

Willow pushed her desk chair back and stood so they were face-to-face. Her eyes flashed as she went from defensive retreat to heated counterattack. "Maybe it's because if I let you help, you'll get in trouble with your boss again and lose your job!"

Scottie's pulse stuttered. "How do you know about that?"

"Doesn't matter," Willow replied. "What matters is that you put your job on the line, without even telling me! What were you thinking?"

Scottie gripped the edge of the desk with both hands. "What was I supposed to do? Stand by and let that jackass Sorensen fire you?"

Willow inhaled and exhaled audibly, as if fighting down the urge to shout. "I appreciate that you tried to protect me, Scottie, but I never wanted you to risk your job for me, and I think you knew that. That's why you did it behind my back instead of telling me you weren't going to document anything."

"Maybe, but—"

"Maybe?" Willow drew out the word with a skeptical look on her face.

Oh no, Willow Greene. I know what you're doing. Willow was trying to make this all about Scottie to distract from the fact that she'd been dealing with her tech issues by herself all week. But Scottie wouldn't allow that. "What if I had told you? What would you have done?"

Willow opened her mouth, then closed it.

"Be honest," Scottie said. "You would have done exactly what you're doing now: pushed me away and tried to muddle through on your own. You wouldn't have asked me for help, even if technological Armageddon happened. Am I right?"

Willow visibly deflated. She dropped back onto her chair and swiped a tiny scrap of paper off her mouse pad. "Okay. Yes. That's probably what I would have done. I don't want you to get fired because of my problems."

Scottie perched on the edge of the desk, closer to Willow but not encroaching onto her personal space. "But that's the thing, Willow. There's no such thing as *your problems* and *my problems.* Just *ours.* We're supposed to be a team." She looked at Willow, desperate to get through to her. "Do you have your VIP girlfriend badge with you?"

Willow stared at her. "What?"

"Just humor me."

"Yes. It's right here." Willow dug through her purse and pulled out the laminated card. "Why?"

Aww. So she did carry it wherever she went. It gave Scottie hope. "Have you read the fine print?"

"Fine print?" Willow echoed.

Scottie made a swiveling motion with her finger. "It's on the back. I didn't want to point it out in front of my entire family since I wasn't sure you'd be comfortable with that."

Willow turned the badge over in her hands.

The fine print on the back of the laminated card said: *This badge grants its wearer lifetime access to: priority tech support, emergency coffee/chai latte/ takeout delivery, and unlimited hugs and kisses.*

Her gaze snapped back up, and Scottie knew exactly what phrase she was staring at: *Lifetime access.*

"That's what I want, Willow," Scottie said quietly. "A lifetime with you. I know we've only been dating for a month, and maybe I should slow down, be more careful to avoid getting burned again, but my heart is already in this, and I'm not going to pretend otherwise. I'm all in for life, and I don't want to keep sorting problems into *mine* and *yours.* Because, dammit, I love you!"

She'd been holding those words in for weeks, afraid to scare Willow off with too much, too soon. Blurting it out now, in the middle of an argument, wasn't the romantic moment she had envisioned. But if a lifetime together wasn't what Willow wanted, she would rather know now.

Willow went absolutely still.

Great. Now she had done it—scared Willow off. But she wouldn't take it back.

"Scottie..." Willow whispered. Her voice broke. "That's... I... The 'for life' thing is scaring the living daylights out of me."

Every bit of anger, fear, and frustration drained from Scottie's body, and her heart went out to Willow. "I know," she replied gently. She'd been aware of Willow's history, of course, or at least the little pieces Willow had let slip.

Willow glanced at the VIP girlfriend badge and smoothed her thumb across the fine print. "It's not that I don't want it, but...I've never been good at relationships. Never managed to achieve a happily ever after. The best I could do was a happy for now."

"I get it," Scottie answered. "After Tanya broke up with me, I felt that way too. I spent months trying to figure out where I went wrong. How we went from our happily ever after to 'I want more from life than this.'"

Willow reached out as if to touch her hand but then didn't.

"Finally, I figured something out," Scottie continued. "A happy ending is not a finish line that you cross once and then you'll be happy forever. It's not a goal; it's a journey. A choice that you make every single day—a choice to be there for each other, no matter what. Tanya stopped making that choice. But I want you to know that, with you, I never will. Like I said, I'm all in for the rest of my life."

Willow clamped her teeth around her lower lip, maybe to hide its trembling.

"But it'll only work if you make the same choice. If you're all in too." Scottie paused and gathered all her courage. "Are you?"

Willow didn't move. She wasn't even sure she was still breathing. All she could do was stare at Scottie.

Her words echoed through Willow's mind on auto-repeat, and the "I love you" made her heart thump against her ribs.

Every fiber of her being yearned to throw her arms around Scottie, kiss her until they both couldn't breathe, and tell her she loved her and would be hers forever too.

But the words got stuck in her throat. It wasn't that she didn't want it. God, she wanted it so much...and that was the scariest part. She'd never allowed herself to want or even hope for a relationship that lasted a lifetime. Old instincts screamed at her to protect herself.

When Willow didn't answer, the hopeful look on Scottie's face dimmed, and her shoulders sagged. "You still don't trust me. You don't trust us."

"What? Of course I trust you!" Willow said quickly. "I trust you more than I've ever trusted anyone."

Scottie pressed her lips together. "Not fully. You're still waiting for me to wake up one day and decide I've had enough of the tech glitches and tell you it's all too much. That *you* are too much."

Willow flinched. She had no defenses against those words because, deep down, she knew they were true.

Scottie's expression softened, the ragged edges of frustration and hurt smoothed out by compassion. "I have a feeling you carried that fear with you in every relationship you had."

"Of course I did!" Willow blurted out. "Because that's what happened every single time. My girlfriends only stick around until I become too inconvenient or weird. Once they get tired of the glitches, they leave." Her eyes burning, she faced Scottie. "I don't just destroy electronics. I'm a relationship jinx too."

Scottie fiercely shook her head. "I don't believe that. You're not jinxing your relationships—at least not the way you think."

Willow's stomach was a knot of tension. "W-what do you mean?"

"I think you're creating self-fulfilling prophecies. You were involved with a few assholes who didn't believe you about the tech thing or got fed up with it, and then you convinced yourself that it'll always be like that, with everyone. That relationships never last. So to protect yourself, you never become fully invested. You always hold back a little, keeping things neatly separated into *yours* and *mine*. And that's not a way to build a happy ending, Willow. Maybe it's not only the glitches your partners get tired of—it's you shutting them out."

Willow's vision blurred. Overhead, the fluorescent lights flickered, but she couldn't tell whether she was causing it or just imaging it. The office chair seemed to spin around and around, making her dizzy, even though she knew it wasn't moving. She desperately gripped the armrests as her world tilted on its axis.

She wanted to fight, to protest, to tell Scottie she was wrong, but she knew there was some truth to it.

Okay, a lot of truth.

She had known since Christmas that she was in love with Scottie and wanted to build a life with her, but rather than telling her, she had kept it to herself and had gone back to fixing her own problems. Yes, she had really thought she'd done it to protect Scottie from getting fired. But she could have talked to her—could have tried to find a better solution together.

Instead, she had retreated and gone straight back into "one-woman army" mode, as Scottie had called it, because she was scared to let herself need Scottie, not just for IT support but for emotional support too.

She had spent most of her life trying to keep things contained—her effect on electronics, her emotions, her relationships. But Scottie didn't fit in a safe little box. She had slipped past all of Willow's defenses, and that was scary as hell, so she'd retreated into the lifelong habit that had always protected her: shutting people out and hiding that part of herself.

"You're right," she got out through a tight throat. "God, you're right. I got scared, and I pushed you away. But I don't want to keep doing that with you. I just have no idea how to stop. It's so deeply ingrained..." She gave Scottie a helpless look. "It's what my parents drilled into me from the time I was very little: Handle your own problems, and never let anyone see."

Scottie stepped close enough that Willow could feel the heat emanating from her. "I know. It's not going to be easy at first, but you already let me see so much of you. Just continue to do more of that. Make the choice to try your best to let me in, day by day. The same way I choose you every day. Not just on the easy days, but on the days you create a dozen paper jams, swear at SAP, or are about two seconds away from throwing your laptop out the window."

She meant it with every cell of her very big heart. Willow could feel it. Scottie was all in, tech glitches be damned.

Now Willow had a choice to make: She could keep hiding behind her fears and make sure no one ever got too close. Or she could take a leap, trusting Scottie to catch her.

"I'm done," she croaked out.

Scottie's expression crumbled. She pressed her hands to her belly as if she'd been struck.

"Oh my God! No! No!" Willow shouted. "I didn't mean I'm done with you. With us. I meant I'm done holding back. I'm all in too."

The broadest, most beautiful smile Willow had ever seen spread across Scottie's face. "You are?"

Willow gave her a tremulous smile in return. "I am." She held up her hand, stopping Scottie from pulling her up from the chair and into her arms. "But if we're really in this together, partners for life, you can't make decisions for me behind my back either, not even to protect me. Like deciding not to write tickets for any of my glitches. Because, dammit, I love you too, and I don't want you to lose your job."

Scottie stared at her.

Willow stared back.

They moved at the same time—Willow jumping up from the chair and Scottie crossing the remaining distance between them. They crashed into an embrace so fierce it felt as if it tore down every remaining wall inside of Willow.

A bright spark jumped between them, and both gasped as a tiny jolt zapped through them.

But this time, instead of flinching back, they leaned into it, almost welcoming it. In a weird way, it felt like a confirmation that they wouldn't let anything—not even Willow's tech affliction or her tendency to build up static electricity—come between them.

"Deal," Scottie whispered, her breath warm on Willow's face. "No more solo missions for either of us. From now on, we'll make all decisions together."

Then their lips found each other without hesitation, and the kiss instantly deepened.

Willow held nothing back, letting herself feel it all.

Scottie's soft lips moved against hers with the same urgency. A sigh that sounded like a mix of relief and hunger vibrated against Willow's mouth.

With an answering moan, Willow slid her fingers up the back of Scottie's neck and into her hair to pull her even closer.

Scottie trailed her hands down Willow's sides before settling them at her waist. The heat of her palms seared through the thin fabric of Willow's blouse, and her thumbs stroked small circles at the dip above her hips.

Willow's knees weakened, and she pressed more closely into Scottie's body for balance.

They tumbled against the desk, still kissing.

The corner dug into Willow's hip, and Scottie shot out one arm to steady her, nearly knocking the takeout bag to the floor.

It teetered on the edge for a moment, then somehow managed to stay upright instead of crashing to the floor.

"See?" Scottie whispered breathlessly, her lips hovering against Willow's and curving up into a smile. "No jinx."

Willow laughed, pressed her face to Scottie's neck, and deeply inhaled her scent. "Will you help me with SAP?" she whispered against Scottie's skin. "If we can figure out a way for you to do that without risking your job."

"Of course I will," Scottie said without the slightest hesitation.

"Maybe from now on, if I'm dealing with a tech issue you can walk me through on the phone or via text, we can skip the ticket. But if you have to show up in person, especially if Celeste or anyone else is around, you document it in the system." Willow finally pulled back a few inches to look at Scottie's face.

Scottie sighed. "I'll feel like I'm reporting you to the principal. But okay. We'll handle it that way."

"Thank you." Willow pressed a soft kiss to Scottie's lips.

They lingered for a moment longer before finally pulling apart.

"So," Scottie said, her cheeks adorably flushed from their kisses. "What did SAP do to annoy you?"

"What didn't it do?" Willow muttered. "Every time I try to enter data into a field, it makes my cursor vanish and jumps me back to the top of the screen."

Scottie glanced at the monitor, then pulled out her phone and started to type.

"What are you doing?" Willow asked.

"Talking you through it via text," Scottie said without lifting her gaze off the phone. A mischievous grin lingered at the corners of her mouth. "So I don't have to file a ticket."

Willow couldn't help laughing. "You're impossible. But I love you."

The typing sounds stopped, and Scottie looked up and into Willow's eyes. "I don't think I'll ever be able to hear that without my heart doing that little flutter thing," she said, the softest expression on her face.

Willow stared at her in wonder. "Have I told you how much I love that you just say what you feel?"

"See? It's doing it again." Scottie made a fluttery motion over the left side of her chest. She shook her head as if to clear it. "Now eat your noodles and don't distract me from providing my first-class VIP girlfriend IT support."

Willow's stomach rumbled its approval. She sank onto her office chair and pulled out takeout containers.

The sound of text messages going out filled the bullpen.

Willow pierced a dumpling with her plastic fork. But instead of taking a bite, she looked at Scottie, who leaned against the desk, head bent over her phone, thumbs flying. The wavy strands framing her face were getting a little long again, falling into her eyes.

This time, it was Willow's heart that did the fluttery thing. She had to stop herself from getting up and kissing Scottie again. Instead, she forced herself to talk about the topic she'd avoided for weeks. "Scottie?" she asked quietly. "Will you help me figure out a game plan for the presentation? What do I do if the laptop doesn't boot up on the big day or PowerPoint glitches?"

Scottie lowered her phone and squeezed Willow's shoulder. "We," she said firmly. "What do *we* do. We'll figure something out together, okay? After you eat."

Willow believed her. For the first time in her life, she trusted that they would manage to beat her tech glitches—together. "Okay." She put her hand on top of Scottie's, grounding herself in her warmth, before finally sliding the fork into her mouth with a contented hum.

Chapter 42

"Small tweaks, my ass," Willow muttered while she worked. The last-minute changes Mr. Sorensen had requested were neither small nor tweaks. She'd been at this for an hour and wasn't even one-third done. This wasn't how she'd wanted to spend her Sunday afternoon.

Her phone vibrated with an incoming text.

She had set it down at a safe distance from herself, on the other side of her bedroom.

Groaning, she got up from the small desk tucked into the corner and crossed to the shelf.

It was a message from Scottie.

Hey, beautiful. I was wondering if you want to do something today to distract yourself.

Willow swallowed at the reminder that tomorrow was the big day—the presentation that would decide whether she would get to keep her job.

A second text arrived. *There's a vintage flea market at the Expo Center. Want to go? We could grab an early dinner afterward.*

I wish I could, Willow replied. *But Mr. Sorensen sent over some last-minute changes that I need to get done today. I'm really sorry.*

Scottie's reply arrived within seconds. *You don't need to apologize. Can I come over and hang out while you work? I promise to be as quiet as a mouse. You won't even know I'm there.*

Willow doubted it. She would be very aware of Scottie's presence. But that wasn't necessarily a bad thing. *I'd love that,* she typed. *But are you sure that's how you want to spend your Sunday?*

Scottie had spent every evening that week running Willow through tech-failure drills, going over anything that could go wrong during the presentation and teaching Willow how to fix it. Did she really want to spend the day watching Willow work instead of finally doing something fun?

Very sure, Scottie replied. *Be there in twenty.*

Willow stared at her phone. Okay, that was new.

Not working weekends. She had always done that to catch up on work she hadn't gotten done at the office because of tech glitches.

What was new was her girlfriend's reaction. Past partners had always complained. They would never have considered hanging out while Willow worked.

But with Scottie, everything was different. For the first time, Willow caught herself believing that a happily ever after might be possible for her after all.

Twenty minutes later, the doorbell rang.

Willow hurried downstairs and opened the door before Fiona could.

Scottie stood in front of her, a paperback novel in one hand and a bag from a bakery in the other. "Marzipan pastries," she said with a grin.

The sight of her made Willow melt. "God, you are the perfect girlfriend. Whoever Tanya is with now, she seriously downgraded."

Scottie's grin eased into something gentler and more vulnerable. "Thank you," she whispered, as if it was exactly what she had needed to hear.

And it probably was. As confident, cheerful, and optimistic as Scottie was most of the time, she also had a soft heart that could be bruised or broken.

Willow vowed right then and there to never be the one who did that to her. Keeping one hand on the metal part of the doorframe, she curled the other arm around Scottie and kissed her.

It wasn't just a short hello; it was slow and heartfelt, neither of them caring that the door was still open and the entire neighborhood could see them.

Scottie's lips, cool from the winter air outside, quickly warmed up beneath hers. Even with her hands full, she wrapped both arms around Willow and pulled her closer.

"Get a room, you two," Fiona shouted from the living room.

Reluctantly, they disentangled themselves.

"I *have* a room," Willow shouted back. Before her sister could fire back another comment, she took the pastries from Scottie, grabbed her hand, and led her past the living room to the stairs at the end of the hall.

So far, they had spent all their time together at Scottie's apartment, mostly because she lived alone. Willow was very aware that Scottie was about to see her bedroom for the first time.

She opened the door and let Scottie enter, closely watching her face as Scottie looked around. She knew exactly what Scottie would notice first: the lack of electronics. There was no TV on the wall, no iPad charging on the bedside table, no game console or smart speakers anywhere. The laptop on the small desk in the corner was the only electronic device—and even that was in her room temporarily.

Instead, one entire wall was lined with shelves displaying her typewriter collection. The portable Underwood Scottie had given her for Christmas proudly took up the center space.

Scottie walked over and studied them, hands clasped behind her back as if trying to be respectful and not touch anything without permission. Several strands of hair fell into her eyes as she bent to examine them more closely. "Wow," she murmured. "That's really amazing."

Willow leaned against the doorframe, studying her, not the typewriters. "Yes. Totally amazing."

Scottie straightened and turned, and their gazes met.

For a second, the urge to abandon her presentation and spend the afternoon with Scottie—maybe drag her to bed—gripped Willow. But then reason won. She looked away. "Make yourself at home. I have maybe two hours left of this misery. If you get bored, I don't mind if you—"

Scottie held up the book she'd brought. "I won't get bored. Get some work done, and don't worry about me." She settled down on the love seat by the window, while Willow went back to her desk.

Soon, the rustle of Scottie turning pages mingled with the rain on the roof and the tapping of Willow's laptop keys. Every once in a while, Willow allowed herself to glance at Scottie, who sat on the love seat sideways—facing Willow—one leg dangling over the armrest. Willow realized she liked having Scottie in her space, and that had never happened before.

It was the most peaceful work session she'd ever had. Not a single glitch happened! Even the animation that had given her trouble earlier behaved on the first click.

Finally, Willow saved her progress and got up to stretch. Only then did she notice that the sun had set while she'd been working and that Scottie had turned on the light.

Scottie looked up from her book. "Time for a break?"

Willow nodded and walked over.

Scottie immediately set her novel aside and made room for her on the love seat. "How is it going?"

"Really well. You get my laptop to behave just by being here." Willow cuddled against her side. A sigh escaped her. "I wish I could take you into the presentation with me."

"I know." Scottie soothingly ran her fingers through Willow's hair. "I'll be there in spirit—and I'll be right outside the door, ready to jump in should it become necessary."

Willow gave her a questioning look. "How are you planning to manage that?"

"I'll find a reason to hang out on the fifteenth floor. Maybe I've got to install an urgent security patch on an EA's computer. And I'll have your emergency bag all packed, crammed full of every replacement device you might need. I'll bring it with me when we set up for the presentation."

"We?"

"Of course." Scottie gave her a wink. "Mr. Sorensen didn't say you'd have to do it alone, did he?"

Willow shook her head.

"So it makes sense to get some help from IT for such an important presentation," Scottie added.

Willow couldn't help smiling. "Perfect sense. Thank you." Knowing Scottie would be there to double-check everything eased some of her tension.

They sat in silence for a while, feeding each other bits of a marzipan pastry. Then Scottie wiped her hands and gestured to the acoustic bass resting on its stand next to the love seat. "Would you play something for me before you go back to work?"

Willow hesitated. She hadn't played for an audience—even an audience of one—in nearly a decade. But she knew Scottie wouldn't judge her for still being a bit rusty, so she picked up the bass and settled it on her right thigh.

Scottie slid to the side to give her room.

Willow slipped the instrument's strap over her head, relaxed her shoulders, and let her thumb rest lightly against the E string. Then she eased into the opening riff of "I Feel Good"—simple but cheerful. The fingers of her left hand instinctively found the right spots on the fretboard.

The low thrum of the strings vibrated through her entire body, mingling with the buzz being close to Scottie always gave her.

Her execution wasn't perfect, but the groove still made her smile. When Willow peeked at her, Scottie was watching her with an awestruck look, as if she were listening to James Brown himself.

"That was beautiful," Scottie said when the last note had faded away. With a grin, she added, "And hot."

Willow laughed. "Hot?"

"A woman with skilled fingers, handling an instrument with such grace and control..." Scottie nodded decisively. "Totally hot."

Willow resisted the urge to fan herself. "Want to try it?"

Scottie hesitated. "Are you sure I won't break it?"

"It's sturdier than it looks," Willow said. "Besides, I'm trying not to be afraid of breaking stuff all the time, and you shouldn't be afraid of it either."

They exchanged a long look.

"Okay," Scottie finally said. "I'd love to try it, then."

Willow slipped the strap over Scottie's head and helped her settle the bass across her lap. "Put your left hand here, on the neck. We won't do any fretting for now. The right hand is your plucking hand. Rest your thumb against the body of the bass or the top string."

"Like this?"

Willow glanced down.

Scottie's strong, competent fingers looked good on her bass.

"Yes, exactly like that. By the way, you were right," Willow said with a smile. "That does look hot."

"Yeah, but let's see how it sounds." Scottie lightly plucked the E string with her index finger.

"Use your first two fingers alternately, and don't be afraid to do that a little harder. Bass strings are pretty thick." Willow reached over and demonstrated, plucking the G string with her index finger and the D string with her middle finger.

But Scottie wasn't watching her hand. She was looking at Willow, a big smirk on her face. "So...harder...and using two fingers... That's your secret?"

Heat crept up Willow's neck, but she held eye contact. "Yes. Of course, you need to have the right rhythm too."

"Of course." Scottie laughed huskily. She tried a few more notes before her fingers drifted higher.

"Um, Scottie?"

Scottie turned her head. "Yeah?" Her low voice vibrated through Willow the same way the bass notes had earlier.

Their faces were only inches apart. The air between them felt charged with something that had nothing to do with static.

Willow cleared her throat. "That's my fingers, not the strings."

"Mm, I know," Scottie murmured and trailed one fingertip down the back of Willow's index finger, sending shivers up Willow's arm and through the rest of her body. "They feel so much better than the strings."

Willow decided then and there that they'd had enough bass lessons for one day. She pulled the strap over Scottie's neck, set the bass carefully on its stand, then reached for Scottie instead.

Scottie surged toward her, and their lips came together in a kiss much more urgent than their earlier one at the door. Her mouth was warm and hungry and tasted faintly of marzipan.

Willow tangled her fingers in the hair at the nape of Scottie's neck. She shifted closer, wanting to feel more of her, and Scottie responded by twisting around so their bodies pressed together more fully.

Scottie kissed with a devastating combination of passion, emotion, and a hint of playfulness that drove Willow wild—deep and demanding one second, then teasing Willow's lower lip with a soft nip the next.

Scottie slid one hand down and beneath Willow's sweater. Her fingertips caressed the bare skin at the small of Willow's back, then lightly trailed up her side, leaving tingles everywhere they touched.

A low whimper of want escaped Willow. She ran her hands down Scottie's arms and gripped her biceps.

The love seat felt too small, too confining, all of a sudden, and Willow was about two seconds away from straddling Scottie's lap.

The light flared brighter for a moment, then a loud, popping noise sounded above them, and the room was thrown into darkness.

They jumped and pulled apart, both breathing heavily, with their lips only an inch apart.

Willow clutched Scottie's arms. It took her kiss-dazed brain a few seconds to understand. The light bulb. She'd actually blown the damn thing out!

Mortification washed over her like a bucket of ice water. She let go of Scottie and pressed one hand to her tingling, swollen lips. "I'm so sorry!"

"I'm not complaining," Scottie replied, her voice husky.

"I meant about..." Willow gestured upward, then realized Scottie couldn't see it in the dark. "The light bulb."

Scottie removed her hand from beneath Willow's sweater and smoothed the fabric down. "Was that...you?"

In the past, she would have denied it and quickly made up an excuse, but with Scottie, she didn't want to do that. "Yes."

Scottie's hand, which had been stroking slow, soothing circles at the small of Willow's back, stilled. "I thought that only happens when you're stressed, nervous, or upset. Were you—?"

"No," Willow said hastily. She didn't want Scottie to think, even for a second, that she'd upset her in any way. "It doesn't usually happen like this. But once or twice, when I got really...um..." Her face burned. "...turned on, the light bulb flickered or popped."

"Oh." Scottie went quiet for a moment, then repeated: "Oh." The second "oh" was longer, less stunned.

Willow could hear the grin in her voice—not a teasing one, more a big, happy, proud one. She lightly slapped her thigh. "Stop grinning."

"Never." Scottie put her hand on top of Willow's, then intertwined their fingers, loosely keeping them resting against her leg. "Hey." She leaned her shoulder against Willow's. "You have absolutely nothing to be embarrassed about. Okay?"

Willow exhaled and relaxed against Scottie's shoulder. "Okay."

They sat like that for a few moments, holding hands in the dark.

"In fact," Scottie added, her voice low and husky, "I think it's pretty hot that I could make you do that."

Of course Scottie would say something like that—something reassuring and completely undoing at the same time. Willow bumped her shoulder. "You think everything's hot."

"Everything about you," Scottie said.

Warmth filled Willow. She stroked Scottie's knuckles with her thumb. "I spent my entire life hiding that part of me. I can't see it the way you do—as something fascinating or hot or even remotely positive. At least not yet."

"I get that," Scottie said quietly.

And for the first time in her life, Willow felt that there was someone who really did. She pressed a kiss to Scottie's cheek, then shifted her weight forward to get up. "I should go replace the light bulb."

"Wait." Scottie held on to her hand, keeping Willow next to her on the love seat. "There's something I'd like to talk about. I didn't think today would be the right time, but maybe now is perfect after all. I have a feeling it'll be easier for you if I can't see you blush—even though I think it's super cute."

Willow sank back against Scottie's side. "What did you want to talk about?"

"Sex," Scottie said simply.

Even just hearing the word in Scottie's still slightly hoarse voice made heat pool low in Willow's belly.

"Once we make love, how do we keep ourselves safe?" Scottie asked.

Oh. Willow blinked. She hadn't had reason to think about safer sex in a very long time. "I got tested after my last time. Um, it's been a while—an embarrassingly long time, to be honest—but everything came back negative. So I'm good."

Scottie squeezed her hand. "Hey. That's not embarrassing. There are no rules about how often you're supposed to have sex."

"Right." Willow squeezed back. "How about you?"

"I got tested after Tanya broke up with me. Just in case," Scottie said. "All negative too."

"Good," Willow replied.

Scottie hummed her agreement. "And it's great that we talked about it. But that's actually not what I meant. When we make love, the only thing I want to short-circuit is every nerve ending in your body. How do we make that happen?"

Willow flushed. "Uh, you mean, what do I like in bed?"

A husky laugh came from Scottie. "Oh, we're definitely going to talk about that. But I meant, how do we avoid getting zapped in sensitive places or burning the place down?"

"Oh." Willow flushed again, this time so hard she wondered if she was glowing in the dark. Now she was indeed grateful Scottie had stopped her from replacing the light bulb. "There are a few things that help. For starters, banning any electronics and battery-operated devices from the bedroom."

"Even the fun ones, hm?"

"Even the fun ones. The one time a girlfriend insisted we use a vibrator..." Willow winced. "Let's just say it didn't end well."

"No battery-operated toys, then," Scottie said, not sounding bothered. "Got it. What else?"

"I try to always ground myself by touching a metal object, something connected to the floor like a radiator or the bed frame, before I touch my partner."

"Metal object," Scottie repeated as if she was compiling a mental list. "Okay. Anything else?"

"The sheets have to be one hundred percent cotton or silk. If we roll around on synthetics, we'd be creating a lightning storm of static."

"Mmm, silk." Scottie let out a hum. "No objections from me."

A vivid image hit Willow: Scottie's warm, bare skin pressed against her front while cool silk slid against her back. She shoved it away before she forgot how to breathe and focused on the list of helpful tricks. "I also usually run a humidifier in the bedroom for about an hour before...you know. And I put on lotion because dry skin builds up charges."

"All right. Keeping things nice and moist. I can do that."

"You!" Willow nudged Scottie's knee with her own, and they burst out laughing.

Once their laughter faded away, Willow lifted their intertwined hands to her lips and kissed Scottie's fingers. "I've never been able to talk about this with anyone. Thank you for bringing it up."

"I want us to be able to talk about anything," Scottie said.

Willow nodded, even though Scottie couldn't see it. "I want that too."

"So now that we've established the safety protocol, I'm interested in the other question—the one you thought I was asking—too. Very, very interested." Scottie's voice dropped an octave at the last three words, sending a shiver through Willow.

"I don't have a ton of experience when it comes to sex." Willow bit her lip, but with Scottie, she didn't mind admitting it. "I'm not one to jump into bed on the first date. Or even the third."

"I gathered that," Scottie said gently. "And just for the record, I'm not pressuring you."

"Pressuring me?" Willow echoed. "Just for the record, if I didn't have the presentation first thing tomorrow morning, I'd ask you to stay over tonight."

Scottie groaned. "And here I thought I couldn't hate Sorensen more than I already do."

A chuckle rose from Willow's chest. "Same here. But maybe it's a good thing—that we're talking first, not jumping into bed, I mean."

"Yeah. I think so too. So what were you trying to say before I interrupted, about not having a ton of experience?"

Willow sighed. "Some of my relationships—if you can even call them that—ended before we ever got that far. But even when we did, it was hard for me to let them touch me. To enjoy it without bracing for a zap or the TV turning on in the middle of things, blasting a WWII documentary." The memory made her grimace.

Scottie tightened her grip on Willow's hand. "I can imagine. Talk about a mood killer."

"Exactly. It's really hard to let yourself go when you're worried about blowing the light bulb or making your girlfriend's smart watch go haywire. I could rarely relax enough to...you know. Climax."

Willow had expected Scottie to make a joke to lighten the mood or to say something reassuring, promising she wouldn't have any problems getting her there.

But Scottie didn't say anything; she just continued to soothingly caress her fingers.

Willow tried to make out her features in the dark. By now, her eyes had adjusted, so she could see Scottie sitting with her head tilted in that typical attentive way, as if her entire universe consisted just of Willow. Somehow, it was more reassuring than any promises she could have made.

"So, to be honest," Willow finally continued, "most of what I know about what I like comes from...touching myself."

Scottie shifted next to her. "If that would help you feel safe and relaxed, I'd be totally up for that." A sexy rasp slipped into her voice, and she paused to clear her throat. "It would be incredibly hot to watch you touch yourself. But only if that's what you wanted."

Renewed heat flared through Willow, and this time, it wasn't just embarrassment. The mental image of Scottie watching her, eyes dark and hungry, as she unbuttoned her blouse and slid her hand down… "I… No. I mean, maybe down the road. But when we make love for the first time, I don't want you to just watch. I want you to touch me."

Scottie let out a groan. "I want that too."

Willow's breath hitched at the need in Scottie's voice. Now she was the one who had to clear her throat before she could speak. "I'm afraid there's not a whole lot more I can tell you. We'll have to figure it out as we go."

Just the thought of it—of Scottie exploring her body to find out what she liked—made her tingle all over.

Scottie brushed her thumb over Willow's knuckles again. "We can definitely do that."

"There's one thing that might help…"

"Anything," Scottie said without hesitation.

Willow had never admitted it to anyone, always afraid it would sound weird. "I think it would help me relax if I could…keep some control," she said quietly.

"Makes sense," Scottie replied. "You have to control where to touch, how to touch, and how to let people touch you in your everyday life so tightly, it figures that you can't just stop doing that in bed."

Willow sat very still, stunned at how Scottie not only got it right away but made it sound as if it were the most normal thing in the world. "Yes," she croaked out.

"I can work with that." Scottie nodded decisively. "Actually, I think that would be pretty—"

"Hot?" Willow finished with a shaky laugh.

"Very," Scottie said. "Like I said: Everything about you is hot to me. You giving up control—hot. You taking control—hot."

Willow stared at her. Sometimes, she still thought Scottie was too good to be true. But she trusted her to mean what she said. "I don't want it to be all about me and what I want, though. What do you like?"

"Oh, I'm pretty adaptable. Most of all, I love making my partner feel good."

Willow nudged her with her shoulder. "What do you like?" She emphasized every word. "For yourself."

"If my partner…if *you* are into it, I'm a total sucker for oral." Scottie paused. "Pun intended."

Willow laughed so hard she nearly slipped off the love seat. "Oh my God! You're impossible!"

Scottie chuckled. "But you love me."

Willow's laughter softened, and she found Scottie's face in the near dark, tenderly cupping her cheek. "I love you." She leaned toward her and kissed her—not with the same heated urgency as before but slowly, gratefully, and full of wonder at how easy all of this felt.

Scottie kissed her back with just as much emotion until the temperature in the room started climbing again.

Groaning, Scottie broke the kiss and pulled back a few inches. "Break's over." She trailed her thumb across the curve of Willow's lower lip. "If we don't stop now, we're both calling in sick tomorrow, and you'll be out of a job."

"Yeah," Willow said, still out of breath. "You're probably right. I should get back to work." She sighed but couldn't wipe the smile off her face as she went in search of a new light bulb.

Chapter 43

Willow placed a second pitcher of water in the middle of the long, polished mahogany table. Her hands shook so much that she nearly spilled half of it over the notepads with the Kudos logo that rested at each setting.

"Hey." Scottie straightened from where she'd been crouched in front of the massive wall-mounted LED display that dominated the far end of the conference room. She walked over to Willow but didn't touch her, as if sensing that any contact might be too much right now. "You okay?"

Willow inhaled deeply and tried to match her breath to Scottie's steady rhythm. "Yeah." She sighed. "No. I barely slept, and when I did, I had nightmares of the display bursting into flames, the laptop flashing the blue screen of death, the video suddenly playing cat memes…and Mr. Sorensen firing me on the spot."

"Don't worry," Scottie said, her voice as soft and soothing as a touch. "None of that will happen—even though I personally think cat memes would be way cooler than Sorensen's third slide."

Willow gave her a weak smile. "True."

"It'll all go well," Scottie said. "No presentation in the history of license negotiations has ever been better prepared than this one. The tech side is all set. I even used a physical HDMI cable instead of relying on a wireless setup—less potential for Wi-Fi drama."

Willow swept her gaze over the room. Six executive leather chairs flanked the long table on either side. A smaller table along the wall held coffee, milk and creamer, and a selection of premium teas.

The large display was powered on, and Scottie had double- and triple-checked all connections, settings, and the volume levels of the ceiling speakers.

They had tested the slides and made sure all embedded animations and videos ran smoothly. The cover slide was up on the screen now, the Kudos logo crisp and clear.

The emergency tech glitch response kit Scottie had put together for her rested on the floor next to a sideboard—close enough for Willow to reach it easily, but out of her immediate vicinity, so the batteries wouldn't drain. It held a backup laptop, two replacement clickers, an extra-long HDMI cable, and every battery and adapter known to mankind.

"You're ready for every glitch the tech gremlins might throw at you. We ran so many tech-failure drills last week, you can fix them all with your eyes closed. And if you can't, I'll be right outside." Scottie nodded toward the other side of the frosted glass wall. "If you open this door, I'll be there before you can even say *help*, okay?"

Willow wiped her clammy hands on her midnight-blue pencil skirt. "Okay. Thank you. For all of this."

Scottie looked her in the eyes, her gaze steady. "No need to thank me. I've got your back. Always."

The sound of footsteps echoed through the hallway, quickly coming closer.

Willow's pulse skyrocketed.

When the door swung open, Scottie backed away and pretended to double-check the display settings.

Mr. Sorensen was the first one in, wearing an immaculate charcoal suit and a tie in the Kudos brand colors.

Four other Kudos executives filtered in behind him, some ignoring her, some murmuring greetings.

Sorensen gave Willow a brief nod. "Is everything ready?"

"Yes, Mr. Sorensen," she answered, struggling to sound calm and confident. "Tested and ready."

"You've got this," Scottie mouthed over the COO's shoulder, then slipped out of the room.

Willow stayed behind, her heart pounding so hard that her entire body seemed to be pulsating. She prayed that for the next thirty minutes, every piece of technology in this room would behave for once and not turn into a reason for her boss to fire her.

It wasn't long before the Unicorn Pictures delegation arrived.

Three of them were practically indistinguishable from the Kudos execs—all middle-aged, white men in gray or navy suits—but the fourth one was a woman.

Willow had read up on Unicorn Pictures, so she instantly knew who she was: Freida Rhodes, their VP of Consumer Products and the lead negotiator when it came to this licensing deal.

In a custom-tailored, champagne-colored pantsuit and designer heels that probably cost more than Willow's rent, she looked effortlessly powerful. She glanced around with sharp eyes, as if assessing everything within seconds. Her gaze paused on Willow for a moment, despite her best attempts to make herself invisible.

Even Mr. Sorensen practically snapped to attention when she shook his hand. It would have been hilarious if Willow hadn't felt ready to throw up.

"Gentlemen." Freida Rhodes's cool voice filled the conference room. "Shall we?"

The low hum of professional pleasantries instantly fell silent, and everyone took their seat at the table—the Kudos team on the left, the Unicorn Pictures people on the right, while Ms. Rhodes sat at the head of the table, with the best view of the display.

Willow had been positioned to Sorensen's left, an empty chair separating her from the inner circle of decision makers. From there, she could quickly reach the tech cart with the laptop or slip out the door to get more coffee if needed.

Her heart thumped against her ribs as Mr. Sorensen took up position slightly to the side of the LED display.

This was it. She tried to calm her breathing.

Through the frosted glass wall, she caught a glimpse of a silhouette on the other side. She knew without a doubt it was Scottie, who'd made up an excuse to hover near the conference room.

The thought that Scottie was near, ready to rush in and slay any digital dragons, calmed her. She no longer minded accepting help from her because she knew Scottie wouldn't see her as a burden or a helpless damsel.

Mr. Sorensen cleared his throat, about to launch into his opening line when the sun peeked out from behind a wall of gray clouds. The glare bounced off the massive LED screen.

He grabbed the remote to close the blinds.

Nothing happened. The blinds didn't move an inch.

Frowning, he pressed the button again.

Still nothing.

Willow's stomach lurched. The licensing pitch wasn't off to a good start. She didn't need to guess what had gone wrong. The remote had been on the table, only a few feet from where she was sitting. Her nervous energy must have drained the batteries.

The wall switch should work, but did she really want to get up, walk across the room without tripping over cords, and return to her seat while everyone was watching?

Definitely not.

Quickly, she opened her emergency kit and took out a pair of fresh AAAs. "May I?" She nodded at the remote that hung useless in Mr. Sorensen's grip.

Still frowning, he handed it over.

She took it, careful not to brush his fingers, swapped out the batteries, and pressed the button.

The motorized blinds smoothly slid down.

Mr. Sorensen gave her one last glare, as if she was to blame for the blinds not working.

Okay, she probably was, but he couldn't know that.

Then he straightened his tie, grabbed the presenter remote, and clicked the first slide into view, making the Kudos logo morph into the film studio's unmistakable emblem. "Here at Kudos Entertainment, we have long admired the world-building and creativity coming out of Unicorn Pictures, and we see a clear path to bringing that magic into homes worldwide."

His smooth, confident voice filled the room as he went through his pitch.

Willow stopped listening but remained on high alert, her attention fully on the tech. She kept an eye on the indicator light of Sorensen's clicker. Scottie had put in a brand-new battery earlier, but with Willow's nervousness spiking, it might drain as quickly as the remote for the blinds had.

"And here's how we envision the Galaxion line." Sorensen pressed the forward button on his clicker, advancing to the next slide. "As you can see, it's designed with interactive features that match the cinematic experience of the movie."

The massive LED display behind him began to flicker. Horizontal white streaks fractured the rotating 3D mock-up of the toy.

A murmur went through the room. Everyone glanced back and forth between Sorensen and the screen. The legal counsel for Unicorn Pictures raised his eyebrows and murmured something about checking the HDMI cable.

But Willow knew that wouldn't help. Scottie had checked it three times earlier, and it had been fine. The problem wasn't a loose plug; it was her own turbulent energy that disrupted the signal.

A surge of panic swept over Willow. But then Scottie's calm voice echoed through her mind: *If the connection between the laptop and the display gets corrupted, toggle the display input off and back on.*

They had rehearsed this! Muscle memory, honed through Scottie's week-long tech-failure drills, kicked in. This time, she didn't ask or wait for permission. She grabbed the display's remote and changed the input from HDMI1 to HDMI2.

The screen went black, sending a new murmur through the room.

Willow ignored it. Fingers trembling, she switched back to HDMI1. Hopefully, that would establish a new connection without her having to unplug the cables or restart the laptop, disrupting the entire presentation.

The display sprang back to life. For a moment, it showed only the HDMI1 label.

Willow held her breath.

The 3D toy mock-up reappeared, the image now crisp and vivid, without a hint of a flicker.

Kudos's head of marketing exhaled loudly.

"As I was saying," Mr. Sorensen continued as if the momentary interruption had been a planned, dramatic pause, "each of the core figures will come with modular armor and gear, allowing kids to recreate sequences from the movie. We've even integrated proximity pairing. When two figures are brought close together, they trigger sound effects and signature lines of dialogue."

He clicked to a video demonstration, and everyone in the room visibly relaxed.

The entire crisis had lasted barely fifteen seconds, but to Willow, it had felt like an eternity. She slumped against the back of her chair and tried to slow her breathing.

Carefully, she peeked up. Had anyone noticed that she'd been the one to fix the display issue?

None of the men paid her any attention. They were focused on the screen. But Freida Rhodes's gaze was fixed on her, expression entirely unreadable.

Oh crap. Willow swallowed and forced a polite smile.

The corner of Ms. Rhodes's mouth twitched in what might have been either a grimace or an answering smile before she refocused on the presentation.

Just as Willow was starting to relax a little, she noticed a new point of tension.

Rick Haggerty—their VP of sales—was tapping his stylus against his tablet with increasing force, a frown on his face. He was their CEO's son, and, according to Scottie, just as technologically challenged as his future brother-in-law, Mr. Sorensen.

Kudos's VP of licensing leaned over, trying to help without interrupting the presentation but apparently not having any luck either.

Mr. Sorensen kept talking, oblivious to the problem.

Willow knew she could ignore it too. She was tasked with making sure the presentation went smoothly; the issues Mr. Haggerty had with his tablet weren't her responsibility.

In the past, she would have stayed silent, worried that she might overstep or make the problem worse.

But now she'd already fixed two tech issues in a row. She was equipped with an emergency kit and a ton of tips from Scottie. Maybe she didn't need to stay under the radar. Perhaps this time, instead of making things worse, she could help.

She leaned across the empty chair between them and whispered: "Want me to try?"

Mr. Haggerty glanced up and stared as if he was noticing her presence for the first time. Finally, he reluctantly slid the device toward her.

Willow checked the battery status. The stylus was connected to the device and fully charged, even though the percentage went down from ninety-seven to eighty-nine as she was holding it. The screen looked fairly clean too, and no other apps were running in the background.

She turned Bluetooth off and back on, then went into the settings and tapped "forget this device" before reconnecting it again.

The stylus still wasn't working. None of her pencil strokes registered.

Her shoulders slumped as she ran out of ideas.

Maybe it was interference from her weird aura after all.

Just as she was about to give up and hand back the tablet, she noticed something that didn't look right. There was a gap between the stylus and its plastic tip.

The nib had become loose! Quickly, she twisted it back in and tested the stylus again.

A perfect black line appeared.

Yes! With a triumphant grin, she slid it back toward Mr. Haggerty.

He tried a few squiggles, then looked at her as if she had pulled off a magic trick and mouthed, "Thanks."

Willow nodded and quietly exhaled.

When she glanced up, Ms. Rhodes's gaze was on her again.

Willow gave her best helpful-but-unimportant-assistant smile—the kind that said "just doing my job; no big deal."

Ms. Rhodes studied her for a moment longer, then turned her attention back to the screen.

The next half hour was a complete blur. Willow tried to take notes to the best of her ability, jotting down all of the questions and reactions from the Unicorn Pictures team while also keeping an eye on the display, the laptop, and Mr. Sorensen's remote.

Thankfully, no other glitches happened, maybe because she now knew she could deal with them and her nerves had settled. For the first time in her life, she experienced a quiet thrill of confidence when it came to tech.

Finally, the presentation and the following Q&A wrapped up.

Ms. Rhodes shook Sorensen's hand. "That was a very compelling presentation. We appreciate the creativity of your team. We'll be in touch—once we've reviewed your numbers, of course."

"Of course," he answered. "We look forward to hearing from you."

Ms. Rhodes turned on her heel and strode toward the door.

The other Unicorn Pictures executives fell into step behind her.

Willow rose too, her notes clutched to her chest.

Ms. Rhodes didn't slow as she passed her, but she gave her the tiniest nod—so tiny that Willow wasn't sure it had really happened.

Then Ms. Rhodes was gone, along with the rest of the delegation, leaving Willow standing next to the laptop, her heart still racing.

The Kudos execs exchanged satisfied glances and patted Sorensen's shoulder as if it already were a done deal.

He puffed his chest out and led the way out of the conference room. At the door, he paused. "Make sure your notes are on my desk within the hour, Ms. Greene. I need them before we debrief."

Willow's grip on her notes tightened. *What an ass.* He hadn't even thanked her! "Yes, sir."

Kudos's head of marketing gave her a smile as he passed her. "Well done."

"Thank you," was all she got out.

Then Willow was alone in the conference room. She sank back into her leather chair and let out a long breath, barely able to believe that it was over—and she still had her job!

Scottie had tried to finish work early, eager to check in with Willow and share the news she'd heard, yet when she finally managed to leave the building, it was already a little after five.

They had talked for a minute right after Sorensen's pitch, but then Willow had needed to rush downstairs to type up her notes.

Scottie wasn't even halfway across the employee parking lot when she spotted a familiar figure.

Willow.

She was leaning against Scottie's car, apparently waiting for her. The sun had just set, yet traces of light still lingered, outlining Willow's silhouette.

That by-now familiar flutter coursed through Scottie's chest.

God, Willow was gorgeous! Of course, Scottie had already noticed this morning how great she'd looked in her midnight-blue pencil skirt and a crisp white blouse. Even though she was still wearing the same outfit, there was something different about her now. Gone was the nervous woman from before the presentation. This Willow exuded confidence. She stood tall, her posture graceful but relaxed, as if all weight had lifted off her. Her brunette hair was no longer pulled back into a tight bun. It fell freely onto her shoulders, a few wisps brushing her soft cheeks. Even the dark shadows that had lurked beneath her eyes this morning had disappeared.

Seeing her like this—so free, joyful, and unguarded—made Scottie lose her breath.

Scottie's steps had faltered at the sight of her, but now she quickly crossed the remaining distance between them.

Willow's gaze tracked her progress as if she couldn't wait to talk to her. "Hey." A smile spread across Willow's face—not the carefully measured workplace smile. She was beaming, and there was something intimate in the way she looked at Scottie. Her hazel eyes sparkled, the green flecks catching the parking lot lights.

"Hey," Scottie replied. "Still basking in your post-presentation glow?"

"Yes," Willow said with another giddy smile.

"It looks good on you." Scottie couldn't rein in her own grin.

A cute flush rose into Willow's cheeks. "Thanks. It feels good too. Like I can finally breathe after being underwater for months. Or years," she added more quietly.

"I really think you'll get a break now. Once Unicorn Pictures signs the licensing deal, Mr. Sorensen won't need you as a scapegoat anymore and will probably go back to ignoring you."

"*If* they sign the deal," Willow said, a hint of her old guardedness shining through for a moment.

"I'm sure they will. I was up in Marketing earlier, and Mr. Saunders was whistling. Rumor has it he's already heard back from Unicorn's director of franchise marketing."

Willow's eyes widened. "That fast?"

"Not officially. I think they went to college together or something. According to the very efficient Kudos rumor mill, the Unicorn execs liked what they saw."

Willow nodded. "The product designers really nailed it. The prototypes for the Galaxion line looked awesome."

"Yeah, but what impressed them wasn't just the toy design. Unicorn is the kind of company that likes knowing their licensing partners can handle a curveball without panicking. And that's exactly what they saw during the presentation." Scottie gave her a meaningful look.

Willow stared at her. "You mean…they were impressed…by me? All I did was replace the batteries and switch HDMI inputs. That's hardly a technical masterstroke."

"I don't think it was your tech know-how that impressed them; it was your quick thinking. They want to work with people who adjust fast under pressure and have a backup plan ready when things don't go their way—and that's exactly what you did." Scottie stepped even closer—so close that she could feel Willow's body heat, even through their coats. "Just for the record, the Unicorn Pictures execs weren't the only ones you impressed today. I'm very impressed by you too."

She'd been nearly bursting with pride all day. Not just because Willow had been able to fix the glitches herself but also because she'd let her help with the setup and the tech-failure drills. It felt like a big win, not only for Willow, but for their relationship too.

Willow's blush intensified. "Thank you. For helping me with the setup and the glitch-fixing drills. And for teaching me that some things don't break when you lean on them; they only get stronger."

Their gazes held.

"Yes," Scottie said, her voice a little scratchy. "They do."

Without breaking their eye contact, Willow brushed her knuckles over the hood of the car behind her, then lifted her other hand to Scottie's face. She trailed her long, graceful fingers across Scottie's jaw, making her pulse jump and her breathing speed up.

Last month, they had decided to keep their interactions strictly professional while at work. But, frankly, Scottie no longer cared who might be watching, and apparently, neither did Willow.

She closed the remaining inches between them and kissed Scottie, softly and without hurry.

The slow slide of Willow's lips against hers sent tingles through every inch of Scottie's body. She wrapped both arms around her and pulled her closer, until Willow's hips were flush against hers.

Willow's fingers traced up the side of her face, then threaded through Scottie's hair as if she couldn't resist touching the rebellious strands.

When they finally pulled apart, both were breathing heavily.

Willow smoothed her hand over Scottie's coat lapels. "Now that you helped me save my job, will you also help me celebrate?"

"Of course," Scottie said. Willow deserved to celebrate. "Where do you want to go? Le Pigeon?"

Willow shook her head.

"Potato Champion?" Scottie chuckled.

"No. I was thinking..." Willow lowered her voice to a raspy whisper. "Your apartment." Her heated gaze left no doubt that she wasn't talking about getting takeout.

Scottie's breath caught. She didn't need to ask whether Willow was sure, nor did she have to think about her own answer. She wanted Willow with an intensity that felt almost like an ache. "Yes," she got out huskily.

"Okay." Willow breathed out the word. "I'll follow you home. I just need to let my sister know not to wait up." She pulled out her phone. Her fingers trembled as she typed a quick message, probably due to an equal mix of desire and nerves. Then she slid the phone back into her coat pocket.

Scottie caught Willow's hand between hers and softly rubbed her fingers. "Drive carefully, all right? I want you in my bed, not in a hospital bed."

"Can't promise I'll stick to the speed limit, but I'll be careful. You too, please."

Scottie nodded.

They moved at the same time, Willow heading toward her car, while Scottie walked around hers to the driver's side.

She fumbled for her keys.

By the time she found them and managed to press the fob, Willow had reached her car. They exchanged one last look across the rows of vehicles, then both hurriedly got in.

Scottie prayed to any patron saint of technology who might be listening that both of their car batteries would start right up.

They were about to make love for the first time, and no tech glitch was allowed to get in the way.

Chapter 44

Willow followed Scottie into the apartment, which smelled of fresh laundry and mint tea. Her heart beat faster as the door clicked shut behind them, and they stripped off their coats and shoes.

"Do you want a glass of wine?" Scottie stuffed her hands into her pants pockets, a gesture that managed to look nervous and sexy at the same time. "Or something to eat?"

It was oddly comforting to see that the normally self-assured woman was a little flustered too. Willow gave her a smile. "No. I only want you." She wasn't usually so bold, but Scottie made it easy to just say what she wanted.

Heat flared in Scottie's eyes. "I want you too. But give me one minute. If you want to freshen up, the bathroom's right there." She pointed at a door to their right.

"Thanks." Willow ducked into the small bathroom, washed her hands, and splashed cold water onto her face. When she glanced in the mirror above the sink, her cheeks were flushed, her pupils wide, and her hair a bit chaotic from the long workday.

She looked wild and alive, not like the pale, nervous woman she'd seen in the mirror this morning.

When she came out of the bathroom, she expected to find Scottie waiting in the hallway, but instead, she leaned in the doorway to the bedroom and made a soft "come here" gesture.

Willow joined her, and they entered together.

"Wow." Willow took it all in, half aware that her mouth hung open.

Scottie had transformed her bedroom into a sanctuary. There were no electronics anywhere, not even on the small desk in the corner. The lights were off. Candles in heavy glass jars flickered on the dresser, the desk, and the sideboard next to the bed, throwing a golden glow over the silk sheets and glinting off the bed's metal frame. A bottle of lotion was waiting on the nightstand.

Willow pressed a hand over her heart. "You Willow-proofed the bedroom!"

"No. I'd never want it to be Willow-proof. I just want you to be comfortable." Scottie rubbed the back of her neck. "I didn't have time to buy a humidifier, and, uh, if you'd rather have the lights on, I'm fine with that. I don't care if you blow out the light bulbs as long as you're enjoying yourself."

Willow's throat was so tight, she barely got the words out. "No, this is perfect. Thank you."

Scottie walked over to the nightstand and picked up the bottle of lotion. "I thought maybe I could help you with this part." Her voice was low and husky.

The thought of Scottie's hands on her, spreading lotion all over her body, made heat curl low in Willow's belly. "Yes," she whispered.

Scottie put the lotion down and stepped closer.

There was still a foot of space between them, but Willow's breath caught in anticipation.

"Can I undress you?" Scottie's eyes seemed to smolder with intensity.

Not trusting her voice to work, Willow nodded. She brushed her fingers across the metal rail at the foot of the bed, discharging the faint prickle of static buzzing through her.

Slowly, as if giving Willow a chance to stop her if she needed to, Scottie lifted her hands.

But stopping her was the last thing on Willow's mind. She stayed very still and glanced down, watching as Scottie's fingers found the first button on her blouse and slipped it free. She unbuttoned each one slowly, as if opening a fragile gift. When she'd undone the last one, she didn't part the blouse yet. Instead, she lifted her gaze to Willow's.

Pulse thudding in her ears, Willow nodded.

Scottie eased the blouse off Willow's shoulders. Her palms followed its path down, sliding along Willow's arms and making goose bumps scatter over her skin.

"Skirt too?" Scottie asked once the blouse fell to the floor.

"Yes."

Scottie found the zipper at the side and slowly drew it down, the sound overly loud in the silent room. Her hands traced the curve of Willow's hips as she guided the skirt down.

It pooled at Willow's feet, and she stepped out of it.

"Keep going?" Scottie sounded as breathless as Willow felt.

She nodded.

Scottie followed the edge of Willow's pantyhose with her thumbs before hooking her fingers beneath the elastic.

Willow reached for the metal footboard, both to make sure no static electricity could build up and to keep her balance as her knees went wobbly.

Holding eye contact, Scottie knelt and eased the sheer material over Willow's hips and down her legs. This time, her fingers grazed bare skin on their way down.

Every light brush made Willow shiver.

Scottie stood and raised her hand to Willow's bra. But instead of taking it off, she lightly stroked the satiny, black material with her fingertips.

Willow sucked in a breath. If this was what it felt like to have Scottie caress her through a layer of fabric, Scottie touching her bare skin would undo her completely.

"Very pretty," Scottie murmured. "But I bet what's beneath it is even more beautiful. Can I?"

Willow nodded, her entire body tingling with anticipation.

Scottie reached around her. She was now so close that her chest brushed Willow's bra-clad breasts.

Her nipples instantly hardened, and she bit back a moan.

The clasp gave away, and the band loosened, but Scottie didn't pull the bra off right away. She smoothed one strap down Willow's shoulder, then bent and placed a soft kiss where it had been before repeating the process on the other side.

When she straightened, creating more space between them, the bra dropped to the floor.

Cool air washed over Willow's bare chest, and she resisted the instinctive urge to cover herself with her arms.

Scottie stood very still. Her gaze swept up Willow's body, hungry yet reverent, taking in every inch as if Willow were the most desirable woman she'd ever seen.

A thrill shot through Willow. The look in Scottie's eyes instantly melted away her rising insecurities.

"I was right," Scottie said, voice smoky. "Way more beautiful than the bra." She trailed a single fingertip along the underside of one breast, barely grazing it.

The moan that Willow had been holding back finally broke free. How could such a barely there touch send an electric current down her body, even though she was still gripping the metal footboard?

Scottie drew a slow line down Willow's belly with her fingertip, then traced the edge of her panties, setting off more shivers. "Want to leave those on for now?"

"No." The answer came out before Willow could even think about it, surprising her. She wanted no more barriers between them. A part of her yearned to just tear off her panties and Scottie's clothes and draw her down on the bed, skipping the lotion. But she forced herself not to rush this. For once, she wanted to feel everything, experience every sensation instead of trying to keep her reactions safe and contained. "Off."

They both reached for the elastic at the same time and slipped the panties down her hips together.

Then Scottie took over. Her knuckles brushed a line down the front of Willow's legs as she slid the fabric down.

Finally, Willow stood fully naked, and Scottie drank her in once more. Her tongue darted out, wetting her full lips.

Tingles shot through Willow's body. How was it possible to feel so vulnerable yet incredibly powerful at the same time?

Scottie shook her head as if to clear it. "Lotion," she said loudly, as if she, too, had to convince herself not to skip that step. "Why don't you lie down?"

Willow sank onto the bed. The silk sheets were cool along her breasts and belly, and she stifled a gasp as the smooth fabric made contact with her sensitized skin. She turned her head on the pillow so she could watch Scottie in the soft candlelight.

Scottie poured lotion into her hands and rubbed them together, warming it.

The scent of apricots filled Willow's senses, reminding her of her favorite shampoo.

The mattress dipped as Scottie knelt next to her. "Where do you want me to start?"

Frankly, Willow didn't care—as long as Scottie would be touching her. But she understood what Scottie was doing: giving her control, because that was what Willow had told her she needed.

"Back," Willow got out through a dry mouth.

Scottie tapped Willow's back with one finger. "Testing, testing, one, two, three." She grinned down at her. "No zaps. Looks like we're good to go."

Willow burst out laughing. Scottie's playfulness was like a healing balm, making any lingering remnants of tension fade away. "You're such a goof."

"Mm-hmm. But I'm your goof." Then Scottie's fingers drifted lower, tracing a slow path down her spine, and Willow's laughter cut off.

Scottie's method of applying lotion was nothing like a massage therapist's. She trailed her palms over Willow's back in tender strokes, as if she was pouring her heart into every touch. "How's this?"

"Mmm." Willow's muscles melted beneath her caresses.

Scottie spread her fingers wide over Willow's shoulder blades, then followed their contours before sliding her palms over her shoulders and along her arms. "Okay?"

Willow could only nod. Everything felt so much more than okay. The lotion made every touch glide smoothly along her skin, but Scottie's fingertips added just a hint of friction that set off tingles everywhere.

Scottie retraced her path without any hurry—up Willow's arms, over her shoulder blades, then down her back, as if memorizing every inch. When she reached the dip at the small of her back, she let her warm palms rest there for a moment before drifting back up, spreading the lotion with long, languid strokes.

Willow's eyes fluttered shut.

On the next sweep down, Scottie's touch veered outward, over her sides, following the line of her ribs. Her fingers grazed the outer curve of Willow's breasts.

Arousal flared through Willow. She gasped into the pillow.

But Scottie didn't linger. She spread lotion down Willow's sides, swept her palms over her hips, and lightly skimmed them over her butt and the back of her thighs.

Every place she touched felt heightened, as if the sparks between them had ignited something under Willow's skin, until her entire body was buzzing.

Scottie worked lotion into her calves, then gentled her touch, caressing the tender spot at the back of her knees with just her fingertips.

Willow's toes curled against the sheets. This really was the most sensual experience of her life.

When Scottie trailed her hands higher, Willow's breathing turned shallow. She pressed her hips against the bed. God, letting Scottie apply the lotion had either been the most genius idea ever or the most torturous one. Possibly both.

Scottie paused, her fingers halfway up Willow's thighs. "Want me to keep going?"

"No," Willow got out hoarsely. Her entire body was on fire, burning for Scottie's touch. But even more than that, she yearned to feel Scottie's skin against her own and make her burn just as brightly. "I want...need to touch you too."

Scottie caught her lower lip between her teeth, and it looked so damn sexy that Willow nearly rolled over and pulled her down against her lotion-covered body.

"But there are a few places that didn't get any lotion yet," Scottie protested half-heartedly.

"Trust me," Willow said with a hoarse chuckle that she barely recognized as her own. "Those places don't need any lotion. But there's one more way to reduce friction."

"Yeah?"

"Get naked. Now."

They both moved at the same time. Scottie stood, gripped the hem of her long-sleeved polo shirt, and pulled it up, over her head, while Willow sat up and reached for the button of Scottie's chinos.

She nearly ripped it open, without any finesse or patience.

Scottie sucked in a breath, but the heated look in her eyes spurred Willow on.

Within seconds, they'd removed every layer, and Scottie stood before her completely naked.

The intoxicating mix of strength and softness made Willow's pulse spike. She swept her gaze up muscular thighs, lingered for a moment on the short, dark-blonde curls between Scottie's legs, then took in her surprisingly curvy hips that tapered to a trim waist.

Scottie's arms and face were lightly tanned, the candlelight turning them golden, while the creamy skin along her chest formed a beautiful contrast. The sight of her pink nipples standing out against fair breasts made Willow's mouth water.

"God, Scottie," she whispered. "You're...stunning."

Scottie grinned and ran one hand through the wavy strands that framed her face. That combination of bashfulness and confidence was as appealing to Willow as her body. Scottie didn't say anything. She stood perfectly still and let Willow look at her as much as she wanted.

Willow drank her in until the urge to do more than look became overwhelming. She needed to touch her, taste her, and explore every inch of her—now. Eagerly, she curled her fingers around the back of Scottie's neck and drew her down.

Scottie went willingly, but just before they could tumble onto the bed together, she caught herself with one knee against the mattress. "Wait! The lotion!"

Willow blinked up at her. "What?"

"I want to touch you everywhere." Scottie's voice dipped low on the last word, making Willow's breath catch. "But first, I need to wash my hands. Be right back." She rushed toward the bathroom.

A moment later, the splashing of water drifted over.

Willow waited, heart hammering wildly as she imagined what would happen once Scottie returned. But the interruption also gave her time to think—and to worry.

What if, despite all of Scottie's efforts, she zapped her in the middle of things or blew every fuse in the apartment? She didn't want to hurt Scottie or ruin the mood.

Or what if she couldn't shut off her anxious brain enough to come, despite how aroused Scottie's light touches had already made her?

She hugged her knees to her chest as nerves crept back in.

Scottie reappeared and stopped two steps into the room. "Hey. Are you okay?" She crossed toward the bed. "We don't have to do this if you don't—"

Willow reached out, keeping her own back against the metal headboard to avoid zapping her, and drew Scottie onto the bed next to her. "No. I want this. I want *you*. I'm just..."

"Nervous?"

Willow hugged her knees to her chest again and nodded. "I don't want to mess this up."

Gently, Scottie pulled Willow's arms down, away from her knees, and wrapped her own around her. "You won't. No matter what happens—or doesn't happen, this is already perfect. *You* are perfect."

Willow raised her gaze to Scottie's, and the tension drained from her body as she looked into her eyes. "You're the one who makes it perfect."

A strand of hair fell into Scottie's eyes as she shook her head. "We'll make it perfect together. And even if it's not quite perfect this first time..." A grin spread across her face. "Well, you know what they say about practice." Her voice dipped low. "Lots and lots of practice."

A wave of heat, gratefulness, and love surged through Willow. She pushed the rebellious lock of hair from Scottie's face and trailed her fingers through the soft strands. They were now long enough to get a good grip, and she took advantage by tugging her forward and pressing their mouths together.

With a groan, Scottie parted her lips beneath Willow's and kissed her back. She sank onto the mattress and pulled Willow on top of her.

Willow moaned at the first contact of Scottie's skin against her own, smoother than the silk sheets and so much warmer. Her eyes fluttered shut. Nothing had ever felt better than this.

Then Scottie stroked one hand down her bare back and splayed her fingers across the dip at the base of her spine, pressing her closer.

Her hard nipples rubbed against Willow's breasts.

Willow gasped into her mouth. *Oh God.* Okay, this felt even better.

Apparently, Scottie was on a mission to make every sensation better than the one before. The sensual glide of her tongue against Willow's own sent ripples of pleasure down to her toes. She kissed her with so much passion that Willow's entire body felt as if it were about to catch on fire.

Her hips started to rock against Scottie's.

Scottie clasped her waist with both hands and drew her more firmly between her parted thighs. Her arousal coated Willow's skin, making her moan and rock harder.

Scottie slid her hands upward, toward Willow's breasts, nearly sending her into overload.

Gasping, Willow wrenched her mouth from Scottie's and broke the kiss. *What was that?* She blinked down at Scottie and panted against her tempting lips.

"You okay?" Scottie's raspy voice sent renewed heat through her. She looked and sounded as dazed and breathless as Willow felt.

Willow nodded. The passion between them had spiraled out of control so fast, it was as scary as it was heady. She needed some control back before she burned the house down. "Yeah. But I need you to..."

"Anything." Scottie tenderly stroked Willow's cheek with her fingertips. "Whatever you need."

Willow tilted her head into the caress, then realized that she was getting lost in Scottie's touch again. God, the effect this woman had on her! Gently, she grasped Scottie's wrists and guided her hands up above her head. "Could you hold on to the headboard?"

Scottie stared up at her, still breathing heavily. "But isn't it you who needs to ground herself?"

"It is," Willow whispered against her lips. "But I don't need to touch the metal as long as I'm touching you. You'll be my ground."

Scottie dropped her head onto the pillow and obediently wrapped her fingers around the vertical metal bars. "I won't let go unless you tell me to."

Even if it weren't strictly necessary in order to prevent static from building up, there would still be something incredibly hot about the sight of Scottie holding on to the headboard, handing over the reins and leaving herself completely open to Willow's touch.

She was giving her full control of this experience, and Willow was determined to savor every second.

For the first time in her life, she wouldn't rush through this, afraid to zap her partner or destroy valuable electronics if it took too long. She would lose herself in Scottie, enjoy every moment, and trust that they would both be all right, no matter what.

She knelt next to her and pressed kisses to Scottie's fingers, which were wrapped tightly around the metal bar.

The toned muscles of Scottie's arms strained beneath her lips as she slid them lower and lower.

Halfway down her arms, she switched over to the tempting line of Scottie's jaw and kissed a path along it until she reached the corner of her mouth.

Scottie angled her head toward her. "Kiss me."

Maybe Willow wasn't in control after all, because every muscle in her body went weak at the need in Scottie's voice. She lowered her mouth to Scottie's, who surged up and kissed her deeply.

Willow buried her fingers in Scottie's hair and lost herself in the kiss. Her worries drained away more and more with every caress of Scottie's tongue, every gentle nip of her teeth, every low moan vibrating against her lips.

Finally, once she felt nearly drunk on Scottie's kisses, she tore her mouth away.

Scottie's cheeks were flushed, and Willow couldn't resist kissing the rosy skin.

Slowly, she slid her lips down, then along the firm line of Scottie's jaw. She paused to nibble a soft earlobe before trailing a string of kisses down her neck.

Scottie instantly tipped her head back, allowing more access. Her pulse raced beneath Willow's lips.

With one last kiss, Willow moved on and explored the muscles of her shoulder.

A gentle nip made Scottie gasp, but as she had promised, she kept her hands on the headboard and let her continue.

Willow was allowed to touch her freely, without restraint. She placed an open-mouthed kiss on the slope of one breast, right above Scottie's pounding heart, then glided her tongue down the soft skin between her breasts, forcing herself not to stray left or right until she finally cupped one firm breast in her hand.

For a moment, she just cradled it, staring down at its perfect shape, then she stroked her thumb along its silky underside. *So incredibly soft.*

"Willow," Scottie whispered.

In response, Willow bent her head and breathed a featherlight kiss onto one already taut nipple.

"God, Willow." Scottie's tone grew more desperate. "What are you doing to me?"

Willow wanted to do so much more. With Scottie, she wanted to do it all—and she knew Scottie would let her. "Worshipping you the way you deserve," she whispered against her nipple, then drew it between her lips.

With a throaty moan, Scottie arched her back, pressing her breast more fully into Willow's mouth.

Her nipple grew impossibly harder against Willow's tongue.

She made love to Scottie's breasts with her mouth and her hands, swiping her tongue across one nipple while circling the other with her fingers.

Scottie bucked and groaned, her legs rubbing restlessly against Willow's.

The way Scottie's breath caught at her every touch made Willow's head spin with desire. Every shudder from Scottie set off answering shivers inside of her.

"Please, Willow. I need you...now."

The needy note in her voice undid Willow.

She looked up and into Scottie's dark eyes.

The tendons and muscles in her forearms stood out in sharp relief as she clung to the headboard. Her full lower lip was trapped between her teeth in a way that made Willow want to surge up her body and kiss her again.

Instead, she kissed a trail down Scottie's belly, which quivered deliciously under her mouth. Willow's hair fanned out, brushing lightly along the bend of Scottie's leg.

A visible shiver ran through Scottie, and Willow imagined she could hear the headboard groan under Scottie's desperate grip.

She settled herself between Scottie's strong, soft thighs.

Scottie eased her legs wider, inviting her touch.

Willow pressed a string of kisses to the silky skin of Scottie's inner thigh, already damp with need. Slowly, she slid her lips higher and higher until the scent of Scottie's arousal filled her senses.

A hum escaped her as she breathed her in, and Scottie shuddered.

She raised her knees, opening herself up to Willow. Her eyes were hooded as she gazed down at Willow. "Please."

Willow couldn't wait any longer. Urgently, she dipped her head down.

They both moaned at the first careful touch of Willow's tongue against her warm wetness.

Scottie's taste, tangy yet sweet, hit her senses. She wanted to tell her how much she loved it, how much she enjoyed this entire experience, but she couldn't bear to take her mouth off her for even a second.

Slowly, she licked her way up to Scottie's swollen clit, then circled it before running her tongue across it.

Scottie's low moan made heat spread through Willow's belly.

She alternated between light flicks and languid swipes, trying to find out the best way to bring Scottie pleasure.

Scottie seemed to like it all. She urgently lifted her hips into each touch, seeking more contact.

Willow wanted more too. Experimentally, she pressed her tongue into her.

Scottie's hips jerked against Willow. An inarticulate sound tore from her throat.

Willow raised her head and glanced up Scottie's body, into her face. "Is this okay?"

Scottie's lips were parted, every muscle in her arms, shoulders, and belly taut as she clung to the headboard. She met Willow's gaze, pupils wide and dark eyes glazed with raw desire. The look of unrestrained abandon on Scottie's face sent a rush of arousal to Willow's core.

This was the hottest thing Willow had ever seen.

"It's...amazing." Scottie's voice was breathless and husky. "But...I need..."

"Anything," Willow said. "Just tell me."

"I need to touch you." Scottie nodded toward the metal bars she clung to. "Can I...?"

"Yes," Willow whispered, awed that Scottie wanted that more than anything else.

Scottie's hand—just the right one—was on her before Willow had even fully gotten out the word, while the left one remained firmly wrapped around the headboard. Her fingertips traced down Willow's arm and seared across her shoulder. Her nails lightly scraped over the nape of Willow's neck, sending sparks of pleasure down her body.

Oh God. Allowing Scottie to touch her was dangerous, threatening to shatter her self-control. Determined to focus on Scottie, she ducked her head back down and swirled her tongue around Scottie's clit once more. Then, slowly, she sucked it between her lips.

The sound Scottie made—part gasp, part groan—sent a jolt of lust through Willow.

Scottie arched against her, pressing herself against Willow's mouth. Her right hand found Willow's shoulder, not guiding her, just establishing a connection, as if she needed it to anchor herself.

There was no moment of insecurity as Willow had often experienced in the past, no guessing what Scottie liked or didn't like. It was astonishingly easy to read Scottie, her body language as clear as the sexy sounds that escaped her—a sharp intake of breath every time Willow flicked her clit with her tongue and a deep, throaty moan whenever she caught it between her lips and sucked lightly.

She gripped Scottie's hips with both hands, enjoying their strength and fullness as Scottie strained against her. Giving her pleasure was the headiest feeling in the world. Willow felt nearly drunk on it—on her taste, on the unfiltered little sounds she made.

"Don't stop," Scottie gasped out. "Please don't stop." Her thighs tightened around Willow's ears as if she never wanted to let her go.

Willow had no intention of stopping. She flicked her tongue faster and harder.

"Willow!" Scottie groaned out her name. She clutched the back of Willow's head, pressing her closer. Her fingers flexed helplessly against Willow's scalp.

Willow let go of Scottie's straining hips with one hand and slid it up her body. She couldn't resist pausing at one breast to rub her thumb over its rock-hard nipple.

"Oh fuck!" Scottie twisted her fingers into Willow's hair and pushed herself harder against her mouth.

Willow groaned into her wetness. She squeezed her legs together in an attempt to ward off her own arousal and focus only on Scottie. Without lifting her mouth off Scottie, she found her left arm and tugged on it until Scottie let go of the headboard. Willow drew her hand down and intertwined their fingers.

Scottie tightly clung to her. A quiver ran through the firm muscles of her inner thighs.

Willow felt it all. The intimacy of it took her breath away.

Scottie's legs around her started to shake.

Willow's own belly tightened in response as she felt Scottie's orgasm build.

Scottie's hips pushed upward, into Willow's mouth, one more time. A hoarse cry tore from her throat. Then her entire body tensed beneath Willow, her thighs clamping around her ears.

Scottie's arousal flooded her mouth.

With one last deep groan, Scottie collapsed onto the mattress. After a few moments, her thighs loosened their grip and fell back to the bed, and her desperate clasp on Willow's hair gentled to a weak caress.

Willow held her breath, completely in awe. She pressed a final, whisper-soft kiss onto Scottie's pulsing clit, making her twitch, then lifted her head and gazed up her body.

Scottie's cheeks were flushed, and her chest heaved. A sheen of sweat made her skin glow like gold in the candlelight. She met Willow's eyes with an expression of pure, stunned bliss. "Holy shit!" Her voice came out raspy. "You clearly were kidding when you said you don't have a ton of experience, right?"

Willow blushed, more with the joy of being able to give Scottie pleasure than from embarrassment. "You made it really easy. You're so…vocal. You weren't exaggerating your responses, were you?"

"Exaggerating?" Scottie echoed. She weakly lifted her head off the pillow and shook it back and forth. "It was all I could do not to come the moment your tongue touched me."

Heat sizzled through Willow. The way Scottie talked so openly about how much she'd aroused her would take some getting used to, but she had to admit it was also a huge turn-on.

Scottie disentangled her fingers from Willow's hair and softly tugged on her shoulder. "Come on up here. I want to hold you."

Willow lingered for a moment longer, inhaling Scottie's intoxicating scent, then wiped her mouth and moved up her body and into her arms.

Scottie gazed at her as if she'd just performed a miracle. She brushed strands of tangled hair behind Willow's ears, cradled her face in her hands, and caressed her cheeks with her thumbs in a gesture so tender that an ache of a different kind started deep within Willow. "I love you," she whispered with so much emotion that tears gathered in Willow's eyes.

"I love you too," she whispered back.

Scottie guided her head down and kissed her, slow and heartfelt.

Willow melted against her. She could have kissed her forever, but the gentle slide of Scottie's fingers over her back—from that sensitive spot between her shoulder blades to the curve of her ass—made tension gather low in her belly, and she became aware that she was pressing herself against Scottie's thigh, desperate for some friction.

More friction. She stilled against her. That was definitely not something she'd ever tried for, especially not when every cell in her body already felt electrified.

"Don't stop." Scottie gripped her hips and rocked her against a strong thigh muscle.

Desire sparked through Willow. She squeezed her eyes shut, struggling for control.

"It's okay." Scottie softly stroked her hips. "Just hold on to the headboard."

Willow's already flushed cheeks burned even hotter. "But I...I can't come like this." Usually, she struggled to come at all, but with Scottie... She opened her eyes to peek down at her.

"Didn't say I wanted you to, did I?" Scottie grinned up at her, yet her eyes were blazing. "I want you to come on my fingers, not on my thigh."

Jesus. Need sliced through Willow. Yes, she wanted that too.

"Straddle me," Scottie said. "That way, you have full control. That's what you still want, right?"

Willow nodded shakily. She sat up, swung one leg across Scottie's hips, and straddled her.

As her arousal coated Scottie's skin, both of them sucked in a breath.

Scottie raked her hands up the outsides of Willow's thighs, making shivers race up her body, then gripped her hips and pulled her more firmly against her belly.

"God." Willow desperately clutched the headboard with both hands and rolled her hips against Scottie.

Scottie stared up at her with a hungry look in her eyes as she reached up and cupped her breasts. "Beautiful," she murmured and rubbed the pads of her thumbs across her nipples.

Moaning, Willow tossed her head back. Every brush of Scottie's thumbs over her nipples sent shock waves of sensation all the way to her core.

Scottie trailed one hand down, but instead of sliding it where Willow wanted it, she cupped one ass cheek and rocked her against her belly.

A gasp escaped Willow. "I thought you wanted me to, uh, come on your fingers?" she got out. Her ability to speak—and think—was slipping away fast.

Scottie lightly squeezed her nipple. "Is that what you want?"

Willow bit her lip, struggling to keep in another moan, and nodded.

"Say it."

Her cheeks burned, but the rest of her body burned even brighter. She looked into Scottie's lust-hazy eyes. "I want to come on your fingers."

Now Scottie was the one who let out a moan. She slipped her right hand down Willow's body and between them.

Willow pressed her knees against the mattress and tightly gripped the headboard, trembling with anticipation.

Scottie's hand shook too as she trailed one finger through Willow's wetness, easing it lower with agonizing slowness. "God, Willow." Her gaze never left Willow's face as she paused at her entrance.

Willow couldn't wait. She pressed her hips down and sank onto Scottie's finger. She couldn't contain the sharp sound—half cry, half gasp—that burst out of her.

Scottie froze beneath her. "Okay? Want me to stop?"

Wildly, Willow shook her head. "No! Don't stop!" She slowly raised herself up, then pressed back down against Scottie's touch.

Scottie gripped her hip with her free hand, supporting her rhythm but not trying to set the pace. "More?"

Unable to speak, Willow nodded.

Her gaze on Willow's face, Scottie slipped a second finger inside.

"Scottie." She breathed out her name on a long gasp.

An answering groan came from Scottie. She shuddered against Willow as if every touch resonated through her too. "God, you feel so good." She stroked Willow deep inside, sending little tremors through her.

"So do you." Then Willow could no longer speak, only moan, as their bodies quickly found a rhythm, and she lost herself in the sensations coursing through her.

The hungry, awed look on Scottie's face, the passion in her dark eyes drove Willow on, made her move faster and faster.

"You're so beautiful," Scottie murmured, voice rough. "So hot." She never looked away from Willow, eagerly drinking in every response.

They met each other stroke for stroke, their gazes locked the entire time.

The intimacy of it nearly overwhelmed Willow. Her breath came in ragged puffs, and she was vaguely aware of the little noises escaping her. Why had she ever worried about not being able to come? She was struggling not to come too soon.

Scottie shifted her hand, adjusting the angle. When she thrust up again, the heel of her palm brushed against Willow's clit.

Pleasure cascaded through Willow. She muffled a cry and desperately clung to the headboard.

Scottie groaned as if she were the one being touched.

The low, breathless sounds nearly tipped Willow over the edge.

Scottie picked up speed, matching the frantic beat of Willow's heart. The heel of her hand now rubbed against Willow's clit every time she ground her hips down.

Willow rasped out a choked plea but had no idea what she was asking for. Harder? Deeper? Faster? More? Or maybe she was gasping out Scottie's name.

Scottie stroked deeper into her. Her grip on Willow's hip tightened as she pressed her down against her fingers.

The first tremors washed through Willow. *Oh no. Not yet.* She dug her teeth into her lower lip and tried to slow down the frantic pace of her hips, but her control was slipping. Emotions rose sharply—need, pleasure, but also fear. The intensity of her desire almost scared her. What if—?

"It's okay," Scottie whispered. "Let go. I've got you."

The words severed the last tether of Willow's self-control. She wrenched her hands off the headboard and clutched Scottie's shoulders for all she was worth, digging her nails into her skin as she gave herself up to the ecstasy of Scottie's touch.

Scottie curled her fingers, brushing a spot that made a wave of pleasure sweep through Willow's body.

A whimper escaped her. Her stomach tightened, and her hips shook against Scottie. She desperately clung to her.

Scottie brought her thumb up and rubbed Willow's clit, using the perfect amount of pressure. "Let go," she whispered again.

Willow rocked down against Scottie one more time, then gave in to the sensations gathering deep inside her. The wild rush crested so sharply that she tossed her head back and opened her mouth in a silent scream. Sparks flashed behind her eyelids as her body clenched tightly around Scottie's fingers.

All her muscles went taut, then melted into a quivering puddle. She fell forward and collapsed on top of Scottie, trusting her to catch her.

Scottie stilled her fingers, wrapped one arm around Willow, and held her until both of their breathing calmed.

After a while, she carefully withdrew.

Another shudder went through Willow.

When her brain started working again, she slowly realized that the pounding wasn't in her body. Okay, not *just* in her body. She was still pulsing with aftershocks.

The noise was coming from the wall in front of her.

Willow tried to lift her head off Scottie's shoulder, but her muscles were still pleasantly useless. "What...?"

Scottie shook with laughter beneath her. "Sorry." She trailed her hand up and down Willow's back in long, soothing sweeps. "That's my neighbor."

"Your...neighbor? Why...?"

"You were pretty loud. Shouted my name a couple of times and cried out when you came."

Willow pushed up on one trembling arm to stare down at her. "What?"

A proud grin spread across Scottie's face. "You cried out my name," she repeated almost reverently. She reached up and cupped Willow's cheek, her thumb brushing the heat flooding there. "It was hot. Beautiful. Glorious."

Willow opened her mouth. Then closed it again. "But I don't..." She shook her head, trying to clear it of the orgasm-induced fog. "I don't do that. I never..."

Scottie smiled up at her, a slow, sexy curl of her lips. "Well, you did with me."

Despite everything they'd just done, another flush raced up Willow's neck. "I...I completely lost control."

Scottie's self-satisfied grin was replaced by a tender smile. "Yeah. That's what made it so beautiful. Seeing you like that...completely unguarded... giving yourself over to the pleasure I made you feel... God, that was..." Now it was Scottie who seemed to be at a loss for words. She trailed off with a shake of her head. "And when you let go of the headboard and held on to me..."

"I let go of the headboard," Willow repeated. Vaguely, the memory of clutching Scottie's shoulders came back to her—of digging her nails into Scottie's skin.

She'd never before let herself get so overwhelmed with pleasure that she had stopped being aware of where her hands were. But with Scottie, she'd stopped bracing for an impending zap and had just allowed herself to feel.

"You did," Scottie said, her voice full of emotion.

Willow sank back against Scottie's shoulder. "Wow," she mumbled as the thought finally sank in. They had made love, had poured every bit of passion and tenderness into touching each other until all restraint had fallen away—and they'd been fine.

More than fine, actually. None of Willow's fears had come true. No zaps. No exploding electronics. And definitely no struggle to climax.

She lifted herself back up on one arm. "You are fine, right? I didn't zap you, did I?"

Scottie shook her head. "No. Although…"

Willow froze against her, but Scottie continued her tender caresses against her back, soothing away the tension.

"Although?" Willow prompted.

"You did blow a few fuses." Scottie flashed her a grin. "All of mine."

Willow couldn't help returning the grin. "All of them?" She shifted to the side so she could trail her hand down Scottie's body.

Scottie sucked in a breath. "Maybe not all of them. A few still seem to be working."

Playfully, Willow lifted her brows. "Oh? Which ones are still functioning?"

"Motor skills are surprisingly intact." Scottie proved it by leaning up and capturing Willow's lips in a soft kiss that quickly grew heated. "Speech is starting to become questionable," she added in a husky whisper against her lips.

Willow dragged her nails in a teasing path down Scottie's belly, then paused at the edge of her damp curls. "What about self-control?"

A long groan escaped from Scottie. "Hanging on by a thread."

"Hmm. Let's see if we can short-circuit it completely." She slid her hand lower, and this time, Scottie reached for her instead of the headboard.

Chapter 45

Willow woke slowly, surfacing from a dream she didn't want to end. Then her mind cleared, and she realized it hadn't been a dream.

Scottie was wrapped around her from behind, her warmth pressing against Willow's back. One arm was looped around Willow's waist, her forearm tucked between Willow's breasts.

Willow blinked her eyes open, and Scottie's bedroom came into a hazy focus. She had no idea where her glasses had ended up.

Last night, it hadn't mattered.

God, last night...

Memories of the way they had touched each other sent a renewed wave of heat through Willow's body. They had kept pushing each other to the brink and beyond until they'd both been too exhausted to continue.

She'd never been this insatiable before. Making love with Scottie felt nothing like the carefully controlled attempts at intimacy she'd shared with past partners. With Scottie, there was no holding back—and she didn't want there to be.

A giddy smile tugged at the corners of her mouth. Her entire body was buzzing, not with static electricity but with happiness. Even though every muscle ached and a few spots were deliciously sore, she felt more relaxed than she had in a very long time. She lay still, enjoying this new, peaceful feeling.

Scottie stirred behind her, pressing even closer. Her arm around Willow tightened. "Mmm. Morning, beautiful," she mumbled against her shoulder, then pressed a tender kiss to it.

"Morning, gorgeous." Willow turned in her arms.

Scottie's expression was soft, her grin as giddy as Willow felt. Her hair was adorably mussed.

They lay still for a few moments, cuddled together on the same pillow, just gazing into each other's eyes from inches away.

Finally, Scottie bridged the tiny gap between them and placed a tender kiss on her lips. "How are you feeling?"

"Good." Willow paused. "Actually, better than good. You?"

Scottie's smile seemed to light up the room. "Happy."

Willow cuddled closer. "Mmm, me too." She could still barely believe that she was the one to make that happen—to give Scottie the happy ending she deserved.

She combed her fingers through the chaotic strands, brushing the soft waves back from Scottie's face. Secretly, she loved Scottie's hair when it started to become slightly too long, and she couldn't help admiring the way it glinted like gold in the sunlight.

Wait! Sunlight?

That meant…

Willow sat up abruptly. "Scottie! The sun's up!"

Scottie rolled onto her back and folded her arms behind her head with a serene smile. "Yeah, isn't it beautiful? Not even the Portland weather would dare spoil a morning like this with rain."

"No! I mean, yes, but… We overslept! We're late for work!" Usually, her internal alarm clock woke her up without fail, even if her phone didn't, but this morning she had slept so deeply, wrapped in Scottie's arms, that she'd lost all notion of time.

"Shit!" Scottie jerked upright too. "Where are our phones? I set my alarm for the entire week, but I didn't hear it go off."

"I left mine in my coat," Willow said.

Scottie glanced around. "Same, I think."

They threw off the covers and scrambled out of bed.

Scottie hurried down the short hallway and returned with their phones.

For a moment, Willow was distracted by the sight of Scottie's gloriously naked body bathed in morning sunlight, then she forced her gaze to the phones Scottie held up.

"Battery's dead—both of them." Scottie flashed her a grin. "Looks like you fried more than just my fuses last night."

A full-body flush engulfed Willow. "I… I'm sorry. That has never happened before. Not if I leave it by the door." She gestured toward the hallway. "My impact radius doesn't usually extend that far, so I didn't think…"

"Hey." Scottie dropped the phones onto the dresser and crossed the room toward her. "There was nothing usual about last night."

The husky tone of her voice made Willow's pulse trip.

Scottie pulled Willow into her arms. "It was so, so worth it. Zero regrets. Okay?"

Willow pressed her overheated cheek to Scottie's neck for a moment. "Okay. No regrets. But we have to get going—or we will regret it. I can't very well tell my boss I was late because of battery-draining, world-class sex."

Scottie chuckled. "Go take a shower. I'll get you a towel."

"Thank you." Willow grabbed her clothes that were strewn across the floor. She hurried through her shower, mind whirring as she tried to come up with an excuse for being late to work.

Could she say her phone battery had died, or would that only cement her reputation as someone who made devices glitch?

She reached for the shower gel.

A fruity scent wafted up as she absentmindedly worked the gel between her palms.

Apricot—like the lotion Scottie had used on her the night before. It was her favorite scent, and Willow had a feeling that wasn't a coincidence.

Scottie had clearly bought the lotion and the shower gel with her in mind, wanting to make her comfortable. She had thought only of Willow the entire time.

And yet here Willow was—thinking of ways to keep her effect on electronics a secret. Instead of reliving the amazing night she'd shared with Scottie, she was sorting through excuses and trying to decide which one sounded least like "I short-circuited my phone battery."

As if she hadn't spent the night in Scottie's arms, feeling more seen, accepted, and free than ever before. Now she was back to exerting the same tight control, letting her life be dictated by the need to keep her tech affliction a secret at all costs.

Did she really want that?

Scottie's words came back to her: "A happy ending is not a finish line that you cross once and then you'll be happy forever," Scottie had said when she'd confronted Willow about slipping back into one-woman-army mode. "It's not a goal; it's a journey. A choice that you make every single day—a choice to be there for each other, no matter what."

A choice… Willow bit her lip.

A soft knock sounded, then the bathroom door creaked open. "I'll leave two towels for you on the counter," Scottie shouted over the patter of the water.

"Thanks." Willow braced her hands on the cold tiles. "Scottie?"

"Yeah?" Scottie pulled back the shower curtain a couple of inches and peeked in. Her gaze roamed down Willow's body, then returned to her face as if she was doing her best not to stare. "Do you need anything else?"

"Yes." Willow reached out, grabbed Scottie's arm, and tugged her beneath the warm spray with her.

A mix between a yelp and a laugh escaped Scottie. Water soaked her hair, flattening the chaotic strands. "Willow! This is not going to speed things up."

Willow wrapped both arms around her and pulled her against her body. Hot water cascaded down on them, and the slide of their naked skin against each other made Willow's eyes flutter closed. "I don't care. Like you said yesterday, Mr. Sorensen will probably go back to ignoring me. Even if he doesn't, I'm the one who saved his presentation. I doubt he'll fire me for being an hour late." She nibbled a spot just beneath Scottie's collarbone, eliciting a moan. "Or two." She kissed a path up her neck. "Or three."

Scottie made a sound low in her throat that wasn't a protest at all. She traced a sensual path down Willow's back. "Or," she whispered, pressing closer, "we could call in sick."

"Sounds reasonable. I'm starting to feel a little flushed and weak-kneed." She trailed kisses along Scottie's jaw.

"Must be contagious," Scottie murmured, "because I feel the same." She cupped Willow's face between her palms and guided their lips together.

They kissed beneath the warm spray, deep and unhurried, and Willow knew without a doubt she'd made the right choice.

Epilogue

Six months later

All around Willow, her co-workers were packing up, preparing to leave for the weekend.

Willow couldn't wait either. They had invited Barb, Mateo, and Gordon with their spouses, plus Fiona, for a barbecue tomorrow. Willow couldn't believe she was actually looking forward to a social gathering for once! Even Kassidy, a fellow hater of parties, had promised to make an appearance.

Quickly, she finished typing a status update to Celeste and hit *send.*

Out of habit, she paused and listened.

Just one whoosh sounded, and no error messages popped up.

Good. With a satisfied nod, she closed Outlook.

A light tap came on her cubicle wall, and when Willow looked up, she wasn't surprised to see Scottie peek around the partition.

She had one hand tucked into the pocket of her chinos, the strap of her messenger bag crossing over her black polo shirt. The soft grin on her face still made Willow's heart beat faster. "Hey, beautiful. Ready to head home?"

Willow's breath hitched. Even after living together for a month, giddiness still bubbled up anytime she thought of going home together—to their apartment, where Scottie's plants and her typewriters peacefully coexisted. "Yes. Just give me a minute to shut everything down."

In record time, she closed all open apps, powered down her computer, and straightened up her desk, sliding a couple of pens back into their cup and aligning the bronze plaque with her Rolodex.

Last year, she had shoved the paper jam award into the back of her drawer as soon as she'd gotten it, terrified that someone would connect the dots and figure out it was Willow who made the office equipment malfunction on a regular basis.

Now she was displaying it on her desk as if it were a badge of honor.

What a difference a few months could make!

Willow grabbed her purse from beneath the desk. "Let's get out of here."

Together, they crossed the bullpen.

"Hey, Willow!" Toby called as they passed his desk. "Trivia tonight. You're coming, right?"

"Wouldn't miss it," Willow replied. "Someone has to keep the IT team from getting too smug."

"Hey!" Scottie bumped her playfully. "Excuse me! I am IT!"

Willow bumped her back. "Yeah, and just look at how smug you are!"

The smoldering look Scottie gave her made heat shoot up Willow's neck. Quickly, she dragged Scottie from the bullpen before she could make a remark like "and rightfully so" in front of all her colleagues.

The elevator doors closed behind them.

Scottie leaned against the mirrored wall and regarded her with a loving expression. "Have I told you lately how proud of you I am?"

Willow moved closer. "Why's that?"

"The way you stepped into Barb's shoes, not just keeping Operations from descending into chaos but also forming relationships with your co-workers... It was truly beautiful to watch."

A new flush warmed Willow's cheeks, yet it felt wonderful to have her efforts be acknowledged, especially by the person who mattered most to her. "It's a lot easier to make friends at work when your colleagues don't think you're the tech reaper."

Scottie chuckled. "For sure. How's the Fortress holding up? Still behaving?"

It was the nickname they had given the static-safe workstation Scottie had set up for her. She'd spent weeks researching, testing, and optimizing. The computer and the monitors were rated for military use, built with internal shielding and components that were more resistant to electromagnetic interference. Scottie had also used long cables so they could move the CPU tower farther away from Willow.

Willow nodded. "It didn't fix all problems, but it made a big difference."

Instead of grinning happily, Scottie frowned. "If it didn't fix all problems, why haven't you submitted any tickets or asked for help in ages?" She studied Willow with a worried expression. "You're not sliding back into old habits, trying to solve your tech issues by yourself, are you?"

"What? No! Of course I'm not. I asked you for help when the Teams app kept freezing, remember?"

"Willow, that was last month!"

"No, that can't be. It was..."

"The day you stressed about moving out and no longer being able to help your sister with the mortgage," Scottie finished.

Willow sank against the elevator wall. God, she was right. She stared at Scottie. "But...but...that means... I haven't had a single glitch for an entire month! Not even a little hiccup!"

"Well," Scottie said with a grin, "we did make the lights flicker this past weekend when we—"

The elevator doors slid open, and Scottie cut herself off.

Still in a daze, Willow followed her through the lobby and into the warm summer air outside. "I can't believe it," she whispered. "I've never gone that long without a glitch. Ever!"

"How does it feel?" Scottie asked softly as they crossed the employee parking lot.

"Strange." Willow laughed shakily. "Like I'm jinxing myself by saying it out loud."

Scottie shook her head. "I don't think you were ever jinxed."

"Whatever it was, it looks like falling in love fixed it. Or at least helped reduce it considerably."

"I'd love to take the credit for fixing every last one of your IT problems, but I don't think it was falling in love," Scottie said. "Or at least not just that."

Willow thought back over everything that had changed in the past six months. "No," she said slowly. "I don't think so either."

They reached Willow's car, but instead of getting in, they leaned against it and faced each other.

Scottie tilted her head in that typical attentive Scottie way yet didn't say anything, giving her space to process.

"I think..." Willow drew a deep breath. "I think it's because I stopped hiding that part of me. I spent so long shutting everyone out, terrified that they'd find out. That added a lot of stress to my life, which made the problem worse."

Emotionally, she had sealed herself away in a steel box, isolating herself from anyone but her sister. How ironic that getting stuck in an elevator—another metal box—had been what had started to tear down her walls of steel.

Scottie nodded. "Like a vicious circle—one you've successfully broken."

"Because I listened to the advice a wise woman once gave me," Willow replied. "Something about happiness being a choice that you make every single day."

"Sounds familiar." Scottie grinned at her. "And you've definitely started making a lot of different choices this year, not just when it comes to us, but in other areas of your life too."

"Yeah." Willow had decided that she no longer wanted her tech affliction to be something shameful that she had to manage alone. "I never would have believed it a year ago, but it really got easier with every choice I made."

Scottie laughed. "After telling your boss, of course everything else felt easy in comparison! You were so scared, I thought you'd fry every device in the department!"

Now Willow could laugh about it too, but she'd been terrified then. She had only told Celeste because Scottie wouldn't have been able to set up the Fortress without the support of Willow's manager. "Of course I was scared! I really thought she'd hammer me with hundreds of questions, trying to get to the bottom of my weird effect on tech."

"Nah," Scottie said, eyes twinkling. "I told you she couldn't care less about the details. You're damn good at your job, so the only question she cared about was whether you could do it without setting the building on fire. If it meant you could work efficiently, she would have gotten Mr. Sorensen and my boss to sign off on building you a nuclear bunker."

"Probably." Willow chuckled.

When the world hadn't ended once her boss knew, Willow had found the courage to tell Gordon and Mateo, then Kassidy and Barb. A couple of months ago, she'd even told Toby, her cubicle neighbor.

They had been stunned, of course, but no one had laughed or refused to believe her.

Willow reached into her purse and pulled out the car keys. They jangled as she fiddled with them. "I don't know when or how it happened, but somewhere along the way, it stopped being this terrible secret," she said quietly. "Now it's just...a quirk. Like Kassidy's hatred of small talk and Hawaiian pizza. Or Mateo's messy desk. Or the way you cry at cat food commercials."

"Hey, I don't cry at cat food commercials!" Scottie pretended to bristle. "Just at cat adoption reels."

"Right. Big difference, softie." Willow gave her an affectionate look, then jingled the keys again. "Fiona once accused me of living my life like I'm cursed. And as much as I didn't want to admit it then, she was right. But now I've stopped thinking of myself that way."

Scottie looked into her eyes. Warmth radiated from her brown irises. "Yeah? What do you think now?"

"Now I think I'm blessed," Willow said. "I have friends who accept me. A job I actually like. An apartment that feels like home. And a girlfriend I love."

"And who loves you back," Scottie added.

The words still made Willow's stomach flutter. "There'll probably always be the occasional glitch, but I'm okay with that now."

"I can't even tell you how happy it makes me to hear that." Scottie's voice was thick with emotions. She wiped at her damp eyes, then laughed shakily. "At least it's not cat videos this time."

With a tender smile, Willow lifted her hand and gently wiped away a single tear lingering in the corner of Scottie's eye. "No spark," she murmured.

"Hm?"

Willow nodded at her hand, which was now cradling Scottie's cheek. "There are no more sparks." In the last few months, they had gotten really good at always grounding themselves before touching, and she had attributed the lack of zaps to that habit. But now she thought it was probably because she was happier with herself and her life, more grounded.

"Oh, I don't know." Scottie reached up and cupped Willow's face, mirroring her gesture. She brushed her thumb along Willow's cheek, then let it linger at the corner of her mouth. "I still feel plenty of sparks every time we kiss."

As if to prove it, Scottie leaned forward and kissed her.

The warm caress of Scottie's lips still made Willow weak in the knees. She twisted her fingers into the fabric of Scottie's polo shirt and deepened the kiss.

"Mmm, yeah," Willow whispered against Scottie's mouth when they finally eased apart. "Lots and lots of sparks."

"Good. Because I promised you VIP girlfriend tech support for life, and I'm a woman of my word." Scottie took the keys from Willow, unlocked the car, and held the passenger-side door open for her.

Willow shook her head. "I'm not sure that's a promise you'll be able to keep."

"What? Of course I'll keep that promise!"

"Yeah, but at some point, we might want to upgrade."

Scottie gave her a puzzled look. "Upgrade?"

Willow nodded. "Upgrade my badge to VIP *wife* tech support."

Scottie's eyes went wide. "Did...did you just propose to me?"

Willow clutched the open car door. "Oh my God! I think I did! I mean...down the road. Once the current support package contract runs out, we could talk about it."

Scottie pressed her against the door and kissed her passionately. "Well," she said when the kiss ended, her voice husky. "You are a loyal customer, so an upgrade seems more than justified."

"Yeah?"

"Yeah." Scottie nodded eagerly. "Your favorite IT support tech is fully in favor of it."

They looked into each other's eyes, both smiling widely.

Finally, they tore themselves away from each other so they wouldn't be late for trivia night.

When they got into the car and Scottie started the engine, the radio came on, playing Jenna Blake's newest hit, "Counting on Forever."

It was the first time since Christmas that it had decided to temporarily work.

They stared at each other, then burst out laughing.

"Immaculate timing." Still chuckling, Scottie eased the car out of the parking lot.

Their fingers found each other across the gear shift and intertwined immediately.

Scottie sang along with the chorus, and after a moment of grinning at her off-key notes, Willow joined in.

For the first time in her life, she was counting on forever too.

If you enjoyed this story, check out Jae's novel *Under a Falling Star,* which takes place at Kudos Entertainment before the events of this story.

Icy COO Dee Saunders is married to her job and has no time for romance, especially not with the cheerful new administrative assistant who has no idea Dee is practically her boss. The instant attraction between them has to be the result of a head wound from a falling star-shaped Christmas tree topper…right?

Other Books from Ylva Publishing

Under a Falling Star

Jae

ISBN: 978-3-95533-238-9
Length: 369 pages (91,000 words)

Falling stars are supposed to be a lucky sign, but not for Austen. The first assignment in her new job—decorating the Christmas tree in the lobby—results in a trip to the ER after Dee, the company's COO, gets hit by the star-shaped tree topper. There's an instant attraction between them, but Dee is determined not to act on it, especially since Austen has no idea that Dee is her boss.

When She Flies

Lee Winter

ISBN: 978-3-69006-109-4
Length: 328 pages (114,000 words)

When artist Sienna stumbles upon a New York luxury goods empire, she learns the CEO is Jasmine, an English art curator who shredded her work years ago. Now Sienna has a second chance to impress the woman… who doesn't even remember her! All she has to do is become an intern—at age thirty-four—and try not to think about how hot her aloof new boss is.

Breaking from Frame

Jazz Forrester

ISBN: 978-3-69006-097-4
Length: 255 pages (92,000 words)

In 1969, Claire struggles through a discontented life to play the perfect homemaker. When beautiful, unmarried Jackie moves in next door, Claire is swept down a path of longing and self-discovery that shatters her suburban bubble. But when her secret dreams threaten to become real, will Claire have the strength to choose love over safety?

Beyond the Shoreline

Morgan Park

ISBN: 978-3-69006-048-6
Length: 262 pages (88,000 words)

Emotional pulls are stronger than the tide in this slow-burn lesbian romance about healing, honesty, and finding the courage to choose yourself. Author Brielle's life would be perfect if only she could fall for the man she's dating. She's also trying not to think about the spark she has with Maeve, the woman who was once her therapist. A chance seaside encounter brings a shock: Brielle's boyfriend is Maeve's brother. Torn between ethics and emotions, will they risk everything to be together?

About Jae

Jae grew up amidst the vineyards of southern Germany. She spent her childhood with her nose buried in a book, earning her the nickname "professor." The writing bug bit her at the age of eleven. Since 2006, she has been writing mostly in English.

She used to work as a psychologist but gave up her day job in December 2013 to become a full-time writer and a part-time editor. As far as she's concerned, it's the best job in the world.

When she's not writing, she likes to spend her time reading, indulging her ice cream and office supply addictions, and watching way too many crime shows.

CONNECT WITH JAE

Website: www.jae-fiction.com
E-Mail: jae@jae-fiction.com

Sparks

Available in paperback and e-book formats.

ISBN (paperback): 978-3-69006-133-9
ISBN (e-book): 978-3-69006-134-6
ISBN (pdf): 978-3-69006-135-3

Published by Ylva Publishing, legal entity of Ylva Verlag, e.Kfr.

Ylva Verlag, e.Kfr.
Owner: Astrid Ohletz
Am Kirschgarten 2
65830 Kriftel
Germany

www.ylva-publishing.com

First edition: 2026

For questions about product safety, please reach out to:
info@ylva-publishing.com

Credits
Edited by Michelle Aguilar
Cover Design by Trixia Quinzon (@trixdraws)
Print Layout by Ylva Publishing

Image rights cover illustration provided by Shutterstock LLC; iStock; Dreamstime; Canva; AdobeStock; Depositphotos
Graphics provided by Freepik

www.ingramcontent.com/pod-product-compliance
Lightning Source LLC
LaVergne TN
LVHW050922080826
845145LV00001B/179

* 9 7 8 3 6 9 0 0 6 1 3 3 9 *